A Family
Of Noblemen

by

Mikhail Evgrafovich Saltykov

Double 9
BOOKS

A Family Of Noblemen
by Mikhail Evgrafovich Saltykov

ISBN: 978-93-61159-03-9

Published by

DOUBLE 9 BOOKS

2/13-B, Ansari Road
Daryaganj, New Delhi – 110002
info@double9books.com
www.double9books.com
Tel. 011-40042856

ABOUT THE AUTHOR

Mikhail Yevgrafovich Saltykov-Shchedrin, born Mikhail Yevgrafovich Saltykov and known during his lifetime by the pen name Nikolai Shchedrin, was a prominent Russian writer and satirist in the nineteenth century. He spent the majority of his life working as a civil servant in various positions. Following the death of poet Nikolay Nekrasov, he served as editor of the Russian literary magazine Otechestvenniye Zapiski until it was outlawed by the Tsarist authorities in 1884. Saltykov's paintings exemplified both stark reality and humorous grotesque combined with imagination. Saltykov's most famous works, the family chronicle novel The Golovlyov Family (1880) and the political novel The History of a Town (1870), are seminal works of nineteenth-century fiction, and he is considered as a key character in Russian Literary Realism. Mikhail Saltykov was born on January 27, 1826, in the village of Spas-Ugol (modern-day Taldomsky District of the Moscow Oblast of Russia), as one of eight children (five brothers and three sisters) in the large Russian noble family of Yevgraf Vasilievich Saltykov (1776–1851) and Olga Mikhaylovna Saltykova (nee Zabelina; 1801–74). His father belonged to a historic Saltykov noble house descended from a branch of the Morozov boyar dynasty.

CONTENTS

BOOK I
THE FAMILY COUNCIL

CHAPTER I

Anton Vasilyev, the manager of a remote estate, was giving his mistress, Arina Petrovna Golovliov, an account of his trip to Moscow. He had gone there to collect the money due from those of her peasant serfs who bought the right to live in the city by paying her a tax. When he had finished with his report, she told him he might retire, but he lingered on irresolutely, as though he had something else to say, yet could not make up his mind to say it.

Arina Petrovna knew her servants through and through; she knew the meaning of their slightest gestures, she could even divine their inmost thoughts. And her steward's manner immediately aroused her disquietude.

"What else?" she asked, looking at him keenly.

"That's all," he replied evasively.

"Don't lie. There is something else. I can see it by your eyes."

Anton Vasilyev still hesitated and continued to shift from one foot to the other.

"What is it? Tell me!" she shouted imperiously. "Out with it, out with it! And don't wag your whole body like a dog, Telltale!"

Arina Petrovna liked to call her managers and domestics by nicknames. She used Telltale for Anton Vasilyev, not because she had found him to carry gossip treacherously, but simply because he had a loose tongue.

The centre of the estate that he managed was an important trading village in which there were many taverns. He liked to take a glass of tea in a tavern and boast of his mistress's great power. And in the course of his boasting he would sometimes unconsciously blab out secrets. His mistress was always with a lawsuit on her hands, so that her trusty's garrulousness sometimes brought her sly stratagems to the surface before they could be executed.

"Yes, I have got something else to say," Anton finally mumbled.

"What is it?" Arina Petrovna asked excitedly.

An imperious woman, with an extraordinarily lively imagination, she instantly pictured all sorts of disagreeable opposition and antagonism, and the thought so instantly took complete possession of her that she turned white and jumped up from her chair.

"Stepan Vladimirych's house in Moscow has been sold," Anton said after a pause.

"Well?"

"It's been sold."

"Why? How? Tell me."

"For debts, I suppose. Of course it can't be because of something nice."

"The police, the court, sold it, I suppose?"

"I suppose so. They say it was sold at auction for 8,000 rubles."

Arina Petrovna dropped back heavily into her armchair and gazed fixedly at the window panes. She was so stunned by the news that she seemed to have lost consciousness for a while. Had she heard that Stepan Vladimirych had killed somebody, or that the Golovliov peasant serfs had risen in revolt and refused to render the service due her on her estates, or that serfdom had been abolished, she would not have been so shocked. Her lips trembled, her eyes stared vacantly into the distance, but she saw nothing. She did not even see the little girl, Duniashka, run past the window carrying something hidden under her apron; she did not see the child stop suddenly on beholding her mistress and wheel round and then dart back guiltily to where she had come from. Such suspicious conduct at any other time would have led to a thorough investigation. Finally Arina Petrovna came to herself and managed to bring out:

"A good joke, I must say." After which there again followed several minutes of ominous silence.

"So the police sold the house for eight thousand?" she asked again.

"Yes, madam."

"So that's what he's done with his patrimony! Splendid! The blackguard!"

Arina Petrovna felt that the news called for a prompt decision, but nothing occurred to her. Her thoughts ran confusedly in exactly opposite directions. On the one hand she thought: "The police sold it. But the police could not have sold it in a minute. An inventory must first have been taken, then an appraisal made, and then the sale must have been advertised. Sold for eight thousand when I myself two years ago paid twelve thousand rubles for it, not a penny less. Had I only known it was going to be up for sale, I could have bought it myself for eight thousand rubles."

Her other thoughts ran: "The police sold it for eight thousand. That's what he's done with his patrimony. To sell one's patrimony for eight thousand rubles!"

"Who told you?" she asked, realizing finally that the house had been sold and the chance to secure it cheaply was gone forever.

"Ivan Mikhailov, the inn-keeper."

"Why didn't he let me know in time?"

"I suppose he was afraid."

"Afraid? I'll teach him to be afraid. I'll make him come here from Moscow, and the moment he comes I'll have him drafted into the army. He was afraid!"

Although on the decline, serfdom still existed. Anton Vasilyev had known his mistress to impose the most peculiar punishments, but, even so, her present decision was so unexpected that it made him miserable. He thought of his nickname Telltale. Ivan Mikhailov was an upright peasant, and Anton never dreamed that misfortune would touch him. Besides, Ivan Mikhailov was his friend and godfather. Now, all of a sudden, he was to be made a soldier just because he, Anton Vasilyev, the Telltale, could not hold his tongue.

"Forgive him—Ivan Mikhailov, I mean," he pleaded.

"Go away, you mollycoddler," she shouted in a voice so loud that he lost all desire to intercede any further for his friend.

CHAPTER II

Arina Petrovna was sixty years old, still of sound health and accustomed to have her own way in everything. Her manner was severe. She lived alone, and managed the huge Golovliov estate all by herself, without having to answer to any one else. She calculated closely, almost parsimoniously, was not intimate with her neighbors, was gracious to the local authorities, and exacted implicit obedience from her children. They were not to do anything without first asking themselves, "What would mamenka say about it?" She was independent, inflexible, even stubborn, though her stubbornness was not so much native as due chiefly to the circumstance that there was not one person in the whole Golovliov family that could oppose her. Her husband was a trifling creature, and drank. Arina Petrovna used to say of herself that she was neither a widow nor a married woman. Some of the children were in St. Petersburg, the others took after their father and were relegated to the class of "horrid creatures," who were unfit for household duties. In these circumstances Arina Petrovna soon began to feel all left alone, and grew totally disaccustomed to family life, although the word "family" was constantly on her lips, and outwardly she seemed to be exclusively guided in all her work by the desire to build up the family estate and keep the family affairs in order.

The head of the family, Vladimir Mikhailych Golovliov, was known from his youth as a dissolute, quarrelsome fellow, with nothing in his character that would be sympathetic to a serious, active woman like Arina Petrovna. He led a lazy, good-for-nothing existence, usually stayed locked up in his room, where he imitated the warble of the starlings, the crowing of cocks, and the like, and composed ribald doggerel. In bursts of confidence he would boast that he had been a friend of the poet Barkov, intimating that the poet had blessed him on his deathbed. Arina Petrovna disliked her husband's verses from the very first. "Nasty stuff!" "Trash!" she called them. And since Vladimir Mikhailych's very object in marrying had been to have someone ever at hand to listen to his poetry, the result was that quarrels soon began, which grew worse and worse and more frequent until they ended with Arina Petrovna utterly indifferent and contemptuous of her clown husband, and Vladimir Mikhailych hating his wife sincerely, with a hatred considerably mixed with fear. The husband called the wife a "hag" and a "devil"; the wife called the husband a "windmill" and a "balalaika without strings."

They lived together in this way for more than forty years, and it never occurred to either of them that there was anything unnatural in such a life. Time did not diminish Vladimir Mikhailych's quarrelsomeness; on the contrary, it took on a still sharper edge. Apart from the poetical exercising in Barkov's spirit that he did, he began to drink and to lie in wait eagerly for the servant girls in the corridors. At first Arina Petrovna looked on this new occupation of her husband's with repugnance. She even got wrought up over it, not so much from jealousy as that she felt it to be an interference with her authority. After a while, however, she shrugged her shoulders, and merely watched out that the "dirty wenches" should not fetch brandy for their master.

From that time on, having said to herself once for all that her husband was not a companion, she directed her efforts exclusively to one object, the building up of the estate. And in the forty years of her married life she actually succeeded in multiplying her property tenfold. With astonishing patience and acumen she kept her eye on the near and distant villages, found out in secret ways the relations that existed between the neighboring landowners and the board of trustees, and always appeared at the auctions like snow on the head. In this fantastic hunt for new acquisitions Vladimir Mikhailych receded more and more into the background, turned seedy and at last dropped out of social life completely. He was now a decrepit old man already, keeping his bed almost the whole time. On the rare occasions that he left his room it was only to stick his head through the half-open door of his wife's bedroom and shout: "Devil!" After which he would go back and close himself up in his own room again.

Arina Petrovna was not much happier in her children. She was of a celibate nature, so to speak, independent and self-sufficient, and her children were nothing to her but a useless burden. The only times when she breathed freely was when she was alone with her accounts and her household affairs, and when no one interfered with her business talks with her managers, stewards, housekeepers, and so on. In her eyes, children were one of the preordained things in life that she felt she had no right to protest against. Nevertheless they did not touch a single chord in her inner being, which was given over wholly to the numberless details of the household.

There were four children, one daughter and three sons. Of the oldest son and the daughter she did not even like to speak; toward the youngest son she was indifferent. It was only for the middle one, Porfisha, that she cherished any feeling at all, a feeling not of love, but of something very akin to fear.

Stepan Vladimirych, the oldest son, passed in the family by the name of Simple Simon, or The Saucebox. He was very young when he was put into the class of "horrid creatures," and from childhood up played the rôle of half pariah, half clown. Unfortunately he was a bright child, susceptible to the impressions of his environment. From his father he inherited an irresistible inclination to play tricks, from his mother the ability to divine the weak sides of people's natures. The first characteristic soon made him his father's favorite, which still further intensified his mother's dislike of him. Often when the mother was absent on business, the father and the boy would betake themselves into the study adorned with the portrait of Barkov, read ribald poems, and gossip, the chief butt of their raillery being the "hag," that is to say, Arina Petrovna. The "hag," instinctively divining their occupation, would drive up to the front steps very quietly, then tiptoe to the study door and listen to their fun-making. The murderous punishment of Simple Simon followed swift and cruel. But Stiopka was not subdued. He was impervious either to blows or to admonitions, and in half an hour was back again at his tricks. He would cut up Aniutka's, the servant girl's, scarf, or he would stick flies into Vasiutka's mouth while he slept, or he would run into the kitchen and carry off a cake (Arina Petrovna kept her children half hungry), which he always divided with his brothers.

"You ought to be killed," his mother said. "I'll kill you, and I won't have to answer for it either. Even God won't punish me for it."

This humiliation, constantly put upon a nature soft, yielding and forgetful, did not remain without its effect. It did not embitter him, nor did it make him rebellious. It made him servile, disposed to buffoonery, with no sense of the fitness of things, and devoid of all foresight and prudence. Such natures yield to all influences and may become almost anything — drunkards, beggars, buffoons, even criminals.

At the age of twenty Stepan Golovliov graduated from the gymnasium in Moscow and entered the university. But his student's life was a bitter one. In the first place, his mother gave him just enough money to keep him from dying of hunger. Secondly, he did not show the least inclination to work. Instead, he developed an accursed talent, which expressed itself chiefly in mimickry. And he suffered from a desire for constant companionship. He hated to be alone a single instant. So he played the light rôle of hanger-on and parasite, and thanks to his readiness for any prank he soon became the favorite of the rich students. However, though they received him into their society, they looked on him, not as one of them, but as a clown; and the reputation clung to him. Once placed on such a plane, he naturally slid down lower and lower, and at the end of the fourth year was thoroughly confirmed in his clownship. Nevertheless, thanks to his receptive ability and good memory, he passed the examinations successfully and received his bachelor's degree.

When he appeared before his mother with the diploma, she merely shrugged her shoulders and said: "Well, that's funny." Then, after letting him spend a month in the country, she shipped him back to St. Petersburg with an allowance of a hundred rubles a month. Now there began for him endless visits to various government offices. He had neither patrons nor the determination to make his own way by hard work. The lad's mind had lost so completely the habit of concentration that bureaucratic tasks such as the drawing up of briefs and case abstracts were beyond his power. After four years of struggle Stepan was forced to admit that there was no hope of his ever rising above the rank of a government clerk. In reply to his lamentations, Arina Petrovna wrote him a stern letter which began with the words: "I was sure that would happen," and wound up with a command to return at once to Moscow. There, at the conclave of Arina Petrovna's favorite peasants, it was decided to place Simple Simon in the Aulic Court, entrusting him to the care of a pettifogger who from time immemorial had been the legal adviser of the Golovliov family.

What Stepan Vladimirych did in the Aulic Court and how he behaved there is a mystery. What is certain is that at the end of the third year he was there no longer. Then Arina Petrovna took a heroic measure. She "threw her son a bone," which was also supposed to fill the part of the "parental blessing," that is to say, the patrimony. "The bone" consisted of a house in Moscow, for which she had paid twelve thousand rubles.

For the first time in his life Stepan Golovliov breathed freely. The house promised to bring him an income of a thousand silver rubles, a sum which in comparison with his former income, seemed like genuine prosperity. He kissed his mamma's hand effusively, and promised to justify her kindness, whereupon Arina Petrovna said: "That's better; but mind you, you numskull, that's all you get from me!" But, alas! so little was he used to handling money, so absurd was his estimation of real values in life, that before long what he thought to be a fabulous revenue proved insufficient. In five or six years he was totally ruined, and was only too glad to enter the militia, which was then being organized. No sooner, however, did the militia troops reach Kharkov than peace was concluded, and Golovliov went back to Moscow, dressed in a somewhat threadbare uniform and high boots. By this time his house had already been sold, and the only thing he owned was a hundred rubles. He began "speculating" with this capital, that is, he tried his luck at cards, but in a short time he lost all he had. Then he conceived the plan of visiting his mother's well-to-do peasants who lived in Moscow. Some of them invited him to dinner, others, yielding to his importunings, gave him tobacco or lent him small sums of money. At last the hour came when he found himself before a blind wall, as it were. He was already almost forty years old, and had to confess to himself that his nomadic existence was too much for his strength. There was only one thing left to him, to take the road leading to Golovliovo.

After Stepan Vladimirych, the oldest child, came Anna Vladimirovna, about whom Arina Petrovna did not like to speak either. The truth of the matter was, the old lady had placed definite expectations in Annushka, but she, far from fulfilling her mother's hopes, had perpetrated a scandal which set the whole district agog. When Annushka left the girls' boarding-school, Arina Petrovna installed her at the village, hoping to make of her a sort of unpaid private secretary and bookkeeper, but instead Annushka eloped one fine night with cornet Ulanov and married him.

"They have married like dogs, without a parent's blessing!" complained Arina Petrovna. "Lucky, though, that he submitted to a wedding ceremony at all. Another man would have taken advantage of her — and vanished into thin air. A fine chance for catching a bird."

With her daughter Arina Petrovna dealt as peremptorily as she had with her hated son. She bestowed "a bone" upon her too, in the shape of five thousand rubles and a wretched little village of thirty souls and a manor-house going with it, so dilapidated that the wind blew through the gaping paneless windows and there was not one sound board in the flooring. In two years the young couple had gone through the money, and the cornet took himself off, deserting his wife and two twin girls, Anninka and Lubinka. Three months later the mother died, and Arina Petrovna, willy-nilly, had to take the little orphans into her own house. She installed them in a side-wing and entrusted them to the care of Palashka, old and one-eyed. "The Lord's mercy is great," remarked Arina Petrovna. "The little orphans won't eat much of my bread, but they'll be a solace to me in my old age. God has given me two daughters instead of one." At the same time she wrote to her son, Porfiry Vladimirych: "Your dear sister died as she lived, indecently, and now her two children are hanging round my neck."

What we are going to say may seem cynical, but we feel it our duty to state that the granting of the heritage to Stepan and Anna did not by any means impair Arina Petrovna's financial condition. On the contrary, in reducing the number of shareholders it contributed indirectly to the rounding out of the family estate. For Arina Petrovna was a woman of strict principles, and once having "thrown them a bone," she considered her obligations toward her unloved children completely and definitely settled. In regard to her grandchildren it never entered her mind that in due time she would have to part with something for them. All she cared for was to draw all the income possible from the small estate of her deceased daughter and deposit it in the Chamber of Trustees. "There I am," she would say, "laying by money for the orphans. For feeding and bringing them up I take nothing from them. For the bread they eat it is God who will pay me."

As for the younger children, Porfiry and Pavel, they served in St. Petersburg, the former in a civil capacity, the latter in the army. Porfiry was married; Pavel was an old bachelor.

Porfiry Vladimirych was known in the family by three nicknames, Yudushka (diminutive of Judas), Bloodsucker, and Goody-goody Boy, which had been invented by Simple Simon. From his early childhood Porfiry had been oddly intent upon currying favor with his "dear mamma" and showed a tendency to play the sycophant. He would open the door of his mother's room softly, creep noiselessly into a corner, and sit there, as if entranced, with his eyes fixed on his mother while she wrote or busied herself with accounts. Even in those days Arina Petrovna regarded her son's efforts to insinuate himself into her good graces with vague suspicion. His stare puzzled her. She could not decide what his eyes expressed, whether venom or filial reverence. "I cannot make out what is in his eyes," she sometimes argued with herself. "His glance is like a noose which he is getting ready to throw. He might look like that handing a person poison or enticing him into a pitfall."

In this connection she often recollected highly significant details of the time she was carrying Porfisha. An old man called Porfisha the Saint was at that time living in the manor. He had the reputation of a seer, and Arina Petrovna turned to him whenever she wanted to learn something about the future. She had asked him when she would be delivered of the child and whether it would be a boy or a girl; but the pious old man gave no direct answer. Instead he crowed three times like a cock and then mumbled:

"Cockerel, cockerel, sharp claw! The cock crows and threatens the brood-hen; the brood-hen—cluck! cluck!—but it will be too late!"

That was all he said. Three days later (the seer crowed three times!) Arina Petrovna gave birth to a son ("cockerel! cockerel!") and named him Porfiry in honor of the old soothsayer. The first half of the prophecy had been fulfilled; but what could be the hidden meaning of the mysterious words, "the brood-hen—cluck! cluck!—but it will be too late?" Arina Petrovna often pondered over it, whenever her eyes fell on Porfisha, who sat in his nook with his enigmatic gaze fixed on her.

Meanwhile Porfisha kept on staring, quiet and meek, staring so intently that his wide-open, motionless eyes began to swim in tears, as if he vaguely sensed the doubts that tormented his mother's soul, and wished to behave so as to disarm her most persistent suspicion. At the risk of annoying his mother, he constantly hovered about her, and the expression in his eyes seemed to say: "Look at me! I conceal nothing from you. I am all obedience and devotion, and, mind you, I am obedient and devoted not only from fear but also from loyalty." And although an inner voice constantly sounded warning that the young scoundrel was dangerous in spite of his wheedling and fawning, her heart could not resist such unremitting devotion and her hand involuntarily felt for the best piece in the dish to bestow upon the affectionate child. And yet the very sight of him at times awakened a vague fear of something puzzling and eery.

The exact opposite of Porfiry was his brother, Pavel, the most perfect embodiment of absolute passivity. As a boy he manifested no inclination whatever for study, or games, or playing with other boys, but liked to keep to himself. He would get into a corner, pout, and set to work building air castles, dreaming that he had gorged himself with oatmeal so that his legs had become thin and he had no lessons to learn, or else that he was Davidka, the shepherd, with a growing lump on his forehead, just like David's, and cracked a whip and had no lessons to learn. Arina Petrovna would gaze at him for a long time, and then her motherly feelings would well up:

"Why do you sit there like a mouse on groats?" she would scold. "Is the poison working in you already? Why don't you come over to your mother and say: 'Mamenka darling, hug me?'"

Pavel would leave his place of refuge and slowly approach his mother, as if someone were pushing him from behind. "Mamenka darling," he would repeat in a bass voice unnatural in a child, "hug me."

"Get out of my sight, you sneak. You think if you get into your corner I don't understand. You are mistaken, my darling. I see through and through you. Your plans and projects are as clear as if they were spread on the palm of my hand."

And Pavel would just as slowly retrace his steps and bury himself again in his corner.

Years passed by, and Pavel Vladimirych gradually developed that apathetic, unaccountably gloomy character which often goes with absolute passivity. He was, perhaps, good, but he had done nobody any good; he was, perhaps, not without some intelligence, but he had not achieved anything intelligent in his life. He was hospitable, but people did not like to avail themselves of his hospitality. He spent money readily, but nothing good or pleasant came of his lavishness to anybody. He never harmed anybody, but that was not considered a merit. He was honest, but no one had ever heard it said: "How honorably Pavel Golovliov dealt in that affair!" It must be added that sometimes, not often, he snarled at his mother, although he feared her like poison. I repeat, he was an ill-tempered person, but back of his moroseness was nothing but sheer inertness.

When the brothers reached maturity, the difference in their characters was most conspicuous in their relation to their mother. Yudushka punctually every week sent a lengthy epistle to "mother dear," in which he informed her in the greatest detail of all the minutiæ of his life in St. Petersburg, and assured her of his disinterested filial devotion in the most carefully selected terms. As for Pavel, he wrote rarely, laconically, and sometimes even enigmatically, pulling every word out of himself with a pair of tongs, as it were.

"My adorable friend and dear mother," is what Porfiry Vladimirych wrote, for instance, "I have received the money from the peasant Yerofeyev, and I send you my most heartfelt thanks for forwarding the sum, which, according to your gracious wish, dearest mamenka, is to be spent for my maintenance. I also kiss your hands with sincere filial devotion. What worries and grieves me is the thought that you are straining your precious health all too much by your ceaseless efforts to satisfy not only our needs, but our whims as well. I don't know what brother thinks, but I— —" etc., etc.

As for Pavel, what he wrote on a similar occasion was: "Dear mother, am in receipt of the money, and, according to my calculations, you still owe six and a half rubles, for which I beg to be graciously forgiven."

When Arina Petrovna wrote reprimanding the children for their extravagance—she did so rather frequently, although there was no serious necessity for it—Porfisha invariably received her rebuke submissively and replied: "I am well aware, my dearest friend and mother, that you bear the heaviest burdens for the sake of us, your unworthy children. I know that often our behavior does not justify your motherly solicitude, and what is worse, erring humans that we are, we often forget it, for which I apologize most devotedly and sincerely, in the hope that in the course of time I will overcome my weakness and be more prudent in my expenditure of the funds that you send, my adorable friend and mother, for my maintenance and for other purposes." Pavel would answer back: "Dearest mother, though you have not as yet paid any of my debts, I accept most submissively the name of spendthrift which you choose to bestow upon me, whereof I beg most sincerely to accept my assurance."

Even the replies that the brothers made to the letter announcing the death of their sister, Anna Vladimirovna, were quite different from each other. Porfiry Vladimirych said: "The news of the death of my dear sister and good playmate, Anna Vladimirovna, has filled my heart with sorrow, a sorrow aggravated by the thought that a new cross has been given you to bear, dearest little mother, in the shape of two little orphans. Is it not sufficient that you, common benefactress to us all, deny yourself everything and, without sparing your health, concentrate all your power on the sole object of assuring the family not only the necessaries of life but also the luxuries? Believe me, it is a wicked thing to do, but now and then, I confess, I cannot refrain from grumbling. As far as I can see, the only solace for you, my dearest, in this state of affairs is to remember as often as you can all that Christ himself had to undergo." Pavel's reply ran: "The news of my sister, who has fallen a victim, I have received. I hope, however, that the Most High will rest her in His celestial tent, although this is uncertain."

Arina Petrovna reading these letters would try to guess which of the two sons would be her destruction. At times she felt certain the danger was coming from Porfiry Vladimirych.

"Look how he wags his tongue, a regular fiend at writing!" she would exclaim. "Simple Simon's nickname suits to a tee—Yudushka! Not a word of truth in all this stuff about my burdens, my cross, and the rest. Sheer lies! Not an ounce of feeling in his heart!"

At other times Pavel Vladimirych seemed to be her real enemy.

"A fool, and yet look how deftly he tries to make love to mother on the sly. 'Whereof I beg most sincerely to accept my assurance!' Wait a while! I'll teach you what 'accept assurances' means! I shall deal with you as I did with Simple Simon, and you'll find out what I mean by your 'assurances'!"

In the end a truly tragical cry would burst from her lips. "And for whom am I hoarding all this wealth? For whom am I gathering all this? I deny myself sleep and food—for whom?"

Such were the domestic circumstances of the Golovliovs at the time that the bailiff, Anton Vasilyev, reported to Arina Petrovna that Simple Simon had dissipated "the bone" flung to him, which, in view of its loss, might now be called with especial significance the "parental blessing."

Arina Petrovna sat in her bedroom, all her senses dazed. A vague, unaccountable feeling stirred within her, whether pity, born suddenly and miraculously, for her hated offspring, who, after all, was her son, or whether merely thwarted despotism, the most expert psychologist would have been unable to decide. Her sensations were utterly confused and succeeded each other with bewildering swiftness. Finally, out of the welter of her thoughts there crystallized one emotion, the fear that "the horrid creature" would again be hanging round her neck.

"Aniutka has forced her whelps on me, and now this dunderhead is coming here," she pondered deeply.

Long she sat silent, her eyes fixed and intent. Dinner was brought in, but she hardly touched it; a servant came and said the master wanted brandy. Without looking up she threw him the keys of the store-room. After the meal she ordered the bath to be prepared for her. Then she went into the oratory, ordered all the image lamps to be lit, and shut herself in. These were all clear signs that the mistress was "in a temper," and so the house turned as quiet as a churchyard. The chambermaids walked on tiptoe; Akulina, the housekeeper, ran back and forth like a lunatic. The preparations for preserving had been set for after dinner; the berries had been rinsed and made ready, but the mistress gave no orders either to go ahead or to wait. The gardener, Matvey, came to ask whether it was time to gather the peaches, but such was his reception in the maids' room that he fled precipitately.

Prayers and bath over, Arina Petrovna felt almost reconciled with the world and had the bailiff summoned again.

"Now tell me, what is the numskull doing?" she asked.

"Well, Moscow is big, it would take more than a year to walk through it."

"But he needs something to fill his stomach with, doesn't he?"

"Our peasants feed him. He eats with one, gets money for tobacco from another."

"And who permits them to give him anything?"

"Goodness me, madam! The people don't complain. They give alms to strangers. Should they refuse a mite to their own master's son?"

"I'll teach them to give mites! I'll have the blockhead deported to your estate, and the community will have to maintain him at its own expense."

"As you command, madam."

"What? What did you say?"

"As you command, my lady. If you order it, we shall feed him."

"That's better. But talk sensibly."

A pause ensued. Then the bailiff, true to his nature and his nickname, lost patience and began to shift from one leg to another, obviously burning with the desire to unburden his mind of something.

"He's a clever one, though," he finally blurted out. "People say he brought back a hundred rubles from the campaign. It isn't a fortune, but still one can live on it for a time."

"Well?"

"He thought he might improve his situation and went in for a shady business."

"Go on, go on, and don't give me any lies."

"He went to the German Club. He thought he would find a fool to beat at cards, but instead he happened on a cunning hawk. He tried to get away, but was held up in the lobby. Of course, he was plucked clean."

"I suppose he was roughly handled, too."

"Of course. The next morning he came to our man, Ivan Mikhailych, and told the tale himself. It's queer, he was in high spirits and laughed as if they had treated him like a lord."

"Things run from him like water off a duck's back. But I won't grieve over it, provided he does not come within sight of me."

"But I believe he will."

"Nonsense, I will not allow him to cross my threshold."

"But I'm sure he will," insisted Anton Vasilyev. "He said so in plain words to Ivan Mikhailych. 'Enough,' he says, 'I am going back to the old woman to eat her dry crusts.' And, madam, to speak the truth, where can he lay his head but here? He cannot keep on forever feeding on our men in Moscow. And besides, he needs clothing and comforts."

That was exactly the thing Arina Petrovna dreaded. It was the very essence of the obscure thought that so deeply alarmed her. "Yes, he will turn up," she said to herself, "he has no other place to go to, there's no doubt of it." He would always be there, within her sight, that accursed, hated stranger of a son. What had been the good of throwing his portion to him? She had thought that, having received "his due," he would drop into eternity. And there he was, rising from the dead. He would come, make insolent demands, and hang on like a leech, shocking everybody by his beggarly appearance. And she would have to meet his demands, because he was a brazen-faced bully, capable of any violence. You cannot put such a man under restraint; he is capable of parading in tatters before strangers, of the wildest debauchery, of running away to the neighbors and telling them the ins and outs of the family affairs. Should she have him deported to the Suzdal Monastery, which was said to be a place for ridding parents in distress of the sight of their refractory children? But the Lord knows whether that fabulous institution existed at all. People said there were such things as houses of correction. But how could one get an overgrown dolt into one of them?

In short, Arina Petrovna was altogether upset by the thought of how the arrival of Simple Simon was going to disturb her peaceful existence.

"I shall billet him upon you," was her threat to the bailiff. "Feed him at your own expense."

"Why so, madam?"

"Because you stand there croaking: 'He's sure to come,'" she mimicked. "Get out of my sight, you raven!"

Anton Vasilyev turned to go, but Arina Petrovna stopped him:

"Wait a minute. Is it true that he is starting out for Golovliovo?"

"I'm not in the habit of telling lies, madam. He said so plainly—'I am going back to the old woman to eat her dry crusts.'"

"He'll soon find out what kind of crusts the old woman has prepared for him."

"But, madam, he won't live with you long."

"Why not?"

"Well, madam, he coughs very badly and keeps on clutching the left side of his chest. He won't live long."

"That kind generally lives very long. He'll outlive us all. The coughing doesn't hurt him. Well, we shall see about it later. Leave me now. I have several matters to attend to."

Arina Petrovna spent the whole evening pondering over this problem. Finally she found it best to convoke the family council for the purpose of deciding what was to be done with Simple Simon. Such constitutionalism was not her habit. She made up her mind to digress from the traditions of autocracy solely for the purpose of shielding herself from public censure, and as she did not doubt the outcome of the conference, she sat down with a light heart to write to Porfiry and Pavel asking them to come to Golovliovo immediately.

CHAPTER III

Meanwhile, the cause of all this mess, Simple Simon, was on his way to Golovliovo. In Moscow he engaged a seat in one of the so-called "diligences," in which small merchants and peasant traders used to travel, and which are still seen in some districts. The diligence had the city of Vladimir as its point of destination, and Stepan was enabled to travel in it through the liberality of the aforesaid innkeeper Ivan Mikhailych, who also paid for his master's meals on the journey.

"Listen," said Ivan Mikhailych, with the air of an accomplice. "Do this, get off at the station and go straight up to your mother just as you are."

"Yes, yes, yes," answered Stepan Vladimirych approvingly. "The house is only about fifteen versts from there. I can walk it in no time. I shall appear before her all dirty and dusty."

"When your mother sees you in that rig, perhaps she'll take pity on you."

"She will, she will. Mother, after all, is a kindly old woman."

Stepan Golovliov was not quite forty, but he looked like fifty. Life had so thoroughly worn him out that there was not a vestige of his noble origin left, not a single trace of his university education nor of the enlightening word of science which in days bygone had been addressed to him, too. He was tall as a Maypole, racked by hunger, unkempt, untidy, with a sunken chest and long bony arms. His bloated face, his dishevelled hair, streaked with grey, his loud, hoarse voice, his bulging, bloodshot eyes were unmistakable signs of heavy drinking and a weather-beaten life. He wore an old, threadbare uniform, with the galloons gone—they had been sold to a smelter—and a pair of reddish boots, patched and sadly worn. Beneath his coat, when unbuttoned, peeped a dirty shirt, as black as if it had been smeared with soot. With the cynicism of a militiaman, he called it "a flea nest."

His glance was stealthy and gloomy, the expression not of inner discontent, but rather of a vague anxiety which seemed to come from an ever-present fear of death by starvation. He talked ceaselessly and disconnectedly, passing without transition from one subject to another. He spoke whether Ivan Mikhailych listened or dozed off under the soporific of his garrulousness. He was dreadfully uncomfortable, because there were four people in the diligence and he had to sit with his legs bent, so that at the end of three or four versts he had an intolerable pain in his knee-joints. Nevertheless the pain did not prevent him from talking. Clouds of dust entered through the side windows of the vehicle, at times flooded by a flaming, scorching sheet of sunlight. But Stepan Golovliov kept on talking.

"Yes, brother," he held forth, "I have lived hard all my life. It is high time to rest. I shan't be eating her out of house and home, shall I? She has enough and to spare. What d'you think, Ivan Mikhailych?"

"Oh, your mother has plenty to eat."

"Yes, but not for me, you mean to say? Yes, friend, she has heaps of money, but not a copper for me. And to think the hag has always hated me. Why? But now I'll sing her a different song. I've made up my mind. I'm desperate. If she tries to drive me out, I won't go. If she doesn't give me food, I'll take it. I've served my country, brother. Now it's everyone's duty to help me. There's only one thing I'm afraid of, that she won't give me tobacco."

"Yes, you'll have to say good-by to tobacco."

"Then I'll put the screw on the bailiff. The devil can well afford to give his master a present now and then."

"Oh, yes, he may do that, but what if your mother forbids him to?"

"Well, in that case I'll be done for. Tobacco is the only luxury that has remained of my former style. When I had money I used to smoke not less than a quarter of a pound of Zhukov's tobacco every day."

"I guess you'll have to do without brandy, too."

"Another calamity. Brandy does me a lot of good. It breaks up my phlegm. When we were marching to Sebastopol, we had hardly reached Serpukhov, when each man had already been given three gallons of brandy."

"You must have lost your senses."

"I don't remember. We marched as far as Kharkov, but I'll be hanged if I remember anything else. The only thing I can recall is that we passed through villages and towns and that at Tula an *otkupshchik* made a speech. He shed tears, the scoundrel did. Yes, our holy mother Russia drank from the cup of sorrow in those days. *Otkupshchiki*, contractors, receivers—it's a wonder God succeeded in saving the country from them."

"Oh, your mother came in for some of the profits. In our village hardly half of the soldiers returned home. A recruit's receipt is now given for each man lost in the campaign, and the government rates such a quittance at more than four hundred rubles."

"Yes, my mater is a cunning blade. She ought to be a minister of state instead of housekeeper at Golovliovo. Let me tell you, she has been unjust to me and she has insulted me, but I respect her. The main thing is, she's clever as the devil. If not for her, where would we have been now? We would have had nothing but Golovliovo with its one hundred and one and a half souls. Just think what an enormous pile she has made."

"Well, your brothers will certainly be rich."

"Yes. But I'll have nothing, that's just as certain. Yes, friend, I've gone to rack and ruin. But my brothers, they'll be rich, especially the Bloodsucker. He can ensnare a person in no time, and it won't be long before he'll undo her, too. He'll pump the estate and the money out of her. I have an eye for these things. But Pavel, he's a fine chap. He will send my tobacco on the sly. You'll see if he doesn't. As soon as I reach Golovliovo, I'll send a note off to him: 'Dear brother, it's so and so with me. Ease my soul.' Ah, if I were rich!"

"What would you do?"

"In the first place, I'd make you roll in wealth."

"Why me? First think of yourself. I'm contented, living as I do under your mother's rule."

"Oh, no, brother, *attendez!* I would make you the chief marshal of all my estates. Yes, my dear friend, you have fed and warmed a soldier, accept my thanks. If not for your generosity, I should now be footing it all the way to the home of my fathers. And, of course, I would free you on the spot and open up all my treasury to you—drink, eat and be merry. What did you think I would do?"

"You'd better stop worrying about me, sir. What else would you do if you were rich?"

"In the second place, I'd get a mistress at once. At Kursk I went to mass once and saw one—a queen! She was very fidgety and restless."

"But maybe she would object to becoming your mistress."

"And how about hard cash? What's the filthy lucre for? If a hundred thousand is not enough for her, she'll take two hundred thousand. When I have money, no expense is too great for me, if it is a question of getting a bit of pleasure out of life. I must confess that at the time I let her know through our corporal that I would give her three rubles. But the wench asked five."

"That was too much for you, of course!"

"Well, I can't tell. As I said, I was in a dream the whole time. Maybe she came to me, but I forget. Those two months of marching have gone completely out of my mind. No such thing has happened to you, I suppose?"

Ivan Mikhailych was silent. Stepan Vladimirych looked at him attentively and discovered that his fellow-traveller was sound asleep.

"Umph," he said. "He has nodded off, the sleepy-head. You have grown fat, brother, on the tea and fare of your eating-house. I can't sleep, not a wink. A good chance for a lark."

Golovliov looked around and saw that everybody was asleep. The merchant at his side was constantly striking his head against a cross-beam, but kept on sleeping. His face shone as if veneered, and flies swarmed about his mouth. A splendid idea, Stepan thought, to cram all the flies down the merchant's throat. His hand began to move toward the merchant, but halfway he repented and gave up the idea. "No more pranks," he said, "enough. Sleep, friends, and rest." Meanwhile—where had he hidden the bottle? Here, the darling! "Let me see you. Lord, save Thy creatures," he hummed, taking out a bottle from a bag fastened to the side of the vehicle and applying it to his mouth. "Ah, that's better. It warms your insides, you know. Shall I have some more? Well, no. The station is about twenty versts from here. I'll have time to get as drunk as a lord. But shan't I have just one drop more? The deuce take it, the vodka. The bottle simply acts like a charm. It's wicked to drink, but how can you help it, if it is the only way of getting some sleep? I wish the vodka, the deuce take it, would do for me quick."

He gulped down some more vodka, returned the bottle to its place, and began to fill his pipe.

"We are all right," he said, talking to himself. "First, we had a sip, and here we are smoking. She won't let me have any tobacco, the old hag, sure as fate she won't, the man is right. Will she give me food? She may send me what is left over from her meals. Well, we, too, had money, but now we have none. Such is life. To-day you eat and drink your fill, you enjoy yourself and smoke a pipe,

"'And to-morrow—where art thou, man?'

Still it would not be a bad thing to have a bite now. I drink like a fish and I hardly ever have a square meal. Doctors say drinking does you good only when followed by a hearty meal, as the Most Reverend Smaragd said when we passed through Oboyan. Was it Oboyan? The deuce knows, it may have been Kromy. But that's immaterial now. The main question is, how to get something to eat. I recollect that my man put a sausage and three rolls into the bag. Caviar is too expensive for the rascal. Look at the fellow—sleeps like a log and sings through his nose. I wouldn't be surprised if he were sitting on the bag."

He rummaged about in search of the bag, but could not find it.

"Ivan Mikhailych, Ivan Mikhailych," he shouted to the sleeping innkeeper. The man woke up and for a while could not make out where he was and how he happened to be sitting opposite his master.

"I was just beginning to nap," he said finally.

"Sleep, friend, sleep. I only want to know where the bag with the food is."

"Are you hungry? But you would like a drink first, I suppose."

"Right. Where is the bottle?"

Stepan Vladimirych took a drink, and then attacked the sausage, which happened to be as salty as salt itself and as hard as stone, so that he had to use the point of his knife to pierce it.

"Some whitefish would taste good now," he remarked.

"Excuse me, sir, I clean forgot about the whitefish. All morning I kept saying to my wife: 'Be sure to remind me of the whitefish.' I am very sorry."

"Oh, it doesn't matter. The sausage is good enough for me. When we were on the campaign, we ate worse things. Father used to tell that two Englishmen made a bet. One of them was to eat a dead cat, and he ate it."

"You don't say!"

"He did. And he was as sick as a dog afterwards. He cured himself with rum. He guzzled two bottles as fast as he could, and that set him right at once. Another Englishman made a bet that he would live a whole year on nothing but sugar."

"Did he win?"

"No. He kicked the bucket two days before the end of the year. And how about you, why don't you take a drink?"

"I never touch it."

"So you swill nothing but tea. No good, brother. That's why your belly has grown so big. One must be careful with tea. A cup of tea must be followed by a glass of vodka. Tea gathers phlegm, vodka breaks it up. Isn't that so?"

"Well, I don't know. You are learned; you know better."

"True. On the campaign we had no time to bother with tea or coffee. But vodka—that's a holy affair. You unscrew the flask, pour the vodka into a cup, drink, and that's all. At that time we had to march so fast that for ten days I went without washing."

"You certainly roughed it, sir."

"Yes, marching on the highroad is not a joke. Still, on our way forward it was not so bad. People gave us money, and there was plenty to eat and drink. But when we marched back there was no more fêting."

Golovliov gnawed at the sausage and finally chewed up a piece.

"It is very salty, this sausage is," he said. "But I'm not squeamish. After all, mother won't feed me on tid-bits. A plate of cabbage soup and some gruel—that's all she'll let me have."

"God is merciful. Maybe she'll give you pie on holidays."

"No, I imagine there'll be no tea, no tobacco, no vodka. People say she has become fond of playing fool, so she may call me in to take a hand at the game and give me some tea. As for the rest, there is no hope."

There was a four-hour rest to feed the horses. Golovliov had finished the bottle and was tormented by hunger. The travellers entered the inn and settled down to a hearty meal.

Stepan Vladimirych took a stroll in the court, paid a visit to the backyard, the stables and the dovecote, and even tried to sleep. Finally he came to the conclusion that the best thing for him to do was to join his fellow-travellers in the inn. There the cabbage soup was already steaming and on a wooden tray on the sideboard lay a great chunk of beef, which Ivan Mikhailych was just then engaged in carving. Golovliov seated himself a little way from the table, lighted his pipe, and sat silent for quite a while pondering over the way in which he could allay the pangs of hunger.

"I wish you a good appetite, gentlemen," he said finally, "the soup seems to be good and rich."

"The soup is all right," answered Ivan Mikhailych. "Why don't you order a portion for yourself?"

"Oh, it was only a remark on my part. I'm not hungry."

"Impossible. All you've eaten is a bit of sausage, and the damned thing only teases one's appetite. Please eat something. I'll have a separate table laid for you. My dear woman," he turned to the hostess, "a place for the gentleman."

The passengers silently attacked their meal and now and then exchanged meaningful looks. Golovliov felt his fellow-travellers suspected how matters stood, although he had played master throughout the journey, not without some arrogance, and had addressed the faithful innkeeper as if he had merely entrusted him with his cash. His brows knitted, and a thick cloud of smoke escaped from his mouth. In the depths of his heart he felt he ought to refuse, but so imperative are the dictates of hunger that he set upon the bowl of cabbage soup like a beast of prey and emptied it in a trice. Along with satiety came his customary self-assurance and, as if nothing were the matter, he said, turning to Ivan Mikhailych:

"Well, my cashier, you will pay up for me, and I am off for the hayloft to have a talk with Mr. Khrapovitzky."

He jogged over to the hayloft, and as his stomach was full he was soon fast asleep. He woke up at five o'clock in the morning. Noticing that the horses stood at their empty bins rubbing their noses against the edges, he roused the driver. "He sleeps like a top, the rascal," he shouted. "We're in a hurry, and he's having pleasant dreams."

Soon the travellers reached the station at which the road turned off to Golovliovo. Here at last Stepan Vladimirych lost some of his devil-may-care attitude and became crestfallen and taciturn. Ivan Mikhailych tried to cheer him up and insisted that he part with his pipe.

"You'd better throw the pipe into the nettles, sir, when you come to the manor-house," he coaxed. "You will find it later on."

Finally the horses that were to take the innkeeper to the end of his journey were ready, and the moment of parting came.

"Good-by, brother," said Golovliov in a tremulous voice, kissing Ivan Mikhailych. "She'll plague the life out of me."

"The Lord is merciful. Keep up a stout heart."

"She'll eat me up alive," repeated Stepan Vladimirych, with such conviction that the innkeeper involuntarily lowered his eyes.

With these words Golovliov turned sharply along the country road, walking in a shuffle and leaning on a gnarled stick which he had cut off a tree.

Ivan Mikhailych followed him with his eyes for a while, and then ran after him.

"Listen, master," he said. "When I was cleaning your uniform a few minutes ago, I saw three rubles in your side pocket. Please don't lose them."

Stepan Vladimirych was visibly irresolute and could not make up his mind how to act in this contingency. Finally, he stretched out his hand to the peasant and said, with tears in his eyes:

"I understand—to buy tobacco for the old trooper? Thanks. But she'll eat me up alive, friend. Sure as hell."

Golovliov found the country road again and several minutes later his grey soldier's cap showed afar off, now vanishing, now appearing above the young wood. It was early in the day. The morning mist, touched into gold by the first rays of the sun, hovered above the country road. The grass glistened with the dew, and the air was redolent of fir-trees, mushrooms, and wild berries. The road meandered across a plain swarming with birds.

Stepan Vladimirych, however, noticed nothing of the beauty about him. All his frivolity had suddenly gone, and he walked as if to the Last Judgment. One thought filled his mind to the exclusion of everything else. In three or four hours he would have reached his goal. He recalled his life at Golovliovo, and he felt as if the doors of a damp cellar were opening to let him in, and no sooner would he penetrate into the gloomy interior than the doors would close behind him and everything would be over. Memories prophetic of what awaited him at Golovliovo surged in his mind. There had been uncle Mikhail Petrovich, popularly known as Mishka the Squabbler, one of the "horrid" members of the family, whom grandfather Piotr Ivanych had exiled to Golovliovo, where he had lived in the servants' quarters and eaten out of the same dish with Trezorka, the house dog. There had been Aunt Vera Mikhailovna, who had lived on the estate by her brother's favor and died of "moderate living"; for Arina Petrovna had begrudged her every mouthful at dinner and every billet of wood for the stove in her room. And a similar fate awaited him.

He foresaw an endless succession of joyless days losing themselves in a grey yawning abyss, and he involuntarily shut his eyes. Henceforth he would have to be alone with a wicked old woman, half dead in the stagnation of despotism. She would be the death of him before long, as sure as fate. Not a soul to speak to, not a place to visit. She would be everywhere, scornful, despotic, deadening. The thought of that inevitable future made his heart so heavy that he stopped under a tree in desperation, and struck his head against it several times. His entire life with all its farcical strutting, idleness, and buffoonery loomed up as if flooded with sudden light. Then he started on his way again. He felt there was nothing else left for him. The least of men can make some effort, can earn his bread. He alone was helpless. It was a new thought. He had been accustomed in thinking of his future to picture various prospects, but always prospects of wealth coupled with idleness, never prospects of work. And now the time had come when he had to pay for the wickedness and aimlessness of his existence. It was a bitter settlement, summed up in the terrible phrase: "She will be the end of me."

It was about nine o'clock in the morning when the white Golovliovo belfry showed above the forest. The traveller's face grew pale, and his hands began to tremble. He took off his cap and crossed himself. The parable of the prodigal son and his return occurred to him, but he at once rejected the idea as a bit of self-delusion.

Finally, he noticed the boundary-post standing by the wayside, and presently he was treading the Golovliovo soil, the hateful soil that had borne him, an unloved child, that had reared him, sent him, hated, into the wide world, and was now receiving him, the unloved one, back into its arms again. The sun was high in the heavens and was ruthlessly scorching the boundless fields of Golovliovo. But Stepan Vladimirych was growing paler and shivering with ague.

At length he reached the churchyard, and here his courage failed utterly. The manor-house looked out from behind the trees as if nothing unpleasant had ever happened there; yet the sight of it worked on him like the vision of a Medusa head. His paternal abode seemed to be a tomb. "A tomb, tomb, tomb," he repeated unconsciously. He had not the courage to go straight to the house, but first called on the priest and sent him to break the news of his arrival and inquire whether his mother would receive him.

The priest's wife was very sympathetic and hastened to prepare an omelette. The village children gathered about him and stared at the master with wondering eyes. The peasants passing by lifted their hats in silence and looked at him curiously. One old servant ran up with the intention of kissing the master's hand. Everyone understood that a wastrel was before them, an unloved son who had returned to his hated home never to leave it except for the graveyard. At the thought of it the people were overwhelmed with a mingled feeling of pity and dread.

At last the priest returned and announced that the lady of the manor was ready to receive Stepan Vladimirych. Ten minutes later he was standing in her presence. Arina Petrovna met him severely and solemnly, and measured him icily from head to foot, but allowed herself no useless reproaches. She received him, not in the living room, but on the porch, and ordered the young master to be taken to his father through another entrance. The old man was dozing in his bed, under a white coverlet, in a white nightcap, all white like a corpse. When he felt the presence of his son he woke up and began to laugh idiotically.

"Well, friend, so now you are under the hag's paw," he cried, while his son kissed his hand. Then he crowed like a cock, burst out laughing again, and repeated several times: "She'll eat him up! She'll eat him up!" The phrase found echo in Stepan's soul.

His fears were justified. He was installed in a separate room in the wing that also housed the counting-room. He was given homespun underwear and an old discarded dressing-gown of his father's, which he put on immediately. The doors of the burial vault had opened, let him in, and closed again.

There now began a long succession of dull, ugly days, which Time's grey, yawning abyss swallowed up, one after the other. Arina Petrovna never received him, nor was he allowed to see his father. Three days after his arrival, his mother informed him through Finogey Ipatych, the bailiff, that he would receive board and clothing and also a pound of Faler's tobacco monthly. Stepan Vladimirych listened to the bailiff, and merely remarked:

"The hag! She's found out that Zhukov's tobacco costs two rubles, while Faler's is only one ruble ninety kopeks a pound. So she pockets ten kopeks a month."

The symptoms of the moral sobering that had appeared during the hours of his approaching Golovliovo on the country road, vanished. Frivolity reasserted its rights and was followed by an acceptance of the conditions his mother imposed upon him. The disquieting thought of the hopeless future, which had once pierced his mind, faded gradually away and finally was no more. The day and the evil thereof, the petty interests of existence in all its undisguised ugliness absorbed his entire being. What part, indeed, could his intentions and opinions play when the course of the rest of his life in all its details was laid out in advance in Arina Petrovna's brain?

All day long he walked to and fro in his room, pipe in mouth, humming bits of songs, passing unaccountably from church tunes to boisterous airs. If the village clerk happened to be in the office, he went up to him and engaged in a conversation, of which the chief topic was Arina Petrovna's income.

"What does she do with all her wealth?" he would exclaim wonderingly, having reached the sum of more than eighty thousand rubles. "My brothers' allowances are rather poor; she herself lives shabbily, and she feeds cured meats to father. She deposits the money in the bank, that's what she does with it."

On one occasion Finogey Ipatych came to deliver the taxes he had gathered, and the table was littered with paper money, and Stepan's eyes glittered.

"Ah, what a heap of money!" he exclaimed. "And it all flows right down her throat. As for giving her son some of these nice greenbacks, no, she wouldn't do that. She wouldn't say: 'Here, my son, you who are visited by sorrow, here is some cash for wine and tobacco.'"

This was usually followed by endless cynical talks about how he could win over his mother's heart.

"In Moscow," he held forth, "I used to meet a man who knew a magic word. If his mother refused to give him money he would utter 'the word,' and she instantly got cramps in her hands and feet, in fact all over."

"It must have been a spell, I suppose," remarked the village clerk.

"Well, whatever it may have been, it is gospel truth that there is such a 'word.' Another man told me this: 'Take,' he says, 'a frog, and put it into an anthill at midnight. By morning the ants will have gnawed it clean, so that only its skeleton will be left. Take the skeleton, and when it is in your pocket ask anything you wish of any woman, and she won't refuse you."

"Well, that's easy."

"The trouble is, one must first damn oneself forever. If it weren't for that, the old hag would be cringing before me."

Hours on end were spent in such talk, but no remedy was found. The preliminary condition was that you either had to call a curse down on yourself, or sell your soul to the devil. There was no help. Stepan Vladimirych had to go on living under his mother's rule, the only relief coming in the small voluntary contributions that he raised from the village officials in the form of tobacco, tea, and sugar. His fare consisted mainly of what remained from his mother's table, and as Arina Petrovna was moderate to the point of avarice, his board was meagre, to say the least; which was all the more painful because ever since vodka had become unattainable, his appetite had grown considerably keener. All day long hunger gnawed at him, and his sole preoccupation was how to fill his stomach. He awaited the hour when his mother would retire for a rest, then sneaked into the kitchen and looked into the servants' quarters, snatching a bit here, a bit there. Sometimes he would sit at his open window watching for passers-by. If one of the serfs came along, he stopped him and levied toll in the form of an egg, a curd-cake, and the like.

At the first meeting between mother and son, Arina Petrovna briefly explained the whole program of his life.

"Live here," she said. "Here is a shelter for you in the counting-house. Your meals you will get from my table. In other matters you will have to put up with things as they are. There were never any dainties in the house, and I shan't change my ways for your sake. Your brothers will soon arrive. Whatever they will decide about you, I shall carry out. I shall take no sin upon my soul. Let them dispose of your fate."

He looked forward to his brothers' arrival with impatience. Not that he reflected on the influence their arrival might have on his existence, as he had evidently decided that the matter was not worth his thought. The only thing that interested him was whether Pavel would bring him tobacco and how much.

"Maybe he'll hand me over some coin, too," he mused. "Porfishka the Bloodsucker, he won't, but Pavel ... I'll say to him: 'Brother, give a soldier some cash for wine.' He'll give me some. He's sure to."

He did not notice the passage of the days, nor did he feel the weight of his absolute idleness. The only time he was lonesome was in the evenings, because the constable left at eight, and Arina Petrovna did not allow her son any candles, on the ground that one can walk to and fro without light. He soon became accustomed to the dark and even began to love it, for in the darkness his imagination had free play and carried him far, far away from the dreary place which was his home. In those hours only one thing disturbed him. He had a dull pain in the chest and his heart palpitated queerly, especially when he went to bed. Sometimes he jumped out of bed and ran about the room, clutching the left side of his chest.

"I wish I would die," he thought at such moments. "But, no, I shan't die. But maybe I shall."

One morning when the village clerk with an air of mystery reported that his brothers had arrived the night before, he shuddered and grew pale. Something childlike suddenly awoke in him. He felt like running to the house to see how his brothers were dressed, and find out what beds had been prepared for them, and whether they had travelling cases like one he had seen a militia captain carrying, and hear how they would talk to mother, and spy out what would be served at dinner. In short, a desire once more arose in him to return to life, which so persistently rejected him, to fall at "dear mamma's" knees, and obtain her pardon. Then perhaps he would eat the fatted calf and be merry.

The house was still quiet, but he had already visited, the kitchen and found out that the following courses had been ordered for dinner: soup with fresh cabbage, also some soup left over from yesterday, cured meat served with cutlets of chopped meat for entree, fried mutton chops and four snipes for the roast, and raspberry pie with cream for dessert.

"Yesterday's soup, cured meat, and the chops—that, brother, is for me," he said to the cook. "There will be no pie for me, I guess."

"For your mother to say, sir."

"Ah, friend, there was a time when I ate snipe. Yes, I did. Once I made a bet with Lieutenant Gremykin that I would eat fifteen snipes one after the other, and what do you think? I won the bet. After that I couldn't look at snipe for a month."

"But you won't refuse to have some now?"

"She wouldn't let me have any. I can't see, though, what makes her so stingy. A snipe is a free bird. You don't have to feed it or look after it. It is self-supporting. She doesn't buy snipes any more than she buys sheep—and yet! The hag knows snipe tastes better than mutton. That's why she won't let me have it. She'd rather let it rot than give it to me. What's ordered for breakfast?"

"Liver, mushrooms in sour cream, and custard."

"Why not send me a custard? Do, brother."

"Well, I'll try hard. Let me tell you, sir. When the brothers sit down to breakfast, you send the village clerk here. He'll fetch you a couple of custards under his coat."

Next day Stepan Vladimirych waited the entire morning for his brothers, but they did not arrive. Finally, about eleven o'clock, the village clerk brought the two promised custards and reported that the brothers had just finished breakfast and were closeted with Arina Petrovna in her bedroom.

CHAPTER IV

Arina Petrovna received her sons solemnly, weighed down by grief. Two maids supported her under the armpits. Her grey locks streamed out from under her cap, her head drooped, and shook from side to side, and her limbs seemed hardly able to support her. She always liked to play the part of a venerable, careworn mother before her children, moving with difficulty and getting her maids to assist her. Simple Simon called such solemn receptions high mass, herself a bishop, and the maids, Polka and Yulka, mace-bearers. As it was late at night the interview was almost a silent one. Without saying a word she gave her sons her hand to kiss; kissed them in turn, and made the sign of the cross over them; and when Porfiry Vladimirych made it clear that he would gladly spend the rest of the night with "mother dear," she merely waved her hand and said:

"Come now. Take a rest, you must be tired after the journey. This is not the time for discussion. We shall talk to-morrow."

Next morning the two sons went to kiss papa's hand, but papa refused his hand. He lay on his bed with closed eyes, and when they entered he cried out:

"Have you come to judge the toll-gatherer? Get out, Pharisees! Get out!"

But in spite of this reception, Porfiry Vladimirych emerged from papa's room agitated and with tears on his eyelids, while Pavel Vladimirych, like "the heartless dolt" that he was, merely picked his nose.

"He is very weak, mother dear, very weak!" exclaimed Porfiry Vladimirych, throwing himself on his mother's breast.

"Is it so bad?"

"Yes, very bad. He won't live much longer."

"Oh, well, it isn't as bad as that."

"No, dear, no. And although your life has never been too joyful, yet as I think how Fate deals you so many blows at once, upon my word, I wonder where you get the strength to bear up under it all."

"Well, my friend, the strength comes if such is the Lord's will. You know what it says in the Scriptures: 'Bear one another's burdens.' It seems that our Heavenly Father has chosen me to bear the burdens of my family."

Arina Petrovna shut her eyes, so delightful was this vision of the family finding their tables covered for them and of her toiling for them and bearing their burdens.

"Yes, my friend," she said after a minute's pause, "it's a hard life I lead in my old age. I have provided for my children, and it is time for me to rest. It's no joke—four thousand souls! At my age to take care of such an estate, to have an eye on everybody and everything, to run back and forth! As for all those bailiffs and managers, they look you straight in the eye, but, believe me, they are the most faithless kind. And you," she interrupted herself, turning to Pavel, "what are you digging in your nose for?"

"What have I to do with it?" snarled Pavel Vladimirych, disturbed in the very midst of his absorbing occupation.

"What do you mean? After all, he's your father. You might find a word of pity for him."

"Well—a father! A father like any other father. He has been that way for ten years. You always make things unpleasant for me."

"Why in the world should I, my boy? I am your mother. Here is Porfisha. He has found words of affection and pity for me as befits a good son, but you don't even look at your mother properly. You look at her out of the corner of your eye, as if she were not your mother, but your foe. Please don't bite me."

"Well, what——"

"Stop! Hold your tongue for a minute. Let your mother say a word. Do you remember the commandment, 'Honor thy father and thy mother, and all will be well with thee?' Am I to understand that you don't wish to be well?"

Pavel Vladimirych kept silence and looked at his mother in perplexity.

"You see, you're silenced," went on Arina Petrovna, "you are guilty. But I shall let you alone. For the sake of this joyful meeting we shall dispense with this talk. God, my child, sees everything. As for me, I see you through and through, and I always have. Children, children, you will remember your mother when she lies in her grave. You will remember her, but it will be too late."

"Mamma dear!" interposed Porfiry Vladimirych. "Away with such black thoughts, away with them!"

"We must all die," said Arina Petrovna sententiously. "These are not black, but pious thoughts. I'm growing weak, children, oh, how weak! Debility and ailments are the only things left of my former strength. Even the maids have noticed it, and they don't care a rap for me. If I say one word, they have ten in reply. I have only one threat, that I shall complain to the young masters. That works sometimes."

Tea was served and then breakfast, during which Arina Petrovna continued her complaining and self-pitying. After breakfast she invited her sons to her bedroom.

When the door was locked, she went straight to the business for which she had convoked the family council.

"Simple Simon is here," she began.

"We heard about it, mamma dear," said Porfiry Vladimirych; and it was hard to say whether it was irony or the calm complacency of a man who has just eaten a hearty meal that sounded in his voice.

"He has come here as if that were the proper thing to do. Whatever he may have done, he seems to think the old mother will always have bread for him. Think of all his hatred for me, of all the trouble his tricks and buffoonery have caused me. And what have I not done to get him a good berth? It all ran off like water from a duck's back. At last, I made up my mind. Goodness, if he cannot take care of himself, am I to ruin my life on account of the big lout? I'll give him a piece of the property, I decided. Perhaps, I thought, once an independent proprietor he'll sober down. No sooner said than done. I myself found a house for him and paid out twelve thousand silver rubles for it with my own hands. And what's the upshot? After less than three years he's hanging round my neck again. How long am I to stand such insults?"

Porfisha lifted up his eyes and shook his head sorrowfully, as if to say, "Fine doings. Why disturb mother dear so ruthlessly? Why not live peacefully and quietly? Then dear mamma would not be angry. Fine doings." But Porfisha's gestures did not please Arina Petrovna, who objected to any interruption to the course of her thoughts.

"Wait a minute," she said, "don't shake your head. Listen first. Think of my feelings when I learned that he had thrown away his parental blessing like a gnawed bone into a cesspool. Think how he outraged me, me, who for years refused myself sleep and food. He has done to his patrimony what one would do to a bauble bought at a fair."

"Oh, mother dear, what a shame, what a shame!" began Porfiry Vladimirych, but Arina Petrovna stopped him again.

"Wait a minute. Let me have your opinion when I order you to. If at least the scoundrel had come to me in time and said: 'I am guilty, dear mamma, I couldn't restrain myself,' I might have bought the house back for a song. The unworthy son did not know how to make use of the property. Perhaps the worthier children would. The house easily brought in fifteen per cent. income yearly. Maybe I would have thrown him out another thousand rubles in his distress. But instead, he disposed of the property without so much as saying a word to me. With my own hands, I paid out twelve thousand rubles for the house, and it was sold at auction for eight thousand rubles!"

"The main thing, dear mamma, is that he has dealt so basely with the parental blessing," Porfiry interjected hastily, as if afraid of being stopped again.

"Yes, that's so, too. My money does not come lightly. I have earned it with the sweat of my brow. When I married your father, all he owned was the estate of Golovliovo with one hundred and one souls, and a few more souls scattered in distant estates, a hundred and fifty in all. As for me, I had nothing at all. Now look what an estate I have built up on that foundation. There are four thousand souls, not a single one less. I can't take them into the grave with me. Do you think it was an easy task to scrape four thousand souls together? No, dear child, not easy, far from easy. I spent many a sleepless night trying to work out a good business scheme, so that no one should smell it out and stand in my way. And what have I not endured in my business travels? I have had plenty of hard road and bad weather and slippery ice. It is only lately that I allow myself the luxury of a coach. In former times I rode in a plain two-horse peasant's cart with a cover put on extra for me. It was in nothing but a cart that I used to go to Moscow. And the filth and stench I had to put up with in the Moscow inns! I begrudged myself the dime for the cabby, and I walked all the way from Rogozhskaya Street to Solyanka. The house-porter would say to me wonderingly: "Mistress, they say you are young and well-to-do, why do you work so hard?" But I was silent and patient. At first all I had at my disposal were thirty thousand rubles in bank notes. I sold your father's remote estates with their one hundred souls, and with what I realized from the sale I set out to buy a property with a thousand souls. I had a mass said at the Iverska Church and went to Solyanka to try my luck. What do you think happened? The Holy Virgin must have seen my bitter tears. She helped me buy the estate. It was like a miracle. The instant I bid thirty thousand rubles the auction came to an end. There had been a lot of noise and excitement, but then the people stopped bidding, and it was as quiet as could be. The auctioneer got up and congratulated me. I was dumfounded.

Ivan Nikolaich, the lawyer, came over to me and said: 'Let me congratulate you, madam, on your purchase.' But I stood there stiff as a post. How great is God's mercy! Think of it, if in my confusion someone had called out just for spite, 'I bid thirty-five thousand,' I should certainly have offered every bit of forty thousand. And where would I have gotten the money from?"

Many a time before had Arina Petrovna regaled her children with the epical beginnings of her career of acquisition. It had never lost the charm of novelty for them. Porfiry Vladimirych listened smiling, sighing, turning up his eye-balls, lowering them, to the tune of the rapid changes through which the tale passed. As for Pavel Vladimirych, he sat with wide-open eyes, like a child, listening to a familiar, yet ever-fascinating fairy tale.

"Do you think your mother built up her fortune without trouble?" went on Arina Petrovna. "It takes trouble even to make a pimple on your nose. After the first purchase I was laid up with fever for six weeks. So judge for yourselves how it must make my heart ache to see my hard-earned money, money I went through torments to get, you may say, thrown out into the gutter for no earthly reason."

There was a minute's pause. Porfiry Vladimirych was ready to rend his garments, but refrained, fearing there would be no one in the village to mend them. Pavel Vladimirych, as soon as the fairy tale was over, fell back into his wonted apathy, and his face resumed its customary dull expression.

"That is why I asked you to come here," began Arina Petrovna anew. "Now judge us, me and the villain. Whatever you decide will be done. If you condemn him, he will be guilty. If you condemn me, I shall be guilty. Only I shall not allow the rascal to get the better of me," she added, quite unexpectedly.

Porfiry Vladimirych felt his turn had come, and he prepared to hold forth, but approached the subject in a roundabout way.

"If you will permit me, dearest mother, to express my opinion," he said, "here it is in two words: children must obey their parents, blindly do their bidding, cherish them in their old age. That's all! What are children, dear mother? Children are loving creatures who owe their parents everything, from their persons to the last rag they possess. Therefore, parents may judge children, while children may never judge parents. Children are in duty bound to respect, not to judge. You say: 'Judge us.' That is magnanimous of you, dear mother, *magnificent*! But how can we think about it without fear, we whom from the first day of our birth you have been clothing with kindness from head to foot? Say what you may, it would not be judgment but blasphemy. It would be such blasphemy, such blasphemy — —"

"Stop, wait a minute. If you say you cannot sit in judgment on me, acquit me and condemn *him*," Arina Petrovna interrupted. She was listening and trying to search his meaning, but could not make out what new plot was back of the Bloodsucker's mind.

"No, mother dear, even that I cannot do, or rather I don't dare to. I have no right to. I can neither acquit nor condemn. I simply cannot judge. You are the mother; you alone know how to deal with us children. You have the right to reward us if we deserve it, and chastise us if we are guilty. Our duty is not to criticise, but to obey. And if at the moment of parental wrath you exceed the measure of justice, even then we dare not grumble, for the ways of Providence are hidden from us. Who knows, perhaps it was necessary. Our brother Stepan has acted basely, unspeakably, but you alone can determine the degree of punishment he deserves."

"Then you refuse to help me? You would have me get out of this affair as best I can?"

"Oh, dearest, dearest, how you misunderstood me! Goodness, goodness! I said, that however you might be pleased to dispose of brother Stepan's fate, so shall it be, and you—what horrible thoughts you ascribe to me."

"All right. And you?" she turned to Pavel Vladimirych.

"Do you want my opinion? But what's my opinion to you?" said he, as if only half-awake. However, he braced himself unexpectedly and went on: "Of course, he's guilty. Have him torn to pieces—ground to dust in a mortar—it's settled in advance. What am I in this?"

Having mumbled these incoherent words, he stopped and stared at his mother, his mouth wide open, as if not trusting his own ears.

"Well, my dear, I shall speak to you later," Arina Petrovna cut him off coldly. "I see that you are anxious to tread in Stiopka's tracks. Take care, my child. You will repent, but it will be too late."

"Why, what's the matter? I'm not saying anything. I say, just as you please. What is there disrespectful in that?" said Pavel Vladimirych, faintly.

"I'll talk with you later on, my boy, later on. You think because you are an army officer, you can run wild. You are greatly mistaken. Then neither of you wants to sit in judgment?"

"I, dearest mother——"

"What am I in this?" said Pavel Vladimirych. "I don't care. Have him torn to pieces."

"Hold your tongue, for Christ's sake, you wicked man!" Arina Petrovna felt she was fully entitled to call her son "scoundrel," but refrained in deference to the joyous meeting. "Well, if you refuse to judge him I shall. Here is my verdict. I shall try to treat him kindly once more. I shall hand over to him the little Vologda village, have a cottage built there, and let him live there and be fed by the peasants."

Although Porfiry Vladimirych had refused to sit in judgment on his brother, his mother's generosity was so amazing that he felt he simply had to point out the dangerous consequences of her project.

"Dearest mamma," he exclaimed, "you are more than magnanimous. You are confronted by a deed—well, the vilest, meanest deed—and then you forget and pardon. *Mag*nificent! But forgive me, I am afraid for you, dearest. Think what you will of me, but if I were you, I wouldn't do it."

"Why not?"

"I don't know. Perhaps I lack your magnanimity, that motherly feeling of yours. But one thought comes back to me all the while—what if brother Stepan does the same with his second legacy as he did with his first?"

Arina Petrovna had already thought of that, yet in the back of her mind was another consideration.

"The Vologda estate is father's property, it belongs to the patrimony," she said through her teeth. "Sooner or later a portion of the patrimony will have to be doled out to him."

"I understand that very well, mother dear."

"Then you also understand that on giving him the Vologda village we can make him sign a document to the effect that he has received his full share and that he renounces all further inheritance claims."

"I understand that too, dearest mother. Your excessive kindness caused you to commit a grave mistake. At the time you bought him the house you ought to have made him give you such a document then."

"Yes, that was a blunder."

"At that time, in his joy, he would have signed any document. But you, dearest, in the kindness of your heart—goodness, what a mistake! What a mistake!"

"Don't talk of it any more. Why didn't you speak up before it was too late? Now you are ready to blame everything on your mother, but when it comes to business, you are not there. However, it isn't the document I have in mind. I can make him sign it even now. Papa, I suppose, isn't going to die at once. Until his death the blockhead must live on something. In case he refuses to sign, we can chase him out and bid him wait for papa's death. No, what I want to know is, do you dislike my idea of giving him the Vologda estate?"

"He will squander away the village, darling, as he did the house."

"If he does, let him blame himself."

"He'll come back to you, again, to no one else."

"Oh, no, I won't stand for it. I won't let him come near my threshold. There won't be a drink of water for him in my house. And people won't condemn me for it, nor will God punish me. To squander away first a house, then an estate! Am I his slave? Is he the only one I have to provide for? Have I not other children?"

"Still, it is to you that he will come. Isn't he brazen-faced enough to do that, darling mamma?"

"I tell you, I won't let him come near my threshold. Why do you sit there croaking, 'he'll come, he'll come?' I won't let him in."

Arina Petrovna grew silent and fixed her gaze on the window. She herself vaguely realized that the Vologda estate would only temporarily free her from "the horrid creature," that in the end he would dispose of it, too, and would return to her again, and that as a mother she could not refuse him a corner in her house. But the thought that the odious fellow would always be with her, that even though locked up in the counting-house he would be preying on her imagination like a spook, was so appalling that she shuddered involuntarily.

"Not for the world!" she exclaimed, striking the table with her fist and leaping to her feet.

Meanwhile, Porfiry Vladimirych kept on staring at "mother dear" and shaking his head rhythmically in token of condolence.

"I see you are angry, dearest mamma," he said at last in a tone so sugared that he seemed to be getting ready to tickle Arina Petrovna.

"What would you have me do? Dance a jig?"

"Excuse me, darling, but what do the Scriptures say about patience? 'In patience,' it says, 'possess ye your souls,' 'In patience'—that's the word. Do you think God does not see? He sees everything, mother dear. We perhaps don't suspect anything, we sit here proposing this and planning that, while He may already have disposed. Oh, dearest mamma, how unjust you are to me."

But Arina Petrovna was fully aware that the Bloodsucker was throwing a snare, and she flew into a rage.

"Are you making sport of me?" she shouted. "I am discussing business, and he's trying to hoax me. Don't pull the wool over my eyes. Speak plainly. Do you want him to remain at Golovliovo, hanging around his mother's neck?"

"Just so, dearest mother, if you please. Let him be where he is and make him sign a paper about the heritage."

"So, so. I knew that was what you would advise. All right. God alone knows how it will pain me always to be having that creature around. However, it seems nobody will take pity on me. When I was young I bore my cross. Shall I refuse it in my old age? But there is still another point. While papa and I are alive, *he'll* live at Golovliovo, and we won't let him starve. But how about afterwards?"

"Dearest mother! Darling! Why such melancholy thoughts?" cried the Bloodsucker.

"Melancholy or not, still one has to provide ahead. We aren't babies. When we die, what will become of him?"

"Dearest mother! Can't you count on us, your children? Have we not been properly brought up by you?"

Porfiry Vladimirych flashed on her one of those puzzling glances which had always made her uneasy, and went on:

"The poor man, dear mamma, I shall help with greater joy than the rich. The rich man, Christ be with him, the rich man has enough of his own. But the poor man—you know what Christ said of the poor."

Porfiry Vladimirych got up and kissed his mother's hand.

"Dearest mamma, allow me to present my brother with two pounds of tobacco," he said entreatingly.

Arina Petrovna did not answer. She looked at him and reflected: "Is he really such a Bloodsucker that he would turn his own brother out on the streets?"

"Well, do as you please. Let him live at Golovliovo," she said finally, turning to Porfiry. "You have trapped me. You started with 'just as you please, dearest mamma,' and finished by dancing me on your wire. But let me tell you this, I hate him and he has disgraced and pestered me all his life, he has even dishonored my motherly blessing. Nevertheless, if you turn him out into the streets or make a beggar of him, you shall not have my blessing. No, no, no. Now you two go to him. The idiot is wearing out his silly eyes looking for you."

The sons left. Arina Petrovna rose and watched them stride over the front yard to the counting-house without exchanging a word. Porfiry was constantly taking off his cap and crossing himself, now at the sight of the church, which shimmered afar off, now before the chapel, now before the wooden post to which a charity box was attached. As for Pavel, he seemed unable to take his eyes off his boot tips shining in the sunlight.

"For whom have I been accumulating riches? Refused myself sleep and food—for whom?" she cried bitterly.

CHAPTER V

The brothers departed, and the manor-house of Golovliovo was deserted. With renewed energy, Arina Petrovna took up her work again. The clatter of the knives in the kitchen ceased, but activities in office, storehouses, cellars, were redoubled. Summer, the great provider, was nearly over; preserving, canning, pickling, storing were in full swing. Winter provisions flowed in from all quarters, dried mushrooms, berries, eggs, vegetables. This requisition in kind imposed upon the peasant women came in wagons from all the various family estates. Everything was measured and added to the stores of former years. Not in vain had the lady of Golovliovo had a long row of cellars, storehouses and granaries built. They were full to the brim. Quite a good deal of damaged material was along with the rest and smelt foully. At the end of summer the stuff was all sorted and what was suspicious was sent to the servants' quarters.

"The pickles are still in good condition, only the skin is coming off in some places, and they smell a little. Well, let the servants enjoy a dainty bit," Arina Petrovna would say, pointing out the barrels to be put aside.

Stepan Vladimirych adapted himself admirably to his new condition. At times he felt a strong craving to get drunk as a piper. He had money for the purpose, as we shall see later. But he restrained himself stoically, as if considering that the time had not yet arrived. He was always busy now, for he took a lively part in the provisioning, rejoicing in its successes and regretting its failures in a wholly disinterested manner. In a sort of ecstasy, hatless, clad in his dressing-gown, he scurried from the office to the cellars, hiding from his mother behind trees and various small buildings that crowded the court-yard. Arina Petrovna noticed him in this garb many times, and felt an itching in her motherly heart to give Simple Simon a severe scolding, but on second thought she left him alone in his escapades. In the cellars Stepan Vladimirych with feverish impatience watched how the carts were unloaded, how jars, barrels and tubs were brought in from the estate, and everything was assorted and finally sent off into the yawning abyss of cellars and storehouses. He felt satisfied in most instances.

"To-day two wagons of mushrooms came from Dubrovino. Ripping fine mushrooms, brother," he informed the village clerk rapturously. "And we were afraid we should have to get along without mushrooms this winter. Bravo, Dubrovino fellow, much obliged! Fine fellows they are! They have helped us out!"

On another occasion, he said:

"To-day mother gave an order to catch some carps in the pond. You ought to see them! Some three feet long! It looks as if we were going to live on carp the whole week."

Sometimes he was worried.

"The cucumbers failed completely this season. There is not a good one among them—all crooked and spotty. They're just good enough to be sent to the servants' quarters. We shall have to use last year's."

He did not approve of Arina Petrovna's management. "Goodness, what heaps of provisions she allows to rot! Just now she's having cured meat, pickles, fish and what not hauled to the servants' quarters. Is that what you call good business? Is that the right way of doing things, I'd like to know. There are lots of fresh provisions, but she will not touch them until the old rot is eaten up."

The confidence entertained by Arina Petrovna that it would be easy to induce Simple Simon to sign any paper proved wholly justified. Not only did he not object to signing all the papers that his mother sent him, but the same evening he even boasted about it to the village clerk.

"Well, brother, to-day I have been doing nothing but signing papers. I have renounced all my rights of inheritance. I am cleaned out. Not a cent to my name, and none coming. I have set the old woman at ease."

He parted with his brothers peaceably, and was in raptures over his big supply of tobacco. Of course, he couldn't help calling Porfisha Bloodsucker and Yudushka, but the disparaging terms were drowned in a deluge of incoherent, meaningless chatter.

In taking leave the brothers became liberal and even gave him money. Porfiry Vladimirych accompanied his gift with the following speech:

"This money will be handy in case you need oil for the ikon lamp or if you want to set up a candle in the church. That's how it is, brother. Be good and gentle, and our dear mother will be satisfied. You will have your comforts, and all of us will be merry and happy. Our mother is a kindly soul, you know."

"There is no denying that she is kindly," agreed Stepan Vladimirych. "Only she feeds me on rotten pickled meat."

"Whose fault is it? Who treated mother's blessing with disrespect? It is your own fault that you lost your estate. What a nice little estate it was. If you only knew how to behave yourself and live modestly, you would now be eating beef and veal and even ordering sauce with them. You would have plenty of everything, potatoes, cabbage, peas. Am I not right, brother?"

Had Arina Petrovna heard this harangue, it would have made her impatient, and she would have let the orator know that it did. But Simple Simon was fortunate that his mind could not, as it were, retain other people's words, and not a syllable of Yudushka's speech reached its destination.

So Stepan Vladimirych parted with his brothers amicably. And there was some vanity in his showing Yakov, the village clerk, two twenty-five ruble notes that had been left in his hands after the brothers had departed.

"This will last me a long time," he said. "We've got tobacco. We're well provided with tea and sugar. Nothing is missing but vodka. However, should we want vodka, we'll get vodka, too. Nevertheless, I will restrain myself for a little while yet. I am too busy now, I have to keep an eye on the cellars. Weaken your watch for a single instant, and everything will be pillaged. *She* saw me, brother, she saw me, the hag, once, when I was gliding by along the kitchen wall. She stood at the window looking at me and I bet she thought: 'Well, well, so that's why I miss so many cucumbers.'"

Then came October. It began to rain, the road turned black, into an impassable stream of mud. Stepan Vladimirych could not go out because his only garments were his father's old dressing-gown and worn slippers. He sat at his window watching the tiny, humble village drowned in mud. There, in the gray autumn mist, men were moving about briskly, looking like black dots.

The heavy summer work was still in full swing, but now its setting was no longer the jubilant, sun-flooded hues of summer, but the endless autumn twilight. The corn kilns emitted clouds of smoke far into the night. The melancholy clatter of the flails resounded in the air. Thrashing was also going on in the manorial barns, and in the office they said it would hardly be possible to get through with the whole mass of grain before Shrovetide. Everything looked gloomy and drowsy, everything spoke of oppressiveness. The doors of the counting-house were no longer ajar, and inside the air was filled with a bluish fog rising from the wet fur cloaks.

It is difficult to say what impression this spectacle of a toilsome, rural autumn made on Stepan's mind, and whether he was at all aware of the labors going on in the incessant rain out in the boggy fields. One thing is certain, that the drab, tearful autumn sky oppressed him. It seemed to hang close down over his head and threaten to drown him in a deluge of mud. All he had to do was to look out through the window and watch the heavy masses of clouds. From the dawn on they covered the heavens, hanging motionless as if spellbound. Even after several hours they were still in the same place, without the slightest apparent change in hue or outline. In the morning, one cloud, heavy and black, had a ragged shape resembling a priest in a cassock with outstretched arms. It was clearly outlined on the pallid background of the upper clouds, and at noon it still had the identically same form. The right hand, it is true, had become shorter, and the left was stretched out in an ugly fashion and was sending down such a flood of rain that against the dark background of the sky there formed a streak still darker, almost black. Another huge shaggy lump of a cloud a little farther up hung over the village, threatening to smother it, you would think. Hours later it was still hanging in the same place, the same shaggy monster with outstretched paws, as though ready to pounce upon the earth. Clouds, clouds, nothing but clouds! Around five o'clock a change took place, darkness gradually enveloped heaven and earth, and soon the clouds disappeared completely, vanishing beneath a black shroud. They were the first to go, next followed the forest and the village, then the church, the chapel, the hamlet, the orchard, and finally the manor-house, several yards away.

It has already become quite dark in the room, and there is no light. So what can one do but pace up and down? A morbid languor seizes Stepan's brain; his entire body, despite its idleness, is filled with an incomprehensible, indescribable feeling of fatigue. Just one thought moves in him and sucks at him—the grave, the grave, the grave! Those black dots which have recently been moving busily on the dark background of the boggy soil and near the village barns are not oppressed by that thought. They will not perish under the burden of despondency and weariness. If they do not challenge the sky directly, at least they struggle, build, make enclosures, repair their houses. Stepan did not question whether all this bustle was worth the while, but he was aware that even the nameless dots were incomparably superior to him, that he couldn't even struggle, that he had nothing to build, nothing to repair.

He spent the evenings in the counting-house, because Arina Petrovna refused to supply him with candles. Several times, through the bailiff, he asked for boots and a fur coat, and was invariably told that boots were not kept in store for him, but that he would be given a pair of felt shoes as soon as the cold spells arrived. Evidently, Arina Petrovna intended to fulfill her program literally, that was, to sustain her son in such a manner as barely to keep him from starvation. At first he abused his mother, but then behaved as though he had forgotten all about her. Even the light of the candles in the counting-room annoyed him, and he began to lock himself in his room and remain all alone in the darkness. There was just a single refuge left, one that he still dreaded but that attracted him irresistibly, to get drunk and forget deeply, irrevocably, to plunge into the sea of oblivion and never emerge again. Everything drove him to it, the debauchery of the past, the enforced idleness of the present, his ailing body with the torturing cough, the unbearable asthma, and the constantly increasing pains in his heart. At last the hour came.

"You must fetch me a bottle of vodka for to-night," he said once to the village clerk in a voice boding little good.

That one bottle of vodka was followed by a long succession of other bottles. After that he got drunk every night. At nine o'clock, when the light in the counting-house had been put out and the servants had retired to their quarters, he placed a bottle of vodka and a slice of rye bread thickly strewn over with salt on the table. He did not attack the liquor at once, but approached it stealthily as it were. Everybody on the place was fast asleep. The mice scudded behind the wall paper and the clock in the counting-house ticked ominously. Stepan threw off his dressing-gown, and began to stride back and forth in the overheated room, with nothing but a shirt on his back. At times he stopped, went over to the table, searched for the bottle in the darkness, then resumed his restless pacing. The first tumblers he emptied in a sort of passion, voluptuously swallowing down the burning liquid. But little by little his heart began to beat faster, the blood mounted to his head, and he mumbled incoherently. His feeble imagination tried to create images, his blunted memory attempted to pierce the mists of the past. But the images were broken and meaningless, and the past remained dim and formless. There was no recollection, either bitter or sweet, as though an impervious wall separated the past from the present.

He was completely filled by the present, which seemed like a prison cell, in which he would be locked up for eternity without consciousness of time or space. His mind took in nothing but the room, the stove, the three windows in the front wall, the squeaking wooden bed with its mattress worn thin, and the table with the bottle.

As the contents of the bottle decreased and his head grew hotter and hotter, even this boresome sense of the present gradually faded. His mumblings, to which at first there had been a bit of form, now lost all meaning. His pupils dilated in the attempt to pierce the engulfing darkness. Finally, the darkness itself vanished and its place was taken by a phosphorescent sheen.

It was an endless void, with not a color or a sound, but radiant with sinister splendor. The void followed him in his wanderings, trod on his heels at every step. There were no walls, no windows, nothing but this endless vacant splendor. Dread fell on him, coupled with an irresistible impulse to annihilate even the void. A few more efforts, and his goal was reached. His stumbling legs carried a benumbed body, his chest gave forth not a murmur but an inarticulate cry, his very existence seemingly ceased. A strange stupor took possession of him, in which conscious life had no part, which plumbed the depths of a life independent of and beyond the boundaries of normal existence. Groans burst from his chest without in the least disturbing his sleep. His organic disease continued its destructive work, without apparently causing him any physical pain.

He rose early in the morning, filled with agonizing longing, disgust and hatred. It was an inarticulate hatred, without either cause or definite object. His bloodshot eyes rolled restlessly, his limbs trembled, his heart worked with sickening irregularity, now stopping altogether, now hammering with such violence that his hand involuntarily clutched at his breast. Not a thought, not a desire! Objects of immediate perception filled his mind so completely that it was closed to other impressions.

He filled his pipe and lighted it. It dropped from his nerveless fingers. His tongue mumbled something, but seemingly by force of habit only. He sat in silence and stared at one point. He felt an intense craving to raise the temperature of his body so that he would feel the presence of life for at least a short while. But he had no way of getting vodka in the daytime. He had to wait for night to attain those blissful moments when the ground vanished from under his feet and the four odious prison walls were replaced by a shoreless, shining void.

Arina Petrovna had not the slightest idea of how Simple Simon spent his time. The casual glimmer of feeling which had appeared for a moment during the conversation with the Bloodsucker vanished so precipitately that she was unconscious of its ever having appeared. It was not a premeditated course of action on her part, but sheer oblivion. She completely forgot that in the counting-house, in close proximity to her, there lived a human being bound to her by ties of blood, who perhaps was pining away in the yearning for life. Once having cut out a certain channel in life and filling it almost mechanically with the same things, she thought others ought to do likewise, it never occurring to her that the very character of the things life holds vary among people according to a multitude of circumstances in different combinations, and that these things may be dear to some, herself among these some, while they are an abomination and a tyranny to others.

Therefore when the bailiff repeatedly reported that "something was the matter" with Stepan Vladimirych, the words slipped by her ears, leaving no impression on her mind. Indeed, she scarcely ever even replied, and when she did, then only with the stereotyped reply:

"Oh, well, he'll be all right. I bet he'll outlive you and me. Nothing is the matter with the shambling colt. Coughing, you say! Well, some people cough thirty years on end and they don't feel it."

Nevertheless, one morning when they came and told her that Stepan Vladimirych had disappeared during the night, she was aroused. Immediately she sent out all the available men in search of him, and herself started an investigation beginning with the room in which Stepan had lived. The first thing that struck her was a bottle standing on the table, with a bit of vodka in it.

"What's this?" she asked, pretending not to understand.

"Why, I guess—the young master indulged," stammered the bailiff.

"Who supplied ——?" she began, flaring up. But she restrained herself, and continued her investigation, hiding her rage.

The room was so filthy that even she, who did not know and did not recognize any demands of comfort, began to feel awkward. The ceiling was smutty, the wall paper in many places was hanging in tatters, the window-sills were black with a thick layer of tobacco ashes, pillows were lying about on the floor beslimed with viscous mud, on the bed lay a crumpled sheet, gray with accumulated dirt. In one window the winter frame had been taken, or, rather, torn out, and the window itself was left half open. Apparently it was through this opening that Simple Simon had disappeared. Arina Petrovna instinctively looked out on the road and became more frightened. It was already the first of November, but the autumn that year had lasted long, and the cold spells had not yet arrived. Both the road and the field were one black sea of mud. How had he got away? Where had he gone to? Here it occurred to her that he had nothing on but a dressing-gown and a slipper. The other slipper had been found under the window. And the night before it had been pouring ceaselessly.

"It's a long, long time since I've been here," she said, inhaling instead of air a foul mixture of vodka, tobacco and sheepskin evaporations.

All day long, while the servants were searching the forest, she stood at the window staring dully out upon the naked fields unrolled before her eyes. So much ado on account of Simple Simon! It seemed like a preposterous dream. She had *said* he ought to have been shipped off to the Vologda village. "No," that cursed Yudushka had wheedled, "leave him here, dearest mother, at Golovliovo." Now handle him, if you please, Yudushka.

"I wish he had lived there, out of my sight, as he pleased—Christ be with him!" Arina Petrovna mused. "But I did my part. If he wasted one good thing, well, I would throw him another. If he'd have wasted the other, too, well, what could I do then? Even God can't fill a bottomless belly. Everything would have been peaceful and quiet here. But now—who knows what he has been up to? Go, look in the forest and whistle for him. It would be good if he were brought home alive, but with drunken eyes one is liable to run into a noose—take a rope, tie it to a branch, put it round his neck, and no more Stiopka. His mother denied herself sleep and food, and he has invented a new style—hanging himself. There would be some excuse for him if he had had it hard here. But goodness, what did he have to do but walk about in his room all day and eat and drink? Another son would not have known how to thank his mother enough. And how does this precious son repay his mother? Goes and hangs himself. The idea!"

Arina Petrovna's surmises about Simple Simon's violent death were not justified. Toward evening he was brought back in a peasant wagon, still alive. He was in a semi-conscious state, all bruised and cut, his face blue and swollen. He had been found at the Dubrovino estate, twenty miles away.

The returned fugitive slept straight through the next twenty-four hours. When he awoke, he stumbled to his feet and began to pace up and down the room as was his habit, but he did not touch the pipe and made no reply to the questions he was asked. Arina Petrovna's heart softened so that on the spur of the moment she all but had him transferred to the manor-house. Then she quieted down, and left him in the counting-house, but gave orders for the room to be scoured and tidied up, the bed linen changed, curtains hung, and so on.

The following evening, when told that Stepan Vladimirych was awake, she had him brought to the house for tea and found it possible, in talking to him, to inject kindliness into her voice.

"Why did you go away from your mother?" she began. "Do you know you caused her great anxiety? It's good the news did not reach papa. It would have been a terrible shock to the poor sick man."

But Stepan seemed altogether indifferent to his mother's kindly words. He kept staring at the candle with his glassy eyes, as if watching the snuff forming on the wick.

"My, my, aren't you a foolish boy?" continued Arina Petrovna, growing kinder and kinder. "Just think what rumors will be spread about your mother because of you. There are enough people who envy her. What will they not say about her? They will say she did not give you food or clothes. My, my, what a foolish boy you are!"

There was the same silence and the same motionless staring glance.

"Was your stay at mother's so bad? Thank God, you don't go hungry or naked. What else do you want? If you are lonesome, don't fret. This is nothing but a village, my boy. We have no entertainments or halls, we sit in our nooks and we hardly know how to while away the time. I, myself, would be glad to dance now and then or sing a song, but you look out upon the road and you lose the desire to go even to church in such weather."

Arina Petrovna paused, hoping that Simple Simon would give utterance to at least some sounds, but he was as dumb as a stone. She was beginning to work up a temper, but restrained herself.

"And if you were discontented with anything, if perhaps you lacked food or linen, could you not explain it frankly to your mother? Could you not say, 'Mamma, darling, won't you have some liver or curd-cakes prepared for me?' Do you think your mother would have refused you? Or if you wanted a drop of vodka, goodness, I wouldn't have begrudged you a glass or two. To think of it, you were not ashamed to beg from a serf, while it was difficult for you to say a word to your own mother."

But her flattering words were of no avail. Simple Simon remained impervious to either emotion (Arina Petrovna had hoped he would kiss her hand) or repentance. In fact, he seemed to have heard nothing.

From that time on he never spoke a single word. All day long he walked up and down his room, his brows knit and his lips moving, apparently never growing tired. At times he halted as if wishing to say something, but he could not find the words. He had not lost the capacity for thinking, but impressions left so slight a trace on his brain that he could not hold them for any appreciable length of time. Consequently his failure to find the necessary words did not even make him impatient. Arina Petrovna, for her part, thought he would surely set the house on fire.

"He does not say a word all day long," she repeated. "Still he must be thinking of something, the blockhead! I am sure he'll set the house on fire one of these days."

But the blockhead did not think of anything at all. He was deeply immersed in absolute darkness, in which there was no room either for reality or the illusory world of imagination. His brain did work, but in a void, disconnected from either the past, the present, or the future. It was as though he was completely wrapt up in a black cloud and all he did was to scan it, to watch its imaginary fluctuations, and, at times, to make a feeble attempt at resisting its sinister sway. The whole physical and spiritual world dwindled down to that enigmatic cloud.

In December of the same year, Porfiry Vladimirych received the following letter from his mother:

"Yesterday morning God visited us with a new ordeal. My son and your brother, Stepan, breathed his last. The very evening before he had been quite well and even took his supper, but in the morning he was found dead in bed. Such is the brevity of this earthly life! And what is most grievous to a mother's heart is that he left this world of vanity for the realm of the unknown without the last communion.

"May this be a warning to us all. He who sets at naught the ties of kinship must always await such an end. Failures in this life, untimely death, and everlasting torments in the life to come, all these evils spring from the one source. For, however learned and exalted we may be, if we do not honor our parents, our learning and eminence will be turned into nothingness. Such are the precepts which every one inhabiting this world must commit to his mind. Besides, slaves should revere their masters.

"Notwithstanding this, all honors were duly given to him who had departed into life eternal, as becomes my son. The pall was ordered from Moscow, and the burial ceremonies were solemnly presided over by the Father archimandrite. And according to the Christian custom, I am having memorial services performed daily. I mourn the loss of my son, but I do not complain, nor do I advise you, my children, to do so. For who knows? We may be mourning and complaining here while his soul may be rejoicing in Heaven."

BOOK II
AS BECOMES GOOD KINSFOLK

CHAPTER I

A hot midday in July; the Dubrovino manor-house all deserted. Workers and idlers alike resting in the shade. Under the canopy of a huge willow-tree in the front yard the dogs, too, were lying stretched out, and you could hear the sound of their jaws when they drowsily snapped at the flies. Even the trees drooped motionless, as if exhausted. All the windows in the manor-house and the servants' quarters were flung wide open. The heat seemed to surge in sweltering waves and the soil covered with short, singed grass was ablaze. The atmosphere was a blinding haze touched into gold, so that one could scarcely distinguish things in the distance. The manor-house, once painted gray and now faded into white, the small flower garden in front of the house, the birch grove, separated from the farm by the road, the pond, the village and the corn field, which touched the outskirts of the village, all were immersed in the dazzling torrent. The fragrance of blossoming linden trees mingled with the noxious emanations of the cattle shed. There was not a breath of air, not a sound. Only from the kitchen there came the grating of knives being sharpened, which foretold the inevitable hash and beef cutlets for dinner.

Inside the house reigned noiseless confusion. An old lady and two young girls were sitting in the dining room, forgetful of their crocheting, which lay on the table. They were waiting with intense anxiety. In the maids' room two women were busied preparing mustard plasters and poultices, and the rhythmic tinkling of the spoons pierced the silence like the chirping of a cricket. Barefooted girls were stealing silently along the corridor, scurrying back and forth from the entresol to the maids' room. At times a voice was heard from upstairs: "What about the mustard plasters? Are you asleep there?" And a girl would dash out of the maids' room. At last heavy footsteps sounded on the staircase, and the regimental surgeon entered the dining room, a tall, broad-shouldered man, with firm, ruddy cheeks, the picture of health. His voice was sonorous, his gait steady, his eyes clear, gay and frank, his lips full and fresh. In spite of his fifty years he was a thoroughly fast liver and expected to see many years pass before he would give up drinking and carousing. He wore a showy summer suit, and his spotless piqué coat was trimmed with white buttons bearing arms. On entering he made a clicking sound with his lips and tongue.

"Girls!" he shouted merrily, standing on the threshold. "Bring us some vodka and something to eat."

"Well, doctor, how is he?" the old lady asked, her voice full of anxiety.

"The Lord's mercy is infinite, Arina Petrovna," answered the physician.

"What do you mean? Then he——"

"Just so. He will last another two or three days, and then—good-bye!" The doctor made an expressive gesture with his hand and hummed: "Head over heels, head over heels he will fall."

"How's that? Doctors treated him—and now all of a sudden——"

"What doctors?"

"The *zemstvo* doctor and one from the town used to come here."

"Fine doctors! If they'd given him a good bleeding, they'd have saved him."

"So nothing at all can be done?"

"Well, I said, 'The Lord's mercy is great,' and I can add nothing to that."

"But perhaps it will work?"

"What will work?"

"I mean—the mustard plasters."

"Perhaps."

A woman in a black dress and black shawl brought in a tray holding a decanter of vodka, a dish of sausages and a dish of caviar. The doctor helped himself to the vodka, held the glass to the light and smacked his tongue.

"Your health, mother," he said to the old lady, and gulped the liquid.

"Drink in good health, my dear sir."

"This is the cause of Pavel Vladimirych dying in the prime of his life, this vodka," said the doctor, grimacing comfortably and spearing a piece of sausage with his fork.

"Yes, it's the ruin of many a man."

"That's because not everyone can stand it. But I can, and I shall have another glass. Your health, madam."

"Drink, drink. Nothing can happen to you."

"Nothing. My lungs and kidneys and liver and spleen are in excellent condition. By the way," he turned to the woman in black who stood at the door, listening to the conversation, "What will you have for dinner to-day?"

"Hash and beef cutlets and chicken for roast," she answered, smiling somewhat sourly.

"Have you any smoked fish?"

"We have, sir. We have white sturgeon and stellated sturgeon, plenty of it."

"Then have a cold soup with sturgeon for our dinner, and pick out a fat bit of sturgeon, you hear me? What is your name? Ulita?"

"Yes, sir, people call me Ulita."

"Well, then, hurry up, friend Ulita, hurry up."

Ulita left the room, and for a while oppressive silence reigned. Then Arina Petrovna rose from her seat and made sure Ulita was not eavesdropping.

"Andrey Osipych, have you spoken to him yet about the orphans?" she asked the doctor.

"Yes, I did."

"Well?"

"There was no change. 'When I get well' he kept on saying, 'I will make my will and write the notes.'"

Silence, heavier than before, filled the room. The girls took the crocheting from the table, and their trembling hands worked one row after the other. Arina Petrovna heaved a deep sigh of dejection. The doctor paced up and down the room and whistled, "Head over heels, head over heels."

"But did you try to drive the matter home to him, doctor?"

"Well, I said to him: 'You'll be a scoundrel if you don't make a definite provision for the orphans.' Could I make it clearer? Yes, mother, you certainly slipped up. If you had called me in a month ago, I would have given him a good bleeding and I would have seen to it that he made his will. But now everything will go to Yudushka, the lawful heir. It certainly will."

"Oh, grandmother, what will become of us?" said the older of the two girls, plaintively and almost in tears. "What is uncle doing to us?"

The girls were Anninka and Lubinka, the daughters of Anna Vladimirovna Ulanova, to whom Arina Petrovna had once "thrown a bone."

"I don't know, dear, I don't know. I don't even know what will become of me. Today I am here, and tomorrow God knows where I'll be. Maybe I'll have to sleep in a shed or at a peasant's."

"Goodness, isn't uncle silly!" exclaimed the younger girl.

"I wish, young lady, you would keep your mouth shut," remarked the doctor. Turning to Arina Petrovna, he suggested, "Why not try to talk to him yourself, mother?"

"No, no. There's no use my talking to him. He doesn't even want to see me. The other day I stuck my nose into his room, and he snarled, 'Have you come to see me off to the other world?'"

"I think Ulita is back of it all. She incites him against you."

"She surely does, nobody but she. And then she reports everything to Porfiry the Bloodsucker. People say he keeps a pair of horses harnessed all day waiting for the beginning of the agony. And just imagine, the other day Ulita went so far as to take an inventory of the furniture, wardrobe, and dishes, so that nothing should be lost, as she said. We are the thieves, just imagine it."

"Why don't you treat her more severely? Head over heels, you know, head over heels."

But fate decreed that the doctor should not develop his thought. A girl, all out of breath, dashed into the room and exclaimed in a fright:

"The master! The master wants the doctor."

CHAPTER II

Not more than ten years had passed since the death of Simple Simon, but the condition of the various members of the Golovliov family had so completely changed that not a trace remained of those artificial ties which had given the family the air of an impregnable stronghold. This stronghold, erected by the tireless hands of Arina Petrovna, had crumbled away, but so imperceptibly that she herself was ignorant of how it had happened, was even involved in the destruction, the leading spirit in which, of course, had been Porfiry the Bloodsucker.

From an irresponsible, hot-tempered ruler over the Golovliovo estate, Arina Petrovna had descended into a mere hanger-on in the home of her younger son, a useless hanger-on, with no voice in the household management. Her head was bowed, her back bent, the fire in her eyes had died out, her gait was languid, the vivacity of her movements was gone. She had taken to knitting to occupy her idleness, but her mind was always wandering somewhere away from her needles, and the knitting was a failure. She would knit for a few moments, then her hands would drop of themselves, her head would fall on the back of her chair, and she would begin to go over bygones in her mind, until she got drowsy and dropped off into a senile slumber. Or else she would get up and begin to pace the rooms, always searching for something; always looking into corners, like a good housewife hunting for her keys, which she usually carries about with her and has now misplaced somehow.

The first blow to her authority was not so much the abolition of serfdom as the preparations preceding it. At first, there were simply rumors, then came the meetings of landowners and addresses, next followed provincial committees, and revising commissions. All these things exhausted and confused her. Arina Petrovna's imagination, active enough without additional stimuli, conceived numerous absurd situations. "How am I going to call Agashka?" she'd think. "Perhaps I'll have to tack a 'Miss' before her name." Or she would see herself walking about in the empty rooms while the servants were taking it easy in their quarters and were gorging themselves with all kinds of food; and when they got tired of gorging she saw them throwing the remnants under the table. Then she would find herself surprising Yulka and Feshka in the cellar, devouring everything in sight, like beasts, and she would itch to reprimand them, but would have to check herself with the thought, "How dare one say anything to them, now that they are free? Why one can't even appeal to the court against them!"

However insignificant such trifles may be, a whole fantastic world is built up of them, which holds you tight and completely paralyzes your activity. Arina Petrovna somehow suddenly let the reins of government slip out of her grasp, and for a space of two years did nothing from morning until night except complain.

"One or the other," she was fond of saying, "gains all or loses all. But these meetings and addresses and commissions, they're nothing but trouble."

At that time, just when the committees were in full swing, Vladimir Mikhailych died. On his deathbed he repudiated Barkov and his teachings, and died appeased and reconciled to the world. His last words were:

"I thank my God that He did not suffer me to come into His presence on an equal footing with the serfs."

These words made a deep impression on his wife's receptive soul, so that both his death and her fantastic notions about the future laid a coloring of gloom and despair on the atmosphere of the house. It seemed as if both the old manor and its inhabitants were getting ready for death.

From a few complaints that found their way into the letters of Arina Petrovna, Porfiry Vladimirych's amazingly keen perceptions sensed the confusion that possessed her mind. Not that Arina Petrovna actually sermonized and moralized in her letters, but above all, she trusted in God's help, "which in these faithless times does not abandon even slaves, far less those who because of their means were the surest prop and ornament of the church." Yudushka instinctively understood that if mother dear began to put her hope in God, then there was some flaw in the fabric of her existence. And he took advantage of the flaw with his peculiar, subtle skill.

Almost at the very end of the preliminaries to the emancipation, he visited Golovliovo quite unexpectedly and found Arina Petrovna sunk into despondency, almost to a point of prostration.

"Well, what news? What do they say in St. Petersburg?" was her first question, after mutual greetings had been exchanged.

Porfiry cast down his eyes and sat speechless.

"No, you must consider my circumstances," continued Arina Petrovna, gathering from her son's silence that good news was not to be expected. "Right now in the maids' room I have about thirty of these creatures. What shall I do with them? If they remain in my care, what am I going to feed them on? At present I have a little cabbage, a little potatoes, some bread, enough of everything; and we manage somehow to make both ends meet. If the potatoes give out, I order cabbage to be cooked; if there is no cabbage, cucumbers have to do. But now, if I have to run to market for everything and pay for everything, and buy and serve, how am I ever to provide for such a crowd?"

Porfiry gazed into the eyes of his "mother dear" and smiled bitterly as a sign of sympathy.

"And then, if the government is going to turn them loose, give them absolute leeway—well, then, I don't know, I don't know, I don't know what it will come to."

Porfiry smiled as if there were something very funny in "what it was coming to."

"Don't you laugh. It is a serious matter, so serious that if only the Lord grants them a little more reason, only then—Here's my case, for instance. I am by no means an old rag, am I? I must have my bread and butter, too, mustn't I? How am I to go about getting it? Think of the bringing-up we received. The only thing we know is how to dance and sing and receive guests. Then how am I going to get along without those wretches, I'd like to know. I can't serve meals or cook. I can't do a thing."

"God is merciful, mother dear."

"He used to be, but not now. When we were good, the Almighty was merciful to us; when we became wicked, well, we mustn't complain. I'm beginning to think that the best thing for me is to throw everything to the dogs. Really, I'll build myself a little hut right next to father's grave, and that's where I'll spend the rest of my days."

Porfiry Vladimirych pricked up his ears. His mouth began to water.

"And who will manage the estates?" he questioned, carefully throwing his bait, as it were.

"Why, you boys will have to manage them yourselves. Thank God, I have provided plenty. I ought not carry the whole burden alone."

Arina Petrovna suddenly stopped and raised her head. Her eyes fell on Yudushka's simpering, drivelling, oily face, all suffused with a carnivorous inner glow.

"You seem to be getting ready to bury me," remarked Arina Petrovna drily. "Isn't it a bit too early, darling? Look out, don't make a mistake."

Thus the matter ended in nothing definite. But there are discussions which, once begun, never really come to an end. A few hours later Arina Petrovna renewed the conversation.

"I'll leave for the Trinity Monastery," she dreamed aloud. "I'll divide up the estate, buy a little cottage on the grounds and settle there."

But Porfiry Vladimirych, taught by past experience, remained silent this time.

"Last year, while your deceased father was still alive," continued Arina Petrovna, "I was sitting alone in my bedroom and suddenly I thought I heard someone whispering in my ear: 'Go to the Trinity Monastery. Go to the Trinity.' Three times, mind you. I turned about—there was nobody in the room. Well, then, I thought that must have been a sign for me. 'Well,' I said, 'if God is pleased with my faith, I am ready.' No sooner had I said that than suddenly the room was filled with such a wonderful fragrance. Of course I immediately ordered my things packed and by evening I was on my way."

Tears rose in Arina Petrovna's eyes. Yudushka took advantage of this to kiss his mother's hand, and even made free to put his arm around her waist.

"Now you are a good girl," he said. "Ah, how good it is, darling, when one lives in peace with God. You come to God with a prayer, and the Lord meets you with help. That's how it is, mother dear."

"Wait a minute, I haven't finished. Next day, in the evening I arrived at the monastery and went straight to the saint's chapel. Evening service was being held, the choir was singing, candles were burning, fragrance was wafted from the censers. I simply did not know where I was—on earth or in Heaven. I went from the service to Father Yon, and I said to him: 'Well, your Reverence, it was mighty good today at church.' 'No wonder, madam,' he said, 'Father Avvakum had a vision today at the evening service. He had just raised his arms to begin praying when he beheld a light in the cupola and a dove looking down at him.' Well, from that time, I came to the conclusion, sooner or later my last days will be spent at Trinity Monastery."

"And who will take care of us? Who will have your children's welfare at heart? Ah, mamma, mamma!"

"Well, you're not babies any longer, and you'll be able to look after yourselves. As for me, I'll go to the monastery with Annushka's orphans and live under the saint's wing. Perhaps the desire will awaken in one of the girls to serve God. Well, then, the convent is right at hand. I'll buy myself a little house, plant a little garden, potatoes, cabbage—there'll be enough of everything for me."

Such idle talk continued for several days, Arina Petrovna making the boldest plans, withdrawing them and remaking them, and then finally carrying the matter so far that she could not withdraw again. Within half a year after Yudushka's visit this was the situation: Arina Petrovna not at the monastery, nor in a little house built near her husband's grave. Instead of that she had divided the estate, leaving only the capital for herself. Porfiry Vladimirych received the better part and Pavel Vladimirych the worse part.

CHAPTER III

Arina Petrovna remained at Golovliovo. This gave rise, of course, to a domestic comedy. Yudushka shed tears and succeeded in inducing his mother dear to manage his household without accountability to him, to receive the income and to use it at her discretion. "And, dearest, whatever portion of the income you give me," he added, "I shall be satisfied with it." Pavel, on the other hand, thanked his mother coldly ("as if he wanted to bite me," were her words), immediately retired from service ("just so, without his mother's blessing, like a madman, he escaped to freedom") and settled down at Dubrovino.

From that time on, Arina Petrovna's judgment became somewhat dimmed. The image of Porfishka the Bloodsucker, whom she had once sized up so shrewdly, now went, as it were, behind a fog. She seemed no longer to understand anything except that, despite the division of the estate and the emancipation of the peasants, she still lived at Golovliovo and still owed no account to anyone. Here, at her side, lived another son, but what a difference! While Porfisha had entrusted both himself and his household into his mother's care, Pavel not only never consulted her about anything, but even spoke to her through his teeth.

And as her mind became more clouded, her heart warmed more to her gentle son. Porfiry Vladimirych asked nothing of her. She herself anticipated his desires. Little by little she became dissatisfied with the shape of the Golovliovo property. At such and such a place, a stranger's land jutted into it—it would be well to buy up that piece of land. In such and such a place it would be fine to have a separate farm, but there was too little meadow. And here, right next to it, was a meadow for sale, ah, a fine bit of meadow. Arina Petrovna's enthusiasm was that of a mother and a woman of affairs who wants her affectionate son to view her capabilities in all their glory. But Porfiry Vladimirych withdrew into his shell, impervious to all her suggestions. In vain did Arina Petrovna tempt him with bargains. To all her propositions for acquiring a piece of woodland or meadowland, he invariably answered: "Dear mother, I am perfectly satisfied with what you granted me in your kindness."

These answers only spurred Arina Petrovna on. Carried away by her household zeal, and also by indignation against the "scoundrel Pavlusha," who lived beside her but refused to have anything to do with her, Arina Petrovna lost sight of her actual relationship to the estate. Her former fever for acquiring possessed her with renewed strength, though now it was no longer aggrandizement for her own sake but for the sake of her beloved son. The Golovliovo estate grew, rounded out, and flourished.

And at the very moment when Arina Petrovna's capital had dwindled to a point at which it was almost impossible for her to live on the interest, Yudushka sent her a most respectful letter along with an enormous package of blank forms, which were to guide her in the future in the making out of the annual balance sheet. Beside the principal items of the household expenses were listed raspberries, gooseberries, mushrooms, etc. There was a special account for every item, on the following plan:

Number of raspberry bushes, year 18—,-----------------------pounds
Number of bushes planted this year ---------------------------------"
Quantity of berries picked --"
Out of this total you, mother dear,
used for yourself---------------- ---------------------------------"
Preserves used, or to be used, in the household of His Excellency
Porfiry Vladimirych Golovlio- ------------------------------------"
Given to boy in reward for good behavior---------------------------"
Sold to the common people for a tidbit-----------------------------"
Decayed because of absence of buyers and for
other reasons ------------------- ---------------------------------"

NOTE.—In case the crop in the year in which the account is
taken is less than that of the previous year, the reasons therefor,
like drought, rain, hail, and so forth, should be indicated.

Arina Petrovna fairly groaned. First of all, she was shocked at Yudushka's avarice. She had never heard of berries forming an item in the account of an estate, and he seemed to emphasize that item most. Secondly, she fully realized that the blanks were a constitution limiting her power hitherto autocratic.

After a long controversial correspondence between them, Arina Petrovna, humiliated and indignant, moved to Dubrovino, and Porfiry Vladimirych subsequently retired from office and settled at Golovliovo.

From that time on the old woman spent many wretched days in enforced idleness. Pavel Vladimirych was particularly offensive in his treatment of his mother. He received her in what he thought was quite a decent manner, that is, he promised to provide food and drink for both her and his orphan nieces, on two conditions, however, first, they were not to enter the entresol which he occupied; secondly, they were not to interfere in the management of the household. The second condition was particularly galling to Arina Petrovna. The management of the house was in the hands of the housekeeper Ulita, a viperous woman who had been found in secret communication with Yudushka and Kirushka, the late master's butler, a man who knew nothing about farming and whom Pavel Vladimirych almost feared. Both of them stole relentlessly. How often did Arina Petrovna's heart ache when she saw the house being ransacked; how she did long to warn her son and open his eyes to the theft of tea, sugar, butter! Loads of things were wasted, and Ulita, not in the least shamed by the presence of the old mistress, repeatedly hid whole handfuls of sugar in her pocket right before her eyes. Arina Petrovna saw it all, but was forced to remain a silent witness to the plunder. No sooner would she open her mouth to make some remark, than Pavel Vladimirych would instantly check her, saying:

"Mother, there should be only one person to manage a house. I'm not alone in that opinion, everybody says so. I know my orders are foolish. Never mind, let them be foolish. Your orders are wise. Let them be wise. Wise you are, very wise, still Yudushka left you without house or home, to shift for yourself."

The last straw was the awful discovery that Pavel Vladimirych drank. The craving had come from the loneliness of life in the country and had crept upon him stealthily, until finally it possessed him completely, and he was a doomed man. When his mother first came to live in the house, he seemed to have some scruples about drinking. He would come down from the entresol and talk to his mother quite often. She noticed that his speech was strangely incoherent but for a long time attributed it to his stupidity. She did not enjoy his visits. The chats with him oppressed her extremely. In fact he always seemed to be grumbling foolishly. Either there had been a drought for many weeks, or an overwhelming downpour of rain, or tree beetles had overrun the garden and ruined the trees, or moles had made their appearance and dug up the whole field. All this afforded an endless source for grumbling. He would come down from the entresol, seat himself opposite his mother and begin:

"There are clouds all around. Is Golovliovo far from here? The Bloodsucker had a shower yesterday and we don't get a single drop. The clouds wander about, all around here. If there were only a drop of rain for us!"

Or else he would say:

"Have you ever seen such a flood? The rye has just begun to flower and it comes pouring down. Half of the hay is rotten already, and the rain still spouts and spurts. Is Golovliovo far from here? The Bloodsucker has long since gathered in his crops, and here we're stuck. We'll have to feed our cattle on rotten hay this winter."

Arina Petrovna listened in silence to his stupid complaints, but at times her patience gave way and she said:

"Well, keep on sitting there with your arms folded."

Instantly Pavel Vladimirych would flare up.

"What would you advise me to do? Transfer the rain to Golovliovo?"

"I'm not talking about the rain, but in general."

"No 'in general,' please. Why don't you tell me straight out what you think I should do? Shall I change the climate? There's Golovliovo. When Golovliovo needs rain, it rains. When Golovliovo doesn't need rain, then it doesn't rain. And everything grows there, while here, the very opposite. Well, we'll see what you'll have to say when there isn't anything to eat."

"Then such will be the Lord's will."

"All right, then such will be the Lord's will. But you say 'in general' as if that were an explanation."

Sometimes Pavel even found his property a burden.

"Why in the world did I get the Dubrovino estate?" he would complain. "What good is it?"

"What's the matter with Dubrovino? The soil is good, there's plenty of everything. What's got into your head of a sudden?"

"This, that nowadays there's no use having any estate. Money, that's the thing. You take your money, put it in your pocket and off you go. But real estate — —"

"What sort of an age have we come to when there's no use owning real estate?"

"Yes, this is a peculiar age. You don't read the newspapers, but I do. Nowadays the lawyers are everywhere—you can imagine the rest. If a lawyer finds out that you have real estate, then he begins to circle around you."

"Well, how is he going to get at you when you have the proper deeds to the property?"

"Deeds or no deeds, they'll get you. Porfiry the Bloodsucker may hire a lawyer and serve me with summons after summons."

"What are you talking about! We're not living in a lawless country."

"That's just why they serve summonses on you. If the country were lawless, they would take it away without a summons. There's my friend Gorlopiatov, for instance. His uncle died and he, fool that he was, up and accepted the inheritance. The inheritance proved worthless, but the debts figured up to the thousands, the bills of exchange were all false. Now they've been suing him for three years on end. First, they took his uncle's estate. Then they even sold his own property at auction. That's what real estate is."

"Can there possibly be a law like that?"

"If there were no such law, they couldn't have sold it. There's a law for everything. A man without a conscience finds a law to back him in everything. But there are no laws for a man with a conscience. Try and look for them in the books."

Arina Petrovna always let Pavel have his way in these controversies. Many a time she could hardly refrain from shouting, "Out of my sight, you scoundrel." But she would think it over and keep silent. Sometimes she would only murmur to herself:

"Goodness, whom do these monsters take after? One is a bloodsucker, the other is a lunatic. What did I hoard and save for? For what did I deny myself sleep and food? For whom did I do all that?"

The more completely drink took possession of Pavel Vladimirych, the more fantastic and annoying his conversations became. Finally Arina Petrovna noticed there was something wrong. A whole flask of vodka would be put away in the dining-room cupboard in the morning, and by dinner time there wouldn't be a drop left. Or she would be sitting in the parlor and would hear a mysterious creaking in the dining-room near the cupboard. She would call out, "Who's there?" and would hear footsteps quickly but carefully withdrawing toward the entresol.

"Goodness, can it be that he drinks?" she once asked Ulita.

"I shouldn't deny it," answered the latter, with a vicious grin.

When Pavel Vladimirych saw that his mother had discovered the truth, he lost all restraint. One morning Arina Petrovna found the cupboard had disappeared from the dining-room, and when she asked where it had gone to, Ulita told her she had been ordered to carry it to the entresol, because it would be more comfortable for the master to drink there.

In the entresol, the decanters of vodka followed one after the other with amazing rapidity. Shut up alone by himself, Pavel Vladimirych began to hate human society. He created a peculiar fantastic reality for himself, spinning out a long-winded nonsensical romance, in which the main heroes were himself and the Bloodsucker. He was not fully conscious of how, deeply rooted his hatred for Porfiry was. It gnawed at his bones and entrails every minute of his life. The loathed image of his brother stood lifelike before his eyes, and Yudushka's lachrymose, hypocritical twaddle rang in his ears. In his talk there lurked a cold, almost abstract hatred of every living thing that did not conform to the traditional code laid down by hypocrisy. Pavel Vladimirych drank and recalled memories, all the insults and humiliations he had had to suffer because of Yudushka's claims to supremacy in the house; the division of the estate in particular; how he had calculated every kopek and compared every scrap of land. Oh, how he detested him! Entire dramas were enacted in his imagination, heated by alcohol. In these dramas he avenged every offense that he had sustained, and not Yudushka but he himself was always the aggressor. He saw himself the winner of two hundred thousand, and informed Yudushka of his good luck in a long scene, making his brother's face writhe with envy. At other times he imagined his grandfather had died and left a million to him, while nothing at all to Porfiry. He also discovered a means of becoming invisible and when unseen he played wicked tricks on Porfiry to make him groan in agony. His genius for inventing tricks was inexhaustible, and for a long time his idiotic laughter would ring through the entresol, much to the delight of Ulita, who would hurry to inform Porfiry Vladimirych of his brother's doings.

He detested Yudushka and at the same time had a superstitious fear of him. He imagined his eyes discharged a venom of magic effect, that his voice crept, snake-like, into the soul and paralyzed the will. He absolutely refused to meet him, and when the Bloodsucker occasionally visited Dubrovino to kiss the hand of his mother dear, Pavel Vladimirych would lock himself into the entresol and remain imprisoned there until he left.

So the days passed until Pavel Vladimirych found himself face to face with a deadly malady.

CHAPTER IV

The doctor stayed at the house overnight merely for the sake of form, and departed for the city early the next day. On taking leave he said frankly that the patient had no more than two days to live, and it was already too late to talk about any "arrangements" since Pavel Vladimirych could not even sign his name properly.

"He'll sign the document wrong and then you will have a lawsuit on your hands," he added. "Of course, Yudushka respects his mother very highly, but, at that, he'll commence proceedings to prove fraud, and should 'mother dear' be sent to distant regions, the only thing he'll do is to have a mass said for the welfare of the travellers."

All morning Arina Petrovna walked about as if in a dream. She tried to say her prayers. Perhaps God would suggest something, but prayers would not enter her head. Even her tongue refused to obey. There was utter confusion in her mind. Fragments of prayers mingled with incoherent thoughts and vague impressions.

Finally she sat down and sobbed. The tears flowed from her dull eyes over her aged shrivelled cheeks, lingered in the hollows of her wrinkles, and dribbled down on the greasy collar of her old calico waist. Her tears spoke of bitterness, despair, and feeble, but stubborn resistance. Her age, her senile ailments, and the hopelessness of the situation, all seemed to point to death as the only way out. At the same time memories of the past intervened, memories of a life of power, prosperity and unrestrained freedom, and these reminiscences plunged their sting into her soul, dragging her down to earth. "To die!" passed through her mind, but the thought was instantly supplanted by a dogged desire to live. She recalled neither Yudushka nor her dying son. It was as if both had ceased to exist for her. She thought of no one, was indignant at no one, accused no one, even forgot whether she had any capital or no and whether it was sufficient to provide for her old age. A deadly anguish seized her entire being. Her tears had come from a deep source. Drop by drop they had been accumulating since the moment when she left Golovliovo and settled at Dubrovino. She was quite prepared for everything that awaited her. She had expected and foreseen everything, but somehow it had never come to her with such vividness that her fears would be realized. And now this very end had arrived, an end full of anguish and hopeless lonesomeness. All her life long she had been busy building up, she had worn herself to the bone for something, and now she felt as if she had wasted her life on a phantom. All her life the word "family" had never left her lips. In the name of "family" she had punished some and rewarded others. In the name of "family" she had subjected herself to privations, torments, she had crippled her whole life; and suddenly she discovered that "family" was exactly what she did not have.

"Good Lord! Can it possibly be the same everywhere?" was the thought that kept revolving in her mind.

She sat with her head resting on her hand and her face soaked with tears turned to the rising sun, as if to bid it, "Look!" She neither groaned nor cursed. She simply sobbed as if choked by her tears. At the same time the thought seared her soul, "There is no one! No one! No one!"

But now her eyes were drained of tears. She washed her face and wandered without purpose into the dining-room. Here she was assailed by the girls with new complaints which seemed at this time particularly importunate.

"What is going to come of it, grandma? Is it possible that we shall be left just so, without anything?" grumbled Anninka.

"How silly uncle is," Lubinka chimed in.

About midday, Arina Petrovna decided to go to her dying son. Stepping softly she climbed the stairs and groped in the dark till she found the door leading into the rooms. The entresol was buried in deepest gloom. The windows were darkened by green shades, through which the light could scarcely filter. A sickening mixture of odors pervaded the room, which had not been ventilated for a long while. There was the smell of berries, plaster, oil from the image-lamp, and those peculiar odors which bespeak the presence of sickness and death. There were only two rooms. In the first one sat Ulita, cleaning berries. The flies swarmed about the heap of gooseberries and impudently attacked her nose and lips, and she would keep driving them off in exasperation. Through the half-closed door of the adjoining room came the sound of incessant coughing which every now and then ended in painful expectoration. Arina Petrovna stopped in an uncertain pose, searching the gloom and waiting for the course of action that Ulita would take in view of her arrival. But Ulita never moved an eyelash, entirely confident that every attempt to influence the sick man would be fruitless. Her lips merely twitched in resentment, and Arina Petrovna heard the word "hag" pronounced under her breath.

"You had better go down, my dear," said Arina Petrovna, turning to Ulita.

"Where did you get that idea from?" snapped the latter.

"I have to talk to Pavel Vladimirych. Go down."

"Excuse me, madam, how can I leave the master? What if something should happen? There's no one to serve him and attend to him."

"What's the matter?" a hollow voice called from the bedroom.

"Order Ulita to go downstairs, my friend. I have matters to talk over with you."

This time Arina Petrovna pressed her point so persistently that she was victorious. She crossed herself and entered the room. The patient's bed stood near the inner wall far from the window. He lay on his back, covered with a white blanket, smoking a cigarette, though almost half unconscious. Notwithstanding the smoke, the flies pestered him with peculiar persistence, so that he had continually to pass his hand over his face. His arms were so weak, so bare of muscle, that they showed the bones, of almost equal thickness from wrist to shoulder, in clear outline. His head nestled despondently in the pillow. His whole body and face burned in a dry fever. His large round eyes were sunken and gazed aimlessly about, as if looking for something. The lines of his nose had grown longer and sharper. His mouth was half open. He had stopped coughing, but he breathed with such difficulty that it seemed as if all his vital energy were concentrated in his chest.

"Well, how do you feel to-day?" asked Arina Petrovna, sinking into the armchair at his feet.

"So—so—to-morrow—that is, to-day—when was the doctor here?"

"He was here to-day."

"Well, then, to-morrow——"

The patient fumbled as if struggling to recall a word.

"You'll be able to get up?" prompted Arina Petrovna. "God grant it, my friend, God grant it."

They both remained silent for a moment. Arina Petrovna found it very difficult to open a conversation when she was face to face with Pavel Vladimirych.

"Yudushka—is he alive?" finally asked the sick man himself.

"Nothing is the matter with him. He lives and prospers."

"I bet he is thinking, 'Now brother Pavel is going to die—and with God's help the estate will come to me.'"

"We'll all die, some day—and after every one of us, the estates will go to the lawful heirs."

"Only not to the Bloodsucker! I'll throw it to the dogs, but he shan't have it."

The situation was turning out excellently. Pavel Vladimirych himself was leading the conversation. Arina Petrovna did not fail to take advantage of the opportunity.

"You ought to consider that, my friend," she said, as if by the way, not looking at her son and examining the color of her hands as if they were the main object of her interest.

"What do you mean by 'that'?"

"Well, I mean, if you don't wish that the estate should go to your brother."

The patient was silent. Only his eyes widened unnaturally and his face flushed more and more.

"And also, my friend, you ought to take into consideration the fact that you have orphaned nieces—and what sort of capital have they? Then there is your mother," continued Arina Petrovna.

"You've managed to give everything away to Yudushka!"

"Whatever may have happened, I know that I myself am to blame. But it wasn't such a crime after all. I thought 'he is my son.' At any rate, it isn't kind of you to remember that against your mother."

Silence followed.

"Well, why don't you say something?"

"And how soon do you expect to bury me?"

"Oh, don't talk like that. All Christians——Everybody doesn't die right away, still in general——"

"There you go—'in general!' Always your 'in general!' You think I don't see."

"See what, my boy?"

"I see you take me for a fool. Well, if I am a fool, let me remain a fool. Why do you come to a fool? Don't come, don't worry about me."

"I'm not worrying. But in general there is a term set to everybody's life."

"Then wait for my term."

Arina Petrovna lowered her head and meditated. She saw clearly that her case was almost a failure, but she was so tortured that nothing could convince her of the fruitlessness of further attempts to influence her son.

"I don't know why you hate me," she declared finally.

"Not at all—on the contrary I—not at all. In fact I—why, the idea—you brought us all up—so impartially."

He spoke in jerks and gasps. A broken yet triumphant laugh made its way into his voice. His eyes sparkled. His shoulders and legs quivered.

"Perhaps I have really sinned against you, then for Christ's sake forgive me."

Arina Petrovna rose and bowed till her hand touched the floor. Pavel Vladimirych shut his eyes without replying.

"Suppose we let the question of the estate alone. You couldn't make any arrangement in your present condition. Porfiry is the lawful heir. Well, let the real estate go to him. But what about your personal property and capital?" Arina Petrovna ventured to state her point directly.

Pavel Vladimirych shuddered, but remained silent. It is very possible that at the word "capital" he gave no thought whatsoever to his mother's insinuations, but simply mused: "September is here already. I have to collect the interest."

"If you think I desire your death, you're very much mistaken, my child. If you would only live I should not need to complain in my old age. What have I to grumble about? I have food and shelter here, and should I want a little additional pleasure, I can get it. I merely wish to call your attention to the fact that there is a custom among Christians, according to which, in expectation of the life to come, we——"

Arina Petrovna paused, searching for a suitable word.

"We provide for the future of those related to us," she concluded, looking out of the window.

Pavel Vladimirych lay motionless, coughing softly. He did not betray by a single movement whether or not he was listening. Apparently his mother was boring him.

"The capital may go from hand to hand during life," said Arina Petrovna, as though passing a trivial remark and resuming the inspection of her hands.

The patient shuddered slightly, but Arina Petrovna did not notice it and continued:

"The law, my friend, expressly permits the free transfer of capital. Money is something one acquires. Yesterday you had it. To-day it is gone. And nobody can call you to account for it. You can give it to whomever you choose."

Pavel Vladimirych suddenly laughed viciously.

"You probably remember the story about Polochkin," he hissed. "He gave his capital to his wife 'from hand to hand' and she ran off with her lover."

"You may rest assured, my child, I have no lover."

"Then you'll run off without a lover—with the money."

"How well you understand my motives!"

"I don't understand you at all. You gave me the reputation of a fool. Well, I *am* a fool. Let me be a fool. What wonderful tricks they have invented—to pass my money from hand to hand! And where do I come in? I suppose you'll order me to go to a monastery for my salvation, and from there watch how you manage my money?"

He shot these words out in a volley, in a voice full of hatred and indignation. Then he broke down completely and burst into a fit of coughing that lasted a full quarter of an hour. It was amazing to see how much strength that wretched human skeleton contained. Finally he caught his breath and closed his eyes.

Arina Petrovna looked about in bewilderment. Until that moment she could not believe it, somehow, but now she was fully convinced that every attempt to persuade the dying man would only serve to hasten the day of Yudushka's triumph. Yudushka kept dancing before her eyes. She saw him walking behind the hearse, giving his brother the last Judas kiss and squeezing out two foul tears. Then she had a picture of the coffin being lowered into the grave and Yudushka exclaiming, "Farewell, brother!" his lips twitching and his eyes rolling upward. She heard his attempt to add a note of grief to his voice, and afterwards say, turning to Ulita: "The kutya,[A] the kutya, don't forget to take the kutya into the house. And be sure to put on a clean table cloth. We must honor brother's memory in the house, too." Next she saw him presiding over the funeral feast, chatting incessantly with the reverend father about the virtues of the deceased. She heard him say, "Ah, brother, brother, you didn't wish to live with us," as he rose from the table, stretching out his hand, palm upward, to receive the father's blessing. And lastly she saw Yudushka walking about the house with the air of a master, taking the inventory of all the effects and in doubtful cases casting suspicious glances at mother.

All these inevitable scenes of the future floated before Arina Petrovna's mental vision. In her ears rang Yudushka's shrill, unctuous voice as he said: "Do you remember, mother dear, the little golden shirt studs that brother had? They were so pretty. He used to wear them on holidays. I simply can't imagine where those studs could have gone to."

> [A] A gruel made of rice or wheat or barley, boiled with raisins and mead. It is eaten after the mass for the dead and, in the South, on Christmas Eve.

CHAPTER V

No sooner did Arina Petrovna come downstairs, than a carriage drawn by a team of four horses made its appearance on a hill near the church. In it, in the place of honor, was seated Porfiry Golovliov, who had removed his hat and was crossing himself at the sight of the church. Opposite him sat his two sons, Petenka and Volodenka. The very blood froze in Arina Petrovna's veins as the thought flashed through her mind, "Speak of the devil and he's sure to appear." The girls also lost courage, and timidly clung closer to their grandmother. The house hitherto peaceful was suddenly filled with alarm. Doors banged, people ran about crying, "The master is coming, the master is coming!" and all the occupants of the house rushed out on the porch. Some made the sign of the cross, some stood in silent expectation, all apparently conscious of the fact that the existing order in Dubrovino had been only temporary, and that now the real management was to begin with a real master at the head. Under the former master some of the old, deserving serfs had enjoyed the privilege of a monthly allowance of provisions. Many of them fed their cattle on the master's hay, had kitchen gardens of their own, and altogether lived "freely." Everyone, of course, was now vitally interested to know whether the new master would permit the old order of things, or whether he would introduce a new one, similar to that which prevailed at Golovliovo.

Yudushka drove up to the house. From the reception accorded to him he concluded that affairs at Dubrovino were fast coming to a head. Without a sign of haste, he descended from the carriage, waved his hand to the servants who rushed forward to kiss it, then put his palms together, and began to climb the steps slowly, whispering a prayer. His face expressed a feeling of mingled grief, firmness, and resignation. As a man he grieved; as a Christian he did not dare to complain. He prayed to God to cure his brother, but above all he put his trust in the Lord and bowed before His will. His sons walked side by side behind him, Volodenka mimicking his father, clasping his hands, rolling his eyes heavenward and mumbling his lips. Petenka revelled in his brother's performance. Behind them, in silent procession, followed the servants.

Yudushka kissed dear mother's hand, then her lips, then her hand again and put his arm about her waist and said, shaking his head sadly:

"And you keep on worrying. That's bad, mother dear, very bad. Instead of that you should ask yourself: 'And what is God going to say to this?' He will say: 'Here have I in my infinite wisdom arranged everything for the best, and she grumbles.' Ah, mother dear, mother dear."

Then he kissed both of his nieces, and with the same charming familiarity in his voice, said:

"And you, too, romps, you are crying your eyes out. I won't permit it. I command you immediately to smile. And that shall be the end of it."

And he stamped his foot at them in jesting anger.

"Just look at me," he continued. "As a brother I am torn with grief. More than once I have shed tears. I am sorry for brother, sorry as can be. I weep. Then I bethink myself: 'And what is God for? Is it possible that God knows less than we what ought to be?' This thought inspires me with courage. That is how you all should act, you, mother dear, and you, little nieces, and—" he turned to the servants—"you all."

"Look at me, how well I bear up."

And in the same charming manner he proceeded to impersonate a man who bears up. He straightened his body, put one foot forward, expanded his chest, and threw back his head. The audience smiled sourly.

This performance over, Yudushka passed into the drawing-room and kissed his mother's hand again.

"Well, so that's how things are, mother dear," he said, seating himself on the couch. "So brother Pavel, too."

"Yes, Pavel, too," softly answered Arina Petrovna.

"Yes, yes—a little too early. Although I play the brave, in my soul I, too, suffer and grieve for my poor brother. He hated me—hated me bitterly. Maybe that is why God is punishing him."

"You might forget about it at such a moment. You must set old grudges aside."

"I have forgotten it all long ago. I only mentioned it in passing. My brother disliked me, for what reason, I know not. I tried one way and another, directly and indirectly. I called him 'dear' and 'kind brother,' but he drew back and that was the end of it."

"I asked you please not to bring all that up. The man is lying at the point of death."

"Yes, mother dear, death is a great mystery. 'For ye know neither the day nor the hour.' That's the kind of mystery it is. There he was making plans, thinking he was exalted so high, so high as to be beyond mortal reach. But in one instant with one blow God undid all his dreams. Perhaps he would be glad now to cover up his sins. But they are already recorded in the Book of Life. And whatever is written in that book, mother dear, won't be scraped off in a hurry."

"But does not the Lord accept the sinner's repentance?"

"That's just what I wish for him from the bottom of my heart. I know he hated me, still I wish him forgiveness. I wish the best for everybody—for those that hate me, those that insult me—everybody. He was unfair to me and now God sends him an ailment—not I, but God. Does he suffer much, mother dear?"

"Well, not very much. The doctor was here and even gave us hopes." So lied Arina Petrovna.

"What splendid news! Don't you worry, dear mother, he'll pull through yet. Here we are eating our hearts away and grumbling at the Creator, and perhaps he is sitting quietly on his bed thanking the Lord for his recovery."

The idea delighted Yudushka so immensely that he even giggled softly to himself.

"Do you know, mother dear, that I have come to stay here a while?" he went on, for all the world as if he were giving his mother a pleasant surprise. "It's among good kinsmen, you know. In case something happens—you understand, as a brother—I may console, advise, make arrangements. You will permit me, will you not?"

"What sort of permissions can I give when I am here myself only as a—guest?"

"Well, then, dearest, since this is Friday, just order them, if you please, to prepare a fish meal for me. Some salt-fish, mushrooms, a little cabbage— you know, I don't need much. And in the meantime, as a relative, I shall drag myself up to the entresol. Perhaps I shall still be in time to do some good, if not to his body, at least to his soul. In his position, it seems to me, the soul is of much more consequence. We can patch up the body, mother dear, with potions and poultices, but the soul needs a more potent remedy."

Arina Petrovna made no objection. The thought of the inevitability of the "end" had taken such complete hold of her, that she observed everything and listened to everything about her dazedly. She saw Yudushka rise from the sofa, stoop and shuffle his feet. He liked to appear invalided at times. He had an idea it added to his dignity. She knew the unexpected appearance of the Bloodsucker in the entresol would greatly excite the patient, might even hasten his end. But after the day of agitation, she was so exhausted that she felt as if in a dream.

Meanwhile Pavel Vladimirych was in an indescribable state of excitement. Though quite alone, he was aware of an unusual stir in the house. Every bang of a door, every hurried footstep in the hall awakened a mysterious alarm. For a while he called with all his might; but, soon convinced his shouts were useless, he gathered all his strength, sat up in bed, and listened. The sound of running feet and loud voices stopped and was followed by a dead silence. Something unknown and fearful surrounded him. Only a few, miserly rays of light sifted through the lowered shades and the dim light of the lamp burning before the ikon in the corner made the dusk filling the room seem all the darker and gloomier. Pavel fixed his gaze upon that mysterious corner as if for the first time he found something surprising in it. The ikon, in a gilt framework on which the rays from the lamp fell perpendicularly, stood out of the gloom with a sort of striking brightness, like something alive. A circle of light wavered upon the ceiling, flaring up or dying down in proportion to the strength or weakness of the lamplight. Strange shadows filled the room, and the dressing-gown hanging on the wall was alive with vacillating stripes of light and shadow. Pavel Vladimirych watched and watched, and he felt as if right there in that corner everything were suddenly beginning to move. Solitude, helplessness, dead silence—and shadows, a host of shadows. The shadows seemed to be coming, coming, coming. Gripped by an indescribable terror, he gazed into the mysterious corner, eyes and mouth agape, uttering no cries, but simply groaning—groaning in a stifled voice, in jerks, like the barking of a dog. He heard neither the creak of the stairs nor the careful shuffling steps in the adjacent room. Suddenly, beside his bed, there loomed up the detestable figure of Yudushka, as if from that gloom which had just mysteriously hovered before his eyes, and as if there were more, more of shadows, shadows without end—coming, coming——

"What? Where did you come from? Who let you in?" he cried instinctively, dropping back on his pillow helplessly. Yudushka stood at the bedside, scrutinizing the sick man and shaking his head sorrowfully.

"Does it hurt?" he asked, putting all the oiliness of which he was capable into his voice.

Pavel Vladimirych was silent, but stared at him stupidly, as if making every effort to understand him.

Meanwhile Yudushka approached the ikon, fell to his knees, bowed three times to the ground, arose and appeared again at the bedside.

"Well, brother, get up. May God send you grace," he said, sitting down in an armchair, in a voice so jovial that he actually appeared to be carrying "grace" about with him in his pocket.

At last Pavel Vladimirych realized that this was no shadow but the Bloodsucker in flesh. He seemed to coil up of a sudden as if in a cramp. Yudushka's eyes were bright with affection, but the invalid very distinctly saw the "noose" lurking in those eyes ready any instant to dart out and tighten round his neck.

"Ah, brother, brother, you've become no better than an old woman," Yudushka continued jocosely. "Come, brace up! Get up and run a little race. Come on, come on, give mother the joy of seeing what a strong fellow you are. Come on now! Up with you!"

"Get out of here, Bloodsucker!" the invalid cried in desperation.

"Ah, brother, brother! I come to you in kindness and sympathy, and you ... what do you say in return? Oh, what a sin! And how could your tongue say such a thing to your own brother! It's a shame, darling, it's a shame! Wait a minute, let me arrange the pillow for you."

Yudushka got up and poked his finger into the pillow.

"Like this," he continued. "That's fine now. Lie quietly, now. You won't need to touch it till tomorrow."

"You get out!"

"My, how cranky your illness has made you! Why, you have even become stubborn, really. You keep chasing me, 'Get out, get out!' But how can I go? Here, for instance, you feel thirsty and I hand you some water. Or I see the ikon is out of order, and I set it to rights, or pour in some oil. You just lie where you are and I'll be sitting nearby, real quietly. So we won't even see how time flies."

"Get out, you Bloodsucker!"

"Look here, you are insulting me, but I am going to pray to the Lord for you. I know it isn't you, it's your illness talking. You see, brother, I am used to forgiving. I forgive everybody. Today, for instance, as I was coming here I met a peasant, and he said something about me. Well, the Lord be with him. He defiled his own tongue. And I, why I not only was not angry at him, I even made the sign of the cross over him, I did truly."

"You robbed him, didn't you?"

"Who, I? Why, no, my friend, I don't rob people; highwaymen rob, but I—I act in accordance with the law. I caught his horse grazing in my meadows—well, let him go to the justice of the peace. If the justice says it's right to let your cattle graze on other people's fields, well, then I'll give him his horse back, but if the justice says it isn't right, I am sorry. The peasant will have to pay a fine. I act according to the law, my friend, according to the law."

"You Judas the traitor, you left mother a pauper."

"I repeat, you may be angry, if you please, but you are wrong. If I were not a Christian, I would even have cause to be angry at you for what you've just said."

"Yes, you did, you did make mother a pauper."

"Now, do be quiet, please. Here, I am going to pray for you. Maybe that will calm you down."

Though Yudushka had restrained himself successfully throughout the conversation, the dying man's curses affected him deeply. His lips curled queerly and turned pale. However, hypocrisy was so ingrained in his nature that once the comedy was begun, he could not leave it unfinished. So he knelt before the ikon and for fully fifteen minutes murmured prayers, his hands uplifted. Thereupon he returned to the dying man's bed with countenance calm and serene.

"You know, brother, I have come to talk serious matters over with you," he said, seating himself in the armchair. "Here you are insulting me, but I am thinking of your soul. Tell me, please, when did you communicate last?"

"Oh, Lord! What is all this? Take him away! Ulita, Agasha! Anybody here?" moaned Pavel.

"Now, now, darling, do be quiet. I know you don't like to talk about it. Yes, brother, you always were a bad Christian and you are still. But it wouldn't be bad, really it wouldn't, to give some thought to your soul. We've got to be careful with our souls, my friend, oh, how careful! Do you know what the Church prescribes? It says, 'Ye shall offer prayers and thanks.' And again, 'The end of a Christian's earthly life is painless, honorable and peaceable.' That's what it is, my friend. You really ought to send for the priest and sincerely, with penitence. All right, I won't, I won't. But really you'd better."

Pavel Vladimirych lay livid and nearly suffocated. If he could have, he would have dashed his head to pieces.

"And how about the estate? Have you already made arrangements?" continued Yudushka. "Yours is a fine little estate, a very fine one. The soil is even better than at Golovliovo. And you have money, too, I suppose. Of course, I don't know anything about your affairs. I only know that you received a lump sum on freeing your serfs, but exactly how much, I never cared to know. To-day, for instance, as I was coming here, I said to myself, 'I suppose brother Pavel has money.' 'But then,' I thought, 'if he has capital, he must have decided already how to dispose of it.'"

The patient turned away and sighed heavily.

"You have not made any disposition? Well, so much the better, my friend. It's even more just, according to the law. It won't be inherited by strangers, but by your own kind. Take me, for example, I am old, with one foot in the grave, but still I think, 'Why should I make disposition of my property if the law will do it all for me, after I am dead?' And it's really the right way, my friend. There will be no quarrels, no envy, no lawsuits. It's the law."

That was unbearable. Pavel Vladimirych felt as if he were lying in a coffin, fettered, in lethargy, unable to move a limb, and forced to hear the Bloodsucker revile his dead body.

"Get out—for Christ's sake, get out!" he finally implored his torturer.

"All right, you just be quiet, I'll go. I know you don't like me. It's a shame, my friend, a real shame, to dislike your own brother. You see, I do love you. And I've always been telling my children, 'Though Pavel Vladimirych has sinned against me, yet I love him.' So you did not make any disposition? Well, that's fine, my friend. Sometimes, though, one's money is stolen while one is yet alive, especially when one is without relatives, all alone. But I'll take care of it. Eh? What? Am I annoying you? Well, well, let it be as you wish. I'll go. Let me offer up a prayer."

He rose, placed his palms together, and whispered a prayer hurriedly.

"Good-by, friend, don't worry. Take a good rest, and perhaps with God's help you will get better. I will talk the matter over with mother dear. Maybe we'll think something up. I have ordered a fish meal for myself, some salt-fish, some mushrooms and cabbage. So you'll pardon me. What? Am I annoying you again? Ah, brother dear! Well, well, I'm going. Above all, don't be alarmed, don't be excited, sleep well and take a good rest," he said, and finally made his departure.

"Bloodsucker!" The word came after him in such a piercing shriek that even he felt as if he had been branded with a hot iron.

CHAPTER VI

While Porfiry Vladimirych was holding forth in the entresol, grandmother Arina Petrovna had gathered the young folks around her downstairs, and was talking to them, not without the hope of getting something out of them.

"Well, how are you?" she asked, turned to her eldest grandson, Petenka.

"I'm pretty well, granny. Next month I'll graduate as an officer."

"Really? How many years have you been promising that? Are the examinations so hard? Or what?"

"At the last examination, granny, he failed in his catechism. The priest asked him, 'What is God?' and he answered, 'God is Spirit—is Spirit—and Holy Spirit.'"

"Oh, you poor thing! How is that? Look at those little orphans. I'm sure even they know that."

"Why, certainly. God is invisible Spirit." Anninka hurried to show off her knowledge.

"Whom none ever beheld," Lubinka put in.

"Omniscient, most Gracious, Omnipotent, Omnipresent," Anninka continued.

"Whither can I go from Thy spirit and whither can I flee from Thy face? Should I rise to Heaven, there wouldst Thou be, should I descend to Hell, there wouldst Thou be."

"I wish you would have answered like that. You would have epaulets by this time. And how about you, Volodya, what are you going to do?"

Volodya flushed and remained silent.

"Apparently, you go no further than your brother with his 'Spirit—Holy Spirit,' Ah, children, children! You seem to be so bright and yet somehow you can't master your studies at all. I might understand if you had a father who spoiled you. Tell me, how does he treat you now?"

"Still the same old way, granny."

"Does he beat you? Didn't I hear he stopped thrashing you?"

"A little bit, but—the worst is, he pesters us to death."

"I must say, I don't understand. How can a father pester his children?"

"He does though, grandma, awfully. We can't go out without permission, we can't take a thing. It couldn't be worse."

"Well, then, ask permission. Your tongue wouldn't fall out in the effort, I imagine."

"Impossible. You just begin to talk to him, then he doesn't let go of you. 'Don't hurry and wait a while. Gently, gently, take it easy.' Really, granny, his talk is too tiresome for words."

"Granny, he listens to us on the sly behind our doors. Just the other day Piotr caught him in the act."

"Oh, you rogues! Well, what did he say?"

"Nothing. I said to him, 'It won't do, daddy, for you to eavesdrop at our doors. Some day you may get your nose squashed. And all he said was, 'Well, well, it's nothing, it's nothing. I, my child, am like a thief in the night, as it says in the Bible.'"

"The other day, granny, he picked up an apple in the orchard, and put it away in a cupboard. I ate it up. So he hunted and hunted for it, and cross-examined everybody."

"What do you mean? Has he become a miser?"

"No, he's not exactly stingy, but—how shall I put it? He is just swamped head over heels in little things. He hides slips of paper, and he hunts for wind-fallen fruit."

"Every morning he says mass in his study, and later he gives each of us a little piece of holy wafer, stale as stale can be."

"But once we played a trick on him. We discovered where he keeps the wafers, made a cut in the bottom of them, took out the pulp, and stuck butter in."

"Well, I must say you are regular cut-throats."

"My, just imagine his surprise, next day. Wafers with butter!"

"I suppose you got it good and hard afterwards."

"No, not a bit. But he kept spitting all day and muttering to himself, 'The rascals!' Of course we made believe he didn't mean us."

"Let me tell you, granny, he is afraid of you."

"Of me! I'm not a scarecrow to frighten him."

"I'm sure he's scared of you. He thinks you'll put a curse on him. He's desperately afraid of curses."

Arina Petrovna became lost in thought. At first the idea passed through her mind: "What if I really should put a curse on him—just take and curse him?" But the thought was instantly replaced by a more pressing question, "What is Yudushka doing now? What tricks is he playing upstairs? He must be up to one of his usual tricks." Finally a happy idea struck her.

"Volodya," she said, "you, dear heart, are light on your feet. Why shouldn't you go softly and listen to what's going on up there?"

"Gladly, granny."

Volodya tiptoed toward the doors and disappeared through them.

"What made you come over to us to-day?" Arina Petrovna continued with her questioning.

"We meant to come a long time ago, grandma, but today Ulita sent a messenger to say the doctor had been here and uncle was going to die, if not to-day, then surely to-morrow."

"Tell me, is there any talk among you about the heritage?"

"We keep talking about it the whole day, granny. Papa tells us how it used to be before grandpa's time. He even remembers Goriushkino, granny. 'See now,' he says, 'if Auntie Varvara Mikhailovna had no children, then Goriushkino would be ours. And God knows,' he says, 'who the children's father is. But let us not judge others. We see a mote in the eye of our neighbor, but fail to notice a beam in our own. That's how the world goes, brother.'"

"Nonsense, nonsense. Auntie was married, was she not? Even if there had been anything before that, the marriage made it all straight."

"That's true, grandma, and each time we go past Goriushkino, he brings up the same old tale: 'Grandma Natalya Vladimirovna,' he says, 'brought Goriushkino as a dowry. By all rights it should have stayed in the family. But your deceased grandfather gave it to sister as a dot. And what wonderful watermelons,' he says, 'used to grow at Goriushkino! Twenty pounds each. That's the kind of watermelons that grew there!'"

"Twenty pounds, bosh! I never heard of such melons. Well, and what are his intentions about Dubrovino?"

"In the same line, granny. Watermelons and muskmelons and other trifles. But of late he has constantly been asking us, 'What do you think, children, has uncle Pavel much money?' He has had it all figured out for a long time, grandma: the amount of redemption loan, and when the property was mortgaged, and how much debt is paid off. We even saw the paper on which he made the calculations; and guess what, granny, we stole it. We nearly drove him crazy with that slip of paper. He'd put it in a drawer, and we'd match the key and stick it into a holy wafer. Once he went to take a bath, when lo and behold! he saw the paper lying on the bath shelf."

"You've a gay life up there."

Volodenka returned and became the center of general attention.

"I couldn't hear a thing," he announced in a whisper, "the only thing I heard was father mouthing words like 'painless, untarnished, peaceful,' and uncle shouting, 'Get out of here, you Bloodsucker!'"

"Didn't you hear anything about the will?"

"I think there was something said about it, but I couldn't make it out. Father shut the door entirely too tight, granny. Only a buzzing came through. And then suddenly uncle yelled, 'Get—get out!' Well then I took to my heels and here I am."

"If only the orphans were given——" anxiously thought Arina Petrovna.

"If father gets his hands on it, granny, he'll not give a thing to anyone," Petenka assured her. "And I have a feeling he's even going to deprive us of the inheritance."

"Still, he can't take it to the grave with him, can he?"

"No, but he'll think up some scheme. It wasn't for nothing that he had a talk with the priest not long ago. 'How does the idea of building a tower of Babel strike you, Father?' he asked. 'Would one need much money?'"

"Well, he just said that perhaps out of curiosity."

"No, granny, he has some plan in mind. If it isn't for a tower of Babel, he'll donate the money to the St. Athos monastery; but he'll make sure we don't get any."

"Will father get a big estate when uncle dies?" asked Volodya, curiously.

"Well, God alone knows which of them will die first."

"Father is sure he'll outlive uncle. The other day, just as soon as we reached the boundary of the Dubrovino estate, he took off his cap, crossed himself, and said, 'Thank God we'll be riding again on our own land!'"

"He's made arrangements for everything already, granny. He noticed the woods. 'There,' he says, 'if there were a good landlord, that would be a ripping fine forest.' Then he looked at the meadows. 'What a meadow! Just look! Look at all those hay stacks!'"

"Yes, indeed, both the woods and the meadows, everything will be yours, my darlings," sighed Arina Petrovna. "Goodness! Wasn't that a squeak on the stairs?"

"Hush, granny, hush! That's he—'like a thief in the night,' listening behind the doors."

There was a silence, but it proved to be a false alarm. Arina Petrovna sighed and muttered to herself, "Ah, children, children!"

The boys stared at the orphans, fairly swallowing them with their gaze, while the little orphans sat in silent envy.

"Did you see Mademoiselle Lotar, cousin?" Petenka started a conversation.

Anninka and Lubinka exchanged glances as if they had been asked a question in history or geography.

"In *Fair Helen* she plays the part of Helen on the stage."

"Oh, yes—Helen—Paris—'Beautiful and young; he set the hearts of the goddesses aflame—' I know, I know it," cried Lubinka joyfully.

"Exactly. And how she sings 'Cas-ca-ader, ca-as-cader.' It's great."

"The doctor who was just here keeps humming '*Head over heels*.'"

"That is Lyadova's song. Wasn't she splendid, cousin? When she died, nearly two thousand persons followed the hearse. People thought there would be a revolution."

"Is it about theatres you're chattering?" broke in Arina Petrovna. "Well, their destiny lies far from theatres, my boys. It leads rather to the convent."

"Granny, you've set your mind on burying us in a convent," complained Anninka.

"Come, cousin, let's go to St. Petersburg instead of to a convent. We'll show you everything to be seen there."

"Their minds should not be occupied with thoughts of pleasure, but rather with thoughts of God," continued Arina Petrovna sententiously.

"We will teach you everything under the sun. In St. Petersburg there are lots of girls like you. They walk about swinging their skirts."

"Stop bothering them, for Christ's sake, you teachers," Arina Petrovna interjected. "Nice things you can teach them."

"I'm going to take them to Khotkov, after Uncle Pavel's death, and we'll settle down comfortably there."

"So you're still at your blabbing," a voice at the door suddenly broke in.

Engrossed in conversation nobody had heard Yudushka steal up "like a thief in the night." He was all in tears, his head was bowed, his face pale, his hands crossed on his breast, his lips mumbling in prayer. For a few moments his eyes sought the ikons, then found them and for a brief while he prayed.

"He's very ill. Ah, how ill he is!" he finally exclaimed, embracing his mother dear.

"Is he?"

"Very, very ill, dear heart. And do you recollect what a strong fellow he was?"

"Well, he was never exactly strong. I can't remember that, somehow."

"Ah no, mother dear, don't say that. He was, always. I remember perfectly when he left the cadets corps how well shaped he was, broad shouldered, glowing with health. Yes, yes, mother dear, that's how it is. We're all in God's hands. To-day we're strong, in the best of health, we want to enjoy life to have a good meal, and tomorrow...."

He shrugged his shoulders and assumed deep emotion.

"Did he say anything at least?"

"Very little, dearest. The only thing he said was, 'Good-by, brother.' And yet, mother dear, he can feel. He feels that he is in a bad way."

"Well, no wonder he feels he is in a bad way when he can hardly catch his breath."

"No, mother dear, that's not what I mean. I have in mind the inner vision which is given to the righteous and which allows them to foresee their death."

"Yes, yes! Didn't he say anything about his will?"

"No, mother. He wanted to say something about it, but I stopped him. 'No,' I said, 'don't talk about that! Whatever you leave me, brother, out of the kindness of your heart, I shall be satisfied. And even if you leave me nothing, I'll have mass said for you at my own expense.' And yet, mother dear, how he wants to live! How he longs for life!"

"Of course, who doesn't want to live?"

"No, mother. Take myself, for example. If it pleased the Lord God to call me to Himself, I'm ready on the spot."

"All well and good if you go to Heaven, but what if Satan gets you between his fangs?"

In this vein the talk continued till supper, during supper, and after supper. Arina Petrovna was very restless. While Yudushka was expatiating on various subjects, the thought entered her mind at shorter and shorter intervals, "What if I should really curse him?" But Yudushka had not the slightest suspicion of the storm raging in his mother's heart. He had an air of serenity, and continued slowly and gently to torture his "mother dear" with his endless twaddle.

"I'll curse him! I'll curse him! Curse him!" Arina Petrovna repeated inwardly, with greater and greater determination.

CHAPTER VII

An odor of incense pervaded the rooms, the sing-song of funeral chants was heard in the house, the doors were thrown open, those wishing to pay their last respects to the deceased came and went. While Pavel Vladimirych lived, nobody had paid any attention to him; at his death everybody mourned. People recalled that he "had never hurt a single person," that "he had never uttered a cross word to anyone," nor thrown anyone a look of ill-will—all qualities that had appeared purely negative, but now assumed a positive character. Many seemed to repent that at times they had taken advantage of the dead man's simplicity—but after all, who knew that the simple soul was destined to so speedy an end? One peasant brought Yudushka three silver rubles and said: "Here's a little debt I owe Pavel Vladimirych. No writing passed between us. Here, take it."

Yudushka took the money, praised the peasant, and said he would donate the three silver rubles for oil to burn forever before an ikon in the church.

"You, my dear friend, will see the flame, and everybody will see it, and the soul of my deceased brother will rejoice. Maybe he will obtain something for you in Heaven. You won't be expecting anything—and suddenly the Lord will send you luck."

Very probably the high estimate of the deceased's virtues was largely based on a comparison between him and his brother. People did not like Yudushka. Not that they couldn't get the better of him, but that he was entirely too much of a nuisance with his scrape-penny ways. Very few could bring themselves to lease land from him. They were afraid of his passion for litigation. He dragged any number of people to court, wasted their time, and won nothing, because his pettifogging habits were so well known in the district that almost without listening to the case the courts dismissed his claims.

Since meanness, or, to be more exact, a kind of moral hardness, especially when under the mask of hypocrisy, always inspires a sort of superstitious fear, Yudushka's neighbors bowed waist low as they passed by the Bloodsucker, standing all in black beside the coffin with palms crossed and eyes raised upward.

As long as the deceased lay in the house, the family walked about on tip-toe, stole glances into the dining-room, where the coffin stood on the table, wagged their heads, and talked in whispers. Yudushka pretended to be overcome by the disaster, and shuffled painfully along the corridor, paid a visit to the "dear deceased," affected deep emotional stress, arranged the pall on the coffin, and whispered to the commissioner of police, who was taking the inventory and affixing the seal. Petenka and Volodenka busied themselves about the coffin, placing and lighting the candles, handing over the censer, and so forth. Anninka and Lubinka cried and through their tears helped the chanters sing the mass for the dead in thin little voices. The woman servants, dressed in black calico, wiped their noses red from weeping on their aprons.

Immediately after the death of Pavel Vladimirych, Arina Petrovna went up to her room and locked herself in. She was not disposed to weep, for she realized that she had to decide upon a course of action immediately. To remain at Dubrovino was out of the question. Consequently, she had only one choice, to go to Pogorelka, the orphans' estate, the "bone" that she had once thrown to her disrespectful daughter, Anna Vladimirovna. Arriving at this decision, she felt relieved, as though Yudushka had suddenly and forever lost all power over her. Calmly she counted her five per cent. Government bonds. They totalled fifteen thousand rubles of her own, and as much belonging to the orphans, which she had saved up for them. And she went on composedly to calculate how much money she would have to spend to put the Pogorelka manor-house in order. Then she immediately sent for the bailiff of Pogorelka, gave the necessary orders about hiring carpenters and sending a horse and cart to Dubrovino for her and the orphans' belongings, ordered the coach to be made ready (the coach was her own, and she had evidence that it was her very own), and began to pack. She felt neither hatred nor goodwill toward Yudushka. It suddenly became disgusting to her to have any dealings with him. She even ate unwillingly and little, because from that day she had to eat not Pavel's but Yudushka's food. Several times Porfiry Vladimirych peeped into her room to have a chat with his "mother dear." He understood the meaning of her packing clearly, but pretended to notice nothing. Arina Petrovna refused to see him.

"Go, my friend, go," she said. "I have no time."

In three days, Arina Petrovna had everything in readiness for departure. They heard mass, performed the funeral service, and buried Pavel Vladimirych. At the funeral everything happened just as Arina Petrovna had imagined on the morning when Yudushka came to Dubrovino. In the very way she had foreseen Yudushka cried out, "Farewell, brother!" when they lowered the coffin into the grave, and turned to Ulita and said hastily:

"Don't forget—don't forget to take the kutya, and put it in the dining-room on a clean table cloth. We will honor brother's memory in the house, too."

Three churchmen, the Father Provost and a deacon, were invited to the dinner served, as is the custom, immediately on the return from the funeral ceremony. A special table was laid in the entrance hall for the sextons. Arina Petrovna and the orphans entered clad in travelling clothes, but Yudushka pretended even then not to understand. He went over to the table, requested the Father Provost to bless the food and drink, poured a glassful of vodka for himself and the churchmen, put on an air of deep emotion and said, "Everlasting memory to the late deceased! Ah, brother, brother, you have forsaken us! Who of us more than you was fit to live a happy life? How sad, brother, how sad!"

Then he crossed himself, and emptied the glass. He crossed himself again and swallowed a piece of caviar, crossed himself again and took a taste of dried sturgeon.

"Eat, Father," he urged the Provost. "All this is my late brother's stock. How the deceased loved good fare! Not only that he ate well himself, but he even liked treating others better. Ah, brother, brother, you have forsaken us! How wrong it was of you, brother, how very wrong!"

He was so carried away by his incessant chatter that he even forgot about his dear mother. But suddenly she came to his mind as he scooped up a spoonful of mushrooms and was about to send it down his mouth.

"Mother, dearest, darling!" he exclaimed. "I, the fool, am here, gorging myself. What a sin! Mother dear, help yourself. Some mushrooms. These are Dubrovino mushrooms. The famous ones."

But Arina Petrovna did not stir. She only shook her head in silence. She seemed listening to something with intense curiosity, a new light seemed to fill her eyes, as if the comedy to which she had long since become accustomed and in which she had always taken active part, suddenly presented itself to her in a changed light.

The dinner commenced with a brief, pathetic discussion. Yudushka insisted that Arina Petrovna should take the hostess's place at the head of the table. Arina Petrovna refused.

"No, you are the host here, so sit where you please," she said drily.

"You are the hostess. You, mother dear, are the hostess everywhere, both at Golovliovo and Dubrovino, everywhere," said Yudushka, trying to convince her.

"Do stop and sit down. Wherever it will be the Lord's will to place me as a mistress, I will sit where I choose. Here you are master—so you take the seat."

"Then this is what we'll do," said Yudushka, much moved. "We'll leave the cover at the host's seat untouched, as if our brother were with us, an invisible companion. He shall be host, and we shall all be his guests."

That is how they arranged it. While the soup was being served, Yudushka chose a proper subject and started a conversation with the priests, addressing most of his remarks, however, to the Father Provost.

"There are many people nowadays who do not believe in the immortality of the soul, but I do," he said.

"Well, they must be desperadoes," answered the Father Provost.

"Not, not that they are desperadoes, but there is is a science about the soul not being immortal. It says that man exists all by himself. He lives and then suddenly—dies."

"There are too many sciences nowadays—if only there were less of them. People believe in sciences and don't believe in God. Take the peasants— even the peasants want to become learned."

"Yes, Father, you are right. They do long to become learned. Take my Naglovo peasants. They have nothing to eat, and still the other day they passed a resolution—they want to open up a school. The scholars!"

"Nowadays there is a science for everything under the sun. One science for rain, another science for fine weather, and so on. Formerly it was a very simple matter. People would come and sing a Te Deum—and the Lord would grant them their prayer. If they needed fine weather, God would grant fine weather; if they needed rain, the Lord had enough of it to go round. God has enough of everything. But since people have begun to live according to science, everything has changed, everything happens out of season. You sow—there is drought; you mow—there is rain."

"You speak the truth, Father, the gospel truth. Formerly people used to pray more to God, and the earth was more plentiful. The harvests were not like now. They were four times, five times, richer. The earth produced in abundance. Doesn't mother remember? Don't you remember, mother dear?" asked Yudushka, turning to Arina Petrovna with the intention of drawing her into the discussion.

"I never heard anything like that in our parts. Maybe you're speaking of the land of Canaan. It is said that was really the case there," drily responded Arina Petrovna.

"Yes, yes, yes," said Yudushka, as if he had not heard his mother's remark, "they don't believe in God, they don't believe in the immortality of the soul, but they want to eat all the same."

"That's just it—all they want is to eat and drink," repeated the Father Provost, rolling up the sleeves of his cassock to reach a piece of the funeral pie and put it on his plate.

Everybody attacked the soup. For a while nothing was heard but the clink of the spoons on the plates and the puffing of the priests as they blew upon the hot liquid.

"Now as for the Roman Catholics," continued Yudushka, stopping to eat, "although they do not deny the immortality of the soul, yet they claim the soul does not land straight in hell or in heaven, but stays for a while in a sort of middle place."

"That, too, is preposterous."

"To tell you the truth, Father," said Porfiry Vladimirych, deep in thought, "if we take the point of view of——"

"There is no use discussing nonsense. How goes the song of our Holy Church? It says, 'In a grassy place, in a cool place, in which there is neither sighing nor sorrow.' So of what use is it to talk of a 'middle' place?"

Yudushka did not fully agree and wanted to make some sort of objection, but Arina Petrovna, growing annoyed at the conversation, stopped him.

"Well, eat, eat, you theologian. I guess your soup is cold by now," she said, and to change the topic she turned to the Father Provost. "Have you gathered in the rye yet, Father?"

"Yes, madam. This time the rye is good, but the spring wheat doesn't promise well. The young oat seeds are ripening too soon. Neither straw nor oats can be expected."

"They are complaining everywhere about the oats," sighed Arina Petrovna, watching Yudushka scoop up the last dregs of his soup.

Another dish was served, ham and peas. Yudushka took advantage of the opportunity to resume the broken conversation.

"I'll wager the Jews don't eat this," he said.

"Jews are dirty," responded the Father Provost. "So people mock them, calling them 'pig's ears.'"

"But the Tartars don't eat ham either. There must be some reason for it."

"The Tartars are dirty, too. That's the reason."

A Family Of Noblemen | 95

"We don't eat horse flesh, and the Tartars refuse pigs' meat. They say rats were eaten during the siege in Paris."

"Well, they were—French!"

The whole supper passed in this way. When carp in cream was served, Yudushka expatiated: "Fall to, Father. These are not ordinary carp. They were a favorite dish of my departed brother."

Asparagus being served, Yudushka said:

"Just look at that asparagus! You'd have to pay a silver ruble for asparagus like that in St. Petersburg. My deceased brother was so fond of it. Bless it, look how thick it is."

Arina Petrovna was boiling with impatience. A whole hour gone and only half the supper eaten. Yudushka seemed to hold it back on purpose. He would eat something, put down his knife and fork, chatter a while, eat a bit again, and chatter again. How often, in bygone days, had Arina Petrovna scolded him for it. "Why don't you eat, you devil—God forgive me." But he seemed to have forgotten her instructions. Or perhaps he had not forgotten them, but was acting that way on purpose, to avenge himself. Or maybe he wasn't even avenging himself consciously. He might just be letting his devilish inner self have free play. Finally the roast was served.

At the very moment that all rose and the Father Provost was beginning to intone the hymn about "the beatific deceased," a noise broke out in the corridor. Shouts were heard that entirely spoiled the effect of the prayer.

"What's that noise?" shouted Porfiry Vladimirych. "Do they take this for a public-house?"

"For mercy's sake, don't yell. That is my—those are my trunks. They are being transferred," responded Arina Petrovna. Then she added with a touch of sarcasm: "Perhaps you intend to inspect them?"

A sudden silence fell. Even Yudushka turned pale and became confused. He realized instantly, however, that somehow he had to soften the effect of his mother's unpleasant words. Turning to the Father Provost, he began:

"Take woodcocks for instance. They are plentiful in Russia, but in other lands——"

"For Christ's sake, why don't you eat? We've got twenty-five versts to go and make them before dark," Arina Petrovna cut him short. "Petenka, dear, go hurry them in there, and see that they serve the pastry."

For a few moments there was silence. Porfiry Vladimirych quickly finished his piece of woodcock. His face was pale, his lips trembled, and he sat tapping his foot on the floor.

"You insult me, mother dear. You hurt me deeply," he declared, finally, but avoided his mother's eyes.

"Who is insulting you? And how am I hurting you—so deeply?"

"It is very—very insulting. So insulting, so very insulting! To think of your going away—at such a moment! You have lived here all the time—and suddenly—and then you mention the trunks—inspection—what an insult!"

"Well, then, if you're anxious to know all about it, why, I'll satisfy you. I lived here as long as my son Pavel was alive. He died—and I leave. And if you want to know about the trunks, why, Ulita has been watching me for a long time at your orders. And concerning myself—it's better to tell your mother straight to her face that she's under suspicion than to hiss at her behind her back like a snake."

"Mother dear! But you—but I——" groaned Yudushka.

"You've said enough," Arina Petrovna cut him short. "And I've had my say."

"But, how could I, mother dear——"

"I tell you, I'm through. For Christ's sake, let me go in peace. The coach is ready, I hear."

The sound of tinkling bells and an approaching vehicle came from the courtyard. Arina Petrovna was the first to arise from the table. The others followed.

"Now let us sit down for a moment, and then we're off," she said, going towards the parlor.

They sat a while in silence. By that time Yudushka had entirely recovered his presence of mind.

"After all, why shouldn't you live at Dubrovino, mother dear? Just see how nice it is here," he said, looking into his mother's eyes with the caressing expression of a guilty cur.

"No, my friend, that's enough. I don't want to leave you with unpleasant words, but I can't stay here. What for? Father, let us pray."

Everybody rose in prayer, then Arina Petrovna kissed everybody good-by, blessed them all, and with a heavy step went toward the door. Porfiry Vladimirych, at the head of the company of relatives, went with her to the porch. There on seeing the coach, he was struck by a devilish idea. "Why, the coach belongs to my brother," was the thought that flashed through his mind.

"So we'll see each other, mother dear?" he said, helping his mother in and casting side glances at the coach.

"If it's the Lord's will—and why shouldn't we see each other?"

"Ah, mother, dear mother, that was a good joke, really! You had better leave the coach—and, with God's help, in your old nest—indeed," urged Yudushka in a wheedling tone.

Arina Petrovna made no answer. She had already seated herself and made the sign of the cross, but the orphans seemed to hesitate.

Yudushka, all the while, kept throwing glance after glance at the coach.

"How about the coach, mother dear? Will you send it back yourself or shall I send for it?" he blurted out, unable to retain himself longer.

Arina Petrovna shook with indignation.

"The coach is—mine!" she cried in a voice so full of pain that everyone felt embarrassed and ashamed. "It's mine! Mine! My coach! I—I have testimony—witnesses. And you—may you——No, I'll wait——We shall see what becomes of you. Children, are you ready?"

"For mercy's sake, mother dear! I have no grievance against you. Even if the coach belonged to this estate——"

"It is my coach—mine! It does not belong to Dubrovino, it belongs to me! Don't you dare to say it—do you hear me?"

"Yes, mother dear. Don't forget us, dear heart. Simply, you know, without ceremony. We will come to you, you will come to us, as becomes good kinsfolk."

"Are you seated, children? Coachman, go on!" cried Arina Petrovna, hardly able to restrain herself.

The coach quivered and rolled off quickly down the road. Yudushka stood on the porch waving his handkerchief and calling until the coach had entirely disappeared from view:

"As becomes good kinsfolk! We will come to you, and you to us—as becomes good kinsfolk!"

BOOK III
FAMILY ACCOUNTS SETTLED

CHAPTER I

It had never occurred to Arina Petrovna that there might come a time when she would become "one mouth too many." Now that moment had stolen upon her just when for the first time in her life her physical and moral strength was undermined. Such moments always arrive suddenly. Though one may long have been on the verge of breaking down, one may still hold out and stave off the end, till suddenly the last blow strikes from a quarter least expected. To be aware of its approach and dodge it, is difficult. One has to resign oneself without complaint, for it is the very blow that in an instant shatters one who till recently has been hale and healthy.

When Arina Petrovna took up her abode in Dubrovino, after having broken with Yudushka, she had labored under great difficulties. But then, at least, she had known that Pavel Vladimirych, though looking askance at her intrusion, was still a well-to-do man to whom another morsel meant little. Now things were very different. She stood at the head of a household that counted every crumb. And she knew the value of crumbs, having spent all her life in the country in constant intercourse with peasants and having assimilated the peasant's notions of the harm a "superfluous mouth" does to a house in which stores are already scanty.

Nevertheless, in the first days after the removal to Pogorelka, she still maintained her usual attitude, busied herself with putting things in shape in the new place, and exercised her former clarity of judgment in household management. But the affairs of the estate were troublesome and petty, and demanded her constant personal supervision; and though on first thought she did not see much sense in keeping accurate accounts in a place where farthings are put together to make up kopek pieces and these in turn to make ten-kopek pieces, she was soon forced to admit that she had been wrong in this. To be sure, there really was no sense in keeping careful accounts; but the point was, she no longer possessed her former industry and strength. Then, too, it was autumn, the busiest time of reckoning up accounts and taking inventories, and the incessant bad weather imposed inevitable limits to Arina Petrovna's energy. Ailments of old age came upon her and prevented her from leaving the house. The long dreary fall evenings set in and doomed her to enforced idleness. The old woman was all upset and exerted herself to the utmost, but succeeded in accomplishing nothing.

Another thing. She could not help noticing that something queer was coming over the orphans. They suddenly became dull and dispirited and were agitated by some vague plans for the future, plans in which notions of work were interspersed with notions of pleasures of the most innocent kind, of course—reminiscences of the boarding-school where they had been brought up, mingled with stray notions about men of toil, which they retained from their fragmentary reading, and timid hopes of clutching at some thread through their boarding-school connections, and so entering the bright kingdom of human life. One tormenting hope stood out definitely from the other vague longings, to leave hateful Pogorelka at whatever costs.

And at length one fine day Anninka and Lubinka actually announced to grandma that they simply could not stay at Pogorelka a moment longer; they led a beastly life there, met nobody but the priest, and he, when he met them, felt it incumbent upon him to tell of the virgins who had extinguished their lamps. It wasn't right, it wasn't fair.

The girls spoke sharply, afraid of their grandmother and simulating courage in order to overcome the anger and resistance they expected. But to their surprise Arina Petrovna listened without anger, without even a disposition toward the useless sermonizing that impotent old age is so given to.

Alas, she was no longer that dominating woman who used to say so confidently: "I am going to Khotkov and will take the little orphans with me." The change was due, not to senile impotence alone, but also to an acquired sense of something better and truer. The last buffets of fortune had not only tamed Arina Petrovna; they had also lighted up some corners of her mental horizon into which her thoughts evidently had never before entered. Now, she knew, there were certain forces in the human being that can remain dormant a long while, but once awakened, they carry one irresistibly on to the glimmering ray of life, that cheering ray for whose appearance one's eyes have been yearning so long amidst the hopeless darkness of the present. Once realizing the legitimacy of such a striving, she was powerless to oppose it. It is true, she tried to dissuade her granddaughters from their purpose, but feebly, without conviction. She was uneasy about the future in store for them; all the more so since she herself had no connections in so-called "society." Yet she felt that the parting with the girls was a proper and inevitable thing. What would become of them? frequently pressed on her mind; but she was now fully aware that neither this question nor others more terrible would restrain one who was struggling for release from captivity.

The girls insisted on one thing, on shaking the dust of Pogorelka from their feet. And finally, after some hesitating and postponing to please grandmother, they left.

The Pogorelka manor-house was now steeped in a forlorn quiet. Self-centered as Arina Petrovna was by nature, yet the proximity of human breath had its calming effect even upon her. For the first time, perhaps, she felt that something had torn itself away from her being, and the freedom with which she herself was now confronted was so boundless that all she saw was empty space. To hide the void from her eyes, she ordered the state-rooms and the attic where the orphans had lived to be nailed up.

"Incidentally, there will be less firewood burned," she said to herself.

She retained only two rooms, in one of which a large ikon case with images was stowed away. The other was a combined bedroom, study and dining-room. For the sake of economy she dismissed her retinue of servants, retaining only her housekeeper Afimyushka, an old, broken-down woman, and Markovna, one-eyed, the soldier's wife, who did the cooking and washing.

All these precautions, however, were of little help. The sensation of emptiness was not slow to penetrate into the two rooms that were meant to be guarded from it. Helpless solitude and dreary idleness were the two enemies Arina Petrovna now confronted. And she was to be bound to these two enemies the rest of her days. Physical and mental disintegration were not slow to follow in the wake of loneliness and idleness, and the less the resistance, the crueller, the more destructive its work.

Days dragged on in the oppressive monotony peculiar to rural life when there are no comforts or there is no executive work to be done, and there is no material for mental occupation. In addition to the external causes at work to take the management of household affairs away from her, was an inner aversion that Arina Petrovna now felt to the petty cares and bustle coming at the sunset of her life. Perhaps she would have overcome her repugnance had she had an aim in view to justify her efforts, but that very aim was wanting. Everybody was sick and weary of her, and she was sick and weary of everybody and everything. Her feverish activity of old suddenly yielded to idleness, and idleness little by little corrupted her will and induced propensities of which Arina Petrovna could never have dreamed only a few months ago.

The strong, reserved woman, whom no one would have thought of calling old, turned into a wreck of her former self. There was neither past nor future for her, but only the immediate moment to live through. The greater part of the day she dozed, sitting in an easy-chair by the table, on which ill-smelling cards were arranged. She would doze for hours on end. Then her body would shudder convulsively, she would wake up, look out of the window, and for a long time stare into the distance, without a single conscious thought.

Pogorelka was a dreary manor-house. It stood all alone, without orchard or shade, or the least indication of comfort. There was not even a flower garden in front of the house. It was a one-story structure, squat, weather-beaten, all black with age. Back of it were the many out-buildings, also half worn-out, and all around was one vast stretch of fields—fields without end. Not even the glimpse of forest anywhere on the horizon. But from her very childhood Arina Petrovna had hardly ever left the country, and this monotonous landscape did not seem dreary to her. It even appealed to her heart and awakened remnants of emotion still glowing within her. The best part of her being lived in these naked fields, and her gaze sought them instinctively.

She stared at the expanse of fields; she stared at the drenched hamlets making black specks on the landscape; she stared at the white churches of the rural parishes; she stared at the motley spots that the cloud shadows formed on the plains; she stared at the peasant unknown to her who walked along the ploughed furrows, and she thought him slow and stiff. While staring, she had no conscious thoughts, or, rather, her thoughts were so fragmentary and disconnected that they could not stay with any one thing for even a short time. She just gazed, gazed till senile slumber again hummed dully in her ears, and the fields, the churches, the hamlets and the peasant in the distance became wrapped in mist.

At times, apparently, she recollected something; but the memories of the past came incoherently, in fragments. Her attention could not concentrate on one point. It jumped from one remote memory to another. Yet sometimes she would be struck by something singular, not joy—her past was very scant in joys—but some grievance, some abuse, bitter and unbearable. Then sudden anger would flare up, anguish would creep into her heart, and tears come to her eyes. She would weep grievously, painfully, the weeping of piteous old age, when tears flow as if under the load of a nightmare. But even while her tears were flowing, her mind unconsciously continued to work in its usual way, and her thoughts drifted imperceptibly away from the cause of her mood, so that in a few minutes the old woman was wondering what had been the matter with her.

Altogether, she lived as if not participating in life personally, but solely because in those ruins there were still left a few odds and ends which had to be collected, recorded, and accounted for. While these odds and ends were present, life went its way compelling the ruin to perform all the external functions necessary to keep that half-asleep existence from crumbling to dust.

But if the days passed in unconscious slumber, the nights were sheer torment. At night Arina Petrovna was *afraid*; she was afraid of thieves, of ghosts, of devils, of all that was the product of her education and life. And the defenses of the place were very poor, for beside the two tottering women domestics Pogorelka had a night-watch in the person of the lame little peasant Fedoseyushka, who for two rubles a month came from the village to guard the manor-house, and usually slept in the vestibule, coming out at the appointed hours to strike the steel plate. In the cattle-yard, it is true, there lived a few farm hands, men and women, but the cattle house was about fifty yards away and it was not easy to summon any one from there.

There is something exceedingly dreary and oppressive in a sleepless night in the country. At nine, or at latest ten o'clock, life ceases. A weird stillness sets in that is full of terrors. There is nothing to do, and it is a waste to burn candles. Willy-nilly one must go to bed. As soon as the samovar was removed from the table Afimyushka, from an old habit acquired during serfdom, spread a felt blanket in front of the door leading to the mistress's bedroom, scratched her head, yawned, flopped down on the floor, and fell dead asleep. Markovna always fumbled in the maids' room a trifle longer, muttering something to herself as if scolding somebody. But at last she, too, got quiet, and a moment later you could hear her snoring and raving intermittently. The watchman banged on the plate several times to announce his presence, then kept quiet for a long time. Arina Petrovna, sitting in front of a snuffy tallow candle, tried to stave off sleep by playing "patience," but scarcely did she have the cards arranged when she fell into a doze.

"It is as easy as not for a fire to start while one is asleep," she would say to herself, and decide to go to bed. But no sooner did she sink into the down pillows than another trouble set in. Her sleepiness, so inviting and insistent all evening long, now left her completely. The room was a close one at the best, and now, from the open flue the heat came thick, and the down pillows were insufferable. Arina Petrovna tossed restlessly. She wanted to call someone, but knew no one would come in answer to her summons. A mysterious quiet reigned all around, a quiet in which the delicate ear could distinguish a multitude of sounds. Now something crackled somewhere, now a whining was audible, now it seemed as if somebody were walking through the corridor, now a puff of wind swept through the room and even touched her face. The ikon lamp burned in front of an image, and the light gave the objects in the room a kind of elusiveness, as if they were not actual things, but only the contours of things. Another bit of light strayed from the open door of the adjacent room, where four or five ikon lamps were burning before the image case. A mouse squeaked behind the wall paper. "Sh-sh-sh, you nasty thing," said Arina Petrovna, and all was silent again. And shadows again, whisperings again coming from no one knew where. The greater part of the night passed in that half-awake senile slumber. Real sleep did not set in and do its work until nearly morning. By six o'clock Arina Petrovna was already on her feet, tired out after a sleepless night.

Other things to add to the misery of this miserable existence of Arina Petrovna's were the poor food she ate and the discomfort of her home. She ate little and used poor food, wishing, probably, to make up for the loss caused by insufficient supervision. And the Pogorelka manor-house was dilapidated and damp. The room into which Arina Petrovna locked herself was never ventilated and remained without cleaning for weeks on end. In this complete helplessness and the absence of all comfort and care, decrepitude began slowly to set in. But her desire to live grew stronger, or, rather, her desire for "a dainty bit" asserted itself. With this came coupled a total absence of the thought of death. Previously, she had been afraid of death; now she seemed to have quite forgotten about it. And with ideals of life differing but little from a peasant's, her conception of a "comfortable life" was of rather a base kind. Everything she had formerly denied herself, dainties, rest, association with wide-awake people, now forced itself upon her in an insistent craving. All the propensities of a regular sponger and hanger-on, idle talk, subservience for the sake of a prospective gift, gluttony, grew in her with astounding rapidity. Like the servants, she fed on cabbage-soup and cured bacon of doubtful quality, and at the same time dreamed of the stores of provisions at Golovliovo, of the German carps that swarmed in the Dubrovino ponds, of the mushrooms that filled the Golovliovo woods, of the fowl that fattened in the Golovliovo poultry-yard.

"Some soup with giblets, or some garden-cress in cream would not be a bad thing," would cross her mind so vividly that her mouth watered. At night when she tossed about rigid with fright at the least rustling, she would think: "Yes, at Golovliovo the locks are secure and the watchmen reliable. They keep banging on the steel plates all the time, and you can sleep in perfect safety." During the day, from sheer lack of human companionship, she was compelled to be silent for hours, and during these spells of compulsory taciturnity, she could not help thinking: "At Golovliovo there are lots of people. There you can talk your troubles away." In fact, Golovliovo kept constantly recurring to her mind, and the reminiscences of her former estate became a radiant spot in which "comfortable living" concentrated itself.

The more frequently the vision of Golovliovo came back to her mind, the stronger became her will to live again, and the farther the deadly affronts she had recently sustained sank into oblivion. The Russian woman, by the very nature of her life and bringing-up, too quickly acquiesces in the lot of a hanger-on. Even Arina Petrovna did not escape that fate, though her past, it would seem, should have tended to warn and guard her against such a yoke. Had she not made a mistake "at that time," had she not portioned out her estate to her sons, had she not trusted Yudushka, she would to this very day have been a harsh, exacting old woman, with everybody under her thumb. But since the mistake was fatal, the transition from a testy, arbitrary mistress to an obedient, obsequious parasite was only a matter of time. As long as she still retained remnants of former vigor, the change was not evident, but as soon as she realized that she was irrevocably doomed to helplessness and solitude, all the pusillanimous propensities began to make their way into her soul, and her will, already weakened, became completely shattered. Yudushka, who used to be received most coldly when he visited Pogorelka, suddenly ceased to be hateful to her. The old injuries were somehow forgotten, and Arina Petrovna was the first to court intimacy.

It began with begging. Messengers from Pogorelka would come to Yudushka, at first rarely, but then with increasing frequency. Now there had been a poor crop of garden-cress at Pogorelka, now the rains had ruined the gherkins, now the turkey-poults had died—there's freedom for you! And then it came to: "Would you mind, my dear friend, ordering some German carps caught in Dubrovino? My late son Pavel never refused them to me." Yudushka frowned, but thought it best not to show open displeasure. The carps were an item, to be sure, but he was filled with terror at the thought that his mother might put her curse upon him. He well remembered her once saying: "I will come to Golovliovo, order the church opened, call in the priest and shout: 'I curse you!'" It was the recollection of this that held him back from many dastardly acts that quite accorded with his nature. But in fulfilling the wish of his "mother dear" he did not omit to hint casually to the people around him that God had ordained that every man bear his cross, and that He did so not without divine purpose, for he who bears not his cross wanders from the righteous path and becomes corrupted. To his mother he wrote: "I am sending you some gherkins, mother dear, as many as my resources allow. As to the turkeys, I am sorry to inform you that besides those left for breeding, there remain only turkey-cocks, which in view of their size and the limited needs of your table are quite useless to you. And will it not be your pleasure to let me welcome you to Golovliovo and share my paltry viands with you? Then we can have one of those idlers (idlers, indeed, for my cook Matvey caponizes them most skilfully) roasted, and you and I, my dearest friend, shall feast on him to our heart's content."

From that day Arina Petrovna became a frequent guest at Golovliovo. Assisted by Yudushka she tasted of turkeys and ducks; she slept her fill both by night and by day, and after dinner she eased her heart with copious small talk, in which Yudushka was proficient by nature, she proficient because of old age. Her visits were not discontinued even when it reached her ears that Yudushka, weary of solitude, had taken in a damsel named Yevpraksia, from among the clergy, as his housekeeper. On the contrary, she made off right for Golovliovo and before alighting from the carriage called to Yudushka with childish impatience: "Well, well, you old sinner, let's see your queen, let's see your queen." That entire day she spent most pleasurably, because Yevpraksia herself waited upon her at table and made her bed after dinner, and because in the evening she played fool with Yudushka and his queen.

Yudushka himself was pleased with this dénouement, and in token of filial gratitude ordered a pound of caviar, among other things, to be put into Arina Petrovna's carriage as she was about to depart. That was the highest token of esteem, for caviar is not a home product; one has to buy it. The courtesy so touched the old woman that she could refrain no longer and said: "Well, I do thank you for this. And God, too, will love you, because you cherish and sustain your mother in her old age. Now, when I get back to Pogorelka, I shall not be bored any more. I always did like caviar. Well, thanks to you, I'll have a dainty morsel now."

CHAPTER II

Five years had passed since Arina Petrovna took up her abode at Pogorelka. Yudushka struck root in Golovliovo and would not budge. He became considerably older, faded and tarnished greatly, but was more of a knave, liar and babbler than ever, for now his "mother dear" was nearly always with him, and for the sake of dainties, she became a ready and indispensable listener to his empty talk.

One must not think of Yudushka as a hypocrite in the sense of Tartuffe, for instance, or some modern French bourgeois, mellifluous and fond of expatiating on "the foundations of society." No, he was a hypocrite of the purely Russian breed, simply a man devoid of moral standards and ignorant of any except the most elementary truths. His ignorance was profound. He was mendacious, had a passion for litigation and empty talk, and was afraid of the devil, too—all negative traits that are not the material for the making of a genuine hypocrite.

In France hypocrisy is a result of education; it constitutes, so to say, a part of "good manners," and always has a distinct political or social coloring. There are hypocrites of religion, hypocrites of "the foundations of society," of property, of family, of politics. And lately there have come up even hypocrites of "law and order." Though this sort of hypocrisy cannot be termed conviction, still it is a banner around which those people rally who find it profitable to play the hypocrite in that way and no other. They sham consciously, that is they know they are hypocrites, and they also know that others know. According to the notions of a French bourgeois, the universe is nothing but a large stage on which is played an endless drama with one hypocrite taking his cue from the other. Hypocrisy is an invitation to decency, decorum, outward elegance and politeness. And what is most important, hypocrisy is a restraint, not for those, of course, who play the hypocrite, hovering in the rarified atmosphere of the social heights, but for those who swarm at the bottom of the social caldron. Hypocrisy keeps society from the debauchery of passion and makes passion the privilege of a very limited minority. When licentiousness keeps within the limits of a small, well-organized corporation, it is not only harmless, but even supports and nourishes the traditions of elegance. The exquisite would perish if there were not a certain number of *cabinets particuliers,* in which licentiousness is cultivated in the moments that are free from the worship of official hypocrisy. But licentiousness becomes really dangerous as soon as it is accessible to all and is combined with the general extension of the right to make demands and insist upon the legitimacy and naturalness of such demands. New social stratifications form, which endeavor to crowd out the old ones, or, at least, limit them considerably. The demand for *cabinets particuliers* grows to such an extent that the question arises: Would it not be simpler in the future to get along without them? It is against these unwelcome questions and formulations of demands that the ruling classes of French society guard the systematic hypocrisy that begins by being an accident of manners and ends by becoming a compulsory law.

The modern French theatre is based on this reverence for hypocrisy. The first four acts of a popular French play are realistic, depicting the decay and disintegration of all standards of marital fidelity. But the fifth act always ends up with some sentimental ringing phrase eulogizing the sweet atmosphere of the fireside and the supreme triumph of virtue over vice. Which is the truth? Which is the sham? Both and neither. In the first four acts the audience sees itself mirrored in the realistic portrayal on the stage, but the fifth act is an equally faithful portrayal of the audience's conception of ideal virtue and pure matrimonial life. So, if French hypocrisy is a superstructure upon the body of public immorality, it is so completely a part of the entire fabric of morality that it keeps the edifice from toppling over.

We Russians have no system of social bringing up. We are not mustered or drilled to become champions of "social principles" or other principles, but simply left to grow wild, like nettles by the fence. That is why there are few hypocrites among us, but many liars, empty-headed bigots, and babblers. We have no need of playing the hypocrite for the sake of social principles, for we know of no such thing as social principles. We exist in perfect liberty, that is, we vegetate, lie, chatter quite naturally, without regard for principle. Whether we ought to rejoice over it or regret it, I cannot say. I think, though, that if hypocrisy breeds resentment and fear, useless lying causes boredom and repugnance. The best thing, therefore, is to ignore the question of the advantages of conscious over unconscious hypocrisy, and vice versa, and have nothing to do with either hypocrites or liars.

Yudushka was more of a chatterbox, liar and rascal than hypocrite. On shutting himself up on his country estate, he at once felt at perfect liberty. In no other environment could his propensities find so vast a field for operation. At Golovliovo he encountered neither direct resistance nor even indirect restraints that would make him think: "I should like to do something mean, but what will people say?" There was none to disturb him with disapproval, no one to intrude into his affairs. Consequently there was no reason for controlling himself. Extreme slovenliness became the dominating feature of his attitude toward himself. He had long had a craving for this perfect freedom from any moral restraint, and the fact that he had not gone to live in the country earlier was entirely due to his fear of idleness. Having spent over thirty years in the dull atmosphere of the bureaucratic department, he had acquired all the habits and appetites of an inveterate official, who does not allow a single moment of his life to pass without being busily engaged in doing nothing. But on studying the matter more closely, he came to the conclusion that the realm of busy idleness can easily be transposed to any sphere.

In fact, scarcely settled at Golovliovo but he at once created a world of trifles in which to rummage without the slightest risk of them ever being exhausted. In the morning he would seat himself at his desk and attend to business matters. First he would carefully check the accounts of the housekeeper, the cattle-yard woman, and the steward. He had established a very complicated accounting system, both for money and inventory. Every kopek, every bit of produce, was entered in twenty books, and on checking up he would find the total either half a kopek behind, or a whole kopek ahead. Lastly he would take up his pen and write complaints to the justice of the peace and the judge of appeals. This took up all his time and had the appearance of assiduous hard work. Yudushka often complained that he had no time to do everything that had to be done, though he pored over the ledgers all day long and did not even stop to take off his dressing-gown. Heaps of well filed but unexamined reports were always lying about on his desk, and among them was the annual report of the cattle-house woman, Fekla, whose activity had long seemed suspicious, though he had had no time to check up her accounts.

All connections with the outside world were completely severed. He received no books, no newspapers, not even letters. One of his sons, Volodya, committed suicide. With the other, Petenka, he corresponded briefly and only on sending him a remittance. He was caught in an atmosphere thick with ignorance, superstition and industrious idleness, and felt no desire to rescue himself from it. Even the fact that Napoleon III. was no longer emperor came to him through the local chief of police a year after the emperor's death. On hearing of it he expressed no particular interest, but only crossed himself and murmured: "May he enter the Kingdom of Heaven," and then said aloud: "And how proud he was! My, my! This was no good, and that did not suit him. Kings went to do him homage, princes kept watch in his antechamber. So the Lord, you see, in one moment cast down all his proud dreams."

The truth of the matter was that for all his reckoning and checking up he was far from knowing what was going on on his own estate. In this respect he was a typical official. Imagine a chief clerk to whom his superior says: "My friend, it is necessary to my plans for me to know exactly how large a crop of potatoes Russia can produce annually. Will you kindly compute this for me?" You think a question like that would baffle the chief clerk? You think he would at least ponder over the methods to be employed in the execution of such a task? Not at all. All he would do is this. He would draw a map of Russia, rule it out into perfect squares, and find out how many acres each square represents. Then he would go to the greengrocer's, would find out the quantity of potatoes each acre requires for seed and what the average ratio is of yield to seed, and, finally, with the help of God and the four fundamental operations of arithmetic, he would arrive at the conclusion that Russia under favorable circumstances could yield so and so many potatoes and under unfavorable circumstances, so and so many. And his work would not only please the chief, but would also be placed in Volume CII of some "Proceedings."

Yudushka even chose a housekeeper who exactly fitted the environment he had created. The maiden Yevpraksia was the daughter of the sexton at the church of St. Nicholas-in-Drops. She was an all-round treasure. Not alert in thinking, not ingenious, not even handy, but diligent, submissive, in no sense exigent. When Yudushka "drew her nearer" to his person, her one request was to be permitted to take some cold cider without asking leave. Such disinterestedness touched even Yudushka. He immediately put at her disposal two tubs of pickled apples beside the cider, and freed her from accountability for any of these items. Her exterior had nothing attractive in it to a connoisseur, but she was quite satisfactory to a man who was not fastidious and knew what he wanted. She had a broad white face, a low forehead bordered with thin yellowish hair, large lack-lustre eyes, a perfectly straight nose, a flat mouth on which there played a mysterious elusive smile, such as one sees in the portraits painted by homebred artists. In short there was nothing remarkable about her, except, perhaps, her back between her shoulder-blades, which was so broad and powerful that even the most indifferent man felt like giving her a good, hearty slap there. She knew it, but did not mind it, so that when Yudushka for the first time patted the fat nape of her neck, she only twitched her shoulders.

Amidst these drab surroundings days wore on, one exactly like the other, without the slightest change, without the least hope of a brightening ray. The arrival of Arina Petrovna was the one thing that brought a bit of animation. At first, when Porfiry Vladimirych had seen his mother's carriage approaching he had frowned, but in time he grew accustomed to her visits and even got to like them. They catered to his loquacity, for even he found it impossible to chatter to himself when all alone. To babble about various records and reports with "mother dear" was very pleasant, and, once together, they talked from morning till night without having enough. They discussed everything—the harvests of long ago and of the present; the way the landed gentry had lived in "those days;" the salt that had been so strong in former years; and the gherkins that were not what they had been in days gone by.

These chats had the advantage of flowing on like water and being forgotten without effort, so that they could be renewed with interest *ad infinitum,* and enjoyed each time as if just put into circulation. Yevpraksia was present at these talks. Arina Petrovna came to love her so well that she would not have her away for a moment. At times, when tired of talking, the three of them would sit down to play fool, and they would keep on playing till long after midnight. They tried to teach Yevpraksia how to play whist with the dummy, but she could not understand the game. On such evenings the enormous Golovliovo mansion became animated. Lights shone in all the windows, shadows appeared here and there, so that a chance passer-by might think Heaven knows what celebration was going on. Samovars, coffee pots, refreshments took their turn on the table, which was never empty. Arina Petrovna's heart brimmed over with joy and merriment and instead of remaining for one day, she would spend three or four days at Golovliovo. And on the way back to Pogorelka she would think up a pretext for returning as soon as possible to the temptations of the "good living" there.

CHAPTER III

It was the end of November. As far as eye could see the ground was covered with a white shroud. A blizzard reigned in the night outdoors; the biting wind drove the snow, piled up huge snow-drifts in an instant, lashed the snow higher and higher, covering every object and filling the air with a wailing. The village, the church, the nearby woods, all vanished in the whirling snowy mist. The wind howled in the trees of the ancient Golovliovo orchard. But inside the landlord's manor it was warm and cozy. In the dining-room there was a samovar on the table. Around it were Arina Petrovna, Porfiry Vladimirych, and Yevpraksia. To one side stood a card-table with tattered cards on it. The open door from the dining-room led on one side to the ikon room, all flooded with light from the ikon lamps, on the other, to the master's study, where an ikon lamp was also burning before an image. The rooms were overheated and stuffy, the odor of olive oil and of the charcoal burning in the samovar filled the air. Yevpraksia, seated in front of the samovar, was engaged in rinsing the cups and drying them with a dish towel. The samovar made spirited music, now humming aloud with all its might, now falling into a doze, as it were, and snoring. Clouds of steam escaped from under the cover and wrapped the tea-pot in a mist. The three at the table were conversing.

"Well, how many times were you the 'fool' to-day?" Arina Petrovna asked Yevpraksia.

"I shouldn't have been fool once if I hadn't given in. I wanted to please you, you see," answered Yevpraksia.

"Fiddlesticks! I remember how pleased you were last time when I bombarded you with threes and fives. You see, I am not Porfiry Vladimirych. He makes it easy for you, hands only one at a time, but I, my dear, have no reason to."

"Yes, indeed! You were playing foul!"

"Well, I say! I never do such things."

"No? Who was it I caught a little while ago? Who wanted to slip through a seven of clubs and an eight of hearts and call them a pair? Well,

I saw it myself and I myself showed you up!" While talking Yevpraksia rose to remove the tea-pot from the samovar and turned her back to Arina Petrovna.

"My, what a back you have! God bless you!" Arina Petrovna exclaimed, in involuntary admiration.

"Yes, a wonderful back," Yudushka repeated mechanically.

"My back again! Aren't you ashamed of yourself? What has my back done to you?" Yevpraksia turned her back first to the right, then to the left, and smiled. Her back was her joy. A few days before even the cook Savelich, an old man, had looked at her admiringly and said: "Well, well, what a back! Just like a hearth-plate!" She did not, be it noticed, complain to Porfiry Vladimirych about the cook's remark.

The cups were filled with tea over and over again, and the samovar grew silent. Meanwhile the snowstorm became fiercer and fiercer. A veritable cataract of snow struck the windowpanes every now and then, and wild sobs ran at intervals down the chimney flue.

"The storm seems to be in real earnest," said Arina Petrovna. "Listen to it howling and whining."

"Oh, well, let it whine. The blizzard keeps on whining and we keep on drinking tea. That's how it is, mother dear," replied Porfiry Vladimirych.

"It must be a terrible thing for one to be out in the fields now."

"Yes, it may be terrible to some, but what do we care? Some feel cold and dreary, but we are bright and cheery. We sit here and sip our tea, with sugar, and cream, and lemon. And should we want tea with rum, we can have it with rum."

"Yes, but suppose — —"

"Just a moment, mother dear. I say, it is very bad in the open now. There is no road or path. Everything is wiped out. And then — wolves! But here we are warm and cozy, afraid of nothing. We just keep sitting here, quietly and peacefully. If we want to play a little game of cards, we play cards; if we want to have some hot tea, well, then we have tea. We won't drink more than we want to, but we may drink to our heart's content. And why all this? Because, mother dear, God's mercy is with us. Were it not for Him, the King of Kings, maybe we, too, would now be wandering in the fields, in the cold and the darkness, in a shabby little coat, a flimsy little girdle, bast shoes."

"Oh, come now, what do you mean — bast shoes? We are gentlefolk, surely. In any circumstances we can afford decent footwear."

"Do you know why we were born in the gentry, mother dear? All because God's mercy was with us. Were it not for that we would now be in a hut and it would be lighted not by a candle but by a *luchina* and as to tea or coffee, we wouldn't dare dream about them. I would be patching my miserable little bast shoes, and you would be getting ready to sup off thin cabbage soup, and Yevpraksia would be weaving tick, and on top of it all, maybe the *desyatsky* would come to press us and the wagon into service."

"Yes, catch the *desyatsky* coming on a night like this!"

"Who knows, mother dear? And maybe the regiments would come! Maybe there would be war or mutiny. The regiments must be there on the dot. The other day, for instance, the chief of police was telling me Napoleon III. had died. So you may be sure the French will be up to some mischief again. Naturally, our soldiers will have to make for the front at once, and you, friend peasant, will have to get your wagon out, quick! Never mind cold, blizzard, and snowdrifts. You go if the authorities tell you to, and if you know what is good for you. But we, don't you see, will be spared a while. They won't turn us out with the wagon."

"Yes, who dares deny it? The mercy the Lord has shown us is great."

"That's just what I say. God, mother dear, is everything. He gives us wood to burn and food to eat. It's all His doing. We think we buy things ourselves, and pay our own hard cash, but when you look into it more deeply, and reckon it up, and figure it out, it's all He, it's all God. If it be His will, we'll have nothing. Here, for instance, I would like to have some fine little oranges, I would have some myself, would offer one to my mother dear, would give an orange to everyone. I have the money to buy oranges. Suppose I produce some coin and say, 'Here, let me have some oranges,' but God says, 'Halt, man!' Then here I am, a philosopher without cucumbers."

They laughed.

"That's all talk," said Yevpraksia. "My uncle was sexton at the Uspenye Church in Pesochnoye. You may be sure he was as pious a man as ever was. So I think God ought to have done something for him. But he was caught in a snowstorm out in the fields and froze to death all the same."

"That's just my point. If such is God's will, you will freeze to death, and if such is not His will, you will remain alive. There are prayers that please God and there are prayers that do not please Him. If a prayer pleases God it will reach Him, if it does not, you may as well not pray at all."

"I remember in 1824 I was travelling and was pregnant with Pavel. It was in the month of December, and I was going to Moscow— —"

"Just a moment, mother dear. Let me finish about the prayers. A man prays for everything, for he needs everything. He needs some butter and some cabbage, and some gherkins, well, in a word, he needs everything. Sometimes he doesn't need the thing, but in his human weakness he prays for it all the same. But God from above sees better. You pray for butter, and he gives you cabbage or onions. You are after fair and warm weather and he sends you rain and hail. What you have to do is to understand it all and not complain. Last September, for example, we prayed God for frost, so that the winter corn might not rot, but God, you see, sent no frosts, and our winter corn rotted away."

"It certainly did rot away," remarked Arina Petrovna commiseratingly. "The peasants' winter fields at Novinky weren't worth a straw. They'll have to plow them all over and plant spring corn."

"That's just it. Here we are planning and philosophizing, and figuring it one way, and trying it another way, but God in a trice reduces all our plots and plans to dust. You, mother dear, wanted to tell us something that happened to you in 1824?"

"What was it? I really don't remember. I suppose I wanted to tell you again about God's mercy. I don't remember, my friend, I don't."

"Well, you'll recall it some other time, if God is willing. And while the blizzard is whirling out there you'd better have some jam, my dear. This is cherry jam from the Golovliovo orchard. Yevpraksia herself put it up."

"I am already helping myself to some. I must admit cherry jam is a rare thing with me now. Years ago I used to indulge every now and then, but now——! Your Golovliovo cherries are fine, so large and juicy. No matter how hard I tried to grow them at Dubrovino, they wouldn't come. Did you add some French brandy to the jam, Yevpraksia?"

"Of course I did. Followed your directions. Another thing I meant to ask you, how do you pickle cucumbers, do you use cardamoms?"

Arina Petrovna thought a bit, then made a gesture of perplexity.

"I don't remember, my dear. I think I used to put cardamoms in. Now I don't. My pickling now is not much. But I used to put cardamoms in, yes, I remember very well now. When I get home I'll look among the recipes, maybe I'll find it. When I had my strength I used to make a note of everything. If I liked something somewhere, I would ask how it was made, write it on a piece of paper, and then try it at home. I once learned a secret, such a secret that the man who knew it was offered a thousand rubles to tell. He wouldn't do it. And I gave the housekeeper a quarter, and she told me every bit of it."

"Yes, mother dear, in your day you certainly were a wizard."

"Well, I don't know if I was a wizard, but I can thank the Lord, I didn't squander my fortune. I kept adding to it. Even now I taste of my righteous labors. It was I who planted the cherry trees in Golovliovo."

"Thanks for it, mother dear, many thanks. Eternal thanks from me and my descendants. That's what I say."

Yudushka rose, went to mother dear and kissed her hand.

"And thanks to you, too, that you take your mother's welfare to heart. Yes, your provisions are fine, very fine."

"Well, how do my provisions compare? You used to have provisions— perfectly stunning! My, what cellars! And not an empty spot!"

"Yes, I used to have provisions, I may as well be frank about it. Mine was a well-stocked house. And as to the many cellars I had, well, the household was much larger, ten times as many mouths as you have to-day. Take the domestics alone. Everyone had to be fed and provided for. Gherkins for one, cider for another, little by little, bit by bit, and it mounts up."

"Yes, those were good times. Plenty of everything. Grain and fruit, all in abundance."

"We used to save more manure, that is why."

"No, mother dear, that is not the reason. It was God's blessing, that's what it was. I remember father once brought an apple from the orchard, and it surprised everybody, it was too big to be put on a plate."

"Well, I don't remember that. I know generally that apples used to be fine, but that they were the size of a plate, that I don't remember. I do remember though, that we caught a carp in the Dubrovino pond weighing twenty pounds, yes, I remember that."

"Carps and fruit—everything was large then. I remember the watermelons the gardener Ivan used to get. They were as big as this!"

Yudushka stretched out his arms in a circle, pretending he could not embrace the imaginary watermelon.

"Yes, those were watermelons. Watermelons, my friend, are according to the year. One year you get lots of them and they are good. Another year they are poor and few. And some years you don't get any at all. Well, it depends upon the lucky ground, too. On the estate of Grigory Aleksandrovich, for example, nothing came up, no fruit and no berries—nothing. Only melons. Nothing but melons used to come up."

"Then he had God's blessing for melons."

"Why, yes, certainly. You can't get along without God's mercy. You can't run away from it either."

Arina Petrovna finished her second cup and cast glances at the card table. Yevpraksia, too, was burning with impatience to have a hand at cards. But the plans were thwarted by Arina Petrovna herself. She suddenly recollected something.

"I have a bit of news for you," she declared. "I received a letter from the orphans yesterday."

"And you kept it to yourself all this time, and only just thought of it? I suppose they are hard up. Do they ask for money?"

"No, they do not. Here, read it. You'll like it."

Arina Petrovna produced a letter from her pocket and gave it to Yudushka, who read aloud:

> "Please, grandma, don't send us any more turkeys or hens. Don't send us money, either, but invest the money. We are not at Moscow but at Kharkov. We've gone on the stage, and in summer we are going to travel to the fairs. I, Anninka, made my début in *Pericola,* and Lubinka in *Pansies.* I was called out several times, especially after the scene where Pericola comes out and sings 'I am ready, ready, read-d-d-y!' Lubinka made a hit, too. The director put me on a salary of one hundred rubles a month and a benefit performance at Kharkov; and Lubinka, at seventy-five a month and a benefit the coming summer, at a fair. Besides, we get gifts from army officers and lawyers. The lawyers sometimes, though, give you counterfeit money, and you have to be careful. And you, dear granny, can have Pogorelka all to yourself, we will never come there again, we don't understand how people can live there. We had the first snow here yesterday, and we had troika rides with the lawyers. One looks like Plevako— my! just stunning! He put a glass of champagne on his head and danced a trepak. It's jolly, beats anything I've seen! The other one isn't so handsome, he looks a little like Yazikov from St. Petersburg. Just think, after he read "The Collection of the Best Russian Songs and Romances," his imagination became unstrung and he got so weak that he fainted in the court-room. And so we spend almost every day in the company of army officers and lawyers. We go on rides and dine and sup in the best restaurants, and pay nothing. And you, granny dear, don't be stingy and use up everything

growing in Pogorelka, corn, chickens, mushrooms. We shall be very glad to send some money. Good-by. Our gentlemen have just arrived. They have come to take us driving again. Darling! Divine! Farewell!

ANNINKA.
And I, too—LUBINKA."

Yudushka spat in disgust and returned the letter. For a while Arina Petrovna was pensive and silent.

"Mother dear, you haven't answered them yet?"

"No, not yet. I just got the letter yesterday. I came here on purpose to show it to you, but between this and that I almost forgot all about it."

"Don't answer it. It's best not to."

"How can I? I must account to them. Pogorelka is theirs, you know."

Yudushka also became pensive. A sinister plan flashed through his mind.

"And I keep wondering how they will preserve themselves in that foul den," Arina Petrovna continued. "You know how it is in these things—once you stumble, you can't get your maiden honor back! Go hunt for it!"

"Much they need it!" Yudushka snarled back.

"Still, you know. Honor is a girl's best treasure, one may say. Who will marry a girl without it?"

"Nowadays, mother dear, unmarried people live like married ones. Nowadays they laugh at the precepts of religion. They get married without benefit of clergy, like heathens. They call it civil marriage."

Yudushka suddenly recollected that he, too, was living in sinful relationship with a daughter of the clergy.

"Of course, sometimes you can't help it," he hastened to add. "If a man, let us say, is in full vigor and a widower—in an emergency the law itself is often modified."

"Yes, of course. When hard pressed a snipe sings like a nightingale. Even saints sin when sorely tried, let alone us mortals."

"Yes, that's just it. Do you know what I would do if I were you?"

"Yes, tell me, please tell me."

"I would insist that they make Pogorelka over to you in full legal fashion."

Arina Petrovna looked at him in fright.

"Well, I have a deed giving me the full powers and rights of a manager."

"Manager is not enough. You ought to get a deed that would entitle you to sell and mortgage it, in a word, to dispose of the property as you see fit."

Arina Petrovna lowered her eyes and remained silent.

"Of course, it is a matter that requires deliberation. Think it over, mother dear," Yudushka insisted.

But Arina Petrovna said nothing. Though age had considerably dulled her powers of judgment, she was somehow uneasy about Yudushka's insinuations. She was afraid of Yudushka, and loath to part with the warmth, spaciousness, and abundance that reigned at Golovliovo, but at the same time she felt that Yudushka had something up his sleeve when he spoke of the Pogorelka deed, and was casting a new snare. The situation grew so embarrassing that she began to scold herself inwardly for having shown him the letter. Happily Yevpraksia came to the rescue.

"Well, are we going to play cards or not?" she asked.

"Yes, come on, come on!" Arina Petrovna hurried them and jumped up quickly. On her way to the card table a new thought dawned upon her.

"Do you know what day it is?" she turned to Porfiry Vladimirych.

"The twenty-third of November," Yudushka replied, somewhat nonplussed.

"Yes, the twenty-third. Do you remember what happened on the twenty-third of November? You have forgotten about the requiem, haven't you?"

Porfiry Vladimirych turned pale and made the sign of the cross.

"Oh, Lord! Did you ever!" he exclaimed. "Really? Is that so? Just a moment. Let's look at the calendar."

In a few minutes he had brought the calendar and taken out a sheet of paper inserted in it, on which was written.

"November 23. The death of my dear son Vladimir."

"Rest in peace, beloved dust, till the joyous morn. And pray the Lord for your father, who will never fail to have memorial services performed on this day."

"There, now!" said Porfiry Vladimirych. "Ah, Volodya! You are not a good son. You are a wicked son. You haven't prayed for your papa in Heaven, it seems, and so he has lost his memory. What are we going to do about it, mother dear?"

"It is not so terrible, after all. You can have the requiem service tomorrow. A requiem and a mass—we'll have both of them sung. It is all my fault, I am old and have lost my memory. I came on purpose to remind you, but on my way it slipped my mind."

"Ah, what a sin! It is a good thing the ikon lamps are burning. It is as if it had dawned on me from above. To-day is not a holiday, but the lamps have been left burning ever since the day of Presentation. The other day Yevpraksia came over to me and asked: 'Do you think I ought to put out the side ikon lamps?' And I, as if a voice were speaking to me from within, thought a while and said: 'Don't touch them. Let them burn.' And now I see what it all meant."

"Well, it is good at least the lamps have been burning. It is some relief to the soul. Where will you sit? Will you be my partner, or will you join your queen?"

"But, mother dear, I don't know if it's proper."

"Yes, it is. Sit down. God will forgive you. It wasn't done on purpose, with evil intentions. It was just because you forgot. It may happen even to saints. To-morrow, you see, we'll rise with the sun, and stand throughout the mass and have the requiem sung—all as it should be. His soul will rejoice that good people remembered him, and we will be at peace because we did our duty. That's the way to do, my friend. No use worrying. I'll always say, in the first place, worry will not bring back your son, and, in the second place, it is a sin before God."

Yudushka yielded to the persuasiveness of these words, and kissed his mother's hands.

"Ah, mother, mother, you have a golden soul, really! If not for you what would I do now? It would be the end of me, that's all. I just wouldn't know what to do and would go under."

Porfiry Vladimirych gave orders for to-morrow's ceremony, and all sat down to play. They played one hand out, then another. Arina Petrovna became heated and denounced Yudushka because he had been handing Yevpraksia only one card at a time. In the intervals between the deals, Yudushka abandoned himself to reminiscences of his dead son.

"And how kind he was," he said. "He wouldn't take a thing without permission. If he needed paper, 'May I have some paper, papa?' 'Yes, you may, my friend,' Or, 'Won't you be so kind, father dear, as to order carps for breakfast?' 'If you wish it, my friend.' Ah, Volodya, my son, you were a good lad in every way, but it was not good of you to leave your father."

A few more hands were played, and Yudushka again gave vent to his reminiscences.

"And, pray, what in the world happened to him? I really can't understand it. He lived quietly and nicely, was a joy to me—it couldn't have been better. And all of a sudden—bang! What a sin, what a sin! Just think of it, mother dear, what a deed! His very life, the gift of the Heavenly Father. Why? What for? What did he lack? Was it money? I think I never held back his allowance. Even my enemies will not dare say that about me. Well, and if his allowance was not enough, I couldn't help it. Your father's money wasn't stolen money. If you haven't enough money, well, learn to restrain yourself. You can't always be eating cookies, you must sometimes be content with simpler fare. Yes, you must. Your father, for example, expected some money the other day, and then the manager comes and says, 'The Torpenlovskoye peasants won't pay their rent.' Well, I couldn't help it, I wrote a complaint to the Justice of the Peace. Ah, Volodya, Volodya! No, you were not a good boy. You deserted your poor father. Left him an orphan."

The livelier the game the more copious and sentimental Yudushka's reminiscences.

"And how bright he was! I remember once, he was laid up with the measles. He was no more than seven years old. My late Sasha came over to him, and he says, 'Mother, mother, is it true that only angels have wings?' 'Well,' she said, 'yes, only angels.' 'Why?' he asked. 'Did father have wings when he came here a while ago?'"

Yudushka remained the fool with as many as eight cards on his hands, among them the ace, king and queen of trumps. Peals of laughter rose, Yudushka was displeased, but he affably joined in the merriment. In the midst of the general excitement, Arina Petrovna suddenly grew silent and listened attentively.

"Stop, be quiet. Somebody is coming," she said.

Yudushka and Yevpraksia listened, but heard no sound.

"I tell you, somebody is coming. Listen, listen! Someone is coming and he is not far off."

They listened again, and surely there was a faint tinkling in the distance, which the wind brought nearer one moment and carried away the next. Five minutes later the bells were distinctly heard. The sound of them was followed by voices in the court-yard.

"The young master, Piotr Porfirych, has arrived," came from the antechamber.

Yudushka rose, and remained standing, dumfounded and pale as death.

CHAPTER IV

Petenka walked in looking flabby and dispirited, kissed his father's hand, observed the same ceremony with his grandmother, then bowed to Yevpraksia, and sat down. He was about twenty-five, rather good-looking, in an army officer's travelling uniform. That was all one could say about him. Even Yudushka knew scarcely more. The relations of father and son were not of the kind one could call strained. There simply were no relations, you might say. Yudushka knew Petenka to be a man who in the eyes of the law was his son and to whom he had to send a certain allowance determined by Yudushka himself, in consideration of which he was entitled to homage and obedience. Petenka, on the other hand, knew that he had a father who could make things unpleasant for him at any time he wished. He made trips to Golovliovo quite willingly, especially since he had become a commissioned officer, not because he greatly enjoyed his father's company, but simply because every man who is not clearly conscious of his aim in life instinctively gravitates to his native place. But now, apparently, he had come because he had been obliged to come, and consequently manifested not a single sign of the joyous perplexity with which every prodigal son of the gentry celebrates his arrival home. Petenka was not talkative.

All his father's ejaculations of pleasant surprise were met with silence, or a forced smile, and when Yudushka asked, "Why did it occur to you all of a sudden?" he answered even crossly, "It just occurred to me and here I am."

"Well, thank you, thank you for remembering your father. I am glad you came. I suppose you thought of grandmother, too?"

"Yes, I thought of grandmother, too."

"Hold on! Maybe you recollected that today is the Anniversary of your brother Volodenka's death?"

"Yes, I thought of that, too."

Thus the conversation went for about half an hour, so that it was impossible to tell whether Petenka were answering or dodging the questions. So, in spite of Yudushka's tolerance of his children's indifference to him, he could not refrain from remarking:

"Well, my child, you are not affectionate. One could hardly call you an affectionate son!"

Had Petenka kept silence this time also, had he taken his father's remark meekly, or better still, had he kissed his father's hand and said, "Excuse me, father dear, you know I am tired from the journey," things would have passed off pleasantly. But Petenka behaved like an ungrateful child.

"Yes, that's what I am," he answered gruffly. "Let me alone, please."

Then Porfiry Vladimirych felt so hurt, so wounded that he could not keep quiet any longer.

"To think of the pains I have taken for your sake!" he said, with bitterness. "Even here I never stop thinking how to improve this and that, so that you may be comfortable and cozy, and suffer no lack, and have no worry. And all of you fight shy of me."

"Who is 'all of you'?"

"Well, you. And the deceased, too, may his soul rest in peace, he was just the same."

"Well, I am grateful to you."

"I don't see your gratitude—neither gratitude nor affection—nothing."

"I'm not affectionate—that's all. But you speak in the plural all the time. One of us is dead already."

"Yes, he is dead. God punished him. God punishes disobedient children. Still, I remember him. He was unruly, but I remember him. Tomorrow, you see, we shall have the memorial services performed. He offended me, but I, notwithstanding, remember my duty. Lord! The sort of thing that goes on these days! Here a son comes to his father and snarls at the very first word. Is that how we acted in our days? I remember we used to come to Golovliovo, and when we were thirty versts away, we began to shiver in our boots. Well, here is mother dear, a live witness, she will tell you. And nowadays. I don't understand it. I don't understand it."

"I don't either. I came quietly, greeted you, kissed your hand and now I sit here and don't bother you. I drink tea, and if you give me supper, I'll have my supper. Why did you raise all this fuss?"

Arina Petrovna sat in her chair listening attentively. She seemed to be hearing the same old familiar tale that had begun long, long ago, time out of mind. Aware that such a meeting of father and son foreboded no good, she considered it her duty to intervene and put in a word of reconciliation:

"Well, well, you turkey-cocks!" she said, trying to give the situation a humorous turn. "Just met and already quarreling. Look at them jumping at each other, look at them! Feathers will soon be flying. My, my, how naughty! Why don't you fellows sit down quietly and properly and have a friendly chat, and let your old mother enjoy it, too? Petenka, you give in. My child, you must always give in to your father, because he is your father. Even if at times father gives you bitter medicine, take it without complaint, with obedience, with respect, because you are his son. Who knows, maybe the bitter medicine will turn sweet—so it will be to your good. And you, Porfiry Vladimirych, come down from your high perch. He is your son, young, delicate. He has made seventy-five versts over hollows and snow-drifts, he is tired, and chilled, and sleepy. We are through with the tea now, suppose you order supper and then let's all go to bed. So, my friend. We'll all go to our nooks and offer up a prayer, and maybe our temper will pass away. And then we'll rise early in the morning and pray for Volodya's soul. We'll have a memorial service performed, and then we'll go home and have a talk. Both of you will be rested and you'll state your affairs in a clear, orderly way. Petenka, you will tell us about St. Petersburg and you, Porfiry, about your country life. And now, let's have supper and to bed!"

The exhortation had its effect not because it was convincing but because Yudushka himself saw he had gone too far and it would be best to end the day peacefully. He rose from his seat, kissed his mother's hand, thanked her for the "lesson," and ordered supper.

The meal was eaten in morose silence. Then they left the dining-room and went to their rooms. Little by little the house became still. The dead quiet crept from room to room and finally reached the study of the Golovliovo master. Having finished the required number of genuflexions before the ikons, Yudushka, too, went to bed.

Porfiry Vladimirych lay in bed, but was unable to shut his eyes. He felt his son's arrival portended something unusual, and various absurd sermons already rose in his mind. Yudushka's harangues had the merit of being good for all occasions and did not consist of a connected chain of thoughts, but came to him in the shape of fragmentary aphorisms. Whenever confronted by an extraordinary situation, such a flood of aphorisms overwhelmed him that even sleep could not drive them from his consciousness.

He could not fall asleep. He was a prey to his absurd sermonizings, though, as a matter of fact, he was not much perturbed by Petenka's mysterious arrival. He was prepared for no matter what happened. He knew nothing would catch him napping and nothing would make him recede in the slightest from the web of empty, musty aphorisms in which he was entangled. For him there existed neither sorrow nor joy, neither hatred, nor love. To him the entire world was a vast coffin which served him as a pretext for endless prattling.

What greater grief could there be for a father than for his son to commit suicide? But even with respect to Volodya's suicide he remained true to himself. It had been a very sad story, which had lasted two years. For two years Volodya had held out, at first showing a pride and determination not to ask his father's aid. Then he weakened, began to implore, to expostulate, to threaten. In reply he always received a ready aphorism, the stone given to the hungry man. It is doubtful whether Yudushka realized that he had handed his son a stone and not bread. At any rate a stone was all he had to give, and so he gave it. When Volodya shot himself he had a requiem service performed, entered the day of his death in the calendar, and promised himself to have memorial services performed on the 23rd of November of every year. Sometimes a dull voice muttered in his ears that the solution of a family quarrel by suicide is rather a questionable method, to say the least; and even then he brought into play a train of aphorisms, such as "God punishes disobedient children," "God is against the proud," and was at peace again.

And now! There was no doubt that something sinister had happened to Petenka. But whatever had happened, he, Porfiry Vladimirych, must be above those chance happenings. "You knew how to get in, then know how to get out." "If the cat wants the fish, let her wet her feet." Just so. That is what he would say to his son the next day, no matter what Petenka told him. And suppose Petenka, like Volodya, were also to refuse to take a stone instead of bread? What if he, too— —Yudushka drove the thought from him. It was a diabolical suggestion. He tossed about and tried in vain to fall asleep. Whenever sleep seemed about to come, there flashed across his mind maxims such as "I should like to reach the sky but my arms are too short," or "You can't stretch more than the length of your bed," or "Speed is good for nothing but catching fleas."

Twaddle surrounded him on all sides, crawled upon him, crept over him, embraced him. Under this load of nonsensicality, with which he hoped to regale his soul tomorrow, he could not fall asleep.

Nor could Petenka find sleep, though the journey had tired him exceedingly. He had an affair that could not be settled anywhere except at Golovliovo, but it was a situation of such a nature that he did not know how to meet it. Petenka, indeed, realized full well that his case was hopeless and his trip to Golovliovo would only add to the difficulties of his situation. But the primitive instinct of self-preservation in man overcomes all reason and urges him on to try everything to the very last straw. That's why he had come. But instead of hardening himself so as to be prepared for whatever might come, he had almost from the first word got into a quarrel with his father. What would be the outcome of this trip? Would a miracle happen? Would stone turn into bread? Would it not have been simpler to put the revolver to his temple and say, "Gentlemen, I am unworthy of wearing your uniform. I have embezzled crown money and I pronounce a just, though severe sentence upon myself"? Bang! And all is over. The deceased Lieutenant Golovliov is hereby struck off the list of officers. Yes, how radical that would be and—how beautiful! The comrades would say, "You were unfortunate, you went too far, still you were an honorable man."

But instead of acting that way at once, he had brought the affair to a point where it became a matter of common knowledge; and then he had been given leave of absence for a fixed time on condition that within that time he would refund the embezzled sum. If not—out of the regiment! The disgraceful end of his early career! So he had come to Golovliovo, though he knew full well that he would be given a stone instead of bread.

But perhaps a miracle would come to change things. Miracles sometimes happen. Perhaps the present Golovliovo would vanish and a new Golovliovo would arise, in which he might——And perhaps grandmother would—hadn't she money? Maybe, if he told her he was in great trouble, she might give him some. Who could tell? "Here," she might say, "hurry, so that you get back before the time is up."

And he rode fast, fast—hurried the driver, just made the train and got to the regiment two hours before the respite was over. "Good for you, Golovliov," his comrades would say, "your hand, honorable young man! Let's forget the matter." And he not only remained in the regiment, but was even promoted to staff-captain, then captain, after that adjutant of the regiment (he had been bursar, already) and, finally, on the anniversary day of the regiment——Ah, if only the night would pass quickly! Tomorrow—well, let happen what may tomorrow. But what he would have to listen to! Gods, what would he not be told! Tomorrow—but why tomorrow? He had a whole day yet. He asked for two days just because he wanted to have enough time to move "him." A likely chance! A fine prospect of persuading and touching him! No use——

Here his thoughts became confused and sank, one after the other, into the mist of sleep. In a few minutes the Golovliovo manor was steeped in heavy slumber.

The next day the whole household was up early in the morning. Everybody went to church except Petenka, who pleaded fatigue. They listened to the mass and the requiem and returned home. Petenka, as usual, came up to kiss his father's hand, but Yudushka extended it sidewise, and everyone noticed that he did not even make the sign of the cross over his son. Tea was served, then *kutya*. Yudushka was dismal, scraped the floor with his feet, avoided conversation, sighed, folded his hands incessantly as if for inner prayer, and never once looked at his son. Petenka, for his part, bristled up and smoked one cigarette after another. The strained situation of yesterday, so far from relaxing, became still more acute. It made Arina Petrovna very uneasy, and she decided to find out from Yevpraksia if anything had happened.

"Has anything happened," she asked, "that makes them look daggers at each other like that?"

"How do I know? I don't interfere in their private affairs," the girl snapped back.

"Maybe it's on account of you. Perhaps my grandson is running after you too?"

"Why should he run after me? A little while ago he tried to catch hold of me in the corridor, and Porfiry Vladimirych saw him."

"Oh. So that's what it is."

In fact, in spite of his critical situation, Petenka had not lost a bit of his levity. His eyes riveted themselves on Yevpraksia's powerful back and he determined to let her know about it. That was the real reason he had not gone to church, hoping Yevpraksia, as the housekeeper, would stay home. So, when the house had turned silent, he had thrown his cloak over his shoulders and hidden himself in the corridor. A minute or two passed, the door of the maids' room banged, and Yevpraksia appeared at the other end of the corridor, carrying a tray with a butter-cake to be served with the tea. Petenka struck her between the shoulder-blades and said, "A wonderful back you've got!" and that instant the dining-room door opened and his father appeared.

"You, scoundrel! If you came here to behave in a nasty way, I'll throw you down the stairs!" Yudushka hissed venomously.

Naturally, Petenka vanished in a moment. He could not fail to realize that the incident of the morning was scarcely likely to improve his case. So he decided to be silent and postpone the explanation until the morrow. Nevertheless he did nothing to allay his father's irritation; on the contrary, he behaved in a foolish, unguarded manner, smoking cigarettes incessantly, heedless of his father's energetically fanning away the clouds of smoke that filled the room; and every now and then making sheep's eyes at Yevpraksia, who smiled queerly under the influence of his glances. Yudushka noticed that, too.

The day dragged on slowly. Arina Petrovna tried to play fool with Yevpraksia, but nothing came of it. No one felt like playing or talking; they could not even think of small talk, though everyone had stores of this merchandise. At last dinner time came. But dinner passed in silence also. After dinner Arina Petrovna made preparations for returning to Pogorelka. But this intention of his "mother dear" alarmed Yudushka.

"God bless you, darling!" he exclaimed. "Do you mean to say you'll leave me here alone with this—this wicked son? No, no, don't think of it. I won't allow it."

"But what is the matter? Has anything happened between the two of you? Why don't you tell me?" she asked.

"No, nothing has happened—as yet, but you'll see. No, please don't go! Be present at——There is something behind his coming here in such a hurry. So, if anything happens—you be the witness."

Arina Petrovna shook her head and decided to stay.

After dinner Porfiry Vladimirych retired, having first sent Yevpraksia to the village priest, and Arina Petrovna also went to her room and dozed off in her easy-chair.

Petenka thought it the most favorable time to try his luck with grandmother, and went to her room.

"What is the matter? Have you come to play a game of fool with an old woman?" she asked.

"No, granny, I am on business."

"Well, what is your business? Tell me."

Petenka hesitated a minute, then blurted out:

"I lost crown money at cards."

Arina Petrovna's eyes grew dim from the shock.

"Much?" she asked in a frightened voice, staring at him.

"Three thousand."

For a moment both were silent. Arina Petrovna looked around restlessly, as if expecting somebody to come to her rescue.

"Do you know they can send you to Siberia for that?" she said at last.

"Yes, I know."

"Poor fellow!"

"Granny, I meant to borrow it from you. I'll pay good interest."

Arina Petrovna became thoroughly frightened.

"Oh no, no!" she protested. "I have only enough money for my coffin and memorial prayers. It's my granddaughters that keep me a-going, and my son, too. No, no, no! You'd better let me alone. Let me see—why not ask your papa?"

"Oh, well, you can't squeeze blood out of an onion. All my hope was in you, granny."

"Just think of what you are saying. I would gladly do it, but where am I to get the money from? I have no money at all. But suppose you ask father, you know, affectionately, respectfully. 'Here, father dear, such is the case. I know I am guilty, I am young and I made a blunder.' You know, with a smile and a laugh. Kiss his hand and fall on your knees, and cry a bit. He likes it. Then maybe father will untie his purse for his sonny dear."

"So you really think it's worth trying? Just a moment. See here, granny, suppose you say to him, 'If you don't give him the money I'll lay a curse on you!' He has always been afraid of your curse, you know."

"No, why curse? You can ask right out. Do ask him, my dear. There is no harm if you bow before your father once too many. He will understand your position, you know. Do it. Be sure to do it."

Petenka, his arms akimbo, walked back and forth as if deliberating. Finally he halted and said:

"No, I won't. He is not likely to give it—it's no use. No matter what I do, even if I smash my head in bowing—he won't do it. But you see, if you threatened him with your curse. What am I to do, granny?"

"I don't know, really. Try and perhaps you'll soften him a bit. How did you come to take such liberties? To lose crown money is no small matter. Did anybody inveigle you into it?"

"It just happened. I took it and lost it at cards. Well, if you have no money of your own, give me some of the orphans'."

"What is the matter with you? Have you lost your wits? How can I let you have the orphans' money? No, no, I can't. Don't talk to me about it, for Christ's sake."

"So you won't. Too bad. And I would pay good interest. Do you want five per cent. per month? No? Well, double the principal in a year?"

"Don't you tempt me!" shouted Arina Petrovna, throwing up her hands. "Leave me alone, for Christ's sake! It won't surprise me if father hears us and says I urged you on! Oh, Lord! I am an old woman, I wanted to rest a bit. I had just dozed off and then he comes with such an offer."

"Very well, then. I am going. So it's impossible? Very good. Just like kinsfolk. On account of three thousand rubles your grandson will go to Siberia. Don't forget to have a Te Deum sung when I go."

Petenka left the room, closing the door with a bang. One of his flimsy hopes was gone. What was he to do next? Only one way out was left—to confess all to father. Who knows, perhaps, perhaps, something would——

"I'll go at once and be done with it," he said to himself. "Or no! What can I hope for? Better tomorrow. Yes, I think tomorrow is better. I'll tell him and leave at once." So he decided. Tomorrow would see and end it all.

After the talk with grandmother the evening dragged on still more slowly. Even Arina Petrovna grew silent after she had learned the real cause of Petenka's arrival. Yudushka tried to be jocular with mother, but perceiving she was absorbed in her own thoughts, also grew silent. Petenka did nothing but smoke. At supper Porfiry Vladimirych asked him:

"Are you going to tell me at last why you have honored me with this visit?"

"I will tell you tomorrow," answered Petenka morosely.

CHAPTER V

Petenka rose early after a sleepless night. His harassed mind vacillated between hope and utter despair. Perhaps he did not really know his father, but one thing he was sure of, that there was not in him a single feeling, a single weak spot that could be grasped at and made use of. When face to face with his father, all he felt was something inexplicable. He did not know how to approach him, what to say first, and this made him very uneasy in his presence. It had been like that since his childhood. As far back as he could remember, it always seemed better not to attempt any forecast at all than to make a matter depend upon his father's decision. So now, too. How was he to begin? How was he to approach the matter? What was he to say first? And why had he come here at all?

A feeling of disgust seized him. Nevertheless he realized he had only a few hours left and something had to be done. Having worked himself up into a fair state of courage, he buttoned up his coat, and walked firmly to his father's study, whispering something to himself. Yudushka was saying prayers. He was pious, and every day gladly devoted a few hours to prayer, not because he loved God and hoped through prayer to enter into communion with Him, but because he feared the devil and hoped God would deliver him from the Evil One.

He knew many prayers and was especially versed in the technique of the poses and gestures of worship. He knew how to move his lips, how to roll his eyes, when it was proper to place the hands palm inward, and when they were to be lifted up, when to be moved with feeling, and when to stand with reverential calm and slowly make the sign of the cross. Even his eyes and his nostrils moistened at the proper moments. But prayer did not rejuvenate him, did not ennoble his feelings, or bring a single ray into his dull existence. He could pray and go through all the requisite bodily movements, and at the same time be looking out of the window to see if someone was entering the cellar without his permission. It was quite a distinct, particular function of life, which was self-sufficient and could exist outside of the general scheme of life.

When Petenka entered the study, Porfiry Vladimirych was on his knees with his hands raised. He did not change his position, but made a jerky movement with one of his hands to indicate that he had not yet finished. Petenka seated himself in the dining-room, where the table was already set for tea, and waited. The half hour that passed seemed like eternity, especially as he was sure his father was prolonging the wait intentionally. The studied coolness with which he had armed himself little by little gave way to vexation. At first he sat stiff, then began to walk to and fro, and finally fell to whistling airs. As a result, the door of the study opened, and Yudushka's irritated voice was heard calling:

"Whoever wants to whistle may do so in the stables."

After a while Porfiry Vladimirych came out clad all in black, in clean linen, as if prepared for a solemn occasion. His countenance was radiant, glowing, breathing meekness and joy, as if he had just been at communion. He approached his son, made the sign of the cross over him, and then kissed him.

"Good morning, friend," he said.

"Good morning."

"Did you sleep well? Was your bed made properly? Were there no little fleas and bedbugs to bother you?"

"Thank you. I slept well."

"Well, thanks to God, if you slept well. It's only at one's parents' home that one can sleep really well. I know it from my own experience. No matter how comfortable I might be at St. Petersburg, I could never sleep so well as at Golovliovo. You feel just as if you were rocked in a cradle. So what are we going to do? Shall we have some tea first, or do you want to say something now?"

"Let's talk it over now. I have to leave in six hours, and maybe we'll need some time for deliberation."

"Oh, well. But, my dear, I tell you directly, I never deliberate, my answer is always ready. If your request is a proper one, well, I never refuse anything proper. It may be hard on me at times, and I can't always afford it, but if it is proper, I can't refuse it. That's the kind of man I am. But if you ask for something that isn't right, I am sorry. Though I feel for you, I shall have to refuse. You observe, my son, I have no underhand ways. I am exactly as you see me. Well, then, let's go into the study. Speak and I will listen. Let's hear, let's hear what the matter is."

On entering the study, Porfiry left the door ajar and instead of seating himself and asking his son to be seated, he began pacing the room, as if instinctively feeling that the matter was delicate and it would be easier to discuss it while walking. The expression of one's face may be more easily concealed, and if the conversation takes a disagreeable turn it may be more readily cut off, and the door half ajar makes it possible to appeal to witnesses; for mother dear and Yevpraksia were sure to come into the dining-room before long to have tea.

"Papa," blurted out Petenka, "I lost some crown money at cards."

Yudushka said nothing, but his lips quivered, and he immediately fell to muttering, as was his habit.

"I lost three thousand," explained Petenka, "and if I don't return the money the day after tomorrow, there may be very disagreeable consequences for me."

"Well, refund the money," said Porfiry Vladimirych affably.

Father and son made a few turns around the room in silence. Petenka wished to make further explanations, but felt a lump rising in his throat.

"Yes, but where am I to get the money from?" he said at last.

"My dear friend, I don't know your resources. Pay it back from the resources you figured on when you gambled crown money away."

"You know very well that in such cases people forget about their resources."

"I don't know a thing, my friend. I never played cards, except with mother, when I play fool to amuse the old woman. And please don't drag me into this dirty business, and let's go and have tea. We'll have tea and sit around, maybe we'll talk about something, but, for the Lord's sake, not about that."

Yudushka started to make for the door and into the dining-room, but Petenka stopped him.

"Look here," he said, "I have to get out of this predicament somehow."

Yudushka grinned and stared at Petenka.

"Yes, my dear, you have to," he agreed.

"Then help me."

"Ah, that's a different matter. You have to get out of the difficulty somehow, to be sure, but how to get out of it—well, that's none of my business."

"But why don't you want to help me?"

"First, because I have no money to cover up your dastardly deeds, and secondly because the entire matter does not concern me in the least. You knew how to get in, then know how to get out. The cat likes fish, then let her wet her feet. You see, my boy, that's just what I said at the start, that if your request is a proper one——"

"I know. You've got a lot of words on the tip of your tongue."

"Wait, save your impudent remarks, and let me say what I wish to say. That they are not mere words I'll prove to you in a minute. So, as I said a while ago, if your request is a proper, a sensible one, all right, my boy. I am always ready to satisfy you. But if you come to me with an unreasonable request, I am very sorry, I have no money for stuff and nonsense. No sir, never. And you won't get any—you may as well be sure of it. And don't dare tell me I use mere words. My words are mighty near deeds."

"But think what will become of me."

"Whatever pleases God, that will happen," answered Yudushka, slightly lifting up his arms and looking sideways at the ikon.

Father and son again made a few turns across the room. Yudushka paced reluctantly, as if in complaint that his son was holding him in captivity. Petenka, his arms akimbo, followed him, biting his moustache and smiling nervously.

"I am your last son," he said. "Don't forget that."

"My boy, God bereft Job of everything, and Job did not complain, but only said: 'God hath given and God hath taken away—may thy will be done, oh, Lord!' So, my boy."

"In the Bible it was God that took, and here you take away from yourself. Volodya——"

"Oh, well, you are talking nonsense."

"No, it isn't nonsense, it's the truth. Everybody knows that Volodya——"

"No, no, no! I don't want to listen to your preposterous remarks. Enough! You've said everything necessary. I have given you my answer. And now let's go and have tea. We'll chat a while, then we'll have a bite, then a drink before you go—and then God speed you! You see how good the Lord is to you? The weather has abated and the road become smoother. Little by little, bit by bit, one, two, and you'll hardly notice when you get to the station."

"Now, listen, I implore you. If you have a drop of feeling——"

"No, no, no! Don't let us talk about it. Let's go into the dining-room. I dare say mother dear must be dull without her tea. It isn't proper to keep the dear old woman waiting."

Yudushka made a sharp turn and almost ran to the door.

"You may go or not, it's all the same to me, but I am not going to drop this conversation," Petenka shouted after him. "It will be worse if we begin talking in the presence of witnesses."

Yudushka came back and planted himself squarely before his son.

"What do you want of me, you scoundrel? Speak up!"

"I want you to pay the money that I lost."

"Never!"

"Is that your last word?"

"You see," exclaimed Yudushka solemnly, pointing at the ikon that hung in the corner, "You see that? It is grandfather's benediction. So, in the presence of that image I say, Never!"

And with a firm step he left the study.

"Murderer!" was hurled after him.

CHAPTER VI

Arina Petrovna was already at the table, and Yevpraksia was busy arranging the tea things. The old woman was silent and thoughtful, and looked as if she were ashamed of Petenka. In the customary way Yudushka kissed her hand, and she made the sign of the cross over him. Then came the usual questions, whether everybody felt well, and had had a good night's rest, followed by the customary monosyllabic answers. Petenka's asking Arina Petrovna for money and awakening the memory of the "curse" had put her into a state of peculiar uneasiness. She was pursued by the thought, "What if I threaten him with my curse?" When she had heard that explanations in the study had begun, she had turned to Yevpraksia with the request:

"Suppose, my dear, you go to the door quietly and listen to what they say."

Yevpraksia went to eavesdrop, but was so stupid she could understand nothing.

"Oh, they're just having a chat," she explained upon her return.

Then Arina Petrovna could not hold out any longer and went to the dining-room, where the samovar had already been brought in. But the interview was nearing its end, and all she noted was that Petenka's voice was loud and angry, and Porfiry Vladimirych's replies were given in a nagging voice.

"He's nagging him, that just it, nagging!" ran in her head. "I remember he used to nag that way, and how is it I did not understand him then?"

At last, father and son appeared in the dining-room. Petenka's face was red and he was breathing heavily. His eyes were staring widely, his hair was disheveled, his forehead was covered with beads of perspiration. Yudushka, on the contrary, entered pale and cross. He wanted to appear indifferent but, in spite of all his efforts, his lower lip trembled. He could hardly utter the customary morning greetings to his mother dear.

All took their places at the table. Petenka seated himself at some distance, leaned against the back of his chair, crossed his legs, lighted a cigarette, and looked at his father ironically.

"You see, mother, the storm has abated," Yudushka began. "Yesterday there was such an uproar, but God only had to will it, and here we have a nice, bright, quiet day. Am I right, mother dear?"

"I don't know. I haven't been out to-day."

"By the way, we are going to see our dear guest off," continued Yudushka. "I rose early this morning, looked out of the window—it was still and quiet outdoors, as if God's angel had flown by and in a moment allayed the riot with his wings."

But no one answered Yudushka's kindly words. Yevpraksia sipped her tea from the saucer, blowing and puffing. Arina Petrovna looked into her cup and was silent. Petenka, swaying in his chair, continued to eye his father with an ironical, defiant air, as if he had to exert great efforts to keep from bursting out laughing.

"Even if Petenka does not ride fast, he will reach the railway station toward night," Porfiry Vladimirych resumed. "Our horses are not overworked. They will feed for a couple of hours at Muravyevo, and they will get him to the place in a jiffy. Ah, Petka, you are a bad boy! Suppose you stay with us a while longer—really. We would enjoy your company, and you would improve greatly in a week."

But Petenka continued to sway in his chair and eye his father.

"Why do you stare at me?" Yudushka flared up at last. "Do you see pictures on me?"

"I'm just looking at you waiting for what's coming next."

"No use waiting, my son. It will be as I said. I will not change my mind."

A minute of silence followed, after which a whisper could be distinctly heard.

"Yudushka!"

Porfiry Vladimirych undoubtedly heard it, he even turned pale, but he pretended the exclamation did not concern him.

"Ah, my dear little children," he said. "I should like to caress and fondle you, but it seems it can't be done—ill luck! You run away from your parents, you've got bosom friends who are dearer to you than father and mother. Well, it can't be helped. One ponders a bit over it, then resigns oneself. You are young folk, and youth, of course, prefers the company of youth to that of an old grouch. So, I resign myself and don't complain. I only pray to Our Father in Heaven, 'Do Thy will, oh Lord!'"

"Murderer!" Petenka whispered, but this time so distinctly that Arina Petrovna looked at him in fright. Something passed before her eyes. It looked like the shadow of Simple Simon.

"Whom do you mean?" asked Yudushka, trembling with excitement.

"Oh, just an acquaintance of mine."

"I see. Well, you'd better make that clear. Lord knows what's in your head. Maybe it is one of us that you style so."

Everybody became silent. The glasses of tea remained untouched. Yudushka leaned against the back of his chair, swaying nervously. Petenka, seeing that all hope was gone, had a sensation of deadly anguish, under the influence of which he was ready to go to any lengths. But father and son looked at each other with an indescribable smile. Hardened though Porfiry Vladimirych was, the minute was nearing when he would be unable to control himself.

"You'd better go, while the going's good," he burst out, finally. "You better had."

"I'm going."

"Then why wait? I see you're trying to pick a quarrel, and I don't want to quarrel with anybody. We live here quietly and in good order, without disputes. Your old grandmother is here. You ought to have regard for her at least. Well, tell us why you came here?"

"I told you why."

"If it's only for that, you are wasting your efforts. Go at once, my son. Hey, who's there? Have the horses ready for the young master. And some fried chicken, and caviar, and other things, eggs, I suppose. Wrap them up well in paper. You'll take a bite at the station, my son, while they feed the horses. Godspeed!"

"No, I am not going yet. I'm going to church first to have a memorial service performed for the murdered servant of God, Vladimir."

"That is, for the suicide."

"No, for the murdered."

Father and son stared at each other. It looked as if in a moment both would jump up. But Yudushka made a superhuman effort and, turning his chair, faced the table again.

"Wonderful!" he said in a strained voice. "Wonderful!"

"Yes, for the murdered!" Petenka persisted brutally.

"Who murdered him?" Yudushka asked with curiosity, still hoping, apparently, that his son would come to his senses.

But Petenka, unperturbed, whipped out:

"You!"

"I?"

Porfiry Vladimirych was astounded. It was a few moments before he came to himself. He rose hastily from his seat, faced the ikon and began to pray.

"You, you, you!" Petenka repeated.

"Well, now! Thank God, I feel better after praying," said Yudushka, seating himself at table again. "Just a minute, though. I, as your father, should not take you up on your talk, but we'll pursue the matter this time. Then you mean to say that I killed Volodenka?"

"Yes, you did."

"And I beg leave to differ. I consider he shot himself. At that time I was at Golovliovo and in St. Petersburg. So what could I have to do with it? How could I kill him when he was seven hundred versts away?"

"As if you don't understand!"

"I don't understand, by the Lord, I don't!"

"And who left Volodya without a penny? Who discontinued his allowances? Who?"

"Stuff and nonsense! Why did he marry against his father's will?"

"But you gave him your permission."

"Who? I? What are you talking about? I never did anything of the kind. Nev-v-v-er!"

"Oh, of course, you acted as you always do. Everyone of your words has ten meanings. Go, guess the right one."

"I never gave my permission. He wrote to me, 'Papa, I want to marry Lida,' you understand, 'I want to,' not 'I beg your permission.' Well, I answered him, 'If you want to marry, you can marry. I cannot stand in your way.' That's all there was to it."

"That's all there was to it," Petenka said jeeringly. "And wasn't that giving your permission?"

"That's exactly what it wasn't. What did I say? I said, 'I cannot stand in your way.' That's all. But whether I give my permission or not, is a different question. He did not ask my permission, he simply wrote, 'Papa, I want to marry Lida.' Well, and as to permission he kept mum. You want to marry. Well, my friend, may God be with you, marry Lida or Fida, I cannot stand in your way!"

"But you could leave him without a crust of bread. So why didn't you write this way, 'I do not approve of your intention, and therefore, though I will not hinder you, I warn you that you can not longer rely on financial aid from me.' That, at least, would have been clear."

"No, I shall never permit myself to do such things, to make threats against a grown son—never! I have a rule never to be in anybody's way. If you want to marry—marry! Well, and as to consequences—I am sorry. It was your business to foresee them yourself. That's why God gave you reason. And as to me, brother, I don't like to thrust myself into other people's affairs. I not only keep from meddling myself, but I don't invite others to meddle in my affairs, I don't invite it, I don't, I don't, I even forbid it! Do you hear me, you wicked, disrespectful son, I f-o-r-b-i-d it!"

"You may forbid it, if you like, but you can't muzzle everybody."

"If at least he had repented! And if at least he had realized that he offended his father! Well, you committed a folly—say you are sorry. Ask forgiveness! 'Forgive me, dear papa, for the mortification I caused you.' But he wouldn't!"

"But he did write to you. He made it clear to you that he had nothing to live on, that he could not endure it any longer."

"That's not the kind of thing to write to a father. From a father one asks pardon, that's all."

"He did so. He was so tortured that he begged forgiveness, too. He did everything, he did."

"And even if he did, he was wrong. You ask forgiveness once, you see your father does not forgive you, you ask again!"

"Oh, you!"

At this Petenka suddenly ceased swaying his chair, turned about, faced the table and rested both elbows on it.

"And here I, too——" he whispered.

His face gradually became disfigured.

"And here I too——" he repeated, and burst into hysterical sobbing.

"Whose fault——"

But Yudushka had no chance to finish his sermon. At that moment something quite unexpected took place. During their skirmish the man had almost forgotten about Arina Petrovna. But she had not remained an indifferent spectator. On the contrary, you could tell at a glance that something quite unusual was taking place within her, and that the moment perhaps had arrived when the ruthless vision of her entire life appeared before her spiritual eye in a glaring light. Her face livened up, her eyes widened and glittered, her lips moved as if they were struggling to utter some word and could not. Suddenly, just at the moment when Petenka's bitter weeping resounded in the dining-room she rose heavily from her arm-chair, stretched her arms forward, and a loud wail broke out from her breast.

"My cu-r-r-se upon you!"

BOOK IV
THE GOOD LITTLE NIECE

CHAPTER I

Yudushka did not give the money to Petenka, though, kind father that he was, he gave orders just before the moment of departure for some chicken, veal and pie to be placed in the carriage. Then he went out on the porch in the chilling wind to see his son off, and inquired whether Petenka was seated comfortably and whether he had wrapped his feet up well. Re-entering the house, he stood at the window in the dining-room a long time making the sign of the cross and sending his blessings after the vehicle that was carrying Petenka away. In a word, he performed the farewell ceremony fittingly, as becomes good kinsfolk.

"Oh, Petka, Petka," he said, "you are a bad, bad son. Look at the mischief you have done. My, my, my! And what could have been better than to live on quietly and peacefully, nicely and easily with father and old granny? But no! Crash! Bang! I am my own master, I've got a head on my shoulders, too! Well, there's your head! My, what trouble!"

Not a muscle quivered in his wooden face, not a note in his voice sounded like an appeal to a prodigal son. But, then, there was nobody to hear his words, for Arina Petrovna was the only one beside himself in the room, and as a result of the shock she had just gone through she seemed to have lost all vitality, and sat near the samovar, her mouth open, looking straight ahead, without hearing anything, without a single thought in her mind.

Then life flowed on as usual, full of idle bustle and babbling. Contrary to Petenka's expectations, Porfiry Vladimirych took the maternal curse quite coolly and did not recede a hair's breadth from the decision that had come from his head full-formed, as it were.

It is true he turned slightly pale and rushed toward his mother with a cry:

"Mother, dear! Darling! Lord be with you! Be calm, dear! God is merciful. All will be well."

But his words were expressive of alarm for her rather than for himself. Her act had been so unexpected that Yudushka even forgot to pretend to be frightened. Only last night his mother had been affectionate, had jested, and played fool with Yevpraksia. Evidently, then, it had all happened in a moment of sudden anger, and there was nothing premeditated, nothing real about it all.

Indeed, he had been very much afraid of his mother's curse but he had pictured it quite differently. In his idle mind he had built an elaborate staging for the occasion, ikons, burning candles, his mother standing in the center of the room, terrible, with a darkened face as she hurled the curse. Then, thunder, candles going out, the veil tearing asunder, darkness covering the earth, and above, amidst the clouds the wrathful countenance of Jehovah illumined by a flash of lightning. But nothing of the sort had happened, so his mother had simply done something rash and silly. And she had had no reason to curse him in earnest, because of late there had been no cause for quarreling. Many changes had occurred since Yudushka expressed his doubt as to whether a certain coach belonged to his mother dear (Yudushka admitted to *himself* that *then* he had been wrong and deserved damnation). Arina Petrovna had become more submissive, and Porfiry Vladimirych had but one thought in his head: how to placate his mother dear.

"The old woman is doing poorly, my, how poorly! At times she even raves," he consoled himself. "The darling sits down to play fool and before you know it, she dozes off."

In justice to Yudushka it must be admitted that his mother's decrepitude gave him some alarm. Even he was not quite ready for her death, had not made any plans, had had no time to make estimates—how much capital mother had when she left Dubrovino, what that capital might bring in annually, how much of the interest she had spent, and how much she had added to the principal. In a word, he had not gone through an infinity of useless trifles, without which he always felt as if he were caught unawares.

"The old woman is hale and hearty," he would muse at times. "Still she won't spend it all—impossible. When she shared us out, she had a neat sum. Maybe she transferred some to the orphans. Oh, the old woman is rich. Yes, she is."

But these musings were not so very serious, and vanished without leaving an impress on his mind. The mass of daily trivialities was already great, and there was as yet no urgent need to augment them by the addition of new trivialities. Porfiry Vladimirych kept putting the matter off, and did not realize it was time to begin until after the damnation scene.

The catastrophe came sooner than he expected. On the second day after Petenka's departure Arina Petrovna left for Pogorelka, and never again visited Golovliovo. She spent a month in total solitude, keeping to her room and scarcely exchanging a word with her servants. From force of habit she rose early in the morning, sat down at her desk, and began to play patience, but hardly ever brought the game to an end, and sat in frozen rigidity—with her glazed eyes fixed on the window. What she thought about or whether she thought at all, even the keenest judge of the deep-lying mysteries of the human soul could not have divined. She seemed to be trying to recollect something, perhaps how she came to be within those walls, and could not. Alarmed by her mistress's silence, Afimyushka would appear in the room, arrange the pillows lining her easy-chair, and try to open a conversation on this or that, but received only impatient monosyllabic replies.

Once or twice Porfiry Vladimirych came to Pogorelka, invited mother dear to Golovliovo, tried to kindle her imagination with the prospect of mushrooms, German carp, and the other allurements of Golovliovo, but his overtures evoked nothing but an enigmatic smile.

One morning she tried to leave her bed as usual, but could not, though she felt no particular pain, and complained of nothing. She took it, apparently, as a matter of course, without any sign of alarm. The very day before she had been sitting at the table and even walked, though with difficulty, and now she was in bed "feeling indisposed." It was even more comfortable. But Afimyushka became thoroughly frightened and without the mistress's knowledge sent a messenger to Porfiry Vladimirych.

Yudushka came early the next morning. Arina Petrovna was considerably worse. He put the servants through a cross-examination as to what mother had eaten and whether she had not overeaten. But Arina Petrovna had eaten almost nothing for a whole month, and had refused all food the previous day. Yudushka expressed his grief, waved his hands, and like a good son, warmed himself at the oven in the maids' room so that he would not bring the cold into the patient's room. At the same time he began to give orders and make arrangements. He had an extraordinary keenness for scenting death. He made inquiries as to whether the priest was home and arranged that in case of emergency he should be sent for at once. He informed himself where mother's chest with her papers was, whether it was locked, and having satisfied himself concerning the state of things, he called in the cook and ordered dinner for himself.

"I need but little," he said. "Have you got a chicken? Well, prepare some chicken soup. If you have some cured beef, get a bit of cured beef ready. Then something fried, and I'll have enough."

Arina Petrovna lay prostrate on her back with her mouth open, breathing heavily. Her eyes were staring wide. One hand projected from under the quilt of hare's fur and hung stiff. She was evidently alive to the commotion incident upon her son's arrival, and perhaps his orders even reached her ears. The lowered window-shades put the room in twilight. The wicks were flickering their last at the bottom of the ikon lamps and sputtered audibly at contact with the water. The air was close and fetid, unbearably suffocating from the overheated stoves, the sickening smell of the ikon lamps, and the breath of illness. Porfiry Vladimirych, in his felt boots, glided to his mother's bed like a snake. His tall, lean figure wrapped in twilight swayed uncannily. Arina Petrovna with a look half of surprise and half of fright followed his movements and huddled under her quilt.

"It is I, mother dear," he said. "What's the matter with you? You are all out of gear today. My, my, my! No wonder I could not sleep all night. Something seemed to urge me on. 'Let's go and see,' I thought, 'how our Pogorelka friends are getting along.' I got up in the morning, hitched a couple of horses to the pony cart, and here I am!"

Porfiry Vladimirych tittered affably, but Arina Petrovna did not answer, and drew herself together in a closer coil under her quilt.

"Well, God is merciful, mother dear," continued Yudushka. "The main thing is to stand up for yourself. Don't put any stock in the ailment. Get up and take a walk through the room, like a sound, hale person. You see, just like this."

Porfiry Vladimirych rose from his seat and demonstrated how sound, hale persons walk.

"Oh, just a moment. I'll raise the window-shade and take a good look at you. Oh, but you are first rate, my darling. Just pluck up some courage, say your prayers, doll up, get into your Sunday best, and you'll be ready for a dance. There, I have brought you some jolly good holy water, just taste some."

Porfiry Vladimirych took a flask out of his pocket, found a wine glass on the table, filled it and gave it to the patient. Arina Petrovna made an effort to lift her head, but in vain.

"I wish the orphans were here," she moaned.

"Well, much need you have of the orphans here. Oh, mother, mother! How is it all of a sudden you—really! Just a little bad turn, and at once you are ready to give up the ship. We'll attend to it all. We'll send a special messenger to the orphans and we'll do everything else in due time. Now, what's the hurry, really? We are going to live yet, yes indeed we are. And we'll have a fine time of it, too. Wait till summer is here, we'll both of us go to the woods to pick mushrooms, and raspberries, and nice juicy black currants. Or else, we'll go to Dubrovino to catch German carps. We'll bring out the horse and carriage, get into it, and one, two, three—there we go. Nicely and easily."

"I wish the orphans were here," repeated Arina Petrovna in anguish.

"We'll bring the orphans, too. Give us time. We'll call them together, all of them. We'll all be here and sit by you. You will be the brood-hen and we'll be your chicks. We'll have it all, if you behave. Now you are a naughty girl, because you went and took sick. That's the kind of mischief you're up to. My, my! Instead of being good and serving as an example for others, look what you're doing. That's bad, my dear, very bad."

But no matter how hard Porfiry Vladimirych tried to cheer up his mother dear with banter, her strength waned from hour to hour. A messenger was dispatched to town to fetch a doctor, and since the patient persisted in moaning and calling the orphans, Yudushka in his own hand wrote a letter to Anninka and Lubinka in which he compared his and their conduct, called himself a Christian and them ungrateful. At night the doctor arrived, but it was too late. Arina Petrovna's fate was sealed. At about four o'clock in the morning the death agony set in and at six Porfiry Vladimirych was kneeling at his mother's bed wailing:

"Mother dear! My friend! Give me your blessing!"

But Arina Petrovna did not hear him. Her wide-open eyes stared dimly into space as if she were trying to understand something and could not.

Yudushka, too, did not understand. He did not understand that the yawning grave was to carry off the last creature that linked him to the living world.

With his usual bustle he delved into the mass of trifles and details that were incident upon the ceremonial of burial. He had requiems chanted, ordered memorial masses for the future, discussed matters with the priest, hurried from room to room with his shambling gait. Every now and then he peeped into the dining-room where the deceased lay, crossed himself, lifted his hands heavenward, and late at night stole quietly to the door to listen to the sexton's monotonous reading of the Psalms. He was pleasantly surprised that his expenses upon the occasions would be very slight, for Arina Petrovna long before her death had put away a sum of money for her burial and itemized in detail the various expenditures.

Having buried his mother, Porfiry Vladimirych at once began to familiarize himself with her effects. Examining the papers he found about a dozen various wills (in one of them she called him "undutiful"); but all of them had been written when Arina Petrovna was still the domineering, despotic mistress, and were incomplete—in the form of tentative drafts.

So Yudushka was quite pleased that he had no need to play foul in order to declare himself the sole legitimate heir to his mother's property. The latter consisted of a capital of fifteen thousand rubles and of a scanty movable estate which included the famous coach that had nearly become the cause of dissension between mother and son. Arina Petrovna kept her own accounts quite separate and distinct from those of her wards, so that one could see at a glance what belonged to her and what to the orphans. Yudushka lost no time in declaring himself heir at the proper legal places. He sealed the papers bearing on the guardianship, gave the servants his mother's scanty wardrobe, and sent the coach and two cows to Golovliovo, which were placed in the inventory under the heading "mine." Then he had the last requiem performed and went his way.

"Wait for the owners," he told the people gathered in the hallway to see him off. "If they come, they'll be welcome; if they don't—just as they please. For my part, I did all I could. I straightened out the guardianship accounts and hid nothing. Everything was done in plain view, in front of everybody. The money that mother left belongs to me legally. The coach and the two cows that I sent to Golovliovo are mine *by law*. Maybe some of my property is left *here*. However, I won't insist on it. God Himself commands us to give to orphans. I am sorry to have lost mother, she was a good old woman, a kindly soul. Oh, mother dear, it was not right of you, darling, to have left us poor orphans. But if it had pleased God to take you, it befits us to submit to His holy will. May, at least, your soul rejoice in heaven, and as for us—well, we are not to be considered."

The first death was soon followed by another.

Yudushka's attitude toward his son's fate was quite puzzling. Since he did not receive newspapers and was not in correspondence with anybody, he could not learn anything of the trial in which Petenka figured. And he hardly wished to. Above all things, he shunned disturbance of every kind. He was buried up to his ears in a swamp of petty details, all centering around the welfare and preservation of his precious self. There are many such people in this world. They live apart from the rest of humanity, having neither the desire nor the knowledge to identify themselves with a "cause," and bursting in the end like so many soap bubbles. They have no ties of friendship, for friendship presupposes the existence of common interests; nor do they have any business connections. For thirty years at a stretch Porfiry Vladimirych had marked time in a government office. Then, one fine day he disappeared, and no one noticed the fact.

He learned of his son's fate after his domestics had. But even then he feigned ignorance, so that when Yevpraksia once tried to mention Petenka, he waved her off and said:

"No, no, no! I don't know, I did not hear anything, and I don't want to hear anything. I don't want to know a thing about his dirty affairs."

But finally he did learn about Petenka. He received a letter from him saying he was about to leave for one of the remote provinces and asking his father to continue to send him an allowance in his new position. The whole of the next day Porfiry Vladimirych was in a state of visible perplexity. He darted from room to room, peeped into the oratory, crossed himself, and sighed. But toward evening he plucked up courage and wrote the following letter:

> "My criminal son Piotr:
>
> "As a faithful and law-abiding subject I should not even answer your letter. But as a father given to human weaknesses, I cannot, from a sense of compassion, refuse good advice to a child who, through his own fault, plunged himself into a whirlpool of evil.
>
> "Here, in short, is my opinion on the subject. The punishment that has been meted out to you is severe, but you quite deserve it. That is the first and most important consideration that should always accompany you in your new life from now on. All your other vagaries and even the memory thereof you must forget, for in your present situation all this will only tend to irritate you and urge you on to impious complaint. You have already tasted of the bitter fruits of haughtiness of spirit. Try now to taste of the fruits of humility, all the more so since there is nothing else left for you in the future. Do not complain of the punishment, for the authorities do not even punish you, but only provide means for your correction. To be grateful for this, and to endeavor to make amends for what you did—that is what you must incessantly bear in mind, and not the luxurious

frittering away of time, which I myself, by the way, never did, although I was never under indictment. So follow this prudent advice of mine and turn over a new leaf, satisfied with what the authorities, in their kindness, will deem it necessary to allot to you. I, for my part, will pray the Giver of all things good to grant you firmness and humility. Even on the very day on which I write these lines I have been to church and offered up fervent prayers for you. And now, I bless you for the new journey and remain, your indignant but still loving father, Porfiry Golovliov."

It is uncertain whether the letter ever reached Petenka, but no more than a month after it was sent, Porfiry Vladimirych was officially notified that his son, while on his way to the place of exile, had fallen ill and died in a hospital.

Yudushka remained alone, but at first did not realize that this new loss had made his life an absolute void. The realization came soon after the death of Arina Petrovna, when he was all absorbed in reckoning and figuring. He read every paper of the deceased, took into account every kopek, traced the relation of this kopek to the kopeks of the guardianship, not wishing, as he put it, either to acquire another's, or to lose his own. Amidst this bustle the question never once arose in his mind: To what end was he doing all this, and who was to enjoy the fruits of his busy hoarding?

From morning to night he bent over his desk musing and criticizing the arrangements of the deceased. Engrossed in these cares he began little by little to neglect the bookkeeping of his own estate.

The manor fell into profound silence. The domestics, who had always preferred the servants' quarters, abandoned the house almost entirely, and when in the master's rooms would walk on tiptoe and speak in a whisper. There was an air of desertion and death about the place and about the man, something eery. The gloom enveloping Yudushka was to grow denser every day.

CHAPTER II

During Lent, when no theatrical performances were given, Anninka came to Golovliovo. Lubinka had been unable to accompany her because she had been engaged for the entire Lent and had gone to Romny, Izum, Kremenchug, etc., where she was to give concerts and sing her entire music-hall repertoire.

During her brief artistic career Anninka had greatly improved in looks. She was no longer the simple, anæmic, somewhat sluggish girl who in Dubrovino or Pogorelka had walked from room to room humming and swaying awkwardly, as if she could not find a place for herself. She was now quite developed, with confident, even dashing manners. At the very first glance one could tell she was quick at repartee. The change in her appearance gave Porfiry Vladimirych a pleasant surprise. Before him stood a tall, well-built woman with a lovely pink complexion, high, well-developed bust, full eyes, and abundant ash-colored hair, which she wore braided low on her neck—a woman evidently aware of her own attractiveness.

She arrived at Golovliovo early in the morning and at once retired to a room, from which she emerged in a splendid silk gown. She entered the dining-room with a swish of her train, manipulating it skilfully among the chairs. Though Yudushka loved God above all, it did not prevent him from having a taste for beautiful and, especially, tall, plump women. So he crossed Anninka first, then kissed her so emphatically on both cheeks, casting queer glances at her bust meanwhile, that Anninka could not refrain from smiling faintly.

They sat down at the tea table. Anninka raised her arms and stretched.

"Oh, uncle, how dull it is here!" she began, yawning slightly.

"There you are! Here only a minute and dull already. You stay with us some time, then we'll see, perhaps you won't find it so dull after all," answered Porfiry Vladimirych, his eyes suddenly taking on an oily glitter.

"No, there isn't an interesting thing here. What is there? Snow all around, no neighbors. Is there a regiment quartered anywhere near here?"

"Yes, there is a regiment and there are neighbors; but, to tell the truth, it doesn't interest me. Yet, if you——"

Porfiry Vladimirych looked at her and did not end his sentence, but coughed. Perhaps he had stopped intentionally, wishing to excite her feminine curiosity. At any rate the same faint smile as before glided over her lips. She leaned her elbows on the table and looked at Yevpraksia fixedly. The, girl all flushed, was drying the glasses, casting sly glances at Anninka with her large, heavy eyes.

"My new housekeeper—very industrious," said Porfiry Vladimirych.

Anninka nodded slightly and began to purr softly:

"Ah, ah! que j'aime—que j'aime—que j'aime—les mili-mili-mili-taires!" and her hips quivered as she sang.

Silence set in, during which Yudushka, his eyes meekly lowered, sipped his tea from a glass.

"My, it's dull!" said Anninka, yawning again.

"It's dull, and it's dull! You never get tired of saying that. You wait a while, stay here a bit longer. We'll order the sleigh set to rights, and you'll ride to your heart's content."

"Uncle, why didn't you become a hussar?"

"Because, my friend, every man has his station ordained by the Lord. Some are to become hussars, others functionaries, others merchants; some are——"

"Oh, yes, and so on, and so forth. Who can keep track of it all? And God ordained all that, did He?"

"Why, yes, my friend, God. And it is not proper to scoff. Do you know what the Scriptures say? 'Without the will of God——'"

"Is it about the hair? Yes, I know that, too. But the trouble is, everybody wears false hair now, and I don't think that was foreseen. By the way, uncle, look what wonderful braids I have! Don't you think they're fine?"

Porfiry Vladimirych came nearer, for some reason, on tiptoe, and fingered her braids for some time. And Yevpraksia, without relaxing her hold on the saucer filled with tea and holding a bit of toast between her teeth, leaned forward and said, "False, I suppose?"

"Oh, no, my own. Some day I'll let my hair down for you, uncle."

"Yes, your hair is fine," said Yudushka, his lips parting in a repulsive smile. Then he recalled that one must turn his back on such temptations and added, "Oh, you hoyden! Always thinking about braids and trains, but you'd never think of inquiring about the main thing, the real thing?"

"Oh, about grandmother? She is dead, isn't she?"

"Yes, my friend, she died. And how she died! Peacefully, calmly, not a soul heard it. That's what I call a worthy end to one's earthly life. She thought of everybody, gave everybody her blessing, called a priest, received her last communion, and suddenly became so calm, so calm! Then she began to sigh. Sighed once, twice, three times, and before we knew it, she was no more."

Yudushka rose, turned toward the ikon, folded his hands, and offered up a prayer. Tears rose to his eyes, so well did he simulate. But Anninka apparently was not of the sentimental kind. It is true she remained pensive for a while but for quite a different reason.

"Do you remember, uncle, how she used to feed my sister and me on sour milk when we were little ones? Not later. Later she was splendid. I mean when she was still rich."

"Oh, well, let bygones be bygones. She fed you on sour milk, but you look none the worse for it, may the Lord be with you. Do you think you would care to visit her grave?"

"Yes, I wouldn't mind."

"But you know, it would be well if you purified yourself first."

"What do you mean, purified?"

"You know—an actress. You think it was easy for the old woman? So before you go to her grave I think you should attend a mass to purify yourself, you know. You see, I'll order a mass early tomorrow morning, and then—Godspeed!"

Absurd as Yudushka's proposition was, it confused Anninka for a minute. But she soon knitted her brows angrily and said sharply:

"No, I'll go now—as I am!"

"Well, I don't know, do as you please. But my advice is: let's attend the mass tomorrow morning, then take tea and have a pair of swift little horses hitched to a pony cart, and then go together. You see, you would become cleansed of your sins, and your grandmother's soul would——"

"Oh, uncle, how foolish you are, though. Lord knows what nonsense you talk. And you even insist on it."

"So you don't like it? Well, don't hold it against me, my dear. I am straight from the shoulder, you know. When it comes to truth, I'll tell it to others and take it from others as well. Though at times it goes against the grain, though truth is hard at times, but I'll always listen to it. And one must listen to it, because—it's the truth. So, my dear. You stay with us a while and live the way we do. Then you'll see that it's better than going with a guitar from fair to fair."

"Heaven knows what you're talking about, uncle. 'With a guitar!'"

"Well, if it isn't a guitar, then it's a bagpipe or something. Besides, you offended me first, called me foolish. So I, an old man, surely have a right to tell you the truth to your face."

"All right, let it be the truth. We won't argue about it. But tell me, please, did grandmother leave anything?"

"Why, of course, she did. But the legitimate heir was present in person."

"That is you. All the better. Was she buried here in Golovliovo?"

"No, near Pogorelka, at the St. Nicholas Church. It was her own wish."

"I'll go. Can I hire horses here, uncle?"

"Why hire? I've got my own. You are not a stranger, I dare say, a niece, my little niece."

Porfiry Vladimirych began to liven up, and put on an *en famille* grin. "A pony cart, a pair of fine little horses—thank God, I am not poor, I dare say! And wouldn't it be well for me to go with you? We would visit the grave, you see, and then would go to Pogorelka and peep in here and there, and we would think matters over, talk things over—about this and that. Yours is a fine little estate, you know. It has some very good spots."

"No, I'll go alone, I think. Why should you go? By the way, Petenka's dead, too, I hear?"

"Yes, my dear friend, Petenka is dead, too. I am sorry for him in one way, very sorry—to the point of tears; but then—it was all his own fault. He was always disrespectful to his father, that's why God punished him. And what God, in His great wisdom, did, you and I cannot undo."

"Of course, we can't. But what makes me wonder is, why you don't find it too horrible to live."

"Why should I fear? You see how much succor I have all around." Yudushka made a gesture, pointing to the ikons. "Succor here and succor in my study. The ikon room is a veritable paradise. You see how many protectors I have."

"But still, you are always alone. It's frightful."

"And if I am afraid, I fall on my knees, say a prayer, and the fear is all gone. And why be afraid? It's light during the day, and at night I have ikon lamps burning in every room. From outside in the dark it looks as if there were a ball in the house. And what ball? Who are the guests? Holy protectors, God's chosen. Those are my guests!"

"You know, Petenka wrote to us before his death."

"Well, of course, he is a relative. It's a good thing he did not lose his feelings of kinship."

"Yes, he wrote to us. It was after the trial, when sentence had been pronounced. He wrote he had lost three thousand rubles in cards and you would not give him the money. But you are rich, uncle, aren't you?"

"Ah, my dear, it's easy to count money in another man's pocket. Sometimes we think a man has mountains of gold, and when you come closer you see he has barely enough for oil and a candle—not for himself—for God."

"Well, then, we are richer than you. We gave some of our own money and took up a collection among our gentlemen friends. We scraped six hundred rubles together and sent it to him."

"What do you mean 'gentlemen friends?'"

"Oh, uncle, we are actresses, you know. Didn't you yourself suggest that I purify myself?"

"I don't like it when you speak that way."

"What can you do? Whether you like it or not, you can't undo what has been done. According to you, God is in that, too."

"Don't blaspheme at least. You may say anything you want, but don't blaspheme. I won't stand for it. Where did you send the money to?"

"I don't remember. To a little town of some sort. He wrote us the name."

"I didn't know. If there was money, I should have gotten it after his death. It is not possible that he spent it all at once. Well, I don't know, I didn't get any. I suppose the jailers and guards were on to it."

"I'm not asking for it, uncle. I just mentioned it while we were on the subject. It's awful, uncle, for a man to perish on account of three thousand rubles."

"It wasn't all on account of the three thousand. Haven't you something else to say than to keep on repeating 'three thousand, three thousand?' But God——"

Yudushka had got his cue and was about to explain in detail how God—Providence—by unseen ways—and all that, but Anninka unceremoniously yawned and said:

"Oh, uncle, how boring it is here."

This time Porfiry Vladimirych was truly offended and became silent. For a long time they both paced up and down the dining room. Anninka yawned, Porfiry Vladimirych crossed himself at every step. At last the carriage was announced and the usual comedy of seeing relations off began. Golovliov put on his fur coat, went out on the porch, kissed Anninka and shouted to the servants, "Her feet! Wrap up her feet well!" and "What about the blankets, have you taken the blankets along? See you don't forget them!" all the while making signs of the cross in the air.

Anninka visited her grandmother's grave, asked the priest to say the mass, and when the choir began to chant the "Eternal memory," she cried a bit. The background of the ceremony was rather sad. The church near which Arina Petrovna had been buried was of the poorest kind. In some places the plaster had fallen off its walls and exposed large patches of brick. The sound of the bells was feeble and hollow, the priest's robe was threadbare. The cemetery was snowed under, so that the path to the grave had to be shovelled clear. No monument had yet been placed. Nothing but a plain white cross, even without an inscription, marked the grave. The cemetery was in a lonely spot removed from any dwelling. Not far from the church stood the houses of the priest and the church officials and all around the cheerless, snow-covered plains stretched as far as the eye could reach. Here and there one could see brushwood jutting out from the snow. A sharp March wind was sweeping over the churchyard, wafting away the chanting of the churchmen and lashing the priest's robe.

"Who would have thought, madam, that the richest landlady in the district would rest here under this modest cross in our poor parish?" said the priest when he was through with the requiem.

At these words Anninka cried again. She recalled the poet's line: "Where feasts once reigned a hearse now stands!" And the tears kept streaming down her cheeks. Then she went to the priest's house, had tea there, and talked with his wife. Another line came back to her: "And pallid death on all doth stare," and again she wept, long and bitterly.

Nobody had notified the people at Pogorelka that the young lady was coming, so that the rooms were not even heated. Anninka, with her fur coat on, walked through all the rooms, remaining a moment in grandmother's bedroom and the ikon room. In the former she found a bedstead with a heap of soiled, greasy pillows, some without pillow-cases. Scraps of paper lay on the desk in disorder, the floor had not been swept and a thick coat of dust covered everything. Anninka sat down in the easy-chair where her grandmother used to sit, and became lost in thought. At first came up reminiscences of the past; then they were crowded out by images of the present. The former came in the shape of fleeting patches and fragments, pausing in her mind for no more than a moment; the latter were more persistent. It was but a brief while ago that she had longed to flee from Pogorelka and it had seemed a hateful place. Now her heart suddenly filled with a morbid desire to live there again.

"It is quiet here, it is not cozy, and it is unsightly; but it is quiet, so quiet, as if everything around were dead. There is much air and much room."

She looked out over the endless fields and felt a desire to dash straight across them, without aim or purpose, just to breathe fast and feel a pain in her chest. And *there,* in the half-nomadic life from which she had just escaped and to which she *must* return—what awaited her there? What had she gained by it? Nothing but recollections of hotels permeated with stench, of an everlasting din coming from the dining and billiard rooms, of unkempt porters, of rehearsals on the stage in the twilight and among the scenes of painted linen, the feel of which was abominable, in the draught and in the dampness. And then, army officers, lawyers, obscene language, and the eternal uproar! What hadn't the men told her! With what obscenity hadn't they touched her! Especially the one with the mustache, with a voice hoarse from drink, inflamed eyes, and a perpetual smell of the stable about him. Lord, what he had told her! Anninka shivered at the very recollection and shut her eyes. Then she came to, sighed, and went into the ikon room. There were now only a few ikons in the image-case, only those which had unquestionably belonged to her mother. The rest of them, her grandmother's, Yudushka, as the legitimate heir, had removed to Golovliovo. The empty spaces where they had stood stared like the hollow eye-sockets in a deathshead. Nor were there any ikon lamps. Yudushka had taken all of them. Only one yellow bit of wax candle stood out, orphan-like, from a miniature tin candlestick that had been forgotten.

"His Excellency wanted to take the image case, too. He was trying to make sure if it really was a part of madam's dowry," reported Afimyushka.

"Well, he could have taken it. Tell me, Afimyushka, did grandma suffer much before she died?"

"No, not much, she was laid up for only a day or so. She just went out, of her own self. She wasn't really sick or anything. She didn't talk either, just mentioned you and your sister once or twice."

"So Porfiry Vladimirych carried off the ikons?"

"Yes, he did. He said they were his mother's personal property. He also took the coach and two cows. From the mistress's papers he gathered,

I suppose, that they belonged to your grandmother, not to you. He also wanted to take away a horse, but Fedulych would not give it to him. 'It's our horse,' he said, 'an old-timer in Pogorelka.' So Porfiry Vladimirych left it here. He was afraid."

Anninka walked through the yard, peeped into the servants' quarters, the barn, and the cattle yard. In a swamp of manure stood about twenty lean cows and three horses. She ordered some bread to be brought, saying, "I'll pay for it," and gave every cow a piece of bread.

Then the cattle-house woman invited the young lady into the house. There was a jug of milk on the table, and in the corner near the oven, behind a low wainscot screening, a new-born calf was sheltered.

Anninka tasted some milk, ran to the little calf, kissed his snout, but quickly wiped her lips, saying the calf had a horrid snout, all slabbery. At the end, she produced three yellow bills from her pocketbook, distributed them to the old domestics, and prepared to go.

"What are you going to do?" she asked, while she made herself comfortable in the pony cart, of old Fedulych, who, as the *starosta*, followed the young owner, with his hands crossed on his breast.

"Well, what can we do? We'll live," answered Fedulych simply.

Anninka became sad again for a moment. There seemed to be irony in Fedulych's words. She waited a while, sighed, and said:

"Well, good-by."

"We thought that you would come back and live with us," said Fedulych.

"No, what's the use? Anyway—you live on!"

Tears flowed from her eyes again and the others cried, too. It seemed peculiar to her; there was nothing to regret in leaving the place, nothing sentimental to remember it by, and yet she was crying. And those people, too. She had not said anything out of the ordinary to them—just the usual questions and answers—and yet their hearts were heavy, they were sorry to see her go. She was seated in the cart, wrapped up and well covered. Everybody heaved a sigh. "Good luck!" came running after her when the cart started. Passing the churchyard she stopped again and went to the grave alone without the ecclesiastics, following the path that had been cleared. It was quite dark, and lights began to appear in the houses of the church officials. She stood there with one hand holding on to the cross rising from the grave. She did not cry, but only swayed slightly, thinking of nothing in particular, unable to formulate any definite thought. But she was unhappy, in every way unhappy. Not because of grandmother, but on her own account. So she stood for a quarter of an hour, and suddenly before her eyes rose the image of Lubinka, who perhaps at that very moment was singing merrily in a rollicking company, somewhere in Kremenchug:

> *"Ah, ah, que j'aime, que j'aime!*
> *Que j'aime, les mili-mili-mili-taires!"*

She almost broke down. She ran to her cart, seated herself, and ordered the coachman to drive to Golovliovo as fast as possible.

CHAPTER III

When Anninka returned to her uncle's, she was dull and silent, though she did feel a bit hungry (in the hurry, uncle had not given her some chicken to take along) and was very glad the table was already set for tea. Of course, Porfiry Vladimirych was not slow to open a conversation.

"Well, were you there?"

"Yes, I was."

"Did you pray at the grave? Did you have the requiem sung?"

"Yes."

"So the priest was at home?"

"Of course he was, or who would have performed the requiem?"

"Oh, yes, certainly. And the two sextons, were they there? Did they sing: 'Eternal memory?'"

"Yes, they did."

"Yes, eternal memory! May she rest in peace. She was a good, kind woman."

Yudushka rose from his seat, faced the ikon and offered up a prayer.

"Well, and how did you find things in Pogorelka, everything in good shape?"

"I don't know, really. I think everything is in its proper place."

"Indeed, 'I think.' You always 'think,' but when you take a good look you find this is wrong and that is wrong. That's how we judge of other people's business. We 'think' and we 'guess!' But anyway, you've got a nice little estate. My late mother fixed it all up very nicely. She even spent a good deal of her own money on it. Well, it's only right to help orphans along."

Listening to these chants of praise, Anninka could not refrain from teasing her kindhearted uncle.

"Uncle, why did you take two cows away from Pogorelka?" she asked.

"Cows, what cows? Oh, you mean the black and the spotted one? Well, my dear, they belonged to my mother."

"And you are her legitimate heir? Oh, well, you can have them. Do you want me to send you a little calf? I will, if you want me to."

"Now, there! Look at her getting excited! Let's talk business, whom do you think the cows belong to?"

"How do I know? They were in Pogorelka."

"And I do know. I have proof that the cows belonged to mother. I found a memorandum written in her own hand. 'Mine,' is plainly written there."

"Oh, let's drop it. It isn't worth talking about."

"There's a pony at Pogorelka, too, little old Baldy, you know. Well, about Baldy I am not sure. I think Baldy belonged to mother, but I'm not sure. And I can't speak of what I don't know."

"Let's drop it, uncle."

"No, why drop it? I'm straight from the shoulder, my dear, I like to bring out the truth of things. Why not talk it over? Nobody wants to part with his own. I don't, you don't. Well, then, let's talk it over and see who's right. And when it comes to talking, I'll tell you plainly: I don't want what's yours and I won't let go of mine, either. Because, though you are not a stranger to me, still I— —"

"And you even took the ikons," Anninka could not refrain from remarking.

"Yes, the ikons, too. I took everything that belonged to me by law."

"Now the image case looks as if it has holes in it."

"What can you do? You'll have to pray before it as it is. God, you know, does not want your image case, but your prayers. If you are sincere about it, your prayer will reach Him, even if it's done before poor ikons. And if you just pray without meaning it, and look around and make a courtesy, then the best images will be of no avail."

Nevertheless, Yudushka rose and offered thanks to God for the fact that his images were "good."

"Well, and if you don't like the old image case, have a new one built and put in new ikons instead of those taken out. My deceased mother acquired the old ikons at her own cost, and now it's up to you to get new ones."

Porfiry Vladimirych even tittered, so clear and simple did his reasoning seem to him.

"But tell me, please, what am I to do now?" Anninka asked.

"Well, wait a while. Rest up first, loll around, get some sleep. We'll talk the matter over and examine it from every angle, and we'll see what can be done. Both of us together may think up something."

"Sister and I are of age, I think?"

"Yes, of age. Quite so. You can now manage yourself and your estate."

"Thank God at least for that."

"I have the honor to congratulate you."

Porfiry Vladimirych rose to kiss her.

"How funny you are, uncle, always kissing."

"Why shouldn't I kiss you? You are not a stranger, I may say, you are my niece. I like kinsfolk, my dear. I am always for my relatives, near or distant, second, third, or fourth cousins, I'm always with them."

"You'd better tell me what I am to do. Must I go to town and see all the officials?"

"Yes, and we'll go to town and we'll attend to the matter—all in due time. But before we do that, rest up a bit. Stay here a while. You are not stopping at an inn but at your uncle's, I may say. You'll have enough to eat and drink, and for your sweet tooth we've got plenty of everything. If you don't like a dish, ask for a different one. Demand, insist! If you don't care for cabbage soup, ask for chicken soup. Order cutlets, duck, pork. Get after Yevpraksia. Here I boasted about pork and I don't really know if we've got any. Have we?"

Yevpraksia, holding the saucer with the hot tea to her mouth, nodded affirmatively.

"Well, you see, we've got pork too, and all in all you can have whatever your heart desires."

Yudushka approached Anninka again and like a good relative clapped her on the knee and quite inadvertently let his hand rest there a little, so that Anninka instinctively recoiled.

"But I've got to go," she said.

"That's just what I've been saying. We'll discuss matters and talk things over and then we'll go with a prayer and a benediction, but not—hop! jump! run! The more haste the less speed. You may hurry to a fire, but our house is not ablaze. Well, Lubinka has got to hurry to the fair, but what is your hurry? Another thing I meant to ask you, Are you going to live in Pogorelka?"

"No, there's nothing for me to do there."

"That's just what I was going to say. Move here, to my house. We'll live here and have a fine time of it."

Yudushka looked at Anninka with such oily eyes that she became embarrassed.

"No, uncle, I don't want to stay here with you. It's too dull."

"Oh, you silly little thing! Why do you keep repeating 'dull, dull?' You speak of dullness and I'll bet you don't know what's dull around here. If you have something to keep you busy, and if you know how to manage yourself, you'll never feel dull. Take me, for example, I don't notice how time flies. On week days I'm busy with the affairs of the estate. I look at this and take a peep into that, and figure out one thing and discuss another thing. Before I know it, the day is gone. And on a holiday—to church! You will do the same thing. Stay with us for a while. We'll find something for you to do. In your leisure time you may play fool with Yevpraksia, or go sleigh-riding—slide along as fast as you wish. And when summer comes we'll go to the woods picking mushrooms. And we'll have tea on the lawn."

"No, uncle, it's no use trying to persuade me."

"Really, you ought to stay."

"No. But the journey has tired me, so I should like to go to bed if possible."

"Yes, you can go rock-a-by. I've got a nice little bed ready for you, everything in proper fashion. If you want to go rock-a-by, go right ahead. But I should advise you to think the matter over. I think it would be best for you to stay with us at Golovliovo."

CHAPTER IV

Anninka spent a restless night. The hysterical mood that had overtaken her at Pogorelka still persisted. There are moments when a person who has been merely existing suddenly realizes that there is a vile ulcer of some kind festering in his life. Where it came from, how it formed itself—one cannot always explain to oneself. In most cases it is not ascribed to the causes that have really brought it on. But an explanation is not even needed. It is sufficient that such an ulcer exists. The effects of such a sudden discovery, while equally painful to everyone, vary in their practical results, with the individual's temperament. Some are rejuvenated and inspired with a determination to begin a new life on new foundations. Others feel but a passing pain that will not bring a profound change for the better, but is even sharper than when the disturbed conscience sees the faint hope of a brighter future.

Anninka was not of those in whom the consciousness of ulcers produces the impulse to rejuvenation. Nevertheless, she realized, being an intelligent person, that there was an abyss between the vague dreams of honest toil which had impelled her to leave Pogorelka forever and her position of provincial actress. Instead of a life of quiet and toil, she had fallen upon a stormy existence, filled with perpetual debauchery, shameless obscenity and cynicism, with vain and everlasting bustle. Instead of the privations and stern surroundings in which she had once lived, she had met comparative ease and comfort. She could not think of it now without a blush of shame. She had hardly noticed the gradual transformation. She had wanted to go to a good place but had entered the wrong door. Her desires had been very modest, indeed. How often she had dreamed, in the attic of Pogorelka, of becoming an earnest girl, working, thirsting for education, bearing hardships with fortitude, all for the sake of the good. (It is true, "good" hardly had definite meaning to her.) But as soon as she had stepped out on to the highroad of independent activity, bitter reality had shattered her dreams at once. An honest livelihood does not come of itself, but is attained only by persistent search and previous training which help in the quest to some extent. But neither Anninka's temperament nor education provided her with this. Her temperament was not marked by passion, it was simply sensitive. The material that her education had given her and on which she meant to build up her life of honest toil was so unreliable and poor that it could hardly serve as a basis for serious work. Her education was of the boarding-school, music-hall kind, with the balance tipping to the side of the music-hall. It was a chaotic heap in which problems were piled up about a flock of geese, dancing steps with a shawl, the sermons of Peter of Picardy, the exploits of Fair Helen, the *Ode to Felitza,* and the prescribed feeling of gratitude to the instructors and patrons of the institution. What was left clear of this chaotic jumble in her soul might quite properly be called a *tabula rasa.* There was scarcely a thing to be read in it; it certainly offered no possibility of finding a starting-point in her for better things. Whatever preparation she had had inspired not love for work but love for a "society" life, the desire to be surrounded by admirers and listen to their flattery, the desire to plunge into the social din, glamor and whirlwind.

If she had listened to herself, she would have discovered that even in Pogorelka, when just beginning to make plans for a life of honest toil as a deliverance from Egyptian bondage, she could have caught herself dreaming not so much of work as of being surrounded by a society of congenial people, frittering her time away in empty talk. Of course, the people of her dreams were clever, and their conversation was honest and serious, but the idle side of life was always in the foreground. Poverty was distinguished by neatness, privations amounted merely to a lack of luxuries. So, when her dreams of a life of work came to a head and she was offered a part in one of the provincial theatres, she hesitated little, though the contrast between dream and reality was great. She hastily freshened up her school information about the relations of Helen and Menelaus, supplemented it by some biographical details from the life of the splendid Prince of Tauris and decided that that was quite sufficient to produce *Fair Helen* and *Episodes from the Life of the Duchess of Herolstein* in the provincial theatres and at the fairs. To clear her conscience she recalled the words of a student she had met in Moscow who used to exclaim repeatedly, "Sacred Art!" She made this her slogan, because it was the easiest way out, and gave at least outward decorum to the path she had chosen—the path toward which the whole of her being was instinctively tending.

The life of an actress upset her. Alone, without the guidance of proper preparation, without a conscious aim, with only a temperament craving for din, glamor, and applause, she soon found herself surrounded by a chaos in which many persons thronged, some coming, others going, without apparent order or connection. There were people of the most diverse characters and views, so that the motives for becoming intimate with this one or that one were not the same. Nevertheless, they were all integral parts of her circle, so that there really could be no question of motives.

Her life had become like the gate to an inn, at which every gay, wealthy, young man could knock and claim entrance. Clearly it was not a matter of selecting a congenial company, but of fitting into any kind of company so as not to die of ennui. Her "sacred art" had really thrown her into a mire, but her head was turned, and she did not notice her position. Neither the dirty faces of the porters nor the slimy, dilapidated stage properties, nor the din, stench, and noise of the hotels and inns, nor the obscene behavior of her admirers—none of these things produced a sobering effect. She did not even notice that she was always in the society of men only, and that there was a permanent barrier between her and the women of *established position*.

The visit to Golovliovo sobered her for a moment.

In the morning, almost immediately after her arrival, she began to feel uneasy. Highly impressionable, she quickly absorbed new sensations and quickly adapted herself to new situations. Consequently, as soon as she reached Golovliovo, she felt herself a "lady." She suddenly recalled that she had something of her own: her own home, her own graves. She became filled with a desire to see herself in her former surroundings, to breathe the air from which she had only recently fled. But her impression was immediately dispelled by contact with the reality she found there. Her experience in this was like that of a person who enters with a smile among friends he has not seen for a long time, and suddenly notices that everybody responds to his cordial greetings coldly. The nasty glances Yudushka cast at her figure reminded her that her position was questionable and not easy to change. When she remained alone, after the naïve questions of the Pogorelka servants, after the pious sighs of warning of the Pogorelka priest and his wife, after the fresh sermons of Yudushka, when she examined her impressions of the day at leisure, she became convinced that the former "lady" was gone forever and that from now on she was only an actress in a miserable provincial theatre, and the position of a Russian actress was not far removed from that of a street woman. Until now she had lived as if in a dream. She would go out half-naked in *Fair Helen*, would appear intoxicated in *Pericola*, would sing all sorts of indecencies in the *Episodes from the Life of the Duchess of Herolstein*, and would even regret that it was not the custom to represent *la chose* and *l'amour* on the stage, imagining how enticingly her hips would quiver and how alluring her every movement would be. But it had never occurred to her to give earnest thought to what she was doing. She had only tried to make everything appear "charming" and *chic* and at the same time please the army officers of the town regiment. But what it all meant, and what the sensation was that her quivering hips produced in the army officers, she did not consider. The army officers were the element that set the tone for the town, and she realized that her success depended upon them. They would intrude behind the scenes, would unceremoniously knock at the door of her dressing-room when she was yet half-clad, would address her in endearing terms—and she looked upon it all as a simple formality, an inevitable feature incidental to her profession. All she asked herself was whether she rendered a feature "charmingly" or not.

Until now she had not thought of her body or her soul as being public, but for a moment feeling herself a "lady" again, she looked on her past in utter disgust and abhorrence, as if she had been stripped naked and were being exposed on the public square; as if all those vile creatures infected with the odors of wine and the stable had suddenly gripped her in their embrace, as her body felt the contact of hands moist with perspiration, of slabbery lips and the dull, greedy, brutal eyes that lingered animal-like over the curved lines of her nude body.

Where was she to go? How was she to throw off that accumulated load, which began to leave its mark on her shoulders? The question tossed in her head desperately—tossed, indeed, for she neither found nor, as a matter of fact, sought an answer. This stay in Golovliovo, too, was a kind of dream. Her past life had been a dream, and her present awakening was a dream. Something had made the little girl ill at ease, and she had become sentimental—that was all. It would pass. There are pleasant moments and there are unpleasant ones—that is how they go. Both merely glide past but do not alter the course of life once determined upon. To give life a new course, to divert its channel, one needs not only moral but also physical courage. It is almost the same as suicide. Before attempting suicide a man may denounce his life, he may be certain that death is the only salvation, yet the weapon of death trembles in his hands, the knife slides harmlessly over the neck, the bullet, instead of striking the forehead, hits lower and only cripples. That is what happened in Anninka's case. She had to kill her former life, but though killing it, she herself had to remain alive. The "nothingness" that in regular suicide is attained by merely pressing the trigger, was to be attained in the peculiar suicide called rejuvenation only after many stern almost ascetic efforts.

A pampered person already undermined by the habit of easy living will turn dizzy at the mere perspective of a rejuvenation. He instinctively turns his head away and shuts his eyes. Then filled with shame and accusing himself of lack of courage, he will take the easy way again.

Oh, the life of toil is a glorious thing! Yet none but strong people can live it and those who are destined for it because of original sin. They are the only ones it does not frighten; the former because they realize the significance and resources of toil and can find pleasure in it; the latter, because to them toil is first a duty, then a habit.

Anninka did not think of remaining at Golovliovo or Pogorelka for even a moment. In this she was fortified by the business routine of her circumstances, to which she clung instinctively. She had been given leave of absence and had arranged her schedule ahead of time, even designating the day on which she was to leave Golovliovo. For people of weak wills the external checks upon their life considerably lighten its burdens. In difficult cases they cling to them instinctively and use them as a justification for their acts.

Anninka decided to leave Golovliovo as soon as possible, and if uncle persisted in his coaxing, to counter him by invoking the necessity of reporting for duty on the set date.

When she arose in the morning she walked leisurely through all the rooms of the vast Golovliovo mansion. She found them dreary, uninviting, deserted. There was an air of decay and haunting unfriendliness about them. The thought of living there indefinitely quite frightened her. "Never!" she kept repeating in a state of inexplicable agitation, "Never!"

CHAPTER V

The next day Porfiry Vladimirych greeted her again with his ambiguous geniality, from which it was impossible to gather whether he wanted to show her affection or suck her blood dry.

"Well, you 'always-in-a-hurry-to-get-there,' did you sleep well? And where are you hurrying to now?" he asked her jestingly.

"Yes, uncle, I am in a hurry, indeed. I am on leave of absence, you know, and I must report on time."

"Is it to play the clown again? I won't let you."

"Whether you let me or not, I am going."

Yudushka shook his head sadly. "And what would your deceased grandma say?" he asked in a tone of kindly reproach.

"Grandma knew about it when she was alive. But why do you use those expressions, uncle? Yesterday you were sending me to the fairs with a guitar and today you speak of playing the clown. I won't allow you to talk like that to me, you hear?"

"Eh-eh! The truth hurts! Well, and I like the truth. I think that if the truth——"

"No, no, I won't listen, I won't listen. I don't want your truth or your untruth. Do you hear me? I don't want you to talk like that to me."

"Well, well! Look at her flaring up! Oh, you romp! Suppose we go in to tea while the drinking is good. I suppose the samovar is making music on the table by now."

Porfiry Vladimirych wanted by joke and jest to make amends for having said "playing the clown," and even tried to embrace her as a sign of reconciliation. But it all seemed so stupid to Anninka, so abominable, that she declined his advance with repugnance.

"I tell you seriously, uncle, I am in a hurry," she said.

"Well, then, let's go and have tea first, then we'll talk."

"But why talk after tea? Why not now?"

"Because. Because everything has got to be done in its proper time. First one, then the other, first we'll have tea and a chat, then we'll talk business. Plenty of time."

She could not help but yield. His prattle was not to be overcome. They went in to tea, and Yudushka temporized maliciously, sipping his tea with deliberation, crossing himself, slapping his thigh, babbling about his late mother dear, and so on.

"Well, now we can talk," he said at last. "Do you intend making a long visit here?"

"Not more than a week. I have to be in Moscow before returning to the company."

"A week is a long time, my dear. You can accomplish a lot in a week, and you can accomplish little. It depends on how you go about it."

"We'd better try and accomplish a great deal, uncle."

"That's just what I say. You can do a lot and you can do little, and sometimes you think you are doing little but before you look around, all the work is attended to. Here, for instance, you are in a hurry to go to Moscow, you've got business there, you say; and what the business is, you yourself don't know, I dare say. But the way I look on it is this, that you spend all your time here in real business instead of going to Moscow."

"No, I must go to Moscow because I want to see if I can't get on the stage there. And as to business, didn't you say we could accomplish a lot in a week?"

"Depending on how you go about it, my friend. If you go about it properly, all will be well and smooth, but if you don't go about it in a proper way, well, you'll strike a snag, and the thing will drag on."

"Well, you guide me, uncle."

"That's just it. When in need then 'You guide me, uncle,' but when not in need, then 'It's dull here, uncle, and I want to go away.' You can't say I'm not right."

"But please do tell me just what I am to do."

"Wait, don't be in a hurry! So, as I was saying, when uncle is needed, he is a dear and darling and a sweety, and when he is not needed he is no good. But you would never trust your uncle and ask him, 'What do you think, uncle dear, ought I to go to Moscow or not?'"

"How funny you are, uncle! I *must* go to Moscow, and suppose I ask your advice and you say no?"

"Well, if I say no, then stay here! It is not a stranger who says so. It's your uncle, and you may as well take your own uncle's advice. Oh, my friend! It's a good thing you've got an uncle. At least there is somebody to feel with you and to warn you when necessary. Think of others who have nobody. Nobody to feel with them, nobody to warn them. And they live all by themselves. And things happen to them—many things that happen in life, my dear."

Anninka wanted to reply, but realized it would be adding fuel to the fire, and remained silent. She sat there, her eyes turned despairingly at her uncle, who was going ahead under full steam.

"I wanted to tell you," Yudushka continued, "I don't like your going to those fairs, no, I don't like it a bit. Though you didn't relish my talking about guitars, I still must say—"

"But it is not enough to say 'I don't like.' Show me a way out."

"Stay with me. That's the way out."

"No, that never!"

"Why?"

"Because I have nothing to do here. What can I do here? Get up in the morning, have tea, at tea think that breakfast is coming, at breakfast think about dinner, and at dinner about afternoon tea. Then supper and then to sleep. No, one can die here."

"They all do it, my friend. First people have tea, after tea those who like to breakfast do so. I, for instance, don't like to have breakfast, so I don't. Then dinner, then afternoon tea, then to bed. Well, I don't see anything ridiculous or objectionable in it. But if I—"

"Nothing objectionable; but it is not after my heart."

"But if I had offended somebody, or misjudged or spoken ill, well, then, really it would be objectionable. But to have tea and breakfast and dinner—goodness! I guess, no matter how clever you are, you can't get along without food."

"Yes, well and good, but it is not after my heart."

"But don't measure things by your own yardstick. Take the advice of your elders. 'This I like, and that I don't like.' Now, you mustn't talk that way! You ought to say instead, 'If it please God, or 'if it does not please God'. That would be the proper kind of talk. Let's say, for instance, in Golovliovo we don't live according to God, if we go against Him, if we sin or question His wisdom, if we envy and do other evil things, well, then we are really guilty and deserve to be blamed. But here, too, it would have to be proved first that we really do not act according to God. And you come and say, 'It is not my style.' Now, take me as an example. There are many things that aren't my style. Here, for instance, I don't like the way you talk to me, the way you pooh-pooh my hospitality. Yet I keep mum. I want to persuade you in a quiet way, maybe you'll come to your senses. Maybe while I am jesting and talking lightly, along will come your guardian angel and lead you along the right path. You know, my friend, I am solicitous not of my welfare, but of yours. Ah, my friend, how bad of you! If, so to speak, I had offended you by word or deed, well, then you would have reason to complain. Though it behooves young people to heed even a sermon when it comes from their elders, yet had I offended you, I wouldn't mind your being angry. But here I am calm and quiet and easy. I don't say a word, but only try to figure out how to make things better and more comfortable for you and for others so that all may rejoice and be happy. And look how you greet my kindness! What you want to do, my dear, is not to be rash in your speech. First think, then pray to the Lord and implore His guidance. And then if, let's say for example—"

Porfiry Vladimirych expatiated in this strain for a long time. His words flowed like thick saliva. Anninka looked at him with instinctive fear and thought, "How is it that the gush of words does not choke him?" And for all his talk, her dear uncle did not utter a word of advice as to what she was to do in connection with the death of Arina Petrovna. She tried to bring the matter up at dinner and later at afternoon tea, but every time Yudushka spun a different web, so that Anninka was sorry she had resumed the conversation, and thought in anguish, "Will it ever end?"

After dinner, when Porfiry Vladimirych retired for his afternoon nap, Anninka remained alone with Yevpraksia and suddenly felt a desire to have a talk with her uncle's housekeeper.

She wanted to know why Yevpraksia did not find it horrible to live at Golovliovo and what gave her the strength to endure the torrents of meaningless words that uncle's mouth belched forth from morning to night.

"Do you find it dull here at Golovliovo, Yevpraksia?"

"Why should we find it dull? We are not of the gentlefolk."

"But still—always alone—no diversion, no pleasures—"

"What pleasures do I need? When it's dull, I look out of the window. I didn't have much merriment when I lived with father."

"Still, I suppose, it was better at home. You had friends, went visiting, played."

"Ah, what's the use!"

"And here with uncle. He says such dull things and he is so long-winded. Is he always like that?"

"Always, all day long the same way."

"And it doesn't bore you?"

"Why should it? I don't listen to him."

"But it's impossible not to listen at all. He may notice it and become offended."

"How can he tell? I look at him. He keeps on talking and I keep on looking and at the same time I think my own thoughts."

"What do you generally think about?"

"Different things. If I have to pickle gherkins, I think about gherkins. If I have to send someone to town, I think about town. Whatever the household needs, that's what I think about."

"So, I see, you live with uncle, but you are always alone?"

"Yes, as good as alone. Unless he sometimes wishes to play cards. Well, then we play cards. But even then he often stops in the middle of the game, puts the cards away and begins to talk. And I look at him. It was much livelier when Arina Petrovna was alive. When she was around he was afraid to talk too much, because the old woman would often cut him short. But now the liberties he takes are the limit."

"Well, you see, Yevpraksia, that's just the horror of it. It is frightful when a man talks and does not know what he says, why he talks and whether he'll ever get through. Doesn't it scare you?"

Yevpraksia looked at her as if struck by a new, wonderful idea.

"You're not the only one," she said. "Many people around here don't like him for the same thing."

"Is that so?"

"Yes. Even the servants. Not one of them can stay here long. He changes them almost every month. The clerks, too. And all on account of that."

"He annoys them?"

"Terribly. The drunkards—they stay because drunkards don't hear. You may blow a bugle, but it's as if they had their ears stuffed. But the trouble is, he doesn't like drunkards."

"Oh, Yevpraksia, and he is trying to persuade me to stay here."

"Well, madam, it really would be nice of you to stay a while. Maybe in your presence he would be ashamed."

"No. Thank you. I haven't the patience to look at him."

"Yes, of course, you are of the gentlefolk. You can have your own way, and at that I suppose you've got to dance to somebody's music."

"Oh, I should say so."

"Yes, I thought so. I meant to ask you another thing. Is it nice to be an actress?"

"You earn your own bread and butter. That's one good thing."

"And is it true, as Porfiry Vladimirych was telling me, that strangers embrace actresses about the waist?"

Anninka flushed up an instant.

"Porfiry Vladimirych does not understand," she said with irritation. "That's why he talks nonsense. He seems to have no notion that it's only play and not reality on the stage."

"And yet, even he, that is, Porfiry Vladimirych, when he saw you first, his mouth began to water. 'My niece,' and 'dear,' and 'darling,' like a gay blade. And his shameless eyes just devour you."

"Yevpraksia, why do you talk nonsense?"

"I? Oh, I don't care. You stay here and you'll see. And I—I don't care. I'll give up my position, and go back to father. It's dull here, anyway, you were right about it."

"It is silly for you to suppose that I am going to stay here. But you're right about one thing, Golovliovo certainly *is* a dull place. And the longer you stay here the duller you feel."

Yevpraksia turned pensive, then yawned and said:

"When I stayed with father I was very, very slim. Now, you see how stout I am, like an oven. So dullness does one good, after all."

"You won't stand it long, anyway. Remember what I say—you won't."

With this the conversation ended.

Luckily Porfiry Vladimirych did not hear it, otherwise he would have obtained a new and fruitful theme for his endless sermonizing.

Porfiry Vladimirych tortured Anninka for two whole days. He kept on saying, "Wait, don't be in a hurry! Quietly, easily. Say your prayers and receive your benediction," and so on. He tired her to death. Finally, on the fifth day, he was ready to go to town with her, though he found another way of tormenting his dear niece.

She was in her fur coat waiting for him in the vestibule, and he, as if to spite her, lingered a whole hour, dressing and washing and clapping his thighs and crossing himself, and walking back and forth, and sitting down, and giving orders. "Here—, or see to it—you know what I mean. See that nothing happens—you know."

He behaved as if he were leaving Golovliovo not for a few hours, but forever. Having tired everybody out, the men and horses who had been waiting at the porch for an hour and a half, his own throat at last got dry from gabbling, and he decided to start out.

The entire affair in town was concluded while the horses were eating their oats at the inn. Porfiry Vladimirych produced an account book, from which it appeared that when Arina Petrovna died the orphans had twenty thousand rubles or a trifle less in five per cent securities. Then the petition to remove the guardianship was filed, along with the papers testifying to the majority of the orphans, and the order was immediately issued to remove the guardianship and transfer both capital and land to the rightful owners. In the evening of the same day Anninka signed all the papers and inventories that Yudushka had prepared and when all was done, heaved a sigh of relief.

The remaining few days Anninka spent in the greatest agitation. She wanted to leave Golovliovo at once, but her uncle met her attempts with a jest, which, good-natured as it sounded, screened a stupid obstinacy that no human power could overcome.

"You yourself said you were going to stay a week. Then stay," he said. "I don't understand why you are in such a hurry. You don't have to pay rent, you are welcome without pay. You will have tea and dinner and anything your heart may desire."

"But, uncle, I must go," Anninka pleaded.

"You are on pins and needles, but I am not going to give you horses," jested Yudushka. "I just won't give you horses, and you'll have to be my prisoner. When the week is up, I won't say a word. We'll attend mass, and have a bite, and some tea, and a chat, and we'll take a good look at each other, and then—God speed you! But, see here, suppose we visit the grave at Voplino again. It would be best to take leave of your grandmother, you know. Maybe her soul will be of guidance to you."

"I shouldn't mind it," Anninka consented.

"So that's what we'll do. Early in the morning on Wednesday we'll attend mass here, then we'll have a bite before you go, and then my team will take you to Pogorelka. From there to Dvoriky you will go with your own team. You are a landlady yourself, I dare say. You've got your own horses."

She had to consent. There is something tremendously powerful in vulgarity. It catches a person unawares, and while he is staring in bewilderment, it has him in its clutches. When we pass a cesspool we close our noses and try not to breathe. We have to do the same violence to ourselves in an atmosphere saturated with idle chatter and vulgarity, deaden our sight, hearing, smell and taste, overcome all sensibility, turn into stone. Otherwise we run the danger of suffocation from the miasma of vulgarity.

Anninka understood this, a bit late, perhaps. At any rate, she decided to let the process of her liberation from the Golovliovo captivity take its own course. She was so thoroughly overcome by Yudushka's irresistible twaddle that she dared not resist when he, like a good relative, embraced her and stroked her back, saying as he did so:

"You see, now you are a good little girl."

She recoiled instinctively at the touch of his trembling bony hand creeping over her back, but was held back from any other expression of loathing by the hope that he might release her when the week was up.

Luckily for her Yudushka was not at all squeamish. He perhaps observed her impatient gestures but paid no attention to them. Evidently he adhered to the theory of sexual relationship epitomized in the saying, "Kiss me, whether you love me or not."

At last came the long expected day of departure. Anninka rose at about six o'clock, but Yudushka was already up and about. He had already performed the ceremonial of his morning prayers, and was sauntering from room to room in dressing-gown and slippers without any plan or purpose. He was visibly agitated, and when he met Anninka looked at her askew. It was almost full daylight, but the weather was bad. The sky was covered with massive dark clouds, from which a chilling sleet was drizzling. The road along the hamlet had turned black and was full of puddles—a forecast of roads impassable because of the thaw. A strong south wind was blowing, another indication of thawing weather. The trees had cast off their snowy mantles, and their nude wet tops swayed drearily. The barns in the yard looked black and slimy. Porfiry Vladimirych led Anninka to the window and pointed out the picture of spring's awakening.

"Does it really pay to go?" he asked. "Would it not be better to stay, after all?"

"Oh no, no!" she cried in a frightened voice. "The bad weather will soon be over."

"Hardly. If you start now I doubt if you will reach Pogorelka before seven o'clock. And in this thawing weather you cannot travel at night, you know. So you'll have to spend a night at Pogorelka anyway."

"Oh, no! I'll travel at night. I'll leave at once. I am brave, you know. And wait till one o'clock? Uncle, darling! Let me leave at once."

"And what would grandma say? 'That's the kind of granddaughter I have!' she'll say. 'She came here, romped about, and wouldn't even come to ask my blessing.'"

Porfiry Vladimirych stopped. For a while he shifted from one foot to the other, then looked at Anninka, then lowered his eyes. Apparently he was making up his mind about something.

"Wait, I'll show you something," he said at last, took a folded note from his pocket and gave it to Anninka. "Here, read this."

Anninka read:

"I was praying to-day, and I asked my good, kind God to leave me my good little Anninka. And the good, kind God said, 'Put your arm around good little Anninka's plump waist and press her close to your heart.'"

"Yes?" he asked turning slightly pale.

"Fi, how nasty!" she answered, looking at him in bewilderment.

Porfiry Vladimirych turned still paler and hissed through his teeth:

"I suppose, we must have hussars!" then crossed himself and shuffled out of the room.

In about fifteen minutes he returned and resumed his jesting as if nothing had happened.

"Well?" he asked. "Are you going to stop at Voplino? Will you go and say good-by to your old granny? Do, my dear, do. It is very good of you to have thought of your grandma. Never forget your kinsfolk, my dear, especially those who, in a manner of speaking, were willing to die for us."

They attended the mass and requiem services, ate some kutya in the church, then came home, ate some more kutya and sat down at the tea table. Porfiry Vladimirych, as if to spite her, sipped his tea more slowly than usual, and dragged his words out wearisomely, discoursing in the intervals between gulps. About ten o'clock they finished tea, and Anninka said imploringly:

"May I leave now, uncle?"

"And what about a bite? What about dinner? Did you really think your uncle would let you leave on an empty stomach? Nay, nay. We are not used to such things at Golovliovo. Why, mother dear would have refused to look at me again if she knew I let my own niece go without a morsel. Don't dare think of it. Why, it's impossible."

Again she had to surrender. An hour and a half passed, but there were no signs of preparation for dinner. Everybody was going about his business. Yevpraksia, her bunch of keys jingling, was seen in the yard darting between the pantry and the cellar. Porfiry Vladimirych was explaining things to his clerk, wearying him with meaningless orders and incessantly slapping his own thighs in an effort to while away the time. Anninka, left to herself, walked up and down the dining-room, looked at the clock, counted her steps, then the ticks of the clock—one, two, three. At times she glanced out of the window and noticed the puddles were growing larger and larger.

Finally knives, forks and plates began to rattle. The butler Stepan entered the dining-room and spread a cloth upon the table. It seemed as if a part of Yudushka's idle bustle had communicated itself to him. He shuffled the plates sluggishly, breathed on the drinking glasses, and examined them, holding them up to the light. Dinner began just at one o'clock.

"Well, so you are going," Porfiry Vladimirych opened the conversation, in a manner befitting the occasion. Before him was a plate of soup, but he did not touch it. He looked at Anninka so affectionately that the tip of his nose turned red.

Anninka swallowed her soup hastily. At last he took up his spoon and dipped it in the soup, but changed his mind, and placed it back on the tablecloth.

"I am an old man, you'll have to pardon me," he began nagging, "you swallowed your soup in a gulp, but I must take it slowly. I don't like it when people are careless with God's gifts. God gave us bread for sustenance, and look how much of it you have wasted. Look at all the crumbs you scattered. Altogether, I like to do things thoroughly and carefully. It comes out safer in the end. Maybe it annoys you that I am not quick enough, that I can't jump through a hoop, or whatever you call it. Well, what can I do? If you feel like being annoyed, go ahead. I know you will be cross a little while and then forgive the old man. Remember, *you* are not going to be young always. You will not be jumping through hoops all of your life. Life will give you experience and teach you wisdom. Then you will say, 'Maybe uncle was right after all.' So, my dear, now while you listen to me, you probably think, 'Uncle is no good. Uncle is an old grouch.' But if you live to my old age, you'll pipe a different tune. You'll say, 'Uncle was nice. Uncle was a dear. Uncle taught me right.'"

Porfiry Vladimirych crossed himself and swallowed two spoonfuls of soup, then put his spoon down and leaned back in his chair as a sign of an ensuing monologue.

"Bloodsucker!" was on the tip of her tongue, but she pulled herself up, poured out a glass of water, and drank it at a gulp. Yudushka sensed her mental state.

"So, you don't like it? Well, like it or not, you'd better take uncle's advice. I've been long meaning to talk to you about your hasty way of doing things, but I could not find the time to do it. I don't like that haste in you. There is fickleness in it, a lack of judgment. When you left your old grandmother, you had no business to leave her and cause the old woman anxiety. I really don't see why you did it."

"Oh, uncle, why recall it? It's done. It isn't kind of you."

"Wait. That's not the point I'm making—kind or unkind—what I want to say is that even when a thing has been done, it can be undone, or done all over again. Not only we mortals, but even God alters His deeds. Now He sends rain, now He sends fair weather. So, suppose—really, the theatre isn't a good place—suppose you decide to stay."

"No, uncle, let's not speak about it, I beg of you."

"And there's another thing I want to tell you. Your fickleness is bad enough, but what is still worse is the way you slight the advice of your elders. I speak for your own good and you say, 'Let's not speak about it.' Uncle is kind and tender, and you snap at him. But do you know who gave you your uncle? Well, tell me—who?"

Anninka looked at him in perplexity.

"God gave you your uncle, that is who. God did it. If not for God, you would now be all alone in the world, you would not know how to manage things, or how to file a petition or where to file it, and what to expect from it. You would be lost in the woods. Anybody could deceive you, abuse you or even disgrace you. You see? And with the aid of God and your uncle the whole deal went through in one day. We went to town, and filed a petition and got the necessary mandates. You see, my dear, what uncle can do?"

"Yes, uncle, I am grateful to you."

"Well, if you are, don't snap at me, and do as I tell you. I mean your good, though at times it seems to you that— —"

Anninka could hardly control herself. There was one way left to rid herself of uncle's sermons—to feign that in principle she accepted his proposal to remain at Golovliovo.

"All right, uncle," she said, "I'll think it over. I myself feel it is not quite proper to live alone, far from relatives. But I can't make up my mind now— I'll have to think it over."

"Well, I am glad to see you have understood me, but what is there to think over? We'll have the horses unhitched, your trunks taken out of the cart—that's all the thinking there is to be done."

"No, uncle, you forget I have a sister."

Whether her argument convinced Porfiry Vladimirych or whether the whole scene had been staged for the mere show of it, it is hard to say. Porfiry Vladimirych himself did not know whether Anninka really ought to stay at Golovliovo or whether it was simply a whim of his. At any rate, from that moment on dinner proceeded at a livelier pace. Anninka agreed to everything he said and answered his questions in a manner that did not provoke much nagging and babbling. Nevertheless, the clock showed half past two when dinner was over. Anninka jumped up from the table as if she had been sitting in a steam bath, and ran to her uncle to say good-by.

In ten minutes Yudushka, in his fur coat and bear-skin boots, saw her to the porch and in person supervised the process of seating the young mistress in the pony cart.

"Easy when you go downhill—you hear? And see that you don't drop her out at the Senkino slope!" he shouted to the driver.

Finally Anninka was seated, wrapped up, and the leather cover of the cart was fastened.

"Suppose you stay!" Yudushka shouted again, wishing that in the presence of the servants gathered about, all go off properly as befits good kinsfolk. But Anninka already felt free, and was suddenly seized with a desire to play a girlish prank. She stood up in the cart and emphasizing every word, said, "No, uncle, I will not! You are a fright!"

Yudushka pretended not to hear, but his lips turned pale.

CHAPTER VI

Anninka was so overjoyed at her liberation from the Golovliovo bondage, that she did not even stop to think of the man who at her departure lost all contact with the world of living beings. She thought only of herself. She enjoyed the feeling of escape. And the sensation of freedom was so strong that when she visited the grave at Voplino again there was no longer a trace of that nervous sensibility which she had betrayed the first time. She listened to the requiem quietly, bowed before the grave without shedding a tear, and quite willingly accepted the priest's invitation to have tea with him.

The house of the Voplino priest was very scantily furnished. The only room of state in the house, which served as the reception room, looked naked and dreary. Along the walls were arranged about a dozen painted chairs, upholstered with haircloth, in holes here and there, and a sofa of the same kind with its back bulging out, like the chest of an old-time general. Against one of the walls between two windows stood a plain table covered with a soiled cloth, on which lay several confession books of the parish. From behind them peeped an inkpot with a quill stuck in it. An image case containing an ikon handed down as a family heirloom and a burning ikon lamp were suspended in the eastern corner of the room. Underneath the image case stood two trunks covered with a drab faded cloth holding the family linen, the dowry of the lady of the house. The walls were not papered. A few daguerreotype portraits of bishops hung in the center of one wall. There was a peculiar odor in the room, as if many generations of flies and black beetles had met their fate there. The priest himself, though a young man, had become considerably faded amidst these surroundings. His thin flaxen hair hung from his head in long, straight locks, like the boughs of a weeping willow. His eyes, once blue, were now lifeless. His voice trembled, his beard had taken on a wedge-like shape, his merino cassock hung on him loosely. His wife, also young, looked even more faded than her husband, because of frequent child bearing.

Nevertheless, Anninka could not help noticing that even these poor timid, worn-out people looked upon her not as at a real parishioner, but in pity, as if she were a lost sheep.

"You were visiting at your uncle's?" began the priest, carefully removing a cup of tea from the tray held by his wife.

"Yes, I stayed there about a week."

"Porfiry Vladimirych is now the chief landowner in the district, and has the greatest power. But it looks as if luck is not with him. First one son died, then the other, and now his mother has departed. I am surprised he did not insist on your staying with him."

"Uncle wanted me to stay, but I did not care to."

"Why so?"

"I prefer to live in freedom."

"Freedom, madam, is not a bad thing, of course, but it has its dangers. And when you think you are the nearest relative to Porfiry Vladimirych, you could forego a bit of that freedom, I imagine."

"No, father, one's own bread tastes better. It's easier to live when you know you are under no obligations to anyone."

The priest looked at her with his extinguished eyes, as if he meant to ask, "Come now, do you really know what 'one's own bread is?'" but he had not the courage to hurt her, so he only drew his cassock closer about him.

"Do you receive much salary as an actress?" inquired the priest's wife.

The priest became thoroughly frightened, and even began to wink at his wife. He expected Anninka to be offended, but Anninka was not offended and answered without a waver, "At present I get a hundred and fifty rubles a month, and my sister earns one hundred. But then we have benefit performances. All told, the two of us net about six thousand a year."

"Why does sister get less? Is she of inferior merit, or what?" continued the priest's wife.

"No, hers is a different *genre*. I have a voice and I sing. The audience likes it more. Sister's voice is a little weaker. So she plays in vaudeville mostly."

"So even in acting some are priests, some deacons and others just sextons?"

"Yes, but we share our income equally. That was our understanding from the very beginning—to share all money equally."

"Like good sisters? Well, there is nothing better than that. How much will that be, father? If you divide six thousand by months, how much will that make?"

"Five hundred rubles a month, and divided by two it makes two hundred and fifty rubles a month each."

"My, what a heap of money! We could not spend that much in a year. Another thing I meant to ask you, is it true that actresses are treated as if they were not real women?"

The priest became so alarmed that his cassock flew open; but seeing that Anninka took the question quite indifferently, he said to himself, "Eh—eh—she is really a hard nut to crack," and felt reassured.

"What do you mean 'not real women?'" she asked.

"Well, they kiss and embrace. I heard they must do it whether they want to or not."

"No, they don't kiss—they only pretend to. And as to whether they want to or not, that is out of the question entirely, because everything is done according to the play. They must act whatever is written in the play."

"Yes, but even if it's in the play—you know—sometimes a man with a slabbery snout sidles up to you. He is loathsome to look at, but you've got to hold your lips ready to let him kiss you."

A blush suffused Anninka's face. There suddenly flashed up in her memory the slabbery face of the brave Captain Papkov, who had actually "sidled up to her" and, alas! not even in accordance with the play.

"You have a wrong notion of what takes place on the stage," she said drily.

"Of course, we've never been to the theatre, but I am sure many things happen there. Father and I have often been speaking about you, madam. We are sorry for you, very sorry, indeed."

Anninka was silent. The priest tugged at his beard as if he, too, had finally gathered up enough courage to say something.

"Of course, it must be admitted, madam, that every calling has its agreeable and disagreeable sides," he at last delivered himself, "but we humans in our failings extol the former and try to forget the latter. And why do we try to forget? Because, madam, we want as far as possible to avoid even the remembrance of duty and of the virtuous life we formerly led." He heaved a sigh and added, "And above all, madam, you must guard your treasure."

The priest glanced at Anninka admonishingly, and his wife shook her head sadly, as much as to say, "Not much chance of that."

"And it is very doubtful whether you can preserve your treasure while an actress," he continued.

Anninka was at a loss what answer to make to these warnings. Little by little she began to see that the talk of these simple-minded folk about her "treasure" was of the same value as the pointed remarks of the officers of the regiments stationed in the various towns about *la chose*. Now it became quite clear to her that both at her uncle's and at the priest's she was considered a peculiar individual to whom one may condescend, but from a distance, so as not to soil oneself.

"Father, why is your church so poor?" she asked to change the subject.

"There is nothing here to make it rich—that's why it's poor. The landlords are all away in the government service, and the peasants haven't much to thrive on. In all there are a little over two hundred parishioners."

"Our bell, you see, is a very poor one," sighed the priest's wife.

"Yes, the bell and everything. Our bell, madam, weighs only five hundred pounds, and to make matters worse, it is cracked. It does not ring, it coughs. To be so poor is even sinful. The late Arina Petrovna promised to erect a new bell and, if she were alive we would most likely have a new bell by now."

"Why don't you tell uncle that grandmother promised you one?"

"I did tell him, madam, and I must admit he listened very kindly to my grievance, but he could not give me a satisfactory answer. He said he had heard nothing about it from mother; that his late dear mother had never spoken about the matter. He would gladly carry out her wishes, he said, if he had only heard mother express them."

"He could not help hearing them," said the priest's wife. "It was known throughout the district."

"So we live on in this wise. At first we had hopes, at least, now we have no hopes left. Not to mention our own personal needs, there is nothing to perform the service with sometimes—neither host nor red wine."

Anninka wanted to rise and take leave, but a new tray appeared on the table, with two dishes on it, one of mushrooms, the other with bits of caviar, and a bottle of Madeira.

"Do oblige us and have a bite—it's the best we have."

Anninka obeyed and quickly swallowed some mushrooms, but refused the Madeira.

"Another thing I meant to ask," continued the priest's wife, "we have a girl in our parish, the daughter of a peasant in the service of Lyshechevsky. She was the chambermaid of a certain actress in St. Petersburg. She says the life of an actress is very easy and pleasant, but an actress must produce a special passport every month. Is that true?"

Anninka stared at her and did not understand.

"That is for the greater freedom," explained the priest. "But I think she did not tell the truth. On the contrary, I heard that many actresses even get pensions from the government for their services."

Anninka became convinced that matters were going from bad to worse, and she rose to take leave.

"We thought you would give up acting now," the priest's wife persisted.

"Why should I?"

"Yes, but—you are a lady. You have reached your majority, you have an estate of your own—what could be better?"

"And you are your uncle's heiress, you know," added the priest.

"No, I sha'n't live here."

"And how we were hoping for it! The father and I would often speak about our little mistress. We thought you would surely come to live at Pogorelka. In the summer it is very nice here. You can go to the woods and pick mushrooms," tempted the priest's wife.

"We have mushrooms even in a dry summer, plenty of mushrooms," chimed the priest.

At last Anninka left. When she reached Pogorelka, her first word was, "Horses! Please have the horses ready at once!" But Fedulych only shrugged his shoulders.

"What's the use of shouting horses? We haven't fed them yet," he grumbled.

"But why? Oh, my God, as if everybody were conspiring against me!"

"That's it, we have conspired. How can you help conspiring if it's clear as day that we can't ride at night in thawing weather? Anyway, you'll get stranded in the mud a whole night, so it is better to be stranded at home, I think."

Grandmother's apartments had been well heated. The bedroom had been prepared, and a samovar was puffing on the table. Afimyushka scraped together the remnants of tea at the bottom of Arina Petrovna's tea-caddy. While the tea was drawing, Fedulych stood at the door, his arms folded, facing the young mistress. Beside him stood the cattle woman and Morkovna looking as if at the first wave of the hand they were ready to flee for their lives.

Fedulych was first to begin the conversation.

"The tea is grandmother's—just a bit left in the bottom of the box. Porfiry Vladimirych was going to take the box away, too, but I wouldn't let him. 'Maybe,' I say, 'the young mistress will come and will want to have some hot tea. So let it stay here till she gets some of her own.' Well, I had no trouble with him—he even joked. 'You old rascal,' he says, 'you will use it up yourself! Be sure,' he says, 'to bring the box to Golovliovo.' I wouldn't be surprised if he sends for it tomorrow."

"You should have given it to him then."

"Why should we? He has enough tea of his own. And now, at least, we, too, will have some after you. Another thing, madam, are you going to make us over to Porfiry Vladimirych?"

"Why, I never meant to."

"Just so. We were going to mutiny, you know. If, supposing, let's say, we are put under the rule of the Golovliovo master, we will all hand in our resignations."

"Why? Is uncle really so terrible?"

"No, he is not terrible, but he tortures you, he is all words. He can talk a man into his grave."

Anninka smiled involuntarily. It was vile dirt indeed, that oozed from Yudushka's orations, not mere babble. It was an ill-smelling wound from which the pus flowed incessantly.

"And what have you decided, about yourself?" Fedulych continued to question.

"Why, what was there to decide about myself?" said Anninka, a bit confused, feeling that she would again be compelled to listen to orations on the "treasure."

"Aren't you really going to give up acting?"

"No—that is, I haven't thought of it so far. But what harm is there in my earning my own bread?"

"I don't see any good in going with a bagpipe from fair to fair to amuse drunkards. Surely you are a lady."

Anninka did not reply, only knitting her brows. A painful thought drummed in her head, "God, when will I leave this place?"

"Of course, you know better how to take care of yourself. But we thought you would come back to live with us. The house is warm, and roomy enough to play tag in. The late mistress looked after the building herself. And if you feel dull, why then you can go sleigh-riding. In the summer you can go to the woods to pick mushrooms."

"We have all kinds of mushrooms here—lots of them," lisped Afimyushka temptingly.

Anninka leaned her elbows on the table and tried not to listen.

"There was a girl here," continued Fedulych cruelly. "She was a chambermaid in St. Petersburg. She says all actresses must have special passports. Every month they have to present their license at the police station."

Anninka could bear it no longer. She had had to listen to such speeches all day long.

"Fedulych!" she shouted in pain. "What have I done to you? Why do you take pleasure in insulting me?"

It was all she could stand. She felt as if something was strangling her. Another word—and she would break down.

BOOK V
FORBIDDEN FAMILY JOYS

CHAPTER I

Not long before the catastrophe that befell Petenka, Arina Petrovna, on one of her visits to Golovliovo, noticed a change in Yevpraksia. Brought up in the practices of serfdom, where the pregnancy of a domestic was the subject of a detailed and not uninteresting investigation, and was even considered an item of income, Arina Petrovna had a keen eye for such matters. She merely looked at Yevpraksia, and the girl, without saying a word, turned away her flushed face in full cognizance of her guilt.

"Come now, come now, my lady. Look at me. Pregnant, eh?" the experienced old woman asked the young culprit. However, there was no reproach in her voice, on the contrary, it sounded jocose, almost gay, as if the old woman scented a whiff of the dear, good, old times.

Yevpraksia, bashful and complacent, kept silence, but under Arina Petrovna's inquisitive look, the red of her cheeks deepened.

"For some time I have been noticing that you walk kind of stiff, strutting about and twirling your skirts as if you were a respectable lady! But, my dear, you can't fool me with your strutting and twirling. I can see your girlish tricks five versts ahead! Is it the wind that puffed you up? Since when is it? Out with it now. Tell me all about it."

A detailed inquiry ensued, followed by a no less detailed explanation. When had the first symptoms appeared? Had she a midwife in view? Did Porfiry Vladimirych know of the joy in store for him? Was Yevpraksia taking good care of herself? Was she careful not to lift anything heavy? The findings were that it was now the fifth month since Yevpraksia had been pregnant; that she had no midwife in view as yet; that Porfiry Vladimirych had been informed of the matter, but had said nothing. He had only folded his hands, mumbled something, and glanced at the ikon, to intimate that all is from God and that He, the Heavenly Father, provides for all occasions.

Yevpraksia had been careless; she had lifted a samovar and had then and there felt that something inside of her snapped.

"You've got brains, I must say," said Arina Petrovna in a grieved tone when the confession was out. "I see I'll have to look into the matter myself. Did you ever! A woman in the fifth month and hasn't even provided for a midwife! But why at least didn't you see Ulita about it, you fool, you?"

"I was going to, but the master doesn't like Ulita, you know."

"Nonsense, girl, nonsense! Whether Ulita offended the master or not has nothing at all to do with the case. He doesn't have to kiss her, does he? No, there is no way out of it. I'll have to take this thing in hand myself."

It was on the tip of her tongue to complain that even in her old age she had hardships to bear, but the subject of the conversation was so attractive that she only parted her lips with a smack and continued:

"Well, my girl, you are in for it. Take your medicine, try it and see how it tastes. Go ahead, just try it. I myself raised three sons and a daughter, and I buried five little ones—I ought to know. We are no better than slaves to those nasty men!" she added, slapping herself on the nape of her neck.

Suddenly, she stopped, struck by a new idea. "Holy saints! If it isn't going to be in Lent! Wait, just a moment, let's figure it out."

They began to figure on their fingers, they figured once, twice, a third time—it surely came out on a Lenten day.

"So that's how it is. That's the kind of saint he is. Just wait, I'll tease the life out of him. A pretty mess for him! I'll tease him. My name is mud if I won't," jested Arina Petrovna.

And truly, that very day, when all were gathered at evening tea, Arina Petrovna began to poke fun at Yudushka.

"See what a trick our saint has played. Maybe it really is the wind that puffed your queen up. Well, brother, you've surprised me, I must say."

At first Yudushka answered his mother's banter with grimaces of aversion, but seeing that Arina Petrovna spoke good-naturedly and meant no harm, he brightened up little by little.

"You are wag, mother dear, you certainly are," he jested in his turn, though evading the real point.

"Why call me a wag? We had better speak seriously about the matter. It's no joke, you know. It's a 'sacrament,' that's what it is. Though not a proper one but still——No, we've got to give it serious thought. What do you think; is she to stay here, or will you send her to the town?"

"I don't know, mother, I don't know a thing, darling," said Porfiry Vladimirych evasively. "You are a wag, you certainly are."

"Well, my girl, never mind, then. We'll talk it over, just the two of us, at leisure. We'll figure it out, and arrange things properly. These mean men— all they need is to satisfy their lust, and we, poor devils, we get the worst of it."

Arina Petrovna felt in her element. She spent a whole evening discussing things with Yevpraksia and could have gone on indefinitely. Even her cheeks began to glow and her eyes to glitter youthfully.

"You know, my dear, what it is? It's something divine, it is," she insisted. "Because, even if it isn't in the proper way, still it's the natural way. But you had better look out. If it comes during Lent—God save you! I'll tease you to death, I'll make this world too hot for you."

Ulita was also called into the council. First matters of real importance were taken up; whether an injection was to be made or whether the abdomen was to be massaged with quicksilver salve. Then they turned to the favorite theme and figured on their fingers again—it came out on a Lenten day! Yevpraksia turned as red as a peony and did not deny it, but pleaded her subordinate position.

"What could I do?" she said. "I must do what he wants me to do. If the master orders us to do something, we, poor devils, can't help but obey."

"Look at her playing the goody-goody. I'll bet, you yourself—-" jested Arina Petrovna.

The woman fairly revelled in the affair. Arina Petrovna recalled a number of incidents from her past, and did not fail to narrate them. First she told of her own pregnancies, what tortures she had had to stand from Simple Simon; how, while carrying Pavel Vladimirych, she travelled by post to Moscow, changing horses at every stage so as not to miss the Dubrovino auction, and as a result nearly departed to the better world, etc., etc. All her deliveries had been remarkable for something or other. Yudushka's was the only one that had come easy.

"I didn't feel the least bit of heaviness," she said. "I would sit and think, 'Lord, am I really pregnant?' And when the time came I just lay down to rest for a few minutes and I don't know how it happened—I gave birth to him. He was the easiest son to me, the very, very easiest."

Then followed stories about domestics, how she herself "caught some of them in the act," how others were spied upon by her trusties, Ulita being generally the leader. Her old woman's memory faithfully guarded these remarkably distinct recollections. In all her drab past—always devoted to hoarding on both a petty and a large scale, the tracking of lust-stricken domestics was the only romantic element that touched a living chord in her.

It was as if in a dull magazine where the reader expects to find treatises on dry fogs and Ovid's grave, he suddenly comes upon "See the troika, gaily dashing," or some such spirited song of gaiety or sadness. The dénouement of these simple love affairs of the maids' room was generally drastic and even cruel. The woman was married off into a remote village, by all means to a widower with a large family, the male culprit was degraded to the position of a cattle tender or even pressed into military service. Arina Petrovna's recollection of the closing chapters of such romances had faded (cultured people have a memory indulgent of their own past), but the spying out of the amorous intrigues passed before her eyes in all its vividness. And no wonder. In those days there was the same absorbing interest in spying of that sort as there is nowadays in the serial "evening story," in which the author, instead of at once crowning the mutual longing of the hero and the heroine, breaks off at the most pathetic place and writes, "to be continued."

"Those girls gave me no end of trouble. Some would keep up the pretense to the last minute, and would feign and sham in the hope of eluding me. But no, my dear, you can't fool me. I am an old hand at it myself," she added almost sternly, as if threatening some one.

Finally came the stories of diplomatic pregnancies, so to speak, in which Arina Petrovna had figured not as the chastiser, but as the accomplice and concealer.

For example, her father Piotr Ivanych, when he was an old, tottering man of seventy, had also had a "mistress," who had also been discovered with an "increment"; and for higher considerations it had been necessary to conceal the "increment" from the old man. As ill luck would have it, Arina Petrovna was then at odds with her brother Piotr Petrovich who, also for some diplomatic reasons, had wanted to spy upon the pregnancy and leave his father in no doubt as to his lady-love's position.

"And what do you think? We carried the whole thing through almost in front of father's nose. The old dear slept in his bedroom, and the two of us, alongside of him, went on with our work, quietly, in a whisper and on tiptoe. I myself with my own hands closed up her mouth, so she could not scream, disposed of the linen, and then grabbed hold of her baby—he was a fine, big fellow—and dispatched him to the foundling asylum. When brother learned about it a week later he only gasped."

There had been another diplomatic pregnancy. Her cousin Varvara Mikhailovna had been involved in the case. Her husband had left on a campaign against the Turks, and she had not been sufficiently careful. She came galloping to Golovliovo like one possessed and had shouted "Save me, cousin!"

"Well, though we were on the outs with her at that time, I did not make her feel it. I welcomed her in the most hospitable way, calmed her, reassured her, pretended she had just come to us on a visit, and fixed the matter up so that her husband did not know a thing about it till his dying day."

Thus ran the tales of Arina Petrovna, and seldom has a narrator found more attentive listeners. Yevpraksia swallowed every word as if the incidents of a wonderful fairy tale were actually passing before her eyes. As to Ulita, she as an erstwhile participant in most of it, only made smacking sounds with the corners of her lips.

Ulita also brightened up and felt more comfortable than she had for a long time. Hers was a restless life. Even in childhood she had burned with servile ambitions. Sleeping and waking, she would dream about gaining favor in her master's eyes and getting the whiphand over those in her own station in life. But her dreams never came true. As soon as she set foot on the rung higher up, she would be tugged back and plunged into the inferno by an unseen, mysterious power. She possessed in perfection the qualities of an all-round servant of the gentlefolk. She was venomous, evil-tongued and always ready for treachery, but also slavishly ready to go anywhere and do anything that neutralized her viciousness. In former days, when it was necessary to follow up an event in the maid servants' room, or settle any dubious affair, Arina Petrovna had gladly made use of her services, though she had never appreciated them and had not admitted her to any office of trust. Ulita would then make loud complaints, and sting with her tongue, but no one paid attention to her grumblings, for she was well known as a malevolent woman, ready to curse herself and others to eternal damnation, but the next moment at a mere wink willing to come running and sit up on her hind legs prepared to do her master's bidding.

And so she had been knocked about, always trying to get somewhere and never getting there, till the abolition of serfdom put an end to her slavish ambitions.

One event in Ulita's youth had kindled in her great hopes. Porfiry Vladimirych, on one of his visits to Golovliovo, had become intimate with her, and, as tradition had it, had even had a child by her. That had brought down upon him the wrath of Arina Petrovna. It is uncertain whether the relationship had been kept up on his subsequent visits; at any rate, when Yudushka decided to establish himself permanently at Golovliovo, Ulita's hopes had been shattered grievously. Immediately after his arrival she came to him with a heap of gossip, in which Arina Petrovna was accused of all sorts of fraud. The master listened very affably to her gossip, but gave Ulita a cold look, evidently failing to remember her former "good services." Offended and deceived in her hopes, Ulita transferred herself to Dubrovino, where Pavel Vladimirych, because of his hatred for his dear brother Porfiry Vladimirych, received her gladly and even made her his housekeeper. Here for a long time her condition seemed to improve. Pavel Vladimirych would sit in the entresol and sip one glass of vodka after another, and she would run busily from storeroom to cellar, clanging a bunch of keys, and rattling her tongue. She had even quarrelled with Arina Petrovna, whom the sly wench nearly drove to her grave.

But Ulita loved treachery too well to be content with the peace and quiet that had come with her "good living." That was when Pavel Vladimirych had become so addicted to drink that his end could readily be foreseen. Porfiry Vladimirych was alive to Ulita's priceless value at this juncture, and he snapped his fingers again and summoned her. He ordered her never for a moment to leave his prey, not to contradict Pavel in anything, not even in his hatred of his brother Porfiry, and by all means to eliminate the interference of Arina Petrovna. This had been one of those domestic crimes which Yudushka had a gift of perpetrating without previous deliberation, spontaneously, and as a matter of course. Needless to say, Ulita carried out his orders most faithfully. Pavel Vladimirych never ceased to hate his brother, and the more he hated him, the more he drank his vodka, and the less capable he became of heeding the remarks and advice of Arina Petrovna as to "making provisions." Every moment of the dying man, every word uttered were at once reported to Golovliovo, so that Yudushka, equipped with a full knowledge of the facts, could determine the exact moment he should have to leave his ambush and step in as master of the situation that he had created. And so he had! He had come to Dubrovino at the very moment that he could get the estate for the asking. Porfiry Vladimirych had rewarded Ulita's services by making her a gift of cloth for a woolen dress, but he never admitted her close to him.

Again Ulita had been plunged from the heights of grandeur into the depths of inferno. It seemed to be her last fall. No one would snap his fingers again and summon her for service. As a sign of special favor and in consideration of her "nursing dear brother in his last days," she had been allotted a nook in the house where all the deserving old servants, who had remained after the abolition of serfdom, had found shelter. Here Ulita had become completely cowed, and when Porfiry Vladimirych made his choice of Yevpraksia, she not only had not shown any obstinacy, but had even been first to come to do homage to the master's love and had kissed her shoulder.

And now, when she had given herself up as forgotten and abandoned, she struck luck once more in Yevpraksia's pregnancy. It was suddenly recalled that somewhere in the servants' room there was a handy person. Somebody snapped her fingers and summoned Ulita. True, it was not the master who had snapped his fingers. But that he offered no obstacles was in itself sufficient grace. Ulita celebrated her entry into the Golovliovo manor by taking the samovar from Yevpraksia's hands. Bending sidewise a bit, with the weight of it, she walked smartly into the dining-room, where Porfiry Vladimirych was already seated. The master said not a word. He even smiled, she thought, when upon another occasion, as she was bringing in the samovar, she shouted from a distance, "Step to one side, master, or I'll scald you."

When Ulita answered the summons to the family council she made wry faces at first and refused to be seated. But when Arina Petrovna shouted at her in a kindly way, "Sit down,—will you? What's the use of your tricks? God made us all equal—be seated." Ulita sat down and kept silence a while. Very shortly, however, her tongue unloosened.

She, too, had her reminiscences. Her memory was stuffed with filth from the days of her serfdom. Beside the carrying out of delicate commissions like dogging the amorous doings of the maids' room, Ulita had also held the office of leech and apothecary in the Golovliovo manor. It was she who made all the injections, and applied the cupping-glasses and mustard plasters. She had given even the old master, Vladimir Mikhailych and Arina Petrovna injections, and the young master, too—every one of them. She retained the most grateful memories, and now there was a boundless field for all her reminiscences.

A new mysterious life animated the Golovliovo manor. Arina Petrovna would come over from Pogorelka every now and then to pay her "good son" a visit and supervise preparations that as yet were given no name. After the evening, the three women would go into Yevpraksia's room, would eat some homemade jam, play fool, and, till late into the night, would revel in reminiscences that would often make the heroine of the occasion blush. The least incident, the smallest trifle, served as a pretext for endless narrations. Yevpraksia brought some raspberry jam, and Arina Petrovna began a story that when she was carrying her daughter Sonya she could not stand even the smell of raspberries.

"No sooner did a raspberry come into the house than I began to yell at the top of my voice, 'Out, out with that damned thing!' After my confinement it was all right again; I liked raspberries again."

Yevpraksia brought some caviar—and Arina Petrovna had an incident to recall in connection with caviar, too.

"A really wonderful thing happened to me in connection with caviar. It was a month or two after I was married and suddenly I was seized with such a strong desire for caviar that I simply had to have it at any cost. I would sneak into the cellar and eat as much as I could. And once I said to my husband, 'Vladimir Mikhailych, why is it that I eat caviar all the time?' He smiled at me, you know, and said, 'My dear, it is because you are pregnant.' And surely enough, just nine months afterward I gave birth to Simple Simon."

But Porfiry Vladimirych continued to be noncommittal, never once admitting that he had anything to do with Yevpraksia's condition. Quite naturally this attitude of his embarrassed the women and dampened their effusions in his presence, so that he came to be completely abandoned. They chased him without ceremony from Yevpraksia's room when he came in the evening to rest up and have a chat.

"Be gone, you fine fellow!" Arina Petrovna said gaily. "You did your part. Now it's none of your business any more, it's the women's business. It's our turn now."

Yudushka took himself off in all meekness. Though not neglecting to reproach his mother dear for being unkind to him, he rejoiced inwardly that she was taking so much interest in the embarrassing affair, and that he was left alone. If not for his mother's participation, God knows what he would have had to undergo in order to hush up the nasty affair, the very thought of which made him spit out in disgust. Now, thanks to the experience of Arina Petrovna and the skill of Ulita, he hoped the "trouble" would pass without gaining publicity, and he himself, perhaps, would learn of the results after all was over.

CHAPTER II

Porfiry Vladimirych's hopes were not realized. First occurred the catastrophe with Petenka, then Arina Petrovna's death. And there was no possibility in sight of his extricating himself by means of some ugly machinations. He could not dismiss Yevpraksia for dissolute conduct, because Arina Petrovna had carried the affair too far and made it too widely known. Nor was Ulita so very reliable. Dexterous woman though she was, yet if he put his trust in her, he might have to deal with the coroner. For the first time in his life Yudushka seriously and sincerely regretted his loneliness; for the first time he realized vaguely that the people around him were not mere pawns to be played with.

"Why didn't she wait a while to die?" Yudushka reproached his mother dear. "She should have fixed it all up quietly and with good sense, and then—as she pleased! If it's time to die—you can't help it. I am sorry for the old woman. But if God wills it so, all our tears, and the doctors, and the cures, and all of us are naught before the power of God. The old woman lived long enough. She had her day—was herself a mistress all her life, and left her children a gentry estate. She lived to old age—well that's enough."

And as usual his idle mind, not used to dwell on a matter presenting practical obstacles, skipped to the easier topic that gave occasion to endless, unhampered verbiage.

"And to think how she died! Why, her death was worthy of a saint," he lied to himself, not knowing, though, whether he lied or spoke the truth. "Without ailment, without trouble—just so. She heaved a sigh, and before we knew it, she was no more. Oh, mother dear! And her smile, and the glow of her cheeks! Her hands placed together as if she wanted to confer a blessing. She shut her eyes and—good-by!"

But in the very heat of his sentimental babblings, something would suddenly prick him. That filthy business again. Fi, fi! "And really why didn't she wait a while! It was only a matter of a month or so, and now, look what she did!"

For some time he attempted to pretend ignorance, and answered Ulita's inquiries just as he had answered his mother's, "I don't know, I don't know anything."

But Ulita, an impudent woman, who had suddenly become conscious of her power, could not be dismissed like that.

"Do I know? Have I brought this business on?" she cut him short. And then he realized that from that moment on the happy combination of the rôle of adulterer with the rôle of the unconcerned observer of the consequences of his adultery had become quite impossible.

Nearer and nearer came the disaster, inevitable, tangible. It pursued him relentlessly and—what was worst of all—it paralyzed his idle mind. He exerted all possible efforts to rid himself of the thought of the approaching calamity, to drown it in a torrent of idle words, but he succeeded only in part. He tried to hide behind the infallibility of the law of Providence and, as was his custom, turned it into a ball of thread which he could wind and unwind without end. There was the parable of the hair falling from a man's head, and the legend of the house built on sand; but just at the moment when his idle thoughts were about to roll down into a kind of mysterious abyss, when the endless winding of the ball seemed quite assured, a single word suddenly jumped out from the ambush and broke the thread. Alas! That one word was "adultery" and designated an act of which Yudushka did not wish to confess himself guilty even to himself.

When all his efforts to forget the disaster or to do away with it proved futile, when he realized at last that he was caught, his soul became filled with anguish. He walked back and forth in the room, thinking of nothing, and he felt that something inside of him trembled and ached. It was a check that his idle mind felt for the first time. Up to now, wherever his idle and empty imagination carried him, it always found boundless space, space that gave room to all possible kinds of combinations. Even the deaths of Volodka and Petka, even the death of Arina Petrovna had not baffled his flow of idle thoughts and words. Those were common, well recognized situations, met by well recognized, well established forms—requiems, funeral dinners, and the like. All this he had done in strict accordance with the custom and thus vindicated himself, so to speak, before the laws of man and Providence. But adultery—what was that? Why, that meant an arraignment of his entire life, the showing up of its inner sham. Though he had formerly been known as a pettifogger, even as a Bloodsucker, gossip had had so little legal background that he could safely retort, "Prove it!"

And now, all of a sudden—adulterer! A known, convicted adulterer. He had not even resorted to "measures," so great had been his confidence in Arina Petrovna; he had not even worked up a story to cover the thing. And on a Lenten day at that. The shame of it!

In these inner talks with himself, in spite of their confusion, there was something like an awakening of conscience. But the question was whether Yudushka would continue along that path or whether his idle mind would even in this grave matter perform its usual function of finding a loophole through which he could crawl out and emerge unscathed.

While Yudushka was thus smarting under his own mental vacuity, Yevpraksia was undergoing an unexpected inner change. Evidently the anticipation of motherhood untied the mental fetters that had hitherto held her bound. Up to that time she had been indifferent to everything and regarded Porfiry Vladimirych as a "master" in relation to whom she was a mere subordinate. Now, for the first time, she grasped a definite idea. It began to dawn on her that here was a state of affairs where she was the most important figure, and where she could not be driven about with impunity. As a consequence, even her face, usually blank and stolid, became lighted up and intelligent.

The death of Arina Petrovna had been the first fact in her semi-conscious life that produced a sobering effect upon her. No matter how peculiar the attitude of the old mistress to Yevpraksia's prospective motherhood was, still there were glimpses of sympathy in it and nothing of the disgusting evasiveness of Yudushka. So Yevpraksia had begun to see a protector in Arina Petrovna, as if expecting that some kind of attack was being planned against her. The forebodings of that attack were all the more persistent since they were not illuminated by consciousness, but merely filled the whole of her being with vague anxiety. Her mind was not vigorous enough to tell her definitely the point from which the attack would come and the form it would take; but her instincts had already been so aroused that the very sight of Yudushka filled her with an inexplicable fear. "Yes, that's where it will come from," reverberated in the inner chambers of her soul—from that coffin filled with dead dust, from that coffin she had so long been tending like a hireling, from that coffin which by some miracle had become the father and lord of *her* child! The feeling this thought awakened in her was akin to hatred and would inevitably have passed into hatred had it not been diverted by the sympathy and interest of Arina Petrovna, who, by constant chatter, never gave Yevpraksia a chance to think.

But Arina Petrovna retired to Pogorelka, and then vanished entirely. The feeling of anxiety and uneasiness in Yevpraksia became still more intense.

The stillness in which the Golovliovo manor became engulfed was broken only by a rustle announcing that Yudushka was stealing through the corridors, listening at the doors. Or sometimes, some one of the servants would come running from the yard and bang the door of the maids' room. But then stillness would again creep in from all sides. It was a dead stillness that filled Yevpraksia's being with superstitions and anguish. And since she was nearing her time, she had not even the sleepy feeling to look forward to that came in the evening after a day of household chores.

She tried once or twice to be affectionate with Porfiry Vladimirych and engage his kindly sympathies. Her attempts only resulted in brief but mean scenes that reacted painfully even on her crude sensibilities. All that was left to her was to sit with her arms folded and think, that is, be alarmed. And as to the causes for alarm, they multiplied daily. The death of Arina Petrovna had untied Yudushka's hands and introduced into the Golovliovo manor a new element of tale-bearing, which thereafter became the one thing in which Yudushka's soul reveled.

Ulita was aware that Porfiry Vladimirych was afraid and that with his idle, empty, perfidious character fear bordered on hatred. Besides, she knew very well that he was incapable not only of attachment but even of simple pity, and he kept Yevpraksia only because, thanks to her, his daily life flowed on in an undeviating rut. Equipped with these simple data, Ulita was in a position to nurse the feeling of hatred that arose in Yudushka whenever he was reminded of the coming "disaster."

Soon Yevpraksia became entangled in a web of gossip. Ulita every now and then "reported" to the master. In one instance she complained about the wasteful disposal of house provisions.

"I am afraid, master, your stuff is spent a bit too fast. I went to the cellar a while ago to get cured beef. I remembered a new tub had been begun not long ago, and—would you believe it? I look into the tub and find only two or three slices at the bottom."

"Is it possible?" said Porfiry Vladimirych, staring at her.

"If I had not seen it myself, I shouldn't have believed it, either. It's surprising what heaps of stuff are used up! Butter, barley, pickles—everything. Other folk feed their servants on gruel and goose-fat, but our servants must have it with butter, and sweet butter at that."

"Is that so?" exclaimed Porfiry Vladimirych, almost frightened.

At another time she entered casually and "reported" about the master's linen.

"Master, I think you ought to stop Yevpraksia, really. Of course, she is a girl, inexperienced, but still, take the linen for instance. She wasted piles of it on bed sheets and swaddling clothes, and it's all fine linen, you know."

Porfiry Vladimirych merely cast a fiery glance, but the whole of his empty being was thrown into convulsions by her "report."

"Of course, she cares for her infant," continued Ulita, in a mellifluous voice. "She thinks Lord knows what, a prince is going to be born. And I think that he, I mean the infant, could well sleep on fustian bedding—with such a mother."

At times she simply teased Yudushka.

"Do you know, master, what I was going to ask you?" she began. "What are you going to do about the infant? Are you going to make him your son, or will you, like other folk, put him in the foundling asylum."

At this Porfiry Vladimirych flashed such a fierce glance at her that she was instantly silenced.

And amidst the hatred that was rising from every corner, the moment drew nearer and nearer when the appearance of a tiny, crying, "servant of God" would in one way or another bring order into the moral chaos of the Golovliovo manor, and would increase the number of the "servants of God" that inhabit this universe.

It was seven o'clock in the evening. Porfiry Vladimirych had had his after-dinner nap and was in his study filling up sheets of paper with columns of figures. He was busy with the following problem: How much money would he now have had, if his dear mother Arina Petrovna had not appropriated the hundred ruble note his grandfather had given him on the day of his birth, but had placed it in the bank to the credit of the minor Porfiry? It came out not much—only eight hundred rubles in notes.

"It isn't a lot of money, let's say," Yudushka mused idly, "but still it's good to know that you have it for a rainy day. Any time you need it—you can just go and get it. You don't have to bow to anybody, or ask favors—just take your own money, given to you by your grandfather. Oh, mother dear! How could you have acted so rashly?"

Porfiry Vladimirych had allayed the fears that had only recently paralyzed his capacity for thinking idle nonsense. The glimmerings of conscience awakened by the difficult position in which Yevpraksia's pregnancy put him, and by the sudden death of Arina Petrovna, little by little faded away. His idle mind had done its work, and Yudushka had finally succeeded by great effort, it is true, in drowning all thought of the impending "disaster" in his bottomless pit of verbiage. One could not say he had made up his mind consciously, but rather intuitively. It was instinct in him that made him revert to his favorite formula: "I don't know anything,

I allow nothing, I forbid everything," which he applied in every difficulty. On this occasion, too, it put an end to the inner turbulence that had briefly agitated him.

Now, this matter of the coming birth was of no concern to him, and his face assumed an indifferent, impenetrable look. He almost ignored Yevpraksia, not even calling her by name. If ever he did inquire about her he would say, "How about that woman—still sick?" He proved to be so strong that even Ulita, who had been through the school of serfdom and had learned quite a lot about reading people's minds, realized that to battle with a man who had no scruples and who would go to any lengths was quite impossible.

The Golovliovo manor was plunged in darkness. Only Yudushka's study and the side room occupied by Yevpraksia were illuminated by a glimmering light. Stillness reigned in Yudushka's rooms, broken only by the rattle of the beads on the counting board and the faint squeak of Yudushka's pencil.

Suddenly, in the dead stillness he heard a distant but piercing groan. Yudushka trembled, his lips quivered, his pencil jerked.

"One hundred and twenty rubles plus twelve rubles and ten kopeks," whispered Porfiry Vladimirych, endeavoring to stifle the unpleasant sensation produced by the groan.

But the groans were now coming with increasing frequency. Finally they got to be annoying. It became so difficult for him to work that he left the desk. First he paced back and forth trying not to hear; but little by little curiosity gained the upper hand. He opened the door cautiously, put his head into the darkness of the adjacent room and listened in an attitude of watchful expectation.

"My, I think I forgot to light the lamp before the ikon of the Holy Virgin, the Assuager of Our Sorrows," flashed through his mind.

Suddenly he heard quick footsteps in the corridor, and he darted back into his study, cautiously closing the door and mincing on tiptoe to the ikon.

A moment later he was already in "proper form," so that when the door opened wide and Ulita rushed into the room, she found him in a pose of prayer with folded hands.

"I am afraid Yevpraksia's life is in danger," said Ulita, not hesitating to interrupt Yudushka's prayers. But Porfiry Vladimirych did not even turn his face; he began to move his lips faster than before, and instead of answering waved his hand in the air as if to chase away an annoying fly.

"What's the use of waving your hand? I say Yevpraksia is doing poorly. She may die any moment," Ulita insisted gruffly.

This time Yudushka turned toward her, but his face was as calm and unctuous as if he had just been in communion with the Deity, and had cast off all earthly cares, and did not even understand what could make people disturb him.

"Though it's sinful to chide after prayer, still as a human being I cannot keep from complaining. How many times have I not asked you not to disturb me when I say my prayers?" he said in a voice befitting his worshipful mood, and permitting himself only a shake of his head as a sign of Christian reproach. "Well, what has happened?"

"What could have happened? Yevpraksia is in labor and cannot give birth. As if you haven't heard it before. Oh, you! Go and look at her at least."

"What is there to look at? Am I a doctor? Can I give her advice, or what? I don't know anything, I don't know any of your business. I know there is a sick woman in the house, but why she is sick and what her sickness is, that, I confess, I never had the curiosity to find out. Send for the priest if the patient is in danger. That's one piece of advice I can give you. Send for the priest, pray with him, light the ikon lamps. And then I'll have tea with the parson."

Porfiry Vladimirych was glad that he expressed himself so well in this most decisive moment. He looked at Ulita firmly as if he meant to say, "Well refute me, if you can."

Even she was baffled by his equanimity. "Suppose you do come and take a look," she repeated.

"I will not go because I have nothing to do there. If it were business, I would go without being called. If I have to go five versts on business, I'll go five versts, and if ten versts, I'll go ten. It may be in wind and storm, but I'll go. For I know there is business to attend to and I've got to go whether I want to or not."

Ulita thought she was asleep and that in her sleep she saw Satan himself standing before her and discoursing.

"To send for the priest—that's business! A prayer—do you know what the Scriptures say about a prayer? 'A prayer cures the afflicted.' That's what it says. So see to it. Send for the priest, pray together, and I, too, will pray in the meantime. You will pray there, in the ikon room, and I will invoke God's mercy here in my study. By joint effort, you on one side, I on the other, we may after all succeed in making our prayers heard in Heaven."

The priest was sent for, but before he came, Yevpraksia, in agony, delivered herself of the child. From the hurried steps and banging doors, Porfiry Vladimirych understood that something decisive had happened. And, indeed, in a few minutes hurried steps were heard in the corridor, and Ulita rushed in holding a tiny creature wrapped up in linen.

"Here! Look at it!" she exclaimed triumphantly, bringing the child close to the face of Porfiry Vladimirych.

For a moment it looked as if Yudushka were hesitating. His body swayed forward and a bright spark flashed in his eyes. But only for a moment. The next instant he turned up his nose squeamishly and waved his hand.

"No, no! I am afraid. I don't like them. Go away, go away!" he began to stammer, with infinite aversion in his face.

"Why don't you at least ask if it's a boy or a girl?" Ulita pleaded with him.

"No, no! What for? It's none of my business. It's your affair, and I don't know anything. I don't know anything, and I don't want to know either. Go away, for Christ's sake, be gone!"

Again Ulita felt as though she were in a nightmare with Satan standing in front of her. It exasperated her.

"I'll take him and put him on your sofa. Go nurse him!" That was a threat.

But Yudushka was not the man to be moved. While Ulita was threatening, he was already facing the ikon, with hands stretched upward. Evidently he was imploring God to forgive all people, those who sinned knowingly, and those who sinned unknowingly; those who sinned in word and those who sinned in deed; and he thanked the Lord that he himself was not a sinner or an adulterer, and that the Lord in His grace had led him in the righteous path. Even his nose trembled with the solemnity of his feeling. Ulita observed him for some time, blew out her lips in disgust and left.

"God took one Volodka and gave another Volodka," flashed up in Yudushka's mind quite irrelevantly; but he at once became aware of this sudden play of thought and spat inwardly in annoyance.

Soon the priest came and chanted and burned incense. Yudushka heard the drawl of the sexton as he was chanting, "Oh, Zealous Protectress!" and gladly chimed in. Soon Ulita came running to the door again and shouted, "He was christened Volodimir!"

Yudushka was moved by the strange coincidence of this circumstance and his recent aberration of mind. He saw the will of God in it, and this time he did not spit, but said to himself:

"Well, then, thank God! He took one Volodka and gave another. That's what God can do. You lose something in one place and you think it's gone, but God, if He wishes, rewards you for it a hundredfold."

At last it was announced that the samovar was on the table and the priest was waiting in the dining-room. Porfiry Vladimirych became quite peaceful and solemn. The Golovliovo priest, Father Aleksandr, was a polite man, and he endeavored to give his intercourse with Yudushka a worldly tone. In the landlord's manor there were all-night vigils every week and on the eve of every principal holiday, in addition to the ceremonial services performed every first of the month. That meant an income of over a hundred rubles a year. Father Aleksandr was not unmindful of this, nor of the fact that the landmarks between the church lands and Yudushka's lands had not yet been settled upon, and Yudushka, on passing the church meadows, would many times exclaim, "My, what fine meadows!" So the priest's worldly behavior toward Yudushka was tempered by fear, which came out every time the priest visited the manor. He would work himself up into gay spirits, though he really had no occasion to feel happy. And when Porfiry Vladimirych gave expression to heresies concerning the ways of Providence, the after-life, and so forth, the priest, though not quite approving of the heresies, still did not consider them sacrilegious and blasphemous, but ascribed them to the temerity of spirit characteristic of the gentry.

When Yudushka entered, the priest hurriedly gave him his blessing and just as hurriedly pulled his hand back as if afraid the Bloodsucker would bite it. He wanted to congratulate his spiritual son on the birth of the new little Vladimir, but uncertain how Yudushka was taking the matter, he decided not to congratulate him.

"It's misty outdoors," the priest began. "By popular signs, in which one may say there seems to be a great deal of superstition, such a state of the atmosphere signifies that thawing weather is near."

"And maybe it will turn out to be a frost. We are foretelling thawing weather and God will go ahead and send us a frost," retorted Yudushka, with a bustling; air of gaiety, and seated himself at the table, this time attended by the butler Prokhor.

"It is true that man in his aspirations strives to attain the unattainable and to gain access to the inaccessible; and as a consequence he incurs cause for penance, or even veritable grief."

"That is why we ought to refrain from guessing and foretelling and be satisfied with what God sends us. If He sends us warm weather, we ought to be satisfied with warm weather; if He send us frost, let us welcome the frost. We'll order the stoves heated more than usual, and those who travel will wrap themselves tight in fur coats, and there you are—we're all warm."

"Quite true."

"There are many nowadays who go circling round. They don't like this and they are dissatisfied with that, and the other thing is not after their heart, but I don't approve. I don't make forecasts myself, and I don't care for it in others. It is haughtiness of spirit—that's what I call it."

"That's true, too."

"We are all pilgrims here, that's how I look at it. Well, as to having a glass of tea, or a light bite, or something, we are allowed to do that, for God gave us our body and limbs. Even the government would not forbid us that. 'You can eat, if you want to,' it says, 'but hold your tongue.'"

"Also perfectly true," exclaimed the priest, tapping the saucer with the bottom of his empty tea-glass in exultation over the harmony between them.

"As I understand it, God gave man reason not to explore the unknown, but to refrain from sin. If I, for instance, feel a craving of the flesh or a temptation of some kind, I call my reason to the rescue and say, 'Show me, forsooth, the ways by which I may overcome this craving,' and I am quite right, for in such cases reason can really be of great use."

"Still, faith is superior, in a way," the priest offered in slight correction.

"Faith is one thing and reason is another. Faith points out the goal, and reason finds the way. It goes searching in every direction till at last it finds something. Take, for instance, all these drugs and plasters and healing herbs and potions—all of them have been invented by reason. But we ought to see to it that such invention is in accordance with faith, to our salvation and not to our ruin."

"I cannot disagree with you in this, either."

"There is a certain book, father, that I read some time ago. It says that one must not disdain the offices of reason if the latter is guided by faith, for a man without reason soon becomes the plaything of passion; and I even think that the first downfall of man came about because the devil in the shape of the serpent beclouded the human reason."

The reverend father did not object to this either, though he refrained from assent, since it was not yet clear to him what Yudushka had up his sleeve.

"We often see that people not only fall into sinful thought, but even commit crimes, all because of lack of reason. The flesh tempts, and if there is no reason, man falls into the abyss. Man craves something sweet, he craves gaiety and pleasure, especially when it comes through women. How will you preserve yourself without the aid of reason? And if, let's say, for instance, I do possess reason, I'll take some camphor and rub it in where necessary, and put some in other parts, and before you know, the craving is over as if it had never been there."

Yudushka became silent as if waiting to hear what the priest had to say in response, but the priest was still uncertain what Yudushka was driving at and therefore he only coughed and said quite irrelevantly:

"There are hens in my yard—very restless on account of the change of season. They run and jump about, and can't find a place for themselves."

"All because neither birds nor beasts nor reptiles possess reason. What is a bird? It has no worry, no cares—just flies about. The other day, for instance, I looked out of the window and saw some sparrows pecking at manure. Manure is enough for them but not for man."

"Yet in some cases even the Scriptures take birds as examples."

"In some cases, that's true. Where faith without reason can be a man's salvation, we must do as the birds do, pray to God, compose verses."

Porfiry Vladimirych grew silent. Though talkative by nature and though the event of the day naturally lent itself to a lengthy discussion, the most suitable form for the remarks on the subject had evidently not yet ripened in his mind.

"Birds need no reason," he said at last, "because they have no temptations. Or, rather, they have temptations but they are never called to answer for their doings. Birds lead a natural life. They have no property to take care of, no legitimate marriages, hence no widowhood. They are responsible neither to God nor to the authorities. They have only one lord— the cock."

"The cock! That's true. The cock is a sort of Sultan of Turkey to them."

"But man has so arranged his life, that he has given up the liberties granted to him by nature, and therefore he needs much reason: first, to keep himself from falling into sin, and second, not to tempt others. Am I right, father?"

"It is gospel truth. The Scriptures advise us to pluck out the tempting eye."

A Family Of Noblemen | 205

"That is, if you understand it literally, but there may be a way of avoiding sin not by plucking out the eyes, but by seeing to it that the eye is not tempted. One must have more frequent recourse to prayer, and curb the unruly flesh. Take me, for instance. I am in good health and vigor, I dare say. Well, I have female servants. Still that does not disturb me in the least. I know I can't get along without servants, well then, I keep them. I keep male servants, and female servants of every kind. A maid is needed in the household to fetch something from the cellar, to pour the tea, bring in something to eat—well—God bless her!—She does her work and I do mine, and so we get along very nicely indeed."

While speaking Yudushka tried to look into the priest's eyes, and the latter in his turn, tried to look into Yudushka's. But happily, there was a burning candle between them, so that they could look at each other to their hearts' content and see nothing but the flame of the candle.

"And then again, I take it this way. If you become intimate with your female servants, they'll begin to have their way in the house. And you'll have squabbles and disorder and quarrels and impertinence. I like to keep away from such things."

The priest stared so steadily that his eyes began to swim. Good manners, he knew, demanded that in a general conversation one should every now and then join in with at least a word. So he shook his head and muttered:

"Tss——"

"And if, at that, one behaves as other folks do, as my dear neighbor, Mr. Anpetov, for example, or my other neighbor, Mr. Utrobin, then you can fall into sin before you know it. Utrobin has six offspring on his place begot in that disgraceful way. But I don't want it. I say that if God took away my guardian angel, it means that such was His holy will, that He wanted me to be a widower. And if I am a widower by the grace of God, I must observe my widowerhood honestly and not contaminate my bed. Am I right, father?"

"It's hard, sir."

"I know it's hard, but still I observe it. Some say it's hard, and I say the harder the better, provided God is with you! We can't all have it sweet and easy. Some of us must bear hardships in the name of God. If you deny yourself something *here,* you will obtain it *there. Here* it is called hardship and *there,* virtue. Am I right?"

"As right as can be."

"And talking about virtues—they are not all of the same kind. Some virtues are great, others are small. What do you think?"

"Yes, quite possible, there may be small virtues and great virtues."

"That's just what I say. If a man is careful in his behavior, if he does not speak vile words, if he does not speak vain words, if he does not judge others, if, in addition to all this, he does not vex anybody or take away what is not his—that man will have a clear conscience, and no mud can soil him. And if anyone secretly speaks ill of a man like that, give it no heed. Spit at his insinuations—that's the long and short of it."

"In such cases the precepts of Christianity recommend forgiveness."

"Yes, forgive also. That's what I always do. If someone speaks ill of me, I forgive him and even pray to God for him. He is the gainer because a prayer on his behalf goes to Heaven, and I, too, am the gainer, for after I have prayed I forget about the whole matter."

"That's correct. Nothing lightens one's heart as much as a prayer. Sorrow and anger, and even ailment, all run before it as does the darkness of night before the sun."

"Well, thank God, then. And we should always conduct ourselves so that our life is like a candle in a lantern—seen from every side. Then we will not be misjudged, for there will be no cause. Take us, for example. We sat down here a while ago, have been chatting and talking things over— who could find fault with us? And now let us go and pray to the Lord, and then—to bed. And tomorrow we shall rise again. Isn't that so, father?"

Yudushka rose noisily, shoving his chair aside in sign that the conversation was at an end. The priest also rose and made ready to raise his arm to bless, but Porfiry Vladimirych, as an indication of special favor, caught the priest's hand and pressed it in his own.

"So he was christened Vladimir, father?" said Yudushka, shaking his head sadly in the direction of Yevpraksia's room.

"In honor of the saintly Prince Vladimir, sir."

"Well, God be praised. She is a good and faithful servant, but as to intelligence—well, she hasn't much of it. That's why they fall into adultery."

CHAPTER III

The whole of the next day Porfiry Vladimirych remained in his study, praying to God for guidance. On the third day he emerged for morning tea, not in his dressing gown, as usual, but in full holiday attire, the way he always dressed when he intended to transact important business. His face was pale, but radiated inner serenity; a benign smile played upon his lips; his eyes looked kindly and all-forgiving. The tip of his nose was slightly red with elation.

He drank his three glasses of tea in silence, and between gulps moved his lips, folded his hands, and looked at the ikon as if, in spite of yesterday's vigil, he still expected speedy aid and intercession from it. Finally he sent for Ulita, and while waiting for her, kneeled again before the ikon, that he might once more strengthen himself by communion with God, and also that Ulita might see plainly that what was about to happen was not his doing, but the work of God. Ulita, however, as soon as she glanced at Yudushka, perceived there was treachery in the depth of his soul.

"Well, now I have prayed to God," began Porfiry Vladimirych, and in token of obedience to His holy will, he lowered his head and spread his arms.

"That's fine," answered Ulita, but her voice expressed such deep comprehension that Yudushka involuntarily raised his eyes.

She stood before him in her usual pose, one hand upon her breast, the other supporting her chin. But her face sparkled with suppressed laughter. Yudushka shook his head in sign of Christian reproach.

"I suppose God bestowed His grace upon you," continued Ulita, unperturbed by his gesture of warning.

"You always blaspheme," Yudushka blustered. "How many times have I warned you with kindness, and you are the same as ever. Yours is an evil tongue, a malicious tongue."

"It seems to me I haven't said anything. Generally when people have prayed to God, it means that God's grace is visited upon them."

"That's just it—'it seems!' But why do you prate about all that 'seems' to you? Why don't you learn how to hold your tongue when necessary? I am talking business and she—'it seems to me!'"

Instead of replying Ulita shifted from one foot to the other, as if to indicate that she knew everything Porfiry Vladimirych had to tell her by heart.

"Listen to me, you!" Yudushka began. "I prayed to the Lord all day yesterday, and to-day too, and—look at it from whatever angle you wish—we've got to provide for Volodka."

"Of course, you've got to provide for him. He is not a puppy, I dare say. You can't throw him into a pond."

"Wait a while! Let me say a word. You plague. So this is what I say. Take it any way you please, we've got to provide for Volodka. First, we must do it out of consideration for Yevpraksia and then we've got to make a man of him."

Porfiry Vladimirych glanced at Ulita in the hope that she might show her willingness to have a good long chat with him, but she took the matter plainly and even cynically.

"You mean me to take him to the foundling asylum?" she asked, looking straight at him.

"Oh, oh," exclaimed Yudushka, "you are very quick to decide. Oh, Ulita, Ulita! You always do things in a hurry and without due consideration. You're always ready to say something rash. How do you know? Maybe I don't intend to send him to the foundling asylum. Maybe I thought of something else for Volodka."

"Well, if you did, there's nothing bad about it."

"This is what I was going to say. On the one hand I feel for Volodka, but on the other hand, if you think the matter over and weigh it carefully, you see it's impossible to keep him here."

"Of course, what will people say? They'll say, 'How did a little baby boy come to the Golovliovo manor?'"

"Yes, they'll say that and other things. And besides, to stay here will be of no benefit to him. His mother is young, and she'll spoil him. I am old, and though I have nothing to do with the matter, still, in consideration of his mother's faithful service, I would also be easy with him. You can't help it, you know, the little fellow will have to be flogged for doing mischief, but how can you? It's this and that, and a woman's tears, and screams, and all. Am I right?"

"Yes, quite right. It is annoying."

"What I want is, that all should be well in our house. I want to see Volodka become a real man in time, a servant of God and a good subject of the Czar. If God wants him to be a peasant, I should like him to know how to plow, mow, chop wood—a little of everything. And if it will be his lot to be of a more exalted station, I want him to know some trade, some profession. Children from the foundling asylum sometimes rise to be teachers."

"From the foundling asylum? They are made generals at once, I suppose."

"Well, I wouldn't say generals, but still—maybe Volodka will live to be a famous man. And as to the manner they are brought up in there, it's excellent. I know all about it myself. Clean beds, healthy wet-nurses, white linen clothes, nipples, bottles, diapers, in a word, everything."

"Yes, it couldn't be better—for illegitimates!"

"And if he is placed in the country as a fosterchild, well, that will be just as good. He will get used to toil from his young days. Toil, you know, is as good as prayer. We, you see, pray in the regular way. We stand before the ikon, make the sign of the cross, and if our prayer pleases God, He rewards us for it. But the peasant—he toils. Sometimes he would be glad to pray in the proper way, but he hasn't the time for it. But God sees his labors and rewards him for his toil just as He rewards us for our prayers. We can't all live in palaces and go to balls and dances. Some of us must live in smoky hovels and take care of Mother Earth and nurse her. And as to where happiness lies, there are two guesses to it. Some live in palaces and in luxury, and yet shed tears; others live behind clay walls on bread and cider, yet feel as if they were in paradise. Am I right?"

"Nothing better if you feel as if you were in paradise."

"So, my dear, that's what we will do. Take that little rascal Volodka, wrap him up warm and cosy and go to Moscow at once with him. I'll order a roofed cart for you and a pair of good horses. The road is smooth, straight, fair, no puddles, no pitfalls. You'll roll along merrily. But see to it that everything is done in the best fashion, in Golovliovo fashion, just the way I like things to be done. The nipple should be clean, and the bottle, clothes, and sheets, and blankets, and diapers—take enough of everything. And if they won't give it all to you, come and tell me. When you get to Moscow, stop at an inn. Ask for enough to eat and a samovar and tea and all that. Oh, Volodka, dear! What trouble you are to me! It breaks my heart to part with you, but it can't be helped, my child. When you grow up, you'll see that it was for your own good, and you'll thank me for it."

Yudushka raised his hands slightly and moved his lips in sign of inner prayer. But that did not prevent him from glancing sideways at Ulita and noticing the sarcastic quivering of her face.

"Well, what—did you want to say something?"

"No, nothing. Of course, you know—he'll thank his benefactors—if he finds them."

"Oh, you wicked thing! You think we'll place him there without a proper card? Why, of course, you'll take out a card, from which document we'll be able to find him. They'll bring him up and teach him sense, and then we'll come with the card and say, 'Here, now, let's have our fellow, our Volodka.' With the card we'll get him from the bottom of the sea. Am I right?"

Ulita made no reply. The caustic quivering of her face showed more distinctly than before and it exasperated Porfiry Vladimirych.

"You are a mean thing," he said. "The devil dwells in you. Fi, fi! Well, enough. To-morrow, before the sun is up, you'll take Volodka and quickly, so that Yevpraksia does not hear you, and set out for Moscow. You know where the Foundling Asylum is?"

"I've carried them," Ulita answered laconically, as if hinting at something in the past.

"Well, if you are used to it—all the better for you. You must know all the ins and outs of the place. Be sure to place him there and bow low before the authorities—like this." Yudushka rose and bowed, touching the floor with his hands.

"Beg of them to make him comfortable. And be sure to get the card, don't forget! The card will help us find him anywhere. I'll allow you two twenty-five ruble bills for expenses. I know how it is—you'll have to give some here and put a couple of rubles there. Ah, ah, how sinful man is! We are all human beings, nothing but human beings! We all like sweets and dainties. Why, even our Volodka! Look at him—he is no bigger than my finger nail—and see the money I've already spent on him."

Yudushka crossed himself and bowed low before Ulita, silently begging her to take good care of the little rascal.

Thus, in the simplest way, was the future of the little illegitimate arranged for.

The next morning, while the young mother was tossing about in delirium, Porfiry Vladimirych was standing at the window in the dining-room, moving his lips and making the sign of the cross on the window pane.

A cart, roofed over with mats, was leaving the front yard. It was carrying Volodka away.

It climbed up the hill, drove by the church, turned to the left and vanished in the village. Yudushka made another sign of the cross and sighed:

"The other day the priest was speaking about thawing weather," he said to himself, "but God sent us a frost instead. And a fine frost, at that. So it always is with us. We dream, we build castles in the air, we philosophize proudly and think we'll excel God Himself in His wisdom, but God in a trice turns our haughtiness of spirit into nothingness."

BOOK VI
THE DESERTED MANOR-HOUSE

CHAPTER I

Yudushka's agony commenced when the resources of loquaciousness, in which he had so freely indulged, began to give out. A void had formed around him. Some had died, others had deserted him. Even Anninka preferred the miserable future of a nomadic actress to the flesh-pots of Golovliovo. Yevpraksia alone remained. But Yevpraksia's conversational gifts were limited, and, more than that, Yevpraksia was now a changed person. It was the difference that had occurred in her which convinced Yudushka that his halcyon days were gone forever.

Till then Yevpraksia had been so helpless that Porfiry Vladimirych could tyrannize over her without the slightest risk, and her mental development was so backward and her character so flabby that she had not even felt the oppression. During Yudushka's harangues she would look into his eyes apathetically, and think of something else. But now suddenly she grasped something important, and the first consequence of awakened understanding was repugnance, sudden and half-conscious, but vicious and insuperable.

Anninka's stay had evidently not been without results for Yevpraksia. The casual conversations with the young actress had quite upset her. Previously she would never have dreamed of wondering why Porfiry Vladimirych, as soon as he met a man, instantly started to weave around him an oppressive net of words, sinister in their emptiness. Now she perceived it was not talking that Yudushka did, but tyrannizing, and it would be well worth the while to pull him up short and make him feel the time had come for him, too, to go easy. So, from now on, she listened to his endless flow of words and soon realized that the one purpose of Yudushka's talk was to worry, annoy, nag.

"The mistress herself said she didn't know why he talked so much," Yevpraksia reasoned. "No, it's his meanness working in him. He knows who is unprotected and at his mercy. And so he turns and twists them anyway he wants to."

But that was only secondary. The main effect of Anninka's visit was that it stirred up the instincts of youth in Yevpraksia, which had hitherto smouldered in her undeveloped mind and now suddenly flared up in a blaze. Many things became clear to her—for instance, why Anninka had refused to remain at Golovliovo and why she had said flatly, "It's horrible here!" She had acted that way because she was young and wanted to enjoy life. Yevpraksia, too, was young, indeed she was! It only seemed that her youth was crushed under a load of fat, in reality it manifested itself quite boldly. It called and lured her; its flame now died down, now flared up. She had thought Yudushka would do for her, but now she perceived her mistake. "The old, rotten stump, how he got round me!" ran through her mind. "Wouldn't it be fine now to live with a real lover, young and handsome? He would hug me and kiss me and whisper caressing words in my ear. The old scarecrow, how did he ever tempt me? The Pogorelka lady must have a lover, I'm sure. That's why she gathered up her skirts and sailed away so rapidly. And I must sit here, in a jail, chained to that old man."

Of course, some time passed before Yevpraksia mutinied openly; but once on the road of revolt she did not halt. A storm was brewing within her, and her hatred grew each minute. Yudushka, for his part, remained in ignorance of her state of mind. Yevpraksia began with general complaints, such as "he has spoiled my life." Then came comparisons. "In Mazulina," she reflected, "Pelageyushka lives with her master as a housekeeper. She never does a stroke of work, and wears silk dresses. She sits in a cosy little room doing bead embroidery. How I hate you now, you old fright; How I hate you, I hate you!" she wound up with a cry.

In addition to this, the main cause of irritation, there was another one, one that was valuable because it could serve as a good occasion for the declaration of war against Yudushka. It was her confinement and the disappearance of her son Volodya.

At the time of the child's removal Yevpraksia had been rather indifferent. Porfiry Vladimirych had curtly announced that the baby had been entrusted to reliable people, and he presented her with a new shawl by way of solace. Then life resumed its course, and Yevpraksia plunged into the mire of household affairs with greater industry than before, as if to atone for her unsuccessful motherhood. But whether the mother feeling continued to smoulder in her, or whether it was merely a whim, at any rate, the memory of Volodka came back to her, and at the precise moment when

Yevpraksia felt the breath of freedom and it began to dawn upon her that there existed another life different from that at Golovliovo. The occasion was too good not to be taken advantage of.

"To think of what the scoundrel has done!" she reflected, trying consciously to work herself into a rage. "He has robbed me of my own child. Just as one drowns a pup in the pond."

Little by little the thought filled her mind completely. She came to believe that she had always longed for her child passionately. Her hatred of Porfiry Vladimirych fed on this new and rapidly growing obsession.

"At least, I should have had something to amuse me now. Volodya, Volodyushka! My dear little son! Where are you now? He must have shipped you to some wretched peasant woman. God curse them, the damned gentry. They bring children in the world and then throw them like pups into a ditch, and no one takes them to account. It would have been better for me to cut my throat than to allow that shameless old brute to outrage me."

Her hatred was now ripe. She felt a desire to vex and pester him and spoil life for him. War began, the most unbearable of wars, squabbles and provocations, and petty pricking. It was the only form of warfare that could have subdued Porfiry Vladimirych.

CHAPTER II

One morning when Porfiry Vladimirych was sitting at tea, he was unpleasantly surprised. He was discharging masses of verbal pus, while Yevpraksia, with a saucer of tea in her hand and a piece of sugar between her teeth, was listening in silence, snorting from time to time. Warm, fresh-baked bread had been served, and he had just begun to develop a theory of his own to the effect that there are two kinds of bread, visible bread which we eat and thereby sustain our bodies, and the invisible, spiritual bread of which we partake for the good of our soul. Suddenly Yevpraksia broke in upon his discourse most unceremoniously.

"People say Palageyushka lives so well at Mazulino," she began, turning her entire body round to the window and swinging her crossed feet with impudent nonchalance.

Yudushka was somewhat startled by the unexpected remark, but attributed no peculiar importance to it.

"In case we don't eat visible bread for a long time," he went on, "we feel bodily hunger; and if we don't partake of the spiritual bread for some length of time— —"

"I say, Palageyushka certainly lives well at Mazulino," Yevpraksia interrupted again.

Porfiry Vladimirych, somewhat startled, looked at her in amazement, but refrained from scolding, evidently smelling a rat.

"If Palageyushka has a fine life, let her," he replied meekly.

"Her master," Yevpraksia kept on provokingly, "makes it nice and easy for her, he does not compel her to work, and dresses her in silk."

Yudushka's amazement grew. Yevpraksia's words were so preposterous that he was taken completely by surprise.

"A different dress every day, one to-day, one to-morrow, and another for holidays. She drives to church in a four-horse carriage. She goes first, and the master follows. When the priest sees her carriage, he has the bells rung. Then she sits in her own room. If her master wishes to spend some time with her, she receives him in her room. And her maid entertains her, or she does bead embroidery."

"Well, what of it?" asked Porfiry Vladimirych, at last coming to his senses.

"I was just telling what a pleasant life Palageyushka leads."

"And you, is your life worse? My, my, aren't you insatiable!"

Had Yevpraksia left his remark unanswered, Porfiry Vladimirych would have belched forth a torrent of empty words to drown her foolish hints. He would have resumed his twaddle. But apparently Yevpraksia had no intention of holding her tongue.

"I can't say that," she snapped back. "My life is not a sad one. Thank goodness I don't wear tick. Last year you bought me two calico dresses and paid five rubles for each. How generous!"

"And how about the woolen dress? And for whom was a shawl bought lately? My, my!"

Instead of answering, Yevpraksia placed her elbows on the table and flashed on Yudushka a side glance brimming over with such deep contempt that, unaccustomed to such looks, he was overcome with something like dread.

"Do you know how the Lord punishes ingratitude?" he mumbled feebly, hoping the reference to God would bring the woman to her senses. But his remark did not placate the mutineer. She cut him short at once.

"Don't talk me blind!" she exclaimed, "and don't drag in God. I'm not a baby. Enough! I've had enough of your tyranny."

Porfiry Vladimirych grew silent. His glass of tea stood untouched. His face grew pale, his lips trembled, as if trying vainly to curl up into a grin.

"These are Anninka's tricks," he said finally, though without a clear perception of what he was saying. "It's she, the snake, who has incited you."

"What tricks do you mean?"

"I mean the way you are talking to me. She, she taught you. No one else!" he foamed in a rage. "Give her silk dresses! The impudence! Do you know, you shameless creature, who in your position wears silk dresses?"

"Tell me and I will know."

"The most—the most dissolute ones. They are the only ones who wear silk dresses."

But Yevpraksia was not impressed. On the contrary, she answered him back with saucy arguments.

"I don't know why you call them dissolute. Everybody knows it's the masters that insist upon it. If a master seduces one of us, well, she lives with him. You and I are not so saintly either, we are doing the same as the Mazulina master and his queen."

"Oh, you! Fie, fie, for shame!"

Yudushka stared at his rebellious companion in utter consternation. A flow of empty words came tripping to his tongue, but for the first time in his life he felt a vague suspicion that there are occasions when even talk is useless.

"Well, my friend, I see there's no use talking to you to-day," he said, rising from the table.

"Neither to-day, nor to-morrow—never! No more of your tyranny! I've listened to you enough; now it's time for you to listen to me."

Porfiry Vladimirych made a movement as if to throw himself at her with clenched fists, but she protruded her chest with such determination that he lost heart. He turned his face to the ikon, lifted up his hands prayerfully, mumbled a prayer, and trudged slowly away into his room.

The whole day he felt uneasy. He had no definite fears for the future, but the feeling that something had broken in upon his well-ordered life and had passed unpunished greatly upset him. He did not go to dinner, pleading ill health, and in a meek, feeble voice asked that his food be brought into his room. In the evening after tea, which passed in silence for the first time in his life, he rose, as was his habit, to say his prayers. In vain did his lips seek to whisper the customary words. His agitated mind refused to follow the prayer. A persistent enervating anxiety pervaded his being, and he involuntarily strained his ear to catch the dying echoes of the day, which were lingering in the various corners of the vast manor-house. Finally, when even the yawning of the people could be heard no more, and the house was plunged in the profoundest quiet, he could not hold out any longer. Stealing noiselessly along the corridor, he went to Yevpraksia's room and put his ear to the door to listen. She was alone, and Yudushka heard her yawning and saying, "Lord! Savior! Holy Virgin," as she scratched her back.

Porfiry Vladimirych tried the knob, but the door was locked.

"Yevpraksia, darling, are you there?" he called.

"Yes, but not for you!" she snapped, so rudely that he immediately retreated to his room.

The next morning there was another conversation. Yevpraksia intentionally selected morning tea for launching her attacks on Porfiry Vladimirych. She felt instinctively that a spoiled morning would fill the entire day with anxiety and pain.

"I'd like to see how some people live," she began in a rather enigmatic manner.

Yudushka changed countenance. "It's beginning," flashed through his mind; but he held his tongue and waited for what would come next.

"It's fine to live with a handsome young friend, upon my word. You walk about in the rooms and look at each other. Not a cross word exchanged. 'My darling' and 'my heart'—that's your whole conversation. Lovely and noble!"

The subject was peculiarly hateful to Porfiry Vladimirych. Although of necessity he tolerated adultery within strict limits, he nevertheless considered lovemaking a diabolical temptation. This time, however, he restrained himself, all the more so because he wanted his tea. The tea-pot had been boiling on the samovar for quite some time, but Yevpraksia seemed to have forgotten about filling the glasses.

"Of course, many of us women are foolish," she went on, impudently swinging in her chair and drumming on the table with her fingers. "Some are so silly that they are ready to do anything for a calico dress; others give themselves away for nothing at all. 'Cider,' you said, 'drink as much as you please,' A fine thing to seduce a woman with!"

"Is it from interest alone that——" Yudushka risked a timid remark, watching the tea-pot from which steam had begun to escape.

"Who says from interest alone? Is it I who am a selfish woman?" cried Yevpraksia heatedly, suddenly shifting the conversation. "Do you mean to reproach me for the bread I eat?"

"I don't reproach you. I only said that not from interest alone do people——"

"'I said'! Talk, but talk sensibly. The idea! I serve from interest! Kindly permit me to ask you what particular advantage I have derived except cider and gherkins?"

"Well, cider and gherkins are not the only things——" ventured Yudushka, unable to restrain himself.

"What else have I gotten? Let me hear, let me hear!"

"Who sends four sacks of flour to your parents every month?"

"Four sacks. What else?"

"Groats, hemp-seed oil and other things——"

"So you are begrudging my poor parents the wretched groats and oil you send them? Oh, you!"

"I am not begrudging them. It's you——"

"Now you are accusing me. I can't eat a crust of bread without being reproached for it, and it's I who am blamed for everything."

Yevpraksia could hold out no longer and burst into tears. Meanwhile the tea kept on boiling, so that Porfiry Vladimirych became seriously alarmed. So he suppressed his growing temper, seated himself beside Yevpraksia and patted her on her back.

"Well, well. All right. Pour the tea. What is all this crying for?"

Yevpraksia emitted a few more sobs, pouted and looked into space with her dull eyes. "You have just been speaking of young fellows," he went on, trying to lend his voice as caressing a ring as possible. "Well—after all, I'm not so old, am I?"

"The idea! Leave me alone."

"Come, come. I—do you know—when I served in St. Petersburg, our director wanted to give me his daughter in marriage?"

"Must have been an old maid—or a cripple."

"No, she was quite a presentable young lady. And how she sang, how she sang!"

"Maybe she sang well, but you accompanied her badly," she retorted.

"No, I——"

Porfiry Vladimirych was completely put out. He was ready to act against his conscience and show that he, too, was skilled in the art of love-making. So he began to rock his body rather clumsily and went so far as to make an attempt to embrace Yevpraksia round her waist. But she drew back firmly from his outstretched arms and cried out angrily:

"Do me a favor and leave me, you goblin! Else I'll scald you with this boiling water. And I don't want your tea. I don't want anything. The idea—to reproach me for the piece of bread I eat. I'll go away from here! By Jesus, I will!"

She banged the door and ran out, leaving Porfiry Vladimirych alone in the dining-room.

Yudushka was completely puzzled. He began to pour the tea himself, but his hands trembled so violently that he had to call a servant to his assistance.

"No, this is impossible. I must think up something, arrange matters," he whispered, pacing up and down the dining-room in excitement.

But he turned out to be quite unable "to think up something" or "to arrange matters." His mind was so accustomed to leaping unrestrainedly from one fantastic subject to another, that the simplest problem of workaday reality threw him off his balance. No sooner did he make an effort to concentrate than a swarm of futile trifles attacked him from all sides and shut actuality out from his consideration. A strange stupor, a kind of mental and moral anæmia possessed his being. He was constantly lured away from the hard realities of life to the pleasant softness of phantoms, which he could shift and rearrange at will and without any hindrance whatever.

He spent the entire day in solitude, for Yevpraksia did not make her appearance at dinner or at evening tea. She stayed at the priest's the entire time and returned late in the evening. Yudushka's distress was extreme. He could not apply himself to any task, he even lost his wonted interest in trifles. One irrepressible thought tormented him: "I must somehow arrange matters, I must." He could not engage in idle calculations, nor even say prayers. He felt that a strange ailment was about to attack him. Many a time he halted before the window in the hope of concentrating his wavering mind on something, or distracting his attention, but all in vain.

It was early spring. The trees stood naked and the new grass had not yet appeared. Black fields, spotted here and there with white cakes of snow, stretched far away. The road was black and boggy and glittered with puddles. Yudushka saw it all as through a mist. There was no one round the rain-soaked servants' buildings, though all the doors were ajar. Nor could he reach anyone in the manor-house, although he constantly heard sounds as of doors banging in the distance. "How fine it would be," he mused, "to turn invisible and overhear what the knaves are saying about me. Do the rascals appreciate my favors or do they return abuse for my kindness? You stuff their bellies from morning till night, and still they squeal for more. Only the other day we opened a barrel of pickled cucumbers, and — —" But no sooner did his thoughts embark upon the exploration of some fantastic subject, no sooner did he began to calculate how many pickles the barrel held and how many pickles one man could consume, than the piercing thought of Yevpraksia brought him back to harsh reality and upset all his calculations.

"She went away without so much as saying a word to me," he reflected, while his eyes scanned the distance, endeavoring to sight the priest's house, in which Yevpraksia was in all probability chatting away at that moment.

Dinner was served. Yudushka sat at table alone slowly sipping thin soup (*she* knew he hated thin soup and had had it cooked watery on purpose). "I imagine the Father must be distressed by Yevpraksia's unbidden visit," he reflected. "She's a hearty eater and an extra dish, perhaps a roast, will have to be served for the guest." His imagination began to run away with him once more, and his mind began to ponder over questions like these: How many spoonfuls of cabbage-soup will Yevpraksia swallow? How many spoonfuls of gruel? What would the Father say to his wife about Yevpraksia's visit? How do they abuse her when alone? All this, the food and the conversation, hovered before his eyes with corporeal vividness.

"I fancy they all guzzle the soup from the same dish. The idea! A fine place she found to hunt for knick-knacks. Outside it's wet and slushy — just the kind of weather that breeds disease. Soon she will return, her skirt all dripping with mud, the disgusting creature. Yes, I must, I must do something!" All his musings inevitably ended with this phrase.

After dinner, he lay down for his nap, as usual, but tossed from side to side, unable to fall asleep. Yevpraksia came back after dark and stole into her nook so quietly that he did not observe her entrance. He had ordered the servants to let him know when she returned, but none of them said a word, as if they had agreed among themselves. He made another attempt to penetrate into her room, but again found the door locked.

Next morning Yevpraksia made her appearance at tea, but now her words were even more alarming and threatening.

"Dear me, where is my little Volodya?" she began, speaking in a studiously tearful tone.

Porfiry Vladimirych shuddered.

"If I could have the tiniest glimpse of him, if I could see how the darling suffers away from his mother! But maybe he is dead already."

Yudushka's lips whispered a prayer.

"It isn't the same as at other people's here. When Palageyushka gave birth to a daughter, they dressed the baby in batiste and silks and made a pink little bed for her. The nurse received more sarafans and frontlets than I ever had. And here — oh, you!"

Yevpraksia abruptly turned her head toward the window and sighed noisily.

"It is true what they say, that all the gentry are an abomination," she went on. "They make children and then throw them in the swamp, like puppies. What does it matter to them? They owe no account to anybody. Is there no God in Heaven? Even a wolf would not act like that."

Porfiry Vladimirych felt like a man sitting on pins and needles. He restrained himself for a long time, but finally could stand it no longer and said through clenched teeth:

"This is the third day that I've been listening to your talk."

"Well, why should *you* do all the talking? Other people have a right to say a word, too. Yes, sir! You've had a child. What have you done with it? I bet you let him rot in the hands of a wretched peasant woman in a dirty hut. I suppose the baby is lying somewhere in filth, sucking at a bottle turned sour, with no one to take care of it, and feed and clothe it."

She shed tears and dried her eyes with the end of her neckerchief.

"The Pogorelka lady was right; she said it's horrible here with you. It *is* horrible. No pleasures, no joy, nothing but mean, underhand ways. Prisoners in jail are better off. At least, if I had a baby now, there would be something to amuse me. But you have taken it away from me."

Porfiry Vladimirych sat shaking his head in torture. From time to time he groaned.

"Oh, how painful!" he finally said.

"Painful? Well, you have made the bed, lie on it. Upon my word, I shall go to Moscow and have a look at my dear little Volodya. Volodya, Volodya! Da-a-ar-ling! Master, shall I take a trip to Moscow?"

"It's no use," answered Porfiry Vladimirych in a hollow voice.

"Then I'll go without asking your permission, and no one can stop me. Because I am—a mother!"

"What sort of mother are you? You are a strumpet—that's what you are," Yudushka finally burst out. "Tell me plainly what you want of me."

Yevpraksia, apparently, was not prepared for this question. She stared at Yudushka and kept silence, as if wondering what she really wanted of him.

"So you call me a strumpet already?" she exclaimed, bursting into tears.

"Yes, a strumpet, a strumpet, a strumpet! Fie, fie, fie!"

Utterly enraged, Porfiry Vladimirych leapt to his feet and ran out of the room.

That was the last flicker of energy. Then he began rapidly to collapse, while Yevpraksia kept up her campaign. She had enormous power at her disposal, the stubbornness of stupidity, sometimes truly appalling because always trained upon the same point with the sole object of annoying, teasing, plaguing. Little by little the confines of the dining-room became too narrow for her. She invaded the study and attacked Yudushka within the precincts of that sanctuary, into which she would not even have thought of entering formerly when her master was "busy." She would come in, seat herself at the window, stare into space, scratch her shoulder blades on the post of the window, and begin to storm at him. She was especially fond of harping on the threat of leaving Golovliovo. As a matter of fact, she had never seriously thought of carrying out her threat, and she would have been astonished had anyone suggested to her that she return to her parental roof. But she suspected that Porfiry Vladimirych feared her desertion more than anything else, and she spared neither time nor energy in taking advantage of this. She approached the subject cautiously and in a roundabout way. She would sit a while, scratch her ear, and then remark, as if in a reminiscent frame of mind:

"To-day, I suppose, they are baking pancakes at father's."

At this prefatory remark Yudushka would grow green with rage. He was just getting ready to plunge into a complicated computation of how much he would get for his milk if all the cows of the neighborhood perished and none but his own, with God's help, remained unharmed and doubled their yield of milk.

"Why are they baking pancakes there?" he asked, trying to force a smile. "Goodness, to-day is Memorial Day! Isn't it stupid of me to have forgotten about it? And there's nothing in the house with which to honor the memory of my late mother. What a sin!"

"I should like to eat father's pancakes."

"Why not? Give orders to have them baked. Get hold of cook Marya or Ulita. Ulita cooks delicious pancakes."

"Maybe she has pleased you in some other way, too," remarked Yevpraksia acidly.

"No, but, oh, she's a witch at cooking pancakes, Ulita is. She cooks them light, soft—a sheer delight!"

Porfiry Vladimirych was evidently trying to mollify Yevpraksia, but to no avail.

"What I want is not yours, but father's pancakes," she answered, playing the spoiled darling.

"Well, that's not difficult. Get hold of the coachman, have him put a pair of horses to the carriage, and drive over to father's."

"No, sir, that won't do. If I've fallen in the trap, that's my own fault. Who has any use for one like me? You yourself called me a strumpet the other day. It's no use!"

"My, my! Isn't it a sin in you to accuse me falsely? Do you know how God punishes false accusations?"

"You did call me strumpet! You did! You did it in the presence of this ikon. How I hate your Golovliovo! I shall run away from here. I shall, by God!"

In the course of this spirited dialogue Yevpraksia behaved in a rather unconstrained manner. She swung about on the chair, picked her nose, and scratched her back. She was obviously playing comedy.

"Porfiry Vladimirych, I should like to tell you something," she went on mischievously. "I want to go home."

"Do you wish to pay a visit to your parents?"

"No, I mean to stay there altogether."

"What's the matter? Has anybody offended you?"

"No, but—I'm not going to stay here forever. Besides, it's too dull here—it's frightful. The house is like a deserted place. The servants poke themselves away in the kitchens and their own quarters, and I sit in the house all alone. Some of these days I shall be murdered. At night, when I go to bed, strange whispers come from every corner."

Days went by, but Yevpraksia never thought of carrying out her threat; which did not lessen its effect on Porfiry Vladimirych. It dawned upon him that in spite of his labors, so-called, he was utterly helpless, that if there were not someone to take care of his household affairs, he would have no dinner, no clean linen, no decent clothing. Hitherto he had not been aware of the fact that his surroundings had been artificially created. His day had passed in a manner established once and for all. Everything in the house centered around his person and existed for him; everything was done in its proper time, everything was in its proper place; in short, there reigned such mechanical precision everywhere that he gave no thought to it. Owing to this clock-work orderliness he could indulge in idle talk and thought without running against the sharp corners of reality. Of course, this artificial paradise held together only by a hair; but Yudushka, always centered in himself, did not know it. His life seemed to him to be built on a rock-bottom foundation, unchangeable, eternal. And suddenly the edifice was about to collapse because of Yevpraksia's foolish whim. Yudushka was completely taken aback. "What if she really leaves?" he reflected panic-stricken. And he began to frame all sorts of preposterous plans to keep her from going. He even decided on concessions to Yevpraksia's rebellious youth which would never before have entered his mind.

"Ugh, ugh, ugh!" he thought, and spat out in disgust when the possibility of having anything to do with the coachman Arkhip or the clerk Ignat presented itself to him in all its offensive nakedness.

Soon, however, he became convinced that his fears were groundless. Thereupon his existence entered a new and quite unexpected phase. Yevpraksia did not leave him, she even abated her attacks, but, to compensate, deserted him altogether. May set in, the weather was fair, and Yevpraksia scarcely ever put in appearance. She ran in for a moment and the next moment had disappeared. In the morning Yudushka did not find his clothing in its usual place, and he had to engage in lengthy negotiations with the servants before he got clean linen. His tea and meals were served either too early or too late, and he was waited upon by the tipsy lackey Prokhor, who came in a stained coat emanating a peculiarly disgusting odor of fish and vodka.

Nevertheless, Porfiry Vladimirych was glad that Yevpraksia left him in peace. He even reconciled himself to the disorder as long as he knew that there was someone to bear the responsibility for it. What frightened him was not so much the disorder as the thought that it might be necessary for him to interfere personally in the details of everyday life. He pictured with horror the minute he would have to administer, give orders and supervise. In anticipation of that awful moment, he endeavored to stifle the voice of protest that at times rose in him, tried to shut his eyes to the confusion reigning in the house, and keep in the background and hold his tongue.

In the meantime open debauchery made its nest in the manor-house. With the coming of fair weather a new life pervaded the estate, hitherto quiet and gloomy. In the evening all the servants, both young and old, went out in the village streets. The young people sang, played the accordion, laughed merrily, screamed and played tag.

The clerk Ignat appeared in a flaming red shirt and an astonishingly narrow jacket, that never closed over his chest, thrown out like a pouter-pigeon's, while the coachman Arkhip took possession of the silk shirt and plush sleeveless jacket worn on holidays, obviously vying with Ignat in the conquest of Yevpraksia's heart. The maiden herself ran from one to the other, bestowing her favors now on the clerk, now on the coachman. Porfiry Vladimirych dared not look out of the window for fear of witnessing a love scene; but he could not help hearing what was going on outside. At times he caught the resounding blow that Arkhip bestowed playfully upon Yevpraksia's back while playing tag. At other times he would catch fragments of conversation such as this:

"Yevpraksia Nikitishna! Yevpraksia Nikitishna! Madam!" the drunken Prokhor would call from the steps of the mansion.

"What do you want?"

"The key of the tea-chest, please. The master is asking for tea."

"Let him wait, the scarecrow!"

CHAPTER III

In a short time Porfiry had completely lost all habits of sociability. He no longer paid any attention to the confusion that had come into his existence. He demanded nothing better of life than to be left alone in his last refuge, his study. He had lost all his former ways of cavilling with and pestering those about him, and he was timorous and glumly meek. All ties between him and reality were cut. To hear nothing, to see nothing, that was his heart's desire. The behavior of Yevpraksia and the servants no longer concerned him. Formerly, had the clerk allowed himself the least inaccuracy in presenting his reports on the various branches of the household management, he would have talked him to death. Now at times the reports were weeks late, and he was unresentful except when he needed some data for his fantastic computations. But when alone in his study he felt himself absolute master, free to give himself over nonchalantly to inane musings. Both of his brothers had died from drink. He, too, fell into the clutches of drunkenness. But his intoxication was mental. Shut up in his study, he racked his brains from early morning till far into the night over fantastic problems. He elaborated various fabulous schemes, made speeches before imaginary audiences, and wove whole scenes about the first person that crossed his mind.

In this wild maze of fantastic acts and images a morbid passion for gain played the most important part.

Porfiry Vladimirych had always had a strong leaning toward the petty annoyance of people and litigation, but because of his lack of practicality he had derived no direct profit from it. Sometimes he was even the first to suffer. This proclivity of his was now transferred to a world of abstractions and phantoms, where there was no scope for resistance on the part of the oppressed and no need for self-justification. The dividing line between the weak and the powerful vanished. In that world there were no police or justices of the peace, or rather, there were, but they existed solely for the purpose of protecting his own interests. On this fantastic plane he could freely enmesh the whole universe in his net of intriguing, cavilling, and petty oppression.

He loved to torment people, ruin them, make them unhappy, suck their blood — at least, in his imagination. He would look over the various branches of his establishment and on each build up a fantastic structure of all manner of oppression and plunder—a veritable paradise, but the foulest ever conceived by a landed proprietor. And everything depended here on overpayments and underpayments assumed arbitrarily, each overpaid or underpaid kopek served as a pretext for remodelling the entire edifice, which thus passed through endless changes.

When his tired thoughts were no longer capable of following out all the details of the intricate computations on which his imaginary operations were based, he applied his imagination to a more plastic material. He recalled every conflict and altercation he had had not only in recent times, but far back in his youth, and he so manipulated his reminiscences as always to come out the victor. He took revenge on those of his former colleagues who had gone over his head in service and had so deeply wounded his self-love that he renounced his official career. He revenged himself on his schoolmates who had taken advantage of their physical strength to tease or persecute him; on the neighbors that had opposed his claims and stood up for their rights; on the servants who had offended him or simply had not treated him with sufficient respect; on "dearest mamma" Arina Petrovna for having wasted too much of the money that "by law" belonged to him on the repairs of Pogorelka; on his brother Simple Simon for having nicknamed him Yudushka; on aunt Varvara Mikhailovna for having unexpectedly given birth to children, with the result that the property of Gavryushkino was forever lost to the family. He revenged himself on the living and he revenged himself on the dead.

Gradually he worked himself into a state of actual intoxication. The ground vanished from under his feet, wings grew on his shoulders, his eyes shone, his lips trembled and foamed, his face grew ghastly pale, and took on a threatening air. The atmosphere around him swarmed with ghosts, and he fought them in imaginary battles.

His existence became so ample and independent that there was nothing left for him to desire. The whole universe was at his feet, that is, the universe of which his wretched mind could conceive. It was something in the nature of ecstatic clairvoyance, not unlike the phenomena that take place at the seances of mediums. His untrammeled imagination created an illusory reality, rendered concrete and almost tangible by his constant mental frenzy. It was not faith or conviction, but unrestrained mental debauchery, a sort of trance in which his tongue involuntarily uttered words and his body made automatic gestures.

Porfiry Vladimirych was happy. He locked up the windows and doors that he might not hear, he drew down the curtains that he might not see. He went through the customary functions and duties which had no connection with the world of his imagination, in haste, almost with disgust. When the ever-drunken Prokhor rapped at his door and announced that dinner was served, he ran into the dining-room impatiently, hurriedly swallowed his three courses and disappeared again into his study. Something new showed in his manners—a mixture of timidity and derision, as if he both feared and defied the few people whom he met. He rose very early and immediately set to work. He cut down the time devoted to worship, said his prayers indifferently, without thinking of their meaning, crossed himself and went through the other gestures of worship mechanically and carelessly. Apparently even the notion of a hell with its complicated system of punishments was no longer present in his mind.

Meanwhile Yevpraksia reveled in the satisfaction of carnal desires. Dancing between the clerk Ignat and the coachman Arkhip, and also casting glances at the red-faced carpenter Ilyusha, who was mending the cellars at the head of a gang of workmen, she did not notice what was going on in the manor-house. She thought the master was playing "a new comedy," and many a light remark about the master was passed in the jolly gatherings of the servants. But one day she happened to enter the dining-room when Yudushka was hurriedly despatching the remnants of roast goose, and suddenly a kind of dread fell upon her.

Porfiry Vladimirych wore a greasy dressing-gown, through the holes of which the cotton interlining peeped out. He was pale, unkempt, and his face bristled with a many days' growth.

"Dear master, what is it? What is the matter?" she turned to him in fright.

Porfiry Vladimirych only smiled half sheepishly, half derisively, and the meaning of his smile was: "I'd like to see how you could get at me now."

"Darling master, what is the matter? Tell me, what has happened to you?" repeated Yevpraksia.

He rose, fixed on her a gaze brimming over with hatred, and said, pausing after each word:

"If you, you hussy, ever dare—enter my study—I will kill you!"

CHAPTER IV

As a result of this scene Yudushka's life outwardly changed for the better. Distracted by no material hindrances, he gave himself completely over to his solitude, so that he did not even notice how the summer passed away.

It was late in August, the days grew shorter; it drizzled ceaselessly and the soil became boggy. The trees looked mournful, with their yellow leaves bestrewing the ground. Absolute silence reigned in the court-yard and about the servants' quarters. The domestics sat quietly under cover, partly because of the weather, partly because they finally perceived that something was the matter with the master. Yevpraksia came completely to her senses, forgot the silk dresses and her lovers, and sat in the maids' room for hours on end, brooding and wondering what she could do. The drunken Prokhor teased her that she had designs on the master's life, that she had poisoned him and she could not escape the road to Siberia.

Meanwhile, Yudushka sat in his study, deep in reveries. The ceaseless patter of the rain on the window-panes lulled him half to sleep—the most favorable state for the play of his fancy. He imagined he was invisible and was inspecting his possessions, accompanied by old Ilya, who had served as bailiff under Yudushka's father, and whose bones had long since been rotting in the village churchyard.

"Ilya is a clever fellow," argued Porfiry Vladimirych with himself, glad that Ilya had arisen from the dead. "An old servant! Nowadays his kind is getting rare. Nowadays they know how to chat and fidget, but when it comes to business, they're good for nothing."

After saying an appropriate prayer, Yudushka and Ilya pick their way leisurely across meadows and ravines, dales and hills, and soon reach the Ukhovshchina waste. For a while they stand dazed, unable to believe their own eyes. Straight before them looms up a magnificent pine forest, their tops tossing in the wind. Some of the trees are so big in circumference that two or even three men could not embrace them. Their trunks are straight, naked, crowned with mighty, spreading tops—all signs of vigor and longevity.

"What a forest, brother!" exclaims Yudushka, enraptured.

"This wood has been protected from felling," explains Ilya. "Under your late grandfather Mikhail Vasilyevich, a procession with holy ikons went around it. And look how tall the trees have grown."

"How large do you think the forest is?"

"At that time it held just seventy desyatins, and the desyatin was then, as you know, one and a half times the present size."

"And how many trees, d'you think, are there on one desyatin?"

"I can't tell. Only God has counted them."

"I reckon there are no less than six or seven hundred trees to a desyatin. I mean the desyatin now used. Wait! If we take the number to be six hundred—or, let us say, six hundred and fifty trees, how many trees are there on one hundred and five desyatins?"

Porfiry Vladimirych takes a sheet of paper and multiplies 105 by 65 and gets 6,825 trees.

"Now, see here, if I were to sell all this timber, do you think I can get ten rubles a tree?"

Old Ilya shakes his head.

"Ten is little," he says. "Look at these trees. Each trunk will give two mill beams and some planks and boards and firewood. What do you think is the price of a mill-wheel beam?"

Porfiry Vladimirych makes believe he does not know, although he figured out everything to a kopek long ago.

"Here," continues the peasant, "a beam is worth ten rubles, but if we take it to Moscow it will be worth its weight in gold. It is a tremendous beam. You will hardly haul it on a three-horse team. And think of the second beam that can be made out of the stem, and the boards and laths and firewood, and branches. Twenty rubles, I should think, is the lowest price for a tree."

Porfiry Vladimirych listens and takes in his words greedily. A clever, faithful servant this Ilya. And how well he has picked out his help! Old Vavilo, Ilya's assistant—he too has been resting in the churchyard for a good many years—is quite worthy of his superior. The foresters, too, are all tried, stalwart men, and the hounds at the corn lofts are fierce. Both the men and the dogs are ready to grapple with the devil himself for the master's good.

"Let's figure out, brother. If we sell the whole forest, what will it come to?"

Porfiry Vladimirych again makes a mental calculation of the value of a large beam, a smaller beam, a plank, a lath, the firewood and the branches.

He adds up, multiplies, now omitting fractions, now adding them. Columns of numbers fill the sheet.

"Here is the total, brother," says Yudushka, showing Ilya's phantom an altogether fabulous sum. The old servant is dazed.

"Is it not a little too large?" he says, pensively shrugging his shoulders.

But Porfiry Vladimirych has already cast off all doubts and giggles gleefully.

"You are a queer fellow, brother!" he exclaims. "It isn't I who say it, it's the number that says it. There is a science called arithmetic. It never tells a lie, brother! Well, this will do for Ukhovshchina. Now let's have a look at Lisy-Yamy, brother. It's a long time since I have been there. I have a strong suspicion the peasants have become thievish. There's Garanka, the guard—I know, I know. Garanka is a good, faithful guard, that's true enough. Still, you know. It seems to me he is not what he used to be either."

They plough noiselessly and unseen through a birch thicket, and stop suddenly, holding their breath. A peasant's cart lies sprawling across the road on its side, and the peasant is standing by, looking at the broken axle in perplexity. He has been standing there for some time, cursing the axle and himself and whipping the horse now and then. Finally he sees he cannot loaf there all day long. He looks around and pricks up his ears to make sure no one is coming along the road. Then he selects a suitable birch tree, and takes out an axe. Meanwhile Yudushka stands motionless and watches. The young birch shudders, sways and suddenly sinks to the ground like a sheaf of corn, reaped by the sickle. The thief is about to lop off the length of an axle from the trunk, but Yudushka has decided that the moment has come. He steals upon him and in a trice snatches the axe from his hand.

"Ah!" is all the thief, taken red-handed, has time to exclaim.

"Ah!" Yudushka mimics him. "Are you allowed to steal timber? 'Ah!' Is it your birch-tree you have just felled?"

"Forgive me, sir!"

"I forgave everyone long ago, brother. I am myself a sinner before the Lord and I dare not judge another. It is the law, not I, that condemns you. Take the tree you have felled to the manor-house and pay up a fine of one ruble. In the meantime, I shall keep your axe. Don't you worry, it is in good hands, brother."

Glad that he was able to prove to Ilya how well-grounded were his suspicions in regard to Garanka, Yudushka transports himself in imagination to the forester's cottage and reprimands him soundly. On his way back home he catches three hens belonging to peasants in the act of feeding on his oats.

Back in his study, he falls again to work, and a peculiar system of household management is suddenly born in his brain. The system is based on the assumption that all mankind suddenly has begun to steal his wood and damage his fields by letting cattle graze upon them. But this does not grieve Yudushka, on the contrary he rubs his hands in delight.

"Let your cattle graze on my fields, fell my trees. I shall be the better off for it," he repeats, hugely pleased. Then he takes a fresh sheet of paper and resumes his ciphering and reckoning. The problems to be solved are these: First, how much oats grows on one desyatin and what will the fines amount to if the peasants' hens scratch the oats up? And, second, how many birches grow in Lisy-Yamy and how much money can they bring in if the peasants fell them illegally and pay the fine? "A birch, though felled," reflects Yudushka gleefully, "will in the end get to the house and be used as firewood—firewood free of charge, mind you!"

Long rows of figures appear on the paper. Yudushka becomes so tired and excited that he rises from the table all perspiring and lies down on the sofa to rest. Here his imagination does not cease its work, it merely selects an easier theme.

"Mamma was a clever woman, mamma was," muses Porfiry Vladimirych. "She knew how to be exacting and how to set one at ease— that is why people served her so willingly. Still she was not without sins. Oh, yes, she had plenty of them."

No sooner does Yudushka think of Arina Petrovna than she appears before him in person, coming straight from the grave.

"I don't know, my friend, I don't know what fault you have to find with me," she says dejectedly, "it seems to me that I——"

"I know, I know," Yudushka cuts her short unceremoniously. "Let me be frank and thrash out the matter with you. For instance, why did you not stop Aunt Varvara Mikhailovna that time?"

"But how in the world could I stop her? She was of age, and she had the full right to dispose of herself."

"Oh, no, permit me, mother dear. What sort of a husband had she? An old drunkard, not much of a man, I should say. Nevertheless, they had four children. Where did they come from, I'm asking you?"

"But how strangely you speak, my friend. As if I were the cause of it all."

"Cause or no cause, you could have influenced her. You ought to have treated her kindly, she would have been shamed by you. But you did the contrary. You kept on scolding her and calling her shameless, and you suspected almost every man in the neighborhood of being her lover. Of course, she kicked up the dust. It's a pity. The Goryushkino estate would have been ours now."

"You cannot forget that Goryushkino," says Arina Petrovna, evidently brought to a standstill.

"What do I care for Goryushkino? I don't need anything. If I have enough to buy a church candle and some oil for the image lamp, I am satisfied. But what about justice, dear mamma, justice? Yes, mother dear, I would be glad to hold my tongue, but I cannot help being frank with you. There's a sin on your conscience, a great sin, indeed."

Arina Petrovna does not answer, and it is impossible to tell whether she is dejected or merely perplexed.

"Another thing," Yudushka goes on, evidently reveling in mother dear's embarrassment. "Why did you buy a house for brother Stepan?"

"I had to, my friend. I had to give him some share," says Arina Petrovna, trying to defend herself.

"And he squandered it away, of course. As if you did not know him! You knew he was a loafer, a disrespectful, foul-mouthed scamp. And to think that you wanted to give him the Vologda village, too. A neat little estate with a nice little forest and a tiny lake, lying like a shelled egg—Christ be with it! It is well that I happened to be around and kept you from taking that imprudent step. Ah, mamma dear, mamma dear, how could you?"

"But he was a son of mine, you understand? A son!"

"I know, I understand very well. And still, I repeat, you ought not to have done it. You paid twelve thousand for the house—where is the money? And Goryushkino is worth at least fifteen thousand. So the loss comes to quite a sum."

"Well, that will do, that will do. Don't be angry with me, please don't!"

"I am not angry, dearest mother, I am only upholding the cause of justice. What's true is true—and I loathe falsehood. I was born with truth, have lived with truth, and with truth I shall die. God loves truth and He would have us, too, love it. Take the case of Pogorelka, for instance. I shall always say you invested too much money in it."

"But I myself lived there."

Yudushka clearly reads "You silly Bloodsucker!" on his mother's face; but he makes believe he does not see.

"Well, yes, you lived there—still—the image-case is in Pogorelka. Whose is it, I'd like to know. And the pony and the tea-caddy. I saw that tea-caddy at Golovliovo with my own eyes, when papa was still alive. What a beautiful little box!"

"Well, but——"

"No, dearest mother, let me speak. Of course it looks like a trifling matter, but a ruble here, half a ruble there, come to quite a sum in the end. Let me use exact figures and make it clear to you. Figures are holy, they never lie."

Porfiry Vladimirych runs over to the table with the intention of finally determining the exact amount of loss that his mother dear had caused him to sustain. He manipulates the counting-board, covers sheets of paper with rows of figures, arms himself to convict Arina Petrovna. But fortunately for her his wavering thoughts cannot remain fixed on one subject for a long time. Unnoticed by himself a new thought enters his mind and, as if by magic, gives an entirely different trend to his ideas. The image of his mother, a minute ago so clear before his eyes, suddenly drops away. He forgets her, his notions become confused, other notions enter his mind.

Porfiry Vladimirych has long had the intention of figuring out what his crops could bring him in. The opportune moment is here. He knows the peasant is always in want, is always on the lookout to borrow provender and always pays his debts with interest. He knows also that the peasant is especially generous with his work, which "costs him nothing," and is not considered as possessing any value in settling accounts. There are many needy people in Russia, oh, how many! There are many people who do not know what the next day will bring them, who see nothing but despair and emptiness wherever they turn their weary eyes, and who hear everywhere only one clamor: "Pay your debt! Pay your debt!" It is around these shiftless, utterly destitute men that Yudushka weaves his net, with a delight passing sometimes into an orgy.

It is April, and the peasant as usual has nothing to eat. "You have gobbled up all your crops, my dear fellows," Porfiry Vladimirych muses. "All winter you feasted, and in spring your stomach is shrivelled from hunger." He has just settled the accounts of last year's crops. The threshing was completed in February, the grain was in the granaries in March, and the amount was recorded in the numerous books the other day. Yudushka stands at the window and waits. On the bridge afar off the peasant Foka appears in his cart. At the bend of the road leading to Golovliovo he shakes the reins rather hastily, and for want of a whip hits his battered jade with his fist.

"He's heading here," whispers Yudushka. "Look at the horse. A wonder it can drag its feet. But if you had fed it well a month or two, it would become quite a horse. You might get twenty-five rubles for it, or even as much as thirty."

Meanwhile Foka drives up to the servants' house. He ties the animal to the hedge, throws it a handful of hay, and a minute later stands in the maids' quarters, shifting from one foot to another. It is in the maids' quarters that Porfiry Vladimirych usually receives such visitors.

"Well, friend, how are things going?"

"Please sir, what I need is some corn."

"How's that? Are you through with your own? What a pity! If you drank less vodka, and worked more, and prayed to God, the soil would feel it. Where one grain grows now, two grains would grow. Then there would be no need for you to borrow."

Foka smiles vaguely, instead of replying.

"You think if God is far from us, He does not see?" Porfiry Vladimirych goes on moralizing. "God is here and there and everywhere, he is with us while we are talking here. He sees everything and hears everything, he only pretends not to see things. 'Let my creatures live after their own way, and we shall see whether they will remember me.' And we sinners take advantage of that, and instead of buying a candle for God from our meager means, we keep on going to the public-house. That's why God gives us no corn. Am I not right, friend?"

"You are quite right, sir. There's no denying it."

"Well, you see, you understand it now. And why is it that you understand it? Because the Lord withdrew His mercy from you. If you had had an abundant crop of corn, you would carry on again, but since God——"

"Right, sir, and if——"

"Wait a minute. Let me say a word. The Lord recalls Himself to those who forgot Him. That is always the case. And we must not grumble over it, but understand that God does it for our good. Were we to remember God, He would never forget us. He would grant us everything, corn and oats and potatoes—more than we need. And He would take care of our animals. Look at your horse. It is skin and bones. And if you have chickens, He would keep them in condition, too."

"You are quite right, sir."

"Man's first duty is to honor God, man's second duty is to honor his superiors, those who have been distinguished by the czars themselves—the gentry, for instance."

"It seems to me, sir, that I——"

"That's just it, 'it seems to me.' But give a little thought to the matter, and you will find out that it's all different. Now when you have come to borrow corn you are very respectful and bland. But two years ago, you remember, when I needed harvesters and came to you peasants to ask for help, what did you answer? 'We have to harvest ourselves,' you said. 'It is not the way it used to be,' you said, 'when we worked for the landlords. Now we are free!' Free, and no corn!"

Yudushka looks at Foka, but Foka does not stir.

"You are very proud, that's why you have no luck. Take me, for example. The Lord has blessed me, and the Czar has distinguished me. But I am not proud. How can I be? What am I but a worm, a moth, a nothing. God took and blessed me for my humility. He loaded me with favors, and put it into the Czar's mind to favor me, too."

"Porfiry Vladimirych, I think that under serfdom we were far better off," Foka remarks, playing the flatterer.

"Yes, brother, those were fine days for you peasants. You had plenty of everything, corn and hay and potatoes. But why recall the old times? I am not rancorous. I have long forgotten about the harvesters. I only mentioned them in passing. Let me see—did you say you needed corn?"

"Yes, I did, sir."

"You have come to buy some, have you?"

"How can I? I should like to borrow some until the new corn comes."

"My, my! Corn is not to be had for money nowadays. I really don't know what to do with you."

Porfiry Vladimirych ponders for a while, as if really perplexed.

"I can lend you some corn, my friend," he finally says. "I have none for sale, for I loathe to traffic in God's gifts. But I will gladly lend you some corn. To-day I'll lend to you, to-morrow you'll lend to me. To-day I have plenty. Take some, help yourself. You want a measure of corn? Take a measure. You want half a measure? Take half a measure. Tomorrow may find me knocking at your window saying, 'Dear Foka, lend me half a measure of corn, I have nothing to eat.'"

"Oh, sir, will you come to me?"

"I shall not. That was merely an example. The world has seen greater reverses. There was Napoleon, about whom the newspapers have written so much. That's how it is, brother. So how much corn do you want?"

"A measure, if you please."

"Well, I can let you have a measure. Only let me warn you, corn is tremendously dear nowadays. This is what we are going to do: I shall give you six chetveriks, and in eight months you will deliver a measure to me. I don't take any interest, but an additional chetverik or two— —"

Yudushka's offer makes Foka gasp. For some time he says nothing, only shrugs his shoulders. "Won't that be a bit too much, sir?" he says at last, evidently alarmed.

"If it's too much, go to others. You see, my friend, I am not forcing you, I am only making you an offer in a friendly way. I didn't send for you, did I? You came here yourself. You came to ask for something and that's my answer. Isn't it so, friend?"

"Yes, quite so, but don't you think it's too much interest?"

"Ah, ah, ah! And I thought you were a just, respectable peasant. Well, you will say to me, what am I going to live on? How will I meet my expenses? Do you know what expenses I have? My dear man, there is no end to them. I've got to pay here, and meet my obligations there, and produce cash in a third place. I've got to satisfy every one. All are after Porfiry Vladimirych, all ask something of him, and I've got to get along with them as best I can. And then again, if I sold the corn to the dealer, I should get money at once. And money, my friend, is a sacred thing. With money I can buy securities, put them in a safe place, and draw interest. No worry, you know, of any kind, no trouble at all. Just clip the coupon and get your money. But with the corn you've got to go carefully about it, and look after it, and all that. A lot of it will dry up, and be wasted, and the mice will eat it up. No, brother, money is the best thing—nothing like it! It would be high time for me to become sensible and turn everything into money and leave you folks."

"Oh, Porfiry Vladimirych, stay with us."

"Well, my dear man, I should like to, but I can't stand it any longer. If I had the strength of my youth, of course I would stay with you and keep at it. But no, it's time to rest. I will go to the Trinity Monastery, I will find shelter under the wing of the saints, and not a soul will hear from me. And how good I'll feel! All will be peaceful and quiet and honest; no noise, no quarrels—like in Heaven."

In a word, in spite of all of Foka's protestations, Porfiry Vladimirych arranges the bargain to suit himself. But that is not enough. At the very moment that Foka consents to the terms of the loan, a thought flashes through Yudushka's mind. A certain Shelepikha meadow appears on the scene. It doesn't amount to much, hardly a desyatin to mow.

"You see, I am doing you a favor, so you do me one in turn," says Porfiry Vladimirych. "This is not interest, but just a favor. God does favors to us all, and we've got to do likewise to one another. You will mow this desyatin in no time, and I'll be much obliged to you. You see, brother, I am a plain man. You'll do me a ruble's worth of service, and I——"

Porfiry Vladimirych rises, faces the church, and makes the sign of the cross to show that the transaction is at an end. Foka also rises and makes the sign of the cross.

Foka has disappeared. Porfiry Vladimirych produces a sheet of paper, arms himself with the counting-board, and the beads begin jumping fast under his skilful fingers. Little by little an orgy of numbers commences. The whole world becomes enwrapped in mist. With feverish haste Yudushka passes from the paper to the counting-board and from the counting-board to the paper. The rows of figures keep growing larger and larger.

BOOK VII
THE SETTLEMENT

CHAPTER I

It is the middle of December. The country stretches still and benumbed, covered with a mantle of snow as far as the eye can reach. The horses, though pulling empty carts, wade with difficulty through the snow-drifts that the wind has driven during the night. There is not the trace of a path to the Golovliovo estate.

Porfiry Vladimirych had grown so unaccustomed to visits that in the beginning of autumn he barred the front entrance to the house and the main gateways leading to it, leaving only the servants' entrance and the side gates for the domestics to communicate with the outer world.

One morning as the clock was striking eleven, Yudushka in his dressing-gown was standing at the window staring aimlessly before him. Since early morning he had been walking to and fro in the room, deep in thought about a certain momentous matter, and ceaselessly counting imaginary profits. Finally, he became mixed in the ciphering and grew tired. Both the magnificent orchard in front of the manor and the village behind it were lost to view in the snow. After yesterday's blizzard the air was frosty, and the snow shimmered and sparkled in the sun, so that Porfiry Vladimirych had to blink. The court was silent and deserted. There was not the least movement, either in the servants' quarters or near the cattle yard. Even the village itself was so silent that it seemed as if death had suddenly stolen upon the people. The only thing that attracted Yudushka's attention was a curl of thin smoke floating upward from the priest's house.

"Eleven o'clock, and the parson's wife has not yet finished cooking," he thinks. "Those black coats are always gorging."

With this as a point of departure, his mind wandered on. Was it a weekday or a holiday, a fast day or not, and what can the parson's wife be cooking? But suddenly his attention was diverted. On the hill at the very beginning of the road from the village of Pogorelka a black dot appeared, approached gradually and grew larger and larger. Porfiry Vladimirych looked intently. "Who could be coming, a peasant or somebody else? Who could it be but a peasant? Yes, a peasant! What was he coming for? If for wood, why, then, the Naglovka forest was on the other side of the village. The knave must be intending to steal some wood. If he was making for the mill, why, then, he ought to have turned to the right. Perhaps he was coming to fetch the priest. Someone dying, or, perhaps, already dead? Or maybe a child had been born? Who could it be? In autumn Nenila walked about pregnant, but it was too early for her. If it should be a boy, he would get into the census. What was the population of Naglovka at the last census? But if a girl, she would not get into the census, and——Still, it is impossible to get along without the female sex. Fie!"

Yudushka spat and looked at the ikon in the corner, as if seeking its protection from the Evil One.

It is quite possible that he would have continued wandering in thought had the black speck been lost to view, but it kept on growing and at last turned toward the marsh road leading to the church. Then Yudushka saw quite clearly that it was a small wagon pulled by two horses, one behind the other. Next it went up the hill, and drove past the church. "Perhaps it is the bishop," passed through his mind. "That's why they have not yet finished cooking at the parson's house." Then the vehicle turned to the right and made straight for the manor-house. Porfiry Vladimirych instinctively drew his dressing-gown together and stepped away from the window, as if afraid of being seen by the traveller.

He had guessed correctly. The wagon drove up to the house and stopped at the side gate. A young woman jumped out of it quickly. She was dressed out of season in a large cotton-lined greatcoat trimmed with lamb's fur, more for show than for warmth. She was apparently frozen. No one appearing to receive her, the stranger hopped over to the maids' entrance. In a few seconds the outer door in the women's quarters banged shut, then another door, and another, until all the rooms adjacent to the maids' entrance were filled with a noise of hurried footsteps and banging doors.

Porfiry Vladimirych stood at his study door listening intently. It was so long since he had seen any strangers, and altogether he had become so unaccustomed to the company of human beings, that he was somewhat bewildered. Nearly a quarter of an hour passed, the running and the banging of the doors continued, and yet he was not told who had come. It was clear that the guest was a relative, who did not doubt her right to the host's hospitality. But what relatives had he? He tried to recall them, but his memory was dull. He had had two sons, Volodka and Petka; he had had a mother, Arina Petrovna—long, long ago! Last autumn Nadka Galkina, daughter of his late aunt Varvara Mikhailovna, had taken up her residence at Goryushkino. Could it be she? Why, no. She had already tried to make her way into the Golovliovo temple, but to no avail.

"She will not dare to, she will not dare to!" reiterated Yudushka, burning with indignation at the very thought of her intrusion. "But who else can it be?"

While he was busy guessing, Yevpraksia approached the door cautiously and announced:

"The young lady of Pogorelka, Anna Semyonovna, has arrived."

It was indeed Anninka, but changed beyond recognition. She was no longer the beautiful, lively, buoyant girl with rosy cheeks, full gray eyes, high breast and heavy, ash-colored tresses massed low on her head, who had come to Golovliovo shortly after the death of Arina Petrovna, but a weak, wasted creature with a sunken chest, hollow cheeks, a hectic face and languid movements—a bent creature, almost hunch-backed. Even her splendid braids looked miserable, and her eyes, blazing feverishly, seemed larger than ever in her emaciated face. Her eyes alone retained something of their former beauty. Yevpraksia stared long at her as at a stranger, then finally recognized her.

"You?" she cried out, clapping her hands.

"I. Well?"

Anninka laughed quietly, as if to add, "Yes, life has played me a dirty trick."

"Is uncle well?"

"Uncle? Nothing is the matter with him. He is alive, there is no doubt about that, but we hardly ever see him."

"What's the matter with him?"

"Just so—it's all because of lonesomeness."

"Don't tell me he has stopped haranguing?"

"He is real quiet now, miss. He used to talk and talk, but suddenly he became silent. Occasionally we hear him in his study talking to himself and sometimes even laughing, but as soon as he comes out of the room he is quiet. People say his late brother, Stepan Vladimirych, had the same trouble. At first he was gay, then suddenly he became quiet. And you, madam, are you well?"

Anninka only waved her hand in reply.

"And is your sister well?"

"She has been lying in her grave at the wayside at Krechetovo a month."

"Lord be merciful! At the wayside!"

"Of course, that's how they bury all suicides."

"Goodness! A lady—and to take her own life! How is that?"

"Yes, at first she was a 'lady,' and then she took poison, that's all. And I, I am a coward, I want to live, and here I have come to you. Not for long, oh, don't be afraid. I shall die soon, too."

Yevpraksia stared at her, as if she did not understand.

"Why are you looking at me? Am I such a fright? Well, never mind my looks. However, I'll tell you later—later. Now pay the coachman and announce me to uncle."

She produced an old pocketbook and took out two yellow bills.

"And here is all my property," she added, pointing to a small trunk. "Here's everything, both my inheritance and my own acquisitions. I am cold, Yevpraksia, very cold. I am quite sick, there's not a bone in my body that doesn't ache, and here as if to spite me, it is so cold. As I was riding, I thought of only one thing, to get to Golovliovo, and die there, at least in warmth. I'd like to have some vodka. Have you any?"

"You had better have some tea, madam. The samovar will soon be ready."

"No, I shall have tea later. Now I'd like to have some vodka. However, don't tell uncle about the vodka yet. It will all come out later."

While they set the table for tea in the dining-room Porfiry Vladimirych appeared. Now Anninka in her turn was completely surprised at her uncle's emaciation and wild, faded looks. Porfiry received Anninka in a strange manner, not coldly, but as if altogether indifferent. He spoke little, as if under compulsion, like an actor trying to recall sentences of parts acted in days gone by, and was absent-minded, as though his mind were absorbed in some grave, urgent business from which he had been torn away to attend to trifles.

"So you have arrived?" he said. "What will you have, tea, coffee? Order the servants to fetch it."

In former days, at family meetings, Yudushka always played the sentimental part. This time it was Anninka who was filled with emotions, genuine emotions. The claw of sorrow must have sunk deep into her being, for she threw herself on Porfiry Vladimirych's breast and embraced him ardently.

"Uncle, I have come to you!" she cried, and burst into tears.

"Well, you are welcome. I have enough rooms. Live here."

"I am sick, uncle, very, very sick."

"If you are sick, you must pray to God! Whenever I am not well, I always heal myself through prayer."

"I have come to you, uncle, to die."

Porfiry Vladimirych looked at her with questioning eyes, and an almost imperceptible smile stole over his lips.

"So that is where your acting has brought you?"

"Yes, that is where my acting has brought me. Lubinka is dead and I—I am alive,"

At the news of Lubinka's death Yudushka piously crossed himself and whispered a prayer. Anninka seated herself at table, her chin in her hands, looking toward the church and continuing to cry bitterly.

"See here, as for weeping and being in despair, it is surely a sin," remarked Porfiry Vladimirych sententiously. "And do you know what a Christian must do on such an occasion? Not cry, but submit and hope— that's how a Christian has to act."

But Anninka threw herself back on the chair and repeated, her arms drooping helplessly:

"Ah, I do not know, I do not know, I do not know!"

"If you are crying your eyes out on account of your sister," Yudushka continued to sermonize, "that is a sin, too. For although it is praiseworthy to love one's sisters and brothers, yet, if it be the will of God to take one or several of them to Himself——"

"Oh, no, no! Uncle, are you kind? Are you kind? Tell me!"

Anninka threw herself on him again and embraced him.

"Well, I am kind, kind. Tell me, do you wish anything? Will you have a bite, or tea, or coffee? Ask for what you want. Order it."

Anninka suddenly remembered how during her first visit her uncle used to ask her, "Will you have beef, pork, potatoes?" And she realized that she would find no other consolation.

"Thank you, uncle," she said, seating herself at the table again. "I do not want anything in particular. I am sure I shall be contented with anything you offer me."

"If so, well and good. Will you go to Pogorelka?"

"No, uncle, for the time being I shall stay with you. You have nothing against it, have you?"

"Christ be with you, of course I don't object. I asked about Pogorelka only because in case you do wish to go there, it would be necessary to arrange for a wagon and horses."

"No, later, later."

"Very well, then. You will go there later on. Meanwhile you can stay with us. You will help about the house, for I'm all alone, you see. This queen," said Yudushka, almost in hatred, pointing to Yevpraksia pouring the tea, "is all the time running about in the servants' quarters, so that sometimes you can never get any service, not a soul in the whole house. Well, good-by for the present. I shall go to my room. I shall pray, do some work and pray again. So, my friend. Is it long since Lubinka died?"

"About a month, uncle."

"Then tomorrow we shall go to church early and order a mass to be read for God's recently deceased servant Lubinka. So good-by for the present. Have some tea, and if you want a bit of luncheon, have the servant bring it to you. At dinner we shall meet again, have a talk, a chat. And if anything has to be done, we shall attend to it, if not—not."

Such was the first family meeting. When it was over, Anninka entered upon her new life in that disgusting Golovliovo, where she was stranded for the second time in her short life.

CHAPTER II

Anninka had gone downhill very fast. It was true that her first visit to Golovliovo had aroused the consciousness of being a "lady," of having her own nest and her own graves, of not being confined in her life to the squalor and uproar of hotels and inns, and of having a shelter where she would be safe from vile breaths infected with the odor of wine and the stable, from hoarse voices, bloodshot eyes, indecent gestures. But alas! No sooner did Golovliovo disappear from sight than this purifying consciousness vanished from her mind.

Anninka had gone from Golovliovo straight to Moscow, and solicited a position on the government stage both for herself and her sister. With this in view she turned for aid to *maman,* that is, the directress of the boarding-school where she had been educated, and to several of her classmates. *Maman* was at first quite kind to her, but as soon as she discovered that her former pupil had acted on the provincial stage, her pleasant manner changed to one of haughtiness and sternness. As for Anninka's classmates, who were mostly married women, they eyed her with an impertinent astonishment that quite frightened her. Only one of them, better-natured than the rest, asked her, evidently wishing to show sympathy:

"Tell me, darling, is it true that when you actresses dress for the stage, officers lace your corsets?"

In a word, her attempts to gain a foothold in Moscow remained unsuccessful. The truth of the matter was, she did not possess the necessary qualifications for theatrical success in the capital. She and her sister Lubinka belonged to that class of lively, but not very talented actresses who play one part all their lives. Anninka had made a hit in *Pericola,* Lubinka in *Pansies* and *Old-time Colonels,* and whatever new rôles they studied strangely resembled their successful parts, or, in the majority of cases, were a complete failure. Anninka often had to play *Fair Helen* also. She would wear a flaming red wig over her ash-colored hair, and cut her tunic down to her waist line, but she was mediocre and dull, not even cynical. From *Fair Helen* she passed to the *Duchess of Herolstein.* In this her colorless acting was coupled with a completely preposterous *mise en scène,* and the outcome was altogether miserable. At last she undertook to play the role of Clairette in *The White*

Slave. But she overdid her part to such an extent that even the none too refined provincial public was shocked by her behavior on the stage, which she turned into a mire of corruption. Anninka gained the reputation of being a clever actress with a fairly good voice, and since she was pretty, she could get an audience in the provinces. But that was all. Lacking individuality, she could not attain permanent success. Even among the provincial public she was popular mainly with army officers, whose chief ambition was to obtain access behind the scenes. She could have got an engagement in the capital only if she had been forced upon some manager by a powerful patron, and even then the public would have given her the unenviable nickname of "a tavern singer."

Thus the two girls had to go back to the provinces. In Moscow Anninka received a letter from Lubinka, saying that their company had removed from Krechetov to the city of Samovarnov, which made Lubinka quite glad, because there she had become friendly with a certain zemstvo leader, who was so infatuated that he was almost, in his own words, "ready to steal the zemstvo funds, if that were necessary to gratify all her desires."

In fact, on her arrival in Samovarnov, Anninka found her sister quite luxuriously situated and planning to give up the stage. Lubinka's admirer, the zemstvo official Gavrilo Stepanych Lyulkin, was a retired captain of the Hussars, recently a *bel homme*, but now somewhat corpulent. His appearance and manners and views taken separately were conspicuously noble, but taken together they gave one the strong impression that the man was altogether free from scruples. Lubinka received Anninka with open arms and told her a room had been prepared for her at the lodgings.

Anninka, still under the influence of her trip to Golovliovo, bridled up at the suggestion. The sisters exchanged tart words, and soon afterwards they separated. Involuntarily Anninka recalled the words of the Volpino parson, who had told her it was hard to safeguard a maiden's "honor" in the acting profession.

Anninka went to live at a hotel and broke off all relations with her sister. Easter passed. The next week the theatres opened, and Anninka found out that her sister's place was already filled by Nalimova, a girl from Kazan, a mediocre actress, but utterly unconstrained in the movements of her body. As usual, Anninka played *Pericola* and enchanted the Samovarnov theatregoers. On her return to the hotel, she found an envelope in her room containing a hundred ruble bill and a laconic note which read: "Should anything happen, you get as much. Merchant Kukishev, dealer in fancy goods." Anninka was enraged and went to complain to the hotel-keeper. He told her Kukishev had this peculiar habit of greeting the newly arrived actresses, and otherwise was a harmless man and it did not pay to take offence. Anninka sealed up the letter and the money in an envelope, sent it back the very next day, and regained her composure.

But Kukishev was more persistent than the hotel-keeper had reported him to be. He was among Lyulkin's friends and was on good terms with Lubinka. He was quite well-to-do and, besides, as a member of the city administration was in a most convenient position with regard to the city treasury. And like Lyulkin, boldness was not his least virtue. According to the taste of market people he possessed a seductive appearance, reminding one of the beetle, which, as the song has it, Masha found in the fields instead of berries:

> "A beetle black, and on his crown
> Nice curly hair, with whiskers smart,
> His eyebrows colored a dark-brown,
> The picture of my own sweetheart."

Being the happy possessor of such looks he thought he had the right to be aggressive, all the more so as Lubinka explicitly promised him her cooperation.

Lubinka, apparently, had burned all her bridges, and her reputation was by no means a pleasant topic in her sister's ears. Every night, it was said, a merry band caroused in her rooms from midnight till morning, Lubinka presiding and appearing as a "gypsy," half naked (at this, Lyulkin, addressing his intoxicated friends, would cry out, "Look, there's a breast!") and with loosened hair. She would sing to the accompaniment of a guitar:

> "How I did love it with my mash,
> Who had the darlingest mustache!"

Anninka listened to the stories about her sister and became greatly worried. What surprised her most was that Lubinka sang the ditty about the "mash who had the darlingest mustache" in a gypsy-like manner, just like the celebrated Matryusha of Moscow. Anninka always gave her sister due credit, and had she been told that Lubinka sang couplets from *Old-time Colonels* with unsurpassed excellence, she would have considered it quite natural and would have readily believed it. The theatergoers of Kursk, Tambov and Penza had not yet forgotten with what inimitable naïveté Lubinka sang the most atrocious ambiguities in her soft little voice. But that Lubinka could sing like a gypsy—pardon me! A lie! She, Anninka, could sing like that, no doubt of it. It was her genre, her business, and everyone in Kursk who had seen her in the play, *Russian Romances Personified,* would willingly testify to it.

Anninka would take the guitar, sling the striped sash over her shoulder, sit down on a chair, cross her legs and begin: "I-ekh! I-akh!" It was the very manner of Matryusha the gypsy.

However that may have been, one thing was certain, that Lubinka was extravagant. And Lyulkin, for fear of introducing a discordant note into the drunken bliss, had already resorted to borrowing from the zemstvo treasury. Not to speak of the tremendous amount of champagne which was both consumed and poured out on the floor in Lubinka's quarters, all sorts of things had to be provided to feed her growing capriciousness and extravagance. First it was dresses from Mme. Minangois of Moscow, then jewelry from Fuld. Lubinka was rather thrifty and did not scorn valuables. Her licentiousness by no means interfered with her love of gold, diamonds and especially lottery bonds. At any rate, it was a life not of gaiety, but of boisterous debauchery and continuous intoxication.

There was one thorn in the rose-bush. It was necessary for Lubinka to curry favor with the chief of police. Although a friend of Lyulkin's, he sometimes liked to make his power felt, and Lubinka always guessed when he was dissatisfied with her hospitality, for the next day the police warden would come to ask for her passport. And she yielded. In the morning she would treat the district chief of police to vodka and a light repast, while in the evening she would personally prepare a "Swedish" punch of which he was very fond.

Kukishev watched this ocean of luxury and burned with envy. He conceived a desire to lead a similar life and have just such a mistress. That would put an end to the monotony of provincial life. One night he would spend with Lyulkin's queen, the next night with his own queen. That was the dream of his life, the ambition of an imbecile, who is the more obstinate in his strivings the greater his stupidity. Anninka seemed to be the most suitable person for the realization of his hopes.

But Anninka would not surrender. She was still new to the stir of passion, although she had had numerous suitors and had been rather free in her relations with them. At one time she even thought she was ready to fall in love with the local tragedian Miloslavsky X, who was consumed with passion for her. But Miloslavsky X was so hare-brained and so persistently drunk that he never told her of his love, only stared at her and stolidly hiccoughed when she passed by. So the love affair never ripened. The other suitors Anninka considered as something in the nature of indispensable furniture, to which a provincial actress is doomed by the very conditions of her profession. She submitted to these conditions, and took advantage of their minor privileges, such as applause, bouquets, drives, picnics, etc., but further than this so to speak external dissipation, she did not go.

She persisted in this manner of conduct. During the whole summer she had kept to the path of virtue, jealously guarding her honor, as if anxious to show the Volpino priest that moral strength can be found even among actresses. Once she even decided to complain about Kukishev to the governor, who listened to her with kindly favor and commended her for her heroism. But seeing that her complaint was an indirect attack on his own person as the governor of the province, he added that, having spent all his strength against the internal enemy, he strongly doubted whether he could be of any use. Hearing this, Anninka blushed and went away.

Meanwhile Kukishev acted so artfully that he succeeded in making the public take an interest in his efforts. People suddenly became convinced that Kukishev was right and that Pogorelskaya I, as she was dubbed on the posters, only looked as if butter would not melt in her mouth. A whole clique was formed with the express purpose of taming the refractory upstart. The campaign was started by several habitués of the theatre who gradually began to hang around her dressing-room and made their nest in the adjoining room belonging to Miss Nalimova. Then, without exhibiting direct enmity, the audiences began to receive Pogorelskaya I, when she appeared on the stage, with a disheartening reserve, as if she were not the star actress, but some insignificant dumb performer. At last the clique insisted that the manager take some parts away from Anninka and give them to Nalimova. And what was most curious, the most important part in this underhand intrigue was played by Lubinka, whose confidant was Nalimova.

Toward autumn Anninka was surprised to find that she was compelled to play the rôle of Orestes in *Fair Helen*, and only Pericola had been left to her of all her main parts. That was because Nalimova would not dare to vie with her in the rôle. In addition, the manager notified her that in view of her cold reception by the audiences, her salary would be reduced to seventy-five rubles a month, with only half the proceeds of one benefit during the year.

Anninka lost courage, because with so small a salary she would have to move from the hotel to an inn. She wrote letters to two or three managers offering her services, but invariably received the answer that they were actually flooded with applicants for the Pericola rôle, and besides, they had learned of her shrewish obstinacy from reliable sources, and so could not foresee any hopes of her success.

Anninka was now living on her last savings. Another week and she would have to move to the inn and live with Khoroshavina, who was playing *Parthenis* and was favored with the attention of a constable. She began to yield to despair, especially since a mysterious hand put a note into her room every day containing the same words, "Pericola, submit. Your Kukishev." And at the critical moment Lubinka most unexpectedly rushed in.

"Tell me, please, for what prince are you saving your treasure?" she asked curtly.

Anninka was taken aback. First of all she was amazed to find that both the Volpino priest and Lubinka employed the same word "treasure" for maidenly honor. Only the priest had regarded it as the "foundation of life," while Lubinka looked upon it as a mere trifle over which the "rascally males" go mad.

Then she involuntarily questioned herself, What is this "treasure," anyhow? Is it really a treasure and is it really worth hoarding? Alas, she could find no satisfactory answer to her questions. On one hand, it is rather shameful to remain without honor, and on the other — — Ah, the devil take it! And could it be that the whole purpose, the whole merit of her existence consisted in struggling every moment of her life to maintain this treasure?

"In only six months I have succeeded in getting thirty bonds," Lubinka continued, "and lots of things. Look what a dress I have on!"

Lubinka turned about, pulled at the front, then at the sides, letting herself be examined. The dress was really an expensive one and unusually well made. It came straight from Minangois in Moscow.

"Kukishev is a kind sort," Lubinka resumed. "He will dress you up like a doll, and he will give you money. You'll be able to send the theatre to the devil. You have had enough of it."

"Never!" cried Anninka heatedly. She had not as yet forgotten the phrase, "sacred art."

"You may remain if you wish to. You will get your former salary again and outstrip Nalimova."

Anninka was silent.

"Well, good-by. They are waiting for me downstairs. Kukishev is there, too. Will you come?"

But Anninka maintained her silence.

"Well, think it over, if there is anything to think about. And when you have done thinking, come to see me. Good-by."

On the seventeenth of September, Lubinka's birthday, the posters of the Samovarnov theatre announced a gala performance. Anninka appeared as

Fair Helen again, and the same evening the part of Orestes was performed by Pogorelskaya II, Lubinka. To complete the triumph of the sisters, Nalimova was given the part of Cleon, the blacksmith. She appeared on the stage dressed in tights and a short coat, her face touched with soot, and a sheet of iron in her hands. The audience was elated. Hardly did Anninka appear on the stage when the audience raised such a clamor that, already unaccustomed to ovations, she nearly broke into tears. And when, in the third act, in the scene where she is awakened at night, she stood up on the sofa almost naked, the house was one groaning mass of humanity. One man in the audience was so thoroughly worked up that he shouted to Menelaus, who was entering the stage, "Get out, damn you!" Anninka understood that the public had pardoned her. As for Kukishev, he was in full dress, white tie and white gloves. In the entr'actes he generously treated friends and strangers alike to champagne and spoke of his triumph with dignity. At last the manager of the theatre, brimming over with jubilation, appeared in Anninka's room and, kneeling before her, said, "Now, madam, you are a good girl and you will get your previous salary with the corresponding number of benefits."

Everybody praised her and congratulated her and protested their sympathy, so that she, who at first was timid, restless, and haunted with a feeling of oppressive melancholy, grew suddenly convinced that she had fulfilled her mission.

After the theatre the whole company went to Lubinka's birthday celebration, and there the congratulations were reiterated. So large a crowd gathered in Lubinka's quarters that the tobacco smoke made it hard to breathe. They sat down to supper, and champagne began to flow freely. Kukishev kept close to Anninka. This made her somewhat shy, but she was no longer oppressed by his attentions. It seemed rather funny, but also flattering, that she had so easily gotten hold of this big, powerful man, who could bend and straighten out a horseshoe without effort, and whom she could order about and do with as she wished. The supper was crowned by that drunken, disorderly gaiety in which neither the head nor the heart takes a part, and which results only in headaches and nausea. The tragedian Miloslavsky X was the only one who looked gloomy and declined champagne, preferring plain vodka, which he gulped down glass after glass. As to Anninka, she abstained from drink for some time, but Kukishev was insistent. He went down on his knees and implored her:

"Anna Semyonovna, it is your turn. I beseech you. For your happiness, for friendship and love. Do us a favor."

She was annoyed by his foolish figure and foolish talk, yet she could not refuse, and before she had time to collect her thoughts, she was already dizzy. Lubinka, for her part, was so magnanimous that she herself asked her sister to sing, "How I did love it with my mash." Anninka performed it so well that everybody exclaimed, "Ah, that was just like Matryusha the gypsy." Then Lubinka sang an obscene song of a different kind, and at once convinced everybody that that kind of singing was her real genre, in which she had no rivals, just as Anninka had none in the gypsy songs. In conclusion, Miloslavsky X and Nalimova presented a "masquerade scene" in which the tragedian recited parts from *Ugolino* (a tragedy in five acts, by Polevoy), and Nalimova followed with a scene from an unpublished tragedy of Barkov. The result was so unexpected that Nalimova nearly eclipsed the two sisters and almost became the heroine of the evening.

It was already dawn when Kukishev, leaving the charming hostess, helped Anninka into her carriage. Pious townspeople were coming from matins. At the sight of Anninka, elaborately attired and somewhat unsteady on her feet, they muttered darkly, "People are coming out of church, and they are gulping wine. A curse on them!"

On leaving her sister's, Anninka went not to the hotel but to her own quarters, small but snug and nicely furnished. She was followed by Kukishev.

The whole winter passed in an indescribable hurly-burly. Anninka was completely in the swing, and if she ever reminded herself of her "treasure," it was only in order to laugh it off with "How foolish I was!" Kukishev, very proud of the fact that his "idea" of securing a mistress like Lubinka had materialized, made ducks and drakes of his money. Instigated by emulation, he ordered two gowns to Lyulkin's one, and two dozen bottles of champagne to his one dozen. Lubinka herself began to envy her sister, because she succeeded in laying by forty lottery bonds during the winter in addition to a considerable amount of jewelry. However, they became friendly again and decided to pool their hoardings.

Anninka always hoped for something, and during an intimate talk with her sister, said:

"When all this will be over, we will go back to Pogorelka. We will have money and establish a home for ourselves."

"And you think this will ever end? Fool!" Lubinka retorted cynically.

To Anninka's misfortune, Kukishev soon came upon a new "idea," which he began to pursue with his usual obstinacy. A vulgar and eminently shallow-pated man, he imagined he would reach the pinnacle of bliss if his queen would "accompany" him, that is, if she would drink vodka with him.

Anninka for some time declined, referring to the fact that Lyulkin never compelled Lubinka to drink vodka.

"And yet she drinks out of love for Lyulkin," Kukishev retorted. "And may I ask you, darling, do you take the Lyulkins as an example? They are Lyulkins, while you and I, we are Kukishevs. Therefore we will drink in our own Kukishev way."

Kukishev had his way. Once Anninka took a small glass of green liquid from the hands of her "beloved" and gulped it down. Of course she saw stars, choked, coughed, became dizzy, thereby putting Kukishev in transports of delight.

"Permit me to remark, darling, that you do not drink well! You did it too fast," he instructed her, as she quieted down somewhat. "The wineglass should be held in the tiny hands, so! Then you bring it over to the lips, slowly—one, two, three—the Lord bless us!"

And he calmly and gravely gulped down the contents of the glass, as if he were pouring vodka into a barrel. He did not even frown, but only took a bit of black bread, dipped it in the salt cellar, and chewed it.

And so Kukishev succeeded in realizing his second "idea" and even began to plan another one, which would beat the Lyulkins hollow. Of course he succeeded in inventing one.

"You know," he suddenly announced, "as soon as summer comes we will go to my mill with the Lyulkins, take along some provisions and bathe in the river."

"Never!" Anninka objected indignantly.

"Why not? We will bathe, then have a cocktail, rest a little, and bathe again. That would be delightful."

It is not known whether Kukishev's third idea materialized or not, but it is certain that this drunken debauchery lasted a whole year, during which time neither the zemstvo nor the city administration exhibited the slightest anxiety concerning Messrs. Kukishev and Lyulkin. For appearance's sake Lyulkin visited Moscow twice, and on his return declared he had sold one of his forests. On being reminded that he had sold the same forest four years before when living with Domashka the gypsy, he answered it was another forest that he had sold that time, and, to give his tale the appearance of veracity, he added detailed information concerning the name of his newly sold forest-estate. As for Kukishev, he gave currency to the story that he had smuggled in a large stock of embroidery from abroad, thereby earning a great deal of money.

In September of the next year the chief of police asked Kukishev for a "loan" of a thousand rubles and, Kukishev was foolish enough to refuse. Then the police superintendent began to confer secretly with the assistant attorney. ("Both of them guzzled champagne in my house every evening," Kukishev testified later at the trial.) On September 17th, at the anniversary of Kukishev's *liaison*, when he and the others celebrated Lubinka's birthday again, a member of the city council came running in and announced to Kukishev that a warrant was being made out at the City Board for his arrest.

"They must have found out something!" Kukishev exclaimed rather pluckily, and without further comment followed the messenger to the council-hall, and from there to prison.

The next day the zemstvo council also took fright. The members assembled and ordered the money in the treasury counted and recounted, and at last came to the conclusion that their treasury, too, had been drained by somebody. Lyulkin was present at the examination, pale, gloomy, but "noble"! When the loss had been discovered, and when it became apparent to Lyulkin that he had no hope of escaping, he walked to the window, drew a revolver from his pocket, and fired a bullet into his temple.

The event created quite a turmoil in the town. The people pitied Lyulkin, saying, "At least he ended nobly!" But the general opinion about Kukishev was, "He was born a shopkeeper, and a shopkeeper he will die!" Concerning Anninka and Lubinka they simply said that "they were the cause of it all," and that it would not do any harm to put them behind the bars, too, so that in future matters might not be very inviting for such wretches.

The prosecutors, however, did not arrest them, but terrorized them so mercilessly that they were completely dismayed. Of course there were some kind people who advised them to conceal all their valuables, but they listened and understood nothing. Owing to this, the attorney for the plaintiffs (both councils hired the same attorney), a daring fellow, wishing to satisfy his clients, came to the sisters one day, accompanied by the process server, to take an inventory. He seized and sealed everything except their dresses and such gold and silver things as bore inscriptions showing they had been the gifts of the appreciative public. Lubinka, however, succeeded in hiding a roll of bank-notes, presented to her the previous evening, in her corset. It was a thousand rubles, on which the sisters would have to exist for an indefinite time.

In expectation of Kukishev's trial, they were kept in the town about four months. Then the trial began, and the sisters, Anninka particularly, had to undergo a ruthless ordeal. Kukishev was cynical in the extreme. He revelled in the disclosure of details, for which there was really no need, but apparently he was desirous of striking a pose before the ladies of Samovarnov and exposed everything indiscreetly. The attorney and the private prosecutor, young and anxious to afford pleasure to the ladies, took advantage of this and endeavored to lend the proceeding a frivolous character, in which they succeeded, of course. Anninka fainted a number of times, but the private prosecutor paid no attention to this and bombarded her with questions. At last the investigation ended, and both sides had their say. Late at night the jurors announced that Kukishev was guilty, but that there were alleviating circumstances. In view of this he was sentenced to be deported to Western Siberia. When the trial was over, the sisters obtained permission to leave Samovarnov. And it was high time, for the thousand rubles were nearly exhausted. Besides, the manager of the Kretchetov theatre, with whom they had made arrangements, demanded that they appear in Kretchetov at once, threatening to discontinue negotiations if they delayed. Nothing was seen or heard of the valuables and documents sealed at the demand of the private prosecutor.

Such were the consequences of their disregard for their "treasure." Tormented, crushed, despised by everybody, the sisters lost all faith in their own strength and all hope for a brighter future. They became emaciated, slovenly, cowardly. And Anninka, to boot, having been in Kukishev's school, had learned to drink.

Matters grew worse. No sooner did they alight from the train at Kretchetov than they at once found "protectors." Lubinka was taken by Captain Popkov, Anninka by the merchant Zabvenny. But the jolly times were no more. Both Popkov and Zabvenny were coarse, quarrelsome, and rather close-fisted. After three or four months they became considerably colder. The sisters were even less successful on the stage than in love affairs. The manager who had accepted the sisters on the strength of the scandal they had caused at Samovarnov quite unexpectedly found himself out of his reckoning. At the very first performance somebody in the gallery shouted when the two girls made their appearance on the stage, "You convicts!" And the name stuck. It decided Anninka's and Lubinka's theatrical fate.

They now lived a dull, drowsy life, devoid of all intellectual interest. The public was cold, the managers scowled at them, the "protectors" would not intercede. Zabvenny dreamed, as once Kukishev had, of how he would "compel" his queen to have a cocktail with him, how she would at first affect horror, and gradually submit. But he was very angry when he found out that she was already past mistress in the art of drinking. The only satisfaction left him was to show his friends how Anninka "guzzled vodka." Popkov, too, was dissatisfied and declared Lubinka had grown thin.

"You once had flesh on your bones," he would say, "tell me, where did you lose it?"

On account of this, he was not only unceremonious with her, but often even beat her when he was drunk.

Toward the end of the winter the sisters had neither "real" admirers nor a "permanent position." They still stuck to the theatre, but there could be no question now either of *Pericola* or the *Old-time Colonels*. Lubinka was more cheerful, but Anninka, being more high-strung, broke down completely. She seemed to have forgotten the past and was not aware of the present. In addition, she began to cough suspiciously, apparently on her way toward an enigmatic malady.

Next summer was terrible. Gradually the sisters were taken to hotels and were given to travelling gentlemen for a moderate fixed price. Scandals and beatings followed one another, but the sisters clung to life desperately, with the tenacity of cats. They reminded one of those wretched dogs who, in spite of being crippled by a beating, crawl back to their favorite place, whining as they go. It was not proper to keep women like that on the stage.

In those dark days only once did a ray of light find its way into Anninka's existence. Miloslavsky X, the tragedian, sent her a letter from Samovarnov in which he persistently offered her his hand and heart. Anninka read the letter and cried. The night long she tossed about in bed, and in the morning she sent a curt reply, "Why? Only that we may drink together?" Then darkness closed down upon her intenser than ever, and endless, base debauchery began again.

Lubinka was the first to wake up, or if not to wake up, at least to feel instinctively that she had lived long enough. There was no work in sight. Her youth, her beauty, and her embryonic talent, all had somehow vanished. That they had a shelter in Pogorelka, she never remembered. It was something distant, vague, long-forgotten. They never did have much of a liking for Pogorelka, and now their hatred toward the place was only intensified. Even when they were almost starving the place attracted her less than ever. And what sort of a figure would she cut there? A figure which all sorts of drunken, lustful breaths had branded as a "creature." Those accursed breaths saturated her entire body. She felt them everywhere, in every place. And what is more horrible, she grew so accustomed to those disgusting breaths that they became a part of her very being. So with Anninka, too. Neither the stench of eating-houses, nor the din of the inns, nor the obscene language of the drunkards seemed abominable to them, so that had they gone to Pogorelka, they would surely have missed the "life." Besides, even in Pogorelka they must have something to live on. All these many years that they had wandered about the world they had heard nothing of the revenue that Pogorelka brought. Perhaps the estate was a myth. Perhaps the folks had all died, all those witnesses of the distant and yet ever-present years, when they had been brought up by their grandmother, Arina Petrovna, on sour milk and stale cured meat.

It was clear that it was best for Lubinka to die. Once this thought dawns on one's consciousness, it becomes an obsession. The sisters not infrequently had moments of awakening, but in the case of Anninka they were accompanied by hysterics, sobs, tears, and so passed away faster. Lubinka was colder by nature. She did not cry or curse, but the thought that she was a "hussy" constantly preyed on her mind. And Lubinka was more reasonable and saw quite clearly that there was not even any profit in their mode of living. For the future she expected nothing but shame, poverty and the street. Shame is a matter of habit, it can be tolerated, but poverty— never! It is better to end it all at once.

"We must die," she once said to Anninka in that same cool and deliberate tone in which two years ago she had asked her for whom she was saving her "treasure."

"Why?" Anninka objected, somewhat frightened.

"I mean it seriously. We must die," Lubinka repeated. "Understand, wake up, think!"

"Well—let us die," Anninka assented, hardly realizing the dismal meaning of her decision.

That same day Lubinka cut off the tips of some matches and prepared two glasses of the mixture. One of these she drank herself, the other she offered her sister. But Anninka immediately lost courage and refused to drink.

"Drink, you slut," Lubinka cried out. "Sister, dearest, darling, drink!"

Anninka, almost insane with fear, ran about the room, instinctively clutching at her throat as if trying to choke herself.

"Drink, drink—you street-walker!"

The artistic career of the two sisters was ended. That same evening Lubinka's corpse was taken into the field and buried. Anninka remained alive.

CHAPTER III

Anninka soon introduced an atmosphere of Bohemian life into Yudushka's nest. She rose late and would roam about the house until dinnertime, undressed, uncombed, with an aching head, and coughing in such agony that each time it would send a shudder through Porfiry Vladimirych in his study and quite frighten him. Her room was always untidy, the bedding in disorder, and her clothes lying about on the chairs and floor. At first she saw her uncle only at dinner and evening tea. The master of Golovliovo came out of his room all dressed in black, spoke little, and ate with his old-time exasperating slowness. He was apparently observing her. After dinner came the early December twilight. Anninka loved to watch the glimmer of the gray winter day gradually die out and the fields grow dim; she loved to see the shadows flood the rooms until finally the whole house was plunged in impenetrable darkness. In the darkness she always felt at ease and hardly ever lit the candles. The only one she allowed to burn was at one end of the sitting-room. It was of cheap palm wax, and sputtered and dripped, its feeble flame formed a tiny circle of light. For some time the house would be astir with the usual after-dinner noises. Plates would rattle in the hands of the dish-washers, and drawers open and close with a clatter; but soon the sound of receding steps would be heard and a dead silence begin to reign. Porfiry Vladimirych would take his after-dinner nap and Yevpraksia bury herself in the bedding in her room. Prokhor would go into the servants' room, and Anninka would remain entirely alone.

She would pace from room to room, humming, trying to tire herself out, but chiefly endeavoring to drive her thoughts away. In walking toward the sitting-room she would fix her eyes upon the circle of light about the candle, and walking away from it, she would try to single out some point in the darkness and keep her eyes fixed on it. But in spite of her efforts reminiscences surged up in her mind irresistibly. She saw the dressing-room with its cheap wall paper, the inevitable pier-glass and the equally inevitable bouquet from Lieutenant Pankov II; the stage with the stage-properties, sooty, slippery from the damp; the hall with its pieces of furniture picked up at random and its boxes upholstered in threadbare purple plush,—the hall which, seen from the stage, looked trim and even splendid, but in reality was dark and miserable. And finally—officers, officers, officers without end. Then she saw the hotel with the vile-smelling corridor, dimly lit by the smoky kerosene lamp; the room she would dart into in order to change her dress for further triumphs, the room with the bed in disorder from the morning; the wash-stand full of dirty water, the bed-sheet lying on the floor, her cast-off underwear forgotten on a chair. Next she saw herself in the general dining-room, filled with kitchen odors, the tables set for supper, with its tobacco smoke, noise, crowds, drinking, debauchery. And again officers, officers, officers without end.

Such were her memories of the time she had once called the years of her successes, triumphs, prosperity.

These reminiscences were followed by others, the prominent part in which was played by the inn, filled with a foul stench, with walls on which the vapor froze in the winter time, insecure flooring, and board partitions, the glossy bellies of bed-bugs showing in the crevices. Nights of drinking and brawls, travelling squires hastily taking greenbacks out of their meager pocket-books, merchants encouraging the "actresses" almost with a whip in hand. And in the morning—headaches, nausea, and utter dejection. At last—Golovliovo.

Golovliovo was death itself, relentless, hollow-wombed death, constantly lying in wait for new victims. Two uncles had died there, two cousins had received mortal wounds. And Lubinka! Although Lubinka, to be sure, had died somewhere in Kretchetov because of her "own affairs," yet the origin of her wounds went back to her life at Golovliovo. All the deaths, all the poisonings, all the pestilence, came from there. There the orphans had been fed on rotten cured meats, there they heard the first words of hatred and contempt for human dignity. Not the slightest childish misdeed had passed without punishment. Nothing could be hidden from the stony-hearted, eccentric old woman, not an extra bite of bread, not a broken clay doll, not a torn rag, not a worn shoe. Each breach of law and order was instantly punished either with a reproach or a slap. And then, when they had been permitted to dispose of themselves, when they had understood that they might run away from the disgusting place, they ran—there! And nobody kept them from running away, nor could they have been kept from running away, because they could imagine nothing worse or more repulsive than Golovliovo.

Ah, if all that could only be forgotten, if one could create a different existence in one's dreams, a magic world that would supplant both the past and the present! But alas, the reality Anninka had lived through had so powerful a hold, that the clutch of it suppressed the feeble efforts of her imagination. In vain did fancy endeavor to imagine angels with silvery wings. From behind those angels peeped inexorably the legions of Kukishevs, Lyulkins, Zabvennys, Popkovs. Lord! Was all lost? Even the ability to deceive and beguile herself? Had that been lost forever in the night revels, in wine, and in debauchery? Yet that past had to be killed somehow, so as not to poison her blood and rend her heart. It had to be crushed, utterly annihilated.

How strange and ruthless was that which had happened! It was impossible even to conceive of some future, of some door by which to escape from the situation, of anything at all that might occur to change things. Nothing could occur. And what was even more unbearable was the fact that to all intents and purposes she was already dead, with the outward signs of life yet present. She should have ended it then, along with Lubinka. Somehow she had remained alive. How was it that the mass of shame which had come upon her then from all sides had not crushed her? And what an insignificant worm she must have been to have crept out from underneath that heap of heavy stones piled up on top of her!

She groaned in agony, and ran about the sitting-room, trying to kill the burning memories. Before her eyes swam familiar images, the Duchess of Herolstein shaking a pelisse, Clairette Angot in her wedding gown with a slit in front up to her waist-line, Fair Helen with slits in front, behind and at the sides. Nothing but obscenity and nakedness. That was what her life had consisted of. Could all that possibly have occurred?

About seven o'clock the house came to life again. The sounds of the preparations for tea were heard, and at last came the voice of Porfiry Vladimirych. Uncle and niece sat down at the tea table and exchanged remarks about the day just ended; but the daily happenings were scanty and so the conversation was brief. Having taken tea and kissed Anninka on the forehead, Yudushka crept back into his den, while Anninka went into Yevpraksia's room to play cards.

At eleven o'clock the debauchery began. Having ascertained that Porfiry Vladimirych was fast asleep, Yevpraksia set the table with various country corned meats and a bottle of vodka. Now came meaningless and obscene songs, strumming on the guitar, and Anninka drinking between the songs and the shameless talk. At first she drank after Kukishev's manner, coolly, with a "Lord bless us" to each glass, but then she gradually sank into gloom and began to moan and curse. Yevpraksia looked at her and pitied her:

"As I look at you, lady," she said, "I am so sorry for you, so sorry."

"Drink with me and you won't be sorry," Anninka retorted.

"No, how can I? They nearly chased me out of the clergy estate because of your uncle, and now if I become— —"

"Well, then it can't be helped. Let me sing you *The Mustache.*"

She strummed the guitar again, and again came the cry, "I-akh! I-okh!" Late at night sleep would suddenly overtake her, obliterating her past and allaying her sufferings for a few hours. The next day, broken down, half-insane, she would again creep out from beneath the deadening load of sleep and live anew.

One of those vile nights when Anninka was singing her filthy songs to Yevpraksia, Yudushka's pale face, ghastly and harassed, appeared in the doorway. His lips were quivering, his sunken eyes looked like sightless cavities by the light of the candle. His hands were folded for prayer. For a few seconds he stood in front of the dumfounded women, and then slowly faced round and passed out.

CHAPTER IV

There are families that are weighed down by an inevitable fate. They are frequent among that portion of the nobility which once lived idle, useless, and uninfluential, under the wing of serfdom in all parts of Russia and is now passing its last days helpless and unprotected in dilapidated manor-houses. In the life of these wretched families both success and failure come unexpectedly and as if by sheer accident.

Sometimes it happens that a shower of good luck, as it were, suddenly comes streaming down on such a family. The ruined cornet and his wife, peacefully fading away in an out-of-the-way village, will suddenly be blessed with a brood of young people, strong, clean, alert, pushing, adaptable to the new conditions of life—the boys as well as the girls—in a word, "knowing ones." The boys pass examinations with flying colors and even establish connections and procure patrons while still at school. In the nick of time they exhibit their modesty (*"j'aime cette modestie"* their superiors say about them), and in the nick of time they show that they can be independent (*"j'aime cette indépendance!"*) They quickly scent the direction from which the wind blows, but they never burn their bridges, so that retreat is free and easy. These successful makers of our modern history begin with obsequious cringing, and almost invariably end with perfidy. As to the girls, they, too, in their line, contribute to the regeneration of the family, that is, they all marry successfully and then exhibit so much tact in the art of dressing that they experience no difficulty in gaining prominent places in so-called society.

From this combination of circumstances, success fairly pours down upon the impoverished family. The first successful members who struggle through courageously, bring up another clean generation, which is still better off because the main paths have not only been broken but also well trodden. Other generations succeed until at last a family comes that has no preliminary struggles and deems it has an inborn right to lifelong rejoicing.

Lately, on account of a modern demand for so-called "new men" resulting from the gradual degeneration of the old men, there have been frequent instances of successful families. Even in earlier days a comet would now and then make its appearance on the horizon, but it was a rare occurrence, the reason being that, first, there were no cracks in the wall surrounding that blissful region over the gateway to which is inscribed: "Here pies are eaten daily," and, secondly, because in order to penetrate into that region, one had to have genuine ability. But now quite a number of cracks have appeared and the matter of penetration is considerably simplified, since great merits are no longer demanded of the newcomer, but only "newness" and nothing else.

Besides these lucky families there is a great multitude of families upon whose members the household gods bestow nothing but misfortune and despair. Like a baleful blight, vice and ill-luck beset them and devour their substance. The malignant influences attack the whole stock, eating their way into the very heart and laying waste generation after generation. There is born a race of weaklings, drunkards, petty rakes, idlers and shiftless ne'er-do-wells. As time goes on the race degenerates more and more, until finally there appear miserable weaklings, like Yudushka's two sons, who perish at the first onslaught of life.

Such a sinister fate pursued the Golovliovo family. For several generations, their history was marked by three characteristics, idleness, utter uselessness, and habitual hard drinking, the last coming as the sorry crown to a chaotic life. The Golovliovo family would have run to seed completely but for the fact that Arina Petrovna flashed like a casual meteor through this drunken confusion. By her personal energy alone this woman brought the family to an unprecedented height of prosperity. Nevertheless her labors were in vain. Not only did she not transmit any of her qualities to her children, but she herself died ensnared by idleness, empty talk and mental vacuity.

Until now Porfiry Vladimirych had held out against the temptation of drink. It may be that he had been frightened off by the fate of his brothers and had consciously abstained from drink, or that he had been satisfied by the intoxication of his frenzied day dreams. But it was not for nothing that he had the reputation of a drunkard among his neighbors. At times he himself felt something was lacking in his existence. Idle musings gave him much, but not all. They did not supply that sharp, stupefying sensation which would completely do away with his sense of reality and plunge him headlong into the void forever.

And now the long-wished-for opportunity presented itself. Ever since Anninka's arrival, Yudushka had been aware of a vague noise at night coming from the other end of the house. For a long time he had puzzled his head over the significance of the mysterious sounds. At last he discovered what they were.

Anninka expected a reprimand the next day. None came. Porfiry Vladimirych spent the morning locked up in his study as usual, but when he appeared at the midday meal, he poured out two wineglasses of vodka instead of only one for himself, and pointed to one with a sheepish smile. Anninka accepted the silent invitation.

"So you say Lubinka is dead?" said Yudushka when the dinner was well under way, as if recalling something.

"Yes, uncle, she is dead."

"Well, God rest her soul! To grumble is a sin, but to honor her memory is quite fitting. Shall we?"

"Yes, uncle, let's honor her memory."

They emptied one more glass, and then Yudushka grew silent. He was evidently still unaccustomed to the society of human beings. When the meal was over, Anninka, performing a family rite, kissed uncle's cheek, and in response he patted her on her cheek and said:

"So that's the kind you are."

The evening of the same day, at tea, which lasted longer this time than usual, Porfiry Vladimirych looked at his niece for a while with a quizzical smile, and finally said:

"Shall we have some corned meats served?"

"Well, if you wish."

"Yes. It's better you should do it in uncle's sight than on the sly. At least, uncle will——"

Yudushka did not finish the sentence. Perhaps he had wanted to say that uncle would keep her from drinking, but something prevented him from saying it.

From that time on cold cuts were served in the dining-room every evening. The outer window shutters were closed, the servants retired, and uncle and niece remained all alone. In the beginning Yudushka did not keep pace with Anninka, but with a little practice he came up to her. They sat slowly sipping their vodka and talking. The conversation, at first dull and indifferent, became more and more animated as their heads grew hotter, and invariably passed into a chaotic quarrel, at the bottom of which were always reminiscences about the victims of Golovliovo.

Anninka started the quarrels. She dug up the family archives with ruthless persistence and delighted in teasing Yudushka by arguing that he along with Arina Petrovna had been the chief cause of the Golovliovo tragedies. Every word breathed such cynicism and such burning hatred that it was difficult to understand how so much vitality could still exist in that worn-out, shattered body. Anninka's attacks galled Yudushka immensely, but he defended himself feebly, angrily sputtering ejaculations of discomfiture. At times, when Anninka went too far in her insolence, he shouted and cursed.

Such scenes repeated themselves day in, day out, without change. Every detail of the pitiful family chronicle was speedily exhausted, but it still held the minds of the two riveted. Every episode of the past lacerated some wound in their hearts, and they felt a bitter delight in constantly evoking, scrutinizing and exaggerating painful memories. Neither the past nor the present contained any moral mainstay on which Anninka could lean. Nothing but sordid stinginess on one side, and mental vacuity on the other. Her youthful heart had thirsted for warmth and love, but had received a stone instead of bread, blows instead of instruction. By the irony of fate, the cruel school in which she had been taught implanted in her not an austere attitude toward life, but a passionate yearning to partake of its sweet poisons. Youth had wrought the miracle of oblivion, it kept her heart from hardening and the germs of hatred from developing. Youth had made her drunk with the thirst for life. That was why a turbulent, furtive debauchery had held her in its sway for several years, and had pushed Golovliovo into the background. Now, when the end was drawing close, her heart began to ache. Now for the first time did Anninka grasp the significance of her past and begin to hate it truly.

The drinking lasted far into the night, and had it not been for the drunken confusion of both thoughts and words, it might have resulted in something frightful. But if alcohol opened the well-springs of pain in these shattered hearts, it also appeased them. The further the night advanced, the more incoherent became their talk and the more impotent their hatred. Toward the end of the debauch, the aching disappeared and their surroundings vanished from their eyes, supplanted by a shining void. They faltered, their eyes closed, they grew muscle-bound. Uncle and niece would then rise from their places and retire to their rooms with tottering steps.

Of course, these night adventures could not remain a secret. Before long the notion of crime became associated with them in the minds of the servants. Life abandoned the vast Golovliovo manor-house. Nothing stirred even in the morning. Uncle and niece rose late and till the midday meal Anninka's racking cough, accompanied by curses, rang from one end of the house to the other. Yudushka listened to the harrowing sounds in terror and a vague presentiment of his own impending doom stirred in him.

It seemed that all the Golovliovo victims were now creeping from out of the nooks and crannies of the deserted house. Gray apparitions stirred everywhere. Here was old Vladimir Mikhailovich, in his white nightcap, making wry faces and citing Barkov; here was Simple Simon and Pavel the Sneak; here were Lubinka and the last offshoots of the Golovliovo stock, Volodya and Petka. All were drunk, lustful, weary and bleeding. And over all these ghosts there brooded a living phantom, Porfiry Vladimirych Golovliov, the last representative of the decadent family.

CHAPTER V

The continual reverting to the past and its victims was bound to have its effect on Yudushka. The natural outcome—was it fear?—No, rather the awakening of conscience. He discovered he had a conscience, and oblivion and contempt, although blunting its sensitiveness, could not destroy it.

The awakening of a torpid conscience is usually fraught with pain. It brings no peace, holds no promise of a new life, but merely tortures, endlessly and fruitlessly. Man sees himself immured in a narrow prison, a helpless victim of the agonies of repentance, with no hope of ever returning to life. And he perceives no other way of allaying his gnawing pain than to break his head against the stony walls of the prison cell.

Never in the course of his long, useless life had it occurred to Yudushka that dire tragedies were interwoven with his existence. He had lived peacefully and calmly, with a constant prayer on his lips, and the thought had been far from him that this manner of life had caused so much sorrow. Least of all could he imagine that he himself had been the source of these tragedies. Suddenly the terrible truth was revealed to his conscience, but all too late—too late for him to make amends for the crimes of his life. He was unsociable, old, with one foot in the grave, and there was not a single human being who approached him with loving pity. Why was he alone? Why did he see nothing but indifference and hatred around him? Why was it that everything he touched had perished? This estate of Golovliovo was once so full, a human nest. How had it happened that now there was not a trace, not a feather left? Of the fledgelings nursed there his niece was the only one that remained alive, and she had come back only to sneer at him and deal him his deathblow. Even Yevpraksia, simple as she was, hated him. She lived at Golovliovo because Porfiry sent her father, the sacristan, provisions every month, but undoubtedly she hated him. He had made her unhappy, too, by robbing her of her child. What was the outcome of his existence? Wherefore had he lied, babbled, persecuted, hoarded? Who would inherit his wealth? Who was to enjoy the fruits of his life? Who?

I repeat, his conscience had awakened. Yudushka waited for the evening with feverish impatience not only in order to get bestially drunk, but also to drown his conscience. He hated the "dissolute wench," who lacerated his wounds with such cold cynicism, yet he was drawn to her irresistibly, as if there was still something to be said between them and some wounds to be torn open. Every evening he made Anninka retell the story of Lubinka's death, and every evening the idea of self-destruction became riper in his mind. At first, the idea occurred to him casually. But as his iniquities became more apparent to him, it sank deeper and deeper into his being and soon was the sole shining spot in all the gloom he saw ahead of him.

And his health began to decline rapidly. He coughed violently and at times had spells of asthma that in themselves were sufficient to make life intolerable, let alone the moral pangs from which he suffered. All the symptoms of the malady that had sent his brothers to their graves were present. He heard the groans of his brother Pavel, as he choked in the entresol of the Dubrovino manor-house. Still Yudushka was doggedly tenacious of life. His sunken, emaciated chest held out against the pain that grew from hour to hour. It was as if his body too were resisting with unexpected vigor so as to take revenge on him for his crimes.

"Is this the end?" he would wonder hopefully, whenever he felt the approach of a paroxysm. But death was slow in coming. Evidently it would be necessary to use violence to hasten the end. All his accounts with life were settled—it was both painful and useless to him. What he needed was death, but, to his sorrow, death was slow in coming. There is something mean and treacherous in the teasing hesitancy of death when it is called upon with all the strength of one's soul.

It was late in March and Passion Week was nearing its end. However abject Yudushka's condition was, he preserved an attitude of reverence toward the sanctity of these days implanted in him in his childhood. His thoughts of themselves took a serious turn, and there was no other desire in his heart than complete silence. In this mood the evenings were no longer spent in wild drinking, but passed in gloomy silence.

Porfiry Vladimirych and Anninka were sitting all alone in the dining-room. The evening service, accompanied by the reading of the gospel, had just ended, and the odor of incense still lingered in the room. The clock struck ten, the servants had retired, and deep, pensive quiet settled over the house. Anninka, her hands clasping her head, was deep in thought. Porfiry Vladimirych sat opposite, silent and sad.

Upon Anninka the Passion Week evening service always made an overwhelming impression. As a child she had wept bitterly at the priest's words: "And when they plaited a crown of thorns, they put it upon His head, and a reed in His right hand," and in a tremulous treble she used to sing after the sexton: "Glory be to Thy long-suffering, oh, Lord! Glory be to Thee!" After the service she used to run, all a-quiver with emotion, to the maids' room, and there, in the growing twilight (Arina Petrovna allowed no candles in that room when there was no work being done), she related "The Passion of our Lord" to the servants. Silent tears flowed from the eyes of the slaves, and they heaved deep sighs. The poor servants felt their Master and Redeemer with their whole hearts and believed He would arise from the dead, arise from the dead in truth. Anninka, too, felt and believed. Beyond the gloom of their life of suffering and persecution, all these poor in spirit beheld the radiant kingdom of freedom. Even the old lady, usually so redoubtable, was gentle during Passion Week. She did not grumble or remind Anninka that she was an orphan. On the contrary, she fondled her and soothed her with kindly words. But Anninka was restless even in bed, she tossed about and talked to herself in her sleep.

Then came her school years and wanderings, the first empty, the second painful. But even as a nomadic actress, Anninka had jealously observed the "holy days," calling back echoes of her distant past and moods of childlike devotion. But now when she saw her life clearly to its last detail, when she had cursed her life and when it became obvious that the future promised neither repentance nor forgiveness, when the source of devotion and the well-spring of tears had dried up, the effect of the tale of the Crucifixion upon her was truly overwhelming. In childhood a gloomy night had surrounded her, but beyond the darkness she had sensed the presence of light. Now nothing but interminable everlasting night stretched ahead endlessly. She neither sighed, nor was agitated, nor even thought. She merely sank into a state of profound torpor.

Porfiry Vladimirych, too, from his very childhood, had revered the "holy days," but, true idol-worshipper that he was, he had observed merely the rites. Every year on the eve of Good Friday he had had the priest come and read the gospel, had sighed, lifted up his arms, touched the ground with his forehead, marked the number of chapters read by means of wax balls, but had understood nothing. Not until now, when his conscience was awakened, had he grasped the fact that the gospel contained the story of how Untruth visited a bloody judgment on Truth.

Of course, it would be an exaggeration to say that this discovery led him to definite conclusions about his own life, yet there is no doubt that it produced in him a commotion bordering on despair. This state of mind was the more painful the more unconsciously he lived through the past which was the source of his commotion.

There was something terrible in his past, he could not tell exactly what. It was as if a mountainous mass, hitherto motionless and hidden by an impenetrable veil, had suddenly moved upon him, threatening every moment to crush him. What he feared was that he might not be crushed, and he felt he must hasten the climax. He had been brooding over the idea for quite some time. "We shall have communion on Saturday," suddenly flashed through his mind. "It would be well to visit dear mother's grave and take leave of her."

"Shall we walk over to the cemetery?" he turned to Anninka and explained his idea to her.

"Why, if you wish, we'll drive out there."

"No, not drive, but——" started Porfiry Vladimirych, but halted abruptly, as if struck by the thought that Anninka might be in his way.

"I have sinned against my dear departed mother. I, I was the cause of her death!"

The thought preyed on him, and the desire to "take leave" grew stronger in his heart, to take leave not by mere conventional words, but by throwing himself on her grave and bursting out in the sobs of a death agony.

"So you say no one is to be blamed for Lubinka's death?" he suddenly asked, as if trying to cheer himself up.

At first Anninka paid no attention to his question. Two or three minutes later, however, she felt an irresistible impulse to return to the subject of Lubinka's death and torment herself with it.

"And her words were, 'Drink, you street-walker,'" he said, after she had repeated the story in detail.

"Yes, her very words."

"And you didn't drink?"

"I didn't. I am alive, as you see."

He rose and paced up and down the room several times, visibly affected. At last he went over to Anninka and stroked her head.

"My poor, poor Anninka!" he said softly.

At the touch of his hands a startling change took place in her. At first she was amazed, then her face began to work, and suddenly a violent torrent of hysterical, inhuman sobs burst from her chest.

"Uncle, are you good? Tell me, are you good?" she fairly shrieked.

In a broken voice, through tears and sobs, she kept on reiterating her query, the same she had asked him the day of her return to Golovliovo, to which he had given such an absurd reply.

"You are good? Tell me, answer me, are you good?"

"Did you hear what the priest read at the evening service?" he said, when she finally grew calm. "Oh, what sufferings He underwent! Only such sufferings can— —And yet He forgave, forgave forever!"

He resumed his pacing, his very soul rent with suffering and his face covered with beads of perspiration.

"He pardoned every one," he reflected aloud. "Not only those who at that time gave Him vinegar mingled with gall to drink, but also those who are doing the same thing now and will do it again in future ages. What a horror!"

Suddenly he stopped before her and said:

"And you—have you forgiven?"

Instead of replying she threw herself on him and clasped him firmly.

"You must forgive me," he went on. "For every one—on your own account—and for those who are no longer here. What has happened?" he cried, looking round distractedly. "Where are they all?"

Utterly shaken and exhausted, they retired to their rooms. But Porfiry Vladimirych could not sleep. He tossed in his bed, all the while trying to recall an obligation that lay on him. Suddenly he clearly remembered the words that had flashed through his mind about two hours before, "I must walk to mother's grave and take leave of her."

An exhausting restlessness seized his being. At last he got up and donned his dressing-gown. It was still dark, and unbroken silence reigned in the house. For a while Porfiry Vladimirych paced back and forth in the room, stopped before the lighted ikon of the Saviour with a thorny crown, and scanned his face. Finally he determined upon a course of action, perhaps half-unconsciously. He stole into the antechamber and opened the outer door.

Outside a March blizzard was raging and blinded him with a torrent of sleet. Porfiry Vladimirych struggled along the road, splashing through the puddles, insensible to the wind and the snow. Instinctively he drew together the skirts of his dressing-gown.

Early next morning a messenger came speeding from the village near the churchyard where Arina Petrovna was buried. He brought the news that the frozen body of the Golovliovo master had been found by the roadside. The servants rushed into Anninka's room. She lay in her bed unconscious in delirium. A messenger was hastily dispatched to Nadezhda Ivanovna Galkina (daughter of Aunt Varvara Mikhailovna), who ever since the previous autumn had been keeping a watchful eye on everything taking place at Golovliovo.